MISFIRE

ALSO BY TAMMY EULIANO

Fatal Intent

MISFIRE

A NOVEL

TAMMY EULIANO

OCEANVIEW ⦵ PUBLISHING

SARASOTA, FLORIDA

ISBN 978-1-60809-522-3

Published in the United States of America by Oceanview Publishing

Sarasota, Florida

www.oceanviewpub.com

10 9 8 7 6 5 4 3 2 1

PRINTED IN THE UNITED STATES OF AMERICA

For my parents, Jerry and Jinny Yachabach
for your unfailing love, support, and belief in my crazy endeavors

ACKNOWLEDGMENTS

First and foremost, I must thank my husband, Neil, who has embraced this encore career of mine with encouragement, patience, and kindness. And my children, whose support and cheerleading have been both a role-reversal and a delight. And my parents, whose constant positivity and unwavering faith in me keep me going no matter what.

Thank you to Bob and Pat Gussin and everyone at Oceanview for believing in Kate Downey and her exploits and for helping make the book better.

For book details, I thank Sara Rampazzi, PhD, and cardiologist Dr. Jamie Conti for sharing their expertise on AICDs; Judd Sheets regarding communication methods from broadcast radio to RFID; and my husband, Neil, for issues related to patents. It's always helpful to have good friends in the legal profession. Assistant State Attorney Joe McCarthy helped with legal matters while Kevin Downey, JD, helped with issues related to wills and estate planning. Finally, thanks to Chris Griseck of the Alachua County Sheriff's Office for help with questions of jurisdiction in rural Florida.

Thanks to authors Jen Delozier and Al Pessin for their insightful comments, as well as my Mystery Writers of America critique group partners and Galey Gravenstein for their suggestions. All of which made the book better.

A special thanks to my daughter, Erin Euliano, who took time away from her PhD research to read the novel and identify some inconsistencies I'd missed literally dozens of times.

Thanks to J.L. Lora, an amazing romance writer, who provided exceptional guidance on a scene or two. You can guess which ones. She is part of a mutual support group, the "Lakehouse Writers," of which I'm blessed to be a part. We met at a Margie Lawson immersion course in 2014 and have been together ever since. Thanks to Margie for her teaching and for these indispensable friendships. Also, Joan Long, another new author with whom I've commiserated over the years.

Writing is a solo endeavor, and yet it takes a village. I am eternally grateful to mine . . . including the four-legged ones.

MISFIRE

CHAPTER ONE

"You aren't gonna let me die this time, are ya, Doc?"

Oh boy.

So started my Wednesday, with about the worst line any anesthesiologist can hear from a patient in preoperative holding.

"*This time?*" the nurse said.

"Last time my heart decided to dance a little jig instead of pumpin' my blood."

Sitting close beside Mr. Abrams, his wife squeezed her eyes closed. "Abe, tell Dr. Downey the whole story."

"I read about it in your chart last night," I said. "Last time they tried to fix your hernia, your heart needed a jump start." To the nurse I added, "V fib," a chaotic heart rhythm that usually requires electrical shock to convert back to a normal rhythm. "It happened when they were putting you to sleep and they canceled the case." Instead of a hernia operation, Mr. Abrams ended up with a very different procedure that day—placement of an automated internal cardioverter defibrillator, or AICD. A device implanted in his chest to detect and treat the problem should it recur.

"Your AICD hasn't fired, right?" The device had been checked by cardiology the day before.

"Right. Rosie watches it like a hawk huntin' a rodent." He nodded to his wife, who slipped her phone under the book in her lap.

"I completely understand," I said to her, nodding at the hidden phone. "My aunt has the same AICD, and I can't stop checking the app either." Maybe a downside of the novel AICD, the Kadence communicated through the patient's phone to the cloud, where I could view status reports on my beloved Aunt Irm's heart. "I don't expect any problems this time, but we're ready if your heart decides on another jig."

"Dr. Downey, I need to ask a favor." Mrs. Abrams didn't look at me, or at anyone. She gripped her paperback as if it would fly open.

"Call me Kate."

"Come on, Rosie, let the doc do her job," Mr. Abrams said.

She ignored him. "Dr. Yarborough is his cardiologist. She said if he could keep his phone during the operation, she would be able to watch his AICD."

I generally like to honor requests. This one required a caveat. "I'll make a deal with you. We'll keep the phone close for Dr. Yarborough as long as you promise not to watch the app."

Her sparse gray eyebrows drew together.

"During surgery, there's electrical noise that can confuse the AICD. I don't know what it might report and I don't want you frightened." Sometimes we turn off AICDs during surgery, but this operation was far enough away from the device implanted near his left shoulder that the noise shouldn't cause a problem. What she might see on the app, though, I couldn't predict.

She nodded uncertainly.

Eric, the anesthesia resident assigned to work with me on the case, arrived with a small syringe of a sedative. "What do you think about some happy juice?"

"I think my wife needs it more than me," Mr. Abrams said.

Her lipstick appeared to redden as her face paled.

"Unfortunately, it goes in the IV," Eric said with a kind smile for her. "We'll take good care of him."

"You'll watch his blood sugar," she said.

"Yes, ma'am." Eric unlocked the bed.

"And be careful with his AICD."

"We will." He unhooked the IV bag from the ceiling-mounted pole and attached it to one on the stretcher.

Tears dampened her eyes as Mrs. Abrams stood and leaned down to kiss her husband's cheek.

"I'm gonna be fine, Rosie. Don't you worry. I'll be huntin' by the weekend, and we can try out that new squirrel recipe before our anniversary."

"We are not serving squirrel stew for our fiftieth anniversary," she said.

Eric and I exchanged a smile.

"Oh now, you wait and see." Mr. Abrams patted his wife's hand.

"What's squirrel taste like?" Eric pushed the bed from the wall.

"Tastes like chicken." Mr. Abrams laughed loudly. "No, just kiddin' with ya . . ." As they turned the corner, the voices faded. I stayed behind to reassure Mrs. Abrams.

"I can't lose him." Eyes squeezed shut, a sob escaped.

I wrapped an arm around her ample shoulders and waited. I knew that feeling; had lived that feeling; had lost.

"I'm sorry." She dabbed her eyes with a tissue.

"No need to apologize. Last time scared you. Tell you what, once he's asleep, I'll give you a call and let you know it went fine."

That calmed her. We walked together to the main doors, where I directed her to the waiting room. I turned the opposite direction to not let her husband of fifty years die during a hernia operation. No pressure there.

In the OR, we helped Mr. Abrams move to the operating table. After applying monitors and going through our safety checks, Eric held the clear plastic mask over his face and said, "Pick out a good dream."

"Oh, I got one." He winked at me. "I'll try to behave this time, Doc."

"I'd appreciate that." I maintained eye contact and held his hand as I injected the drugs to put him off to sleep. Despite having induced anesthesia thousands of times, I always experience a tense few moments between the time the patient stops breathing and when the breathing tube is confirmed in the windpipe. During those couple of minutes, if we couldn't breathe for him, there's a real, if remote, chance the patient could die. Not a failure to save, but, in essence, a kill. Anesthesia is unique in that. We take people who are breathing fine, mess it up, then fix it, so the surgeon can correct the real problem.

When Mr. Abrams' induction proceeded without incident, I felt an extra sense of relief and was happy to share that with his wife. The operation, too, went well, and an hour later, he awoke from anesthesia, gave a sleepy smile, and said, "How'd it go, Doc?"

"Fine. No more hernia. Are you in any pain?"

He shook his head. "Nope, you done good."

"Team effort," I said as we disconnected the monitors. With the help of several others in the room, we slid him across to the stretcher and rolled from the OR to Slot 8 in the recovery room. As Eric gave his transfer-of-care report to the recovery nurse, I helped reconnect the monitors. Mr. Abrams looked great. Whether he'd be hunting squirrel in a few days, I couldn't say. I headed toward the pre-op area to see our next patient.

"Dr. Downey!"

I spun back to see Mr. Abrams' head loll to the side, his eyes closed, his hands on his chest. In two steps I was back at his side. "Mr. Abrams?" I placed two fingers to his neck where his pulse should be while the ECG monitor above showed ventricular fibrillation— a randomly bumpy line—and his pulse oximeter, the sticker on his finger that recorded pulse and oxygen, became a flat line. Cardiac arrest.

What the hell?

I forced the image of his wife saying, "I can't lose him," from my mind as I lowered the head of the bed and started chest compressions. "Eric, manage the airway."

He placed a mask over Mr. Abrams' nose and mouth and started squeezing the breathing bag. "Why isn't his AICD firing?"

Good question.

The overhead monitor flashed and shrieked an alarm.

The fire-engine red crash cart arrived and a nurse snapped off its plastic lock. As she tore open the foil pack of defibrillation pads from the top of the crash cart, the charge nurse assembled medications. A smoothly running team, each member with his or her own tasks.

The overhead alert began, "Anesthesia and Charge Nurse stat to the PACU." I tuned it out as a crowd in scrubs assembled around us. The anesthesiologist in charge of the recovery room said, "How can I help?"

"Call Nikki Yarborough in cardiology." As I continued chest compressions, the nurse reached around my arms to place the large defibrillator pads on Mr. Abrams' chest. I noticed the small scar where his AICD was implanted and silently ordered the damn thing to fire. The charging defibrillator whined with an increasing and eventually teeth-itching pitch.

Seconds before I yelled, "Clear!" the ECG monitor traced a "square wave"—three sides of a bottomless square, up-across-down. I held my breath, though it was only seconds. Normal sinus rhythm followed. His AICD had finally fired, kick-starting his heart back to normal electrical activity.

I stopped chest compressions and placed my fingers on his neck. Strong pulse. "Mr. Abrams?" I grasped his hand and leaned forward. His head turned toward me. "How do you feel?"

He rubbed his sternum with his other hand. "Chest hurts."

"Like a heart attack, or like someone pounded on it?"

"Pounded." He opened one eye.

"Sorry about that."

"No. Thank you." The corners of his mouth turned up weakly. "You did good."

"I'll have cardiology come check out your AICD and figure out why it took so long to fire."

He nodded. "Can you tell my wife I'm okay?" It struck me his first thought was for his wife, and that I'd told her everything would be fine. *Crap.* It also struck me she might have peeked at his app.

The recovery room attending waited for me as I stepped away. "Dr. Yarborough's in a procedure but will come by as soon as she's done."

I thanked him and hurried to the waiting room to check on Mrs. Abrams.

She must have followed directions, because I found her in the back corner of the crowded space, the book unopened in her lap. At my approach, she looked up.

"He's fine." Always the best lead, but she didn't smile. I sat beside her and lowered my voice in an attempt at privacy. "After the surgery, he had a rhythm problem like before."

She gasped and I placed a hand on her arm.

"We did CPR until his Kadence fired and everything is fine now. He's awake and he asked me to tell you that."

Tears filled her eyes.

Though I wasn't supposed to invite her to the recovery room until the nurse was ready, Mrs. Abrams needed to see for herself. I knew what that felt like. "Would you like to see him?"

She nodded and walked with me in silence.

The very understanding nurse lowered one of the stretcher's side rails, and Mr. Abrams extended an arm to embrace his wife. "Now, Rosie, I told you I'd be fine." He looked past her shoulder and winked at me, but his eyes shone as well. Such a beautiful couple. I returned to work before we were all bleary eyed.

A little shaken by the morning's events, I opened Aunt Irm's Kadence app on my phone. All was well. Still, a shiver tickled the back of my neck. On the way back to the OR, I texted Nikki to call when she saw Mr. Abrams. Though only a year out of training, Nikki Yarborough placed most of the AICDs at University. Between three years of medicine residency followed by three years of cardiology fellowship and two more years as a fellow subspecializing in heart rhythm problems—electrophysiology—she was extremely well trained. She led the clinical studies for the Kadence, a new AICD invented by her chairman, and knew more about it than any physician, including him. I'd known her for three years and was sufficiently impressed to place my own great-aunt Irm under her care.

An hour later, I received the text and found Nikki at Mr. Abrams' bedside with a tiny laptop on the rolling table. Attached to the computer, a small device that resembled a computer mouse rested near his left shoulder, where the AICD was implanted. Beside Nikki, her fellow, Annabelle Kessler, watched the screen. Annabelle had completed all of her training so far at University and Nikki had only good things to say about her.

Mrs. Abrams sat on the other side of the bed, her hand entwined with his.

"How are you feeling?" I asked him.

He gave me a thumbs-up. "Right as rain."

"Hey, Kate, good to see you." Nikki invited me to view the laptop screen with her. The banner at the top read, "Kadence Interrogation." I swallowed a lump in my throat.

"This is his ECG around the time of the event this morning." She scrolled the tracing rapidly, too fast for me to pick out the usual peaks and valleys of a normal ECG. Finally, she stopped. "Everything looks fine."

I concurred, as if she needed me to.

She clicked *Play* and the tracing scrolled across the screen at a normal pace. "Until here." She stopped the playback. A square wave interrupted the regular rhythm. Normal to the left, ventricular fibrillation to the right. She pointed to the text below, where the AICD reported its automated analysis real-time. "It didn't register an abnormal rhythm, just sent a shock."

"Why would that happen, Doc?" Mr. Abrams' Southern drawl came through.

"Well, it's a complex device that does fire sometimes unexpectedly. Usually, you just feel a kick to the ribs."

He shook his head. He had reached for his chest but likely forgot in his anesthesia hangover.

"This shock happened to fall at the worst possible instant in your normal heart rhythm," she said. "It confused the electrical system, and your heart went into ventricular fibrillation, or v-fib. The same thing happens occasionally when a baseball player gets hit in the chest by a ball at just the wrong moment and collapses."

Mr. Abrams looked at me. "I'm thinking any moment is bad to get hit by a baseball, am I right?"

I liked this man.

"In this case, it looks like your AICD had one of those random firings at that wrong instant," Nikki said.

"Ah, just bad luck then." He sounded so calm, while I felt a sudden desperate urge to call Aunt Irm.

"Looks like it," Nikki said. "The rest of the interrogation is completely normal. Everything seems fine."

Good news, if unsatisfying. What was to prevent it from happening again? I didn't say that out loud, of course.

"We'll keep you overnight," Nikki continued. "To be on the safe side."

She and I stepped away together. "Should I be worried?" I asked.

"About what?"

I stared at her. Of course she knew "about what." When Aunt Irm fainted at bridge club six weeks ago, and the workup showed sick sinus syndrome as well as a possible risk for sudden death from a heart rhythm problem, Nikki insisted she needed a pacemaker with defibrillator functionality. I agreed. She implanted an AICD the next day.

Now she stared back, then realization dawned. "Oh, sorry. No. Your aunt is fine."

Though we talked about other options at the time, Nikki had recommended the new Kadence. I wasn't so sure. New devices always scare me. I never get the newest phone until it's been out a few months, never get the first-year model of a new car. Anyway, she sold me on the Kadence because it allowed me to keep an eye on my aunt's device wherever she was, without her having to connect to bedside communication equipment like the other AICDs on the market. It wasn't as much information as Nikki could see on the interrogation computer, but it was enough to reassure me her device was functioning.

The only con at the time was that the device had only recently received FDA approval. Nikki reassured me that, other than the novel communication capabilities, it was the same basic design as the AICDs already on the market from more established manufacturers.

"Random firings happen with all AICDs. The Kadence is no exception." She wrapped a thin arm around my shoulders and squeezed. Her extra four inches made me feel small. "Nothing to be worried about. I promise." She stepped away. "Sorry, I have to get back to the cath lab. You and I need to catch up though."

"Let me know when you have time." She had a husband. Competition for her evenings that I no longer shared.

Despite her reassurance, I called Aunt Irm. "You feeling okay?"

"Of course I am, kindchen." She'd called me "kid" in her native German since childhood. "You must stop worrying. My new ticker-minder keeps me safe."

So far, her *ticker-minder* hadn't had to do anything, but the procedure to implant it had nearly killed her. "Okay, just checking."

"Do not forget I have bridge tonight."

"Isn't it only Wednesday?"

"Yes, we have been over this. Marjorie's niece will be visiting from Panama City tomorrow so we must play tonight."

"Right. Sorry," I said with vague recollection. "Carmel's picking you up, right?" Carmel was Aunt Irm's closest friend and co-conspirator. They did everything from church committees to bake sales together. And now, Carmel kept my aunt entertained during her convalescence.

"Yes, kindchen, and dropping me off after. Do not worry. Go out with friends. Do something young people do."

That made me smile. I worried about Aunt Irm's health while she obsessed over my social life. Somehow, in her mind, visiting my husband's grave didn't qualify as *social life*.

CHAPTER TWO

SINCE AUNT IRM'S "ticker trouble," as she called it, I rushed home each day after work to be with her and my dog, Shadow. Tonight, I had the evening to myself. My beloved black Lab had exercised at doggie daycare and been dropped off at home, so I justified a rare hour alone. I drove to the cemetery without stopping for flowers. Greg wasn't a flowers kind of guy. "They just die after all," he'd say, though I still brought them for baby Emily sometimes.

Once through the wrought-iron gates, I passed several cars parked on the grassy shoulder. Singles and couples stood before gravestones. One elderly gentleman in a suitcoat sat on a stone bench, leaning forward against his cane. He was there nearly every time I visited, rain or shine. Part of me wanted to approach, introduce myself, and hear his story. Maybe he needed someone to talk to. But a much larger part of me recognized a partner in grief—an ever-growing club that values the silence in our mourning.

The plot I purchased for our little family was toward the back, shaded by a huge live oak. The section had recently been added to the cemetery, and I'd been pleasantly surprised by the location. Not because I'd be buried under a tree—as Greg would say, "What do I care, I'll be dead." —but because it provided a nicer environment to visit, separate from the main area, shady, away from the road noise. In the end, none of that mattered. Visiting a cemetery sucked. Greg's death sucked. Being a widow . . .

Someone stood at Greg's grave. A man. In a suit. Greg didn't know many people who wore suits outside of funerals, and this guy was six months late. I pulled onto the verge and waited in the car, both so as not to disturb him and because I wanted my husband to myself. After several minutes, the man turned, so I stepped from the car. He typed on his cellphone as he walked. By the time he glanced up, I was only feet away.

"Hi," I said, "I'm Kate Downey. Greg was my husband." I gestured to the grave.

"Dr. Downey, hi." He offered his hand. "Tom Angley. I represent your mother-in-law's estate. We spoke regarding the sale of her house last year."

"Right."

"I'm sorry for your loss," he said.

I'd gone months without hearing that empty phrase. It hadn't been long enough. Still, I said the obligatory, "Thank you."

He eyed me cautiously. "I don't mean Greg. I mean your mother-in-law."

Greg's mom? She was gone? The memory care center where she'd lived the last two years did not encourage my visits. It seemed only to confuse her more. Still, she was family and it hurt in that same place as my parents and Uncle Max and Greg and Emily. "She passed?"

"She did. I guess my secretary assumed the next-of-kin would have told you." He cringed. "My mistake. Of course, Adam would not have been able to communicate."

I stifled a laugh that would have been in terrible taste considering our location and the fact I'd just learned of my mother-in-law's death. But wow. Greg's brother, Adam, was in prison, convicted of manslaughter and as an accessory to the attempted murders of Aunt Irm and me, as well as another friend of ours. Tom Angley, Esq., needed a new secretary.

"She passed away peacefully on Monday," he said.

I was glad to hear it was peaceful. She'd struggled with alcoholism and declined rapidly after the death of her husband. It was probably a blessing she couldn't remember Greg's accident. In her mind, he was forever twenty-six and a newly graduated doctor.

"As you know, she left Greg in charge of her estate, listing you second." After Adam's trouble with drugs, his mother put her estate in Greg's name. It made sense at the time. The unexpected part was that she listed me second, should he become incapacitated. Not surprisingly, Adam rejected the setup.

"What do I need to do?"

"Nothing at the moment. Right now, I'm helping Adam figure out burial plans."

That made no sense. "Shouldn't she be buried beside her husband in Jacksonville?"

"That's what I thought, but Adam wanted to see where Greg was buried." He held up his phone and I understood. He was taking pictures to send to Adam in prison.

Heat rose in my face. It was as if Adam were there, torturing me yet again.

The lawyer shifted on his feet. "He says he wants the family together."

If I was hearing right, Adam wanted to exhume his father's body and move it ninety miles west, to our little plot under the oak tree in Newberry. In truth, I wouldn't mind my bones sharing eternity with Greg's parents, but not Adam. It may be stupid and senseless to care, but I did.

"You know what? I don't think it's possible to fit three more graves in this area." He clicked buttons on his phone, allowing me to watch as he deleted photographs.

My lungs emptied in relief. "Thank you," I whispered.

"I'll be in touch."

As he left, I stood there, letting my heart rate return to normal. Greg's mom was dead. They might be together in heaven right now . . . if there is a heaven . . . and if it works that way. If so, she's meeting her only grandchild. The idea actually struck a jealous chord in me. How crazy is that, being jealous of a dead woman?

I continued to Greg's grave, to his granite headstone. "Greg Downey, husband, father, doctor, soldier." Beside him, a smaller headstone read simply, "Emily Downey" and a single date. Premature birth and death moments apart, and mere days after an explosion put her father in a persistent vegetative state. In a way, Adam had been right last year. Greg had died that day on deployment far from home. The extra eleven months were purgatory, for him, for me, and for Adam. I had been selfish, not willing to let go. I'd saved him from a clogged tracheostomy early on, then wasn't willing to withdraw care and watch him starve to death.

"I'm sorry," I said to his grave as I spun the gold band still on my left ring finger. "I should have let you go the first time."

The Greg in my mind said, "You weren't ready. There was still hope. Now it's time to let go."

"Never," I whispered.

"You deserve a family," he said. But it wasn't him, of course. Where had that come from? Did I want a child? I glanced down at Emily's name. I wanted her—her and Greg. Desperately. I didn't bother wiping the tears, just let them fall.

"You don't have to be alone," the Greg in my mind said.

Christian O'Donnell's face flashed in my memory. A friend who could be more. He'd helped me prove a nurse anesthetist was killing patients—a mercy-killer-for-hire—one of the victims had been Christian's father. Greg's death had been collateral damage.

Christian helped me through the funeral, and each night I found solace in his magnificent pencil drawing of a smiling baby Emily in her father's strong arms.

Christian and I hadn't spoken in the months since Greg's funeral. An occasional text to check in. And I had a feeling he communicated with Aunt Irm. He'd sent a beautiful bouquet when she was recovering from her "ticker trouble."

Oh God. What am I doing? Christian has no place here. No one does.

"I'm sorry, Greg. I love you."

"It's okay," he said in my head. "Your life has to go on."

Would he really say that? Would I, were the roles reversed? I pictured Greg looking into the eyes of another woman with that unqualified adoration reserved just for me. And though splinters of jealousy stabbed, I would want him happy . . . after an appropriate period of mourning, of course. I smiled then, imagining a celestial grief timer. Bong, time to move on. "I don't want to move on. I want you." It had been a year and a half now since we'd talked. Longer since we'd embraced. The fading memory of his voice, his touch, his Greg-ness, terrified me. What if I forgot?

"You won't forget, but there's room in your heart for more."

Shut up, Greg.

CHAPTER THREE

BY THE TIME I reached our neighborhood of modest "starter" homes with small lots and smaller houses, the sun was setting. Families and couples strolled the quiet, tree-lined streets with children on scooters, or skates, or bikes with training wheels. Though most names escaped me, they waved and I recognized faces and marveled as the children grew both in size and skills. It was a perfect neighborhood for young families.

At the door from the garage into the house, Shadow greeted me with his exuberant whole-body wag and his cries of relief at my safe return. Or maybe it was my talent at dishing out dog food. While he inhaled his dinner, I changed into running clothes. He finished first and whined for me to catch up. Bossy dog.

I jotted a note for Aunt Irm, attached Shadow's leash, and we left by the front door. I let him lead, as if I had a choice. He chose a left turn on the sidewalk, headed toward the village center and, I assumed, the pet supply store. Little did Shadow know it would be closed at this hour and he'd have to settle for water without the free sample treats.

Two miles later, we reached the small shopping area and Shadow pulled even harder, across the street to the small restaurant where Greg and I used to enjoy sitting outside and meeting neighbors. Tonight, Shadow and his weapon of a tail yanked me toward a patio table where his brother sat obediently, his thumping tail the only evidence he knew trouble was coming. That and his smile, of course.

"Kate!" My old friend Randi Sinclair struggled to stand and hug me, her enormous belly between us. "It's so good to see you. What are you doing running alone so close to dark?"

"I've got Shadow. How are you feeling?" I nodded to her husband, Craig.

"We're all good. We figure this is our last dinner out for a while. Mom has Robbie." Baby number two was nearly due.

"Ah, I won't interrupt. I'm looking forward to next week."

"Not as much as I am." She patted her swollen abdomen.

I love taking care of pregnant women, including friends and colleagues, despite the added level of stress. I'd placed her epidural for the failed labor that led to Robbie's C-section. Now she'd asked me to take care of her for the scheduled repeat procedure.

Shadow alternated between nudging the other dog's muzzle and putting his shoulders down, haunches high in the air, growling softly.

"He is not going to play with you," I said. "He's a good dog."

Randi laughed.

"One of these days I'm going to borrow him to play in the backyard with Shadow. You'll have to teach me the command for, 'Go run and play and stop being so dang obedient.'"

"That's easy. It's 'Be like Shadow.'"

"Ha."

"Kate, one quick thing," Craig said. "I saw that Adam's mother died." As a favor to me, Craig had represented Adam for a drug arrest years ago and knew of our legal history since.

"Oh, I'm sorry," Randi said.

I nodded my thanks. "Apparently I'm the executor of her estate, unfortunately."

"You can remove yourself," Craig said. "To avoid dealing with Adam, you can decline the role if you want."

"Seriously?"

"Give her attorney a call."

I thanked him, told them to enjoy their meal, and pulled Shadow from under the table. He was happy enough to start running again. I could remove myself as executor and be done with Adam forever. As appealing as that sounded, was it what Greg would want? He'd looked out for his brother. Would he expect any less from me? Selfishly, I wanted out, but like it or not, Adam was family. Besides Shadow, he was all I had left of Greg. It would be wrong to ignore his mother's wishes for my own mental health. Adam was in no position to manage an estate at the moment.

We reached the house just as Carmel's old Toyota sedan turned into the driveway, her headlights temporarily blinding me. Thank God for Carmel. Aunt Irm's dear friend offered to be her chauffeur for the six months my aunt couldn't drive after the AICD placement. What a relief for me. I hated the thought of her stuck in the house.

She wouldn't consider a ride-sharing service. "We always told you kids not to get in cars with strangers," she would say. Carmel and her army of church women came to the rescue. Each Sunday, Carmel asked for my work schedule for the week and basically watched over Aunt Irm whenever I couldn't. I had no idea how to thank her.

Shadow insisted we greet my aunt as she made her slow way up the sidewalk. Carmel and I exchanged a wave, then I took Aunt Irm's arm and the package she carried as we plodded up the steps and into the house. "Did you win?" I asked.

"I did. With Carmel as my partner, we won the pot."

"So you're buying dinner?"

"As long as it does not cost more than five dollars and thirty-seven cents."

"Sounds like Ramen noodles."

"What is Ramen noodles? Is this something I should learn to make?"

I laughed. "No, please. They're inexpensive, prepackaged noodles with almost no nutritional value but tons of salt. I lived on them in college."

"Salt is not good."

"Salt is very good." We had this argument often when Aunt Irm first moved in, my tendency to salt everything, untasted, versus her effort to hide the salt shaker. We came to a truce, though I still salted liberally behind her back. I'd given up explaining that my kidneys work and my blood pressure is normal.

Shadow returned to his bowl and searched for escapee kibble, then licked the bowl, scraping it along the linoleum, while I refilled his water dish. As soon as I stepped back, he lapped noisily, then ran into the family room, lay on his back, and slithered, scratching and moaning. *Crazy dog.*

Aunt Irm pulled her eyes from Shadow. "You have not eaten."

"Because I'm not on the carpet scratching my back?"

"Hmph. I will heat your plate while you shower."

"Are you trying to tell me something?"

"I am. Go."

After, Aunt Irm sat with me at the kitchen table while I ate the leftovers she'd brought home from bridge—chicken with mushroom sauce and a salad. She always came home with a doggie bag, though she disapproved of the term. "It is not for Shadow. He should not eat people food." Poor Shadow.

"This is wonderful, thank you." I tried not to eat too fast. It required conscious effort.

"Yes, Carmel promised me the recipe." Proudly Italian, Carmel was an amazing cook and not just of Italian fare.

"How was your day?" I asked. "Any dizziness?"

"No, of course not. I am fine. Did you see something on your spying cloud?"

"Ha, no, the reports from your Kadence have all been normal." She loved to use new English words but had the occasional and often humorous context-fail. I should probably correct her more, but why?

"How was your day, kindchen?"

"Work was fine." I left out the Kadence misfire. "But this evening I learned that Greg's mother passed away."

"I am sorry for her." After a brief moment of silence, she said, "How did Adam do it from prison?" How bizarre that I found such an accusation abundantly plausible.

"I don't think he did." Though my confidence was entirely baseless. The elder Mrs. Downey was next on the mercy killer's list when we got in the way. "She left me in charge of her estate."

"You should donate everything to charity for her. Adam deserves nothing."

"As if that wouldn't put a target on my back. Besides, he's still Greg's brother."

Aunt Irm's thoughtful eyes searched mine. "Adam is not as Greg knew him. When he attacked you, he was not owing money or using his drugs. He wished only pain for you. Greg would not protect *this* Adam. He is no longer family."

Every muscle tightened at the recollection of that awful night.

"It is unfortunate you will still share a name," she said.

"It's a common one. I'll pretend I married into a different branch."

"The branch that is not so evil and doomed to hell for all of eternity?"

I smiled. She was rarely so bitter. "Weren't you going to talk to Father Jeff about this?"

"I did. We decided that I cannot forgive him."

Somehow, I doubted a Catholic priest would be part of that "we."

"Father Jeff said I must only pray for him."

"And do you?"

Straight-faced, she said, "I do, but perhaps not in the way Father Jeff intended."

I laughed, then finished my dinner. Aunt Irm looked past me. "Oh, we have a message." She stood and moved to the junk desk near the door to the garage.

We had cellphones, but both she and our new security system insisted on a landline. I never checked the answering machine.

Its electronic voice said, "You have one new message. Wednesday, three-sixteen p.m." A new voice took over, one that soothed the persistent ache in my heart. "Hi, this is Christian O'Donnell." Aunt Irm's eyes sparkled when she stole a glance at me. "I'm going to be in town tomorrow and was hoping I could take both of you to dinner. Kate, I need to ask you about something, if you're available. If not, Aunt Irm and I can go without you. Please call or text and let me know." He seemed to hesitate, then said, "Have a great evening."

Aunt Irm brought me the handset. "You must call him."

"It's late." I felt my face flush. Wow, even after several months. I went to the sink, rinsed my plate, and loaded it in the dishwasher.

Behind me, Aunt Irm spoke. "Christian, thank you for the call. Kate and I would love to see you tomorrow. Please come to the house and I will cook."

I should have whirled around and stopped her. I should have taken the phone and told Christian no. I did neither. Instead, my heart beat a little harder, a little faster, and I looked forward to something for the first time in months.

CHAPTER FOUR

I WOKE THE next morning feeling out of sorts. Bad dreams? None came to mind, but a wrongness weighed on me. Christian was coming. That's what was wrong. Not wrong but . . . not right either.

Aunt Irm appeared wary as I emerged from my room, darting looks at me, and offering a "Good morning" that felt more like a question than a statement. I thanked her, as always, for filling my travel mug with coffee, wished her a good day, and left without mentioning the man-size elephant in the room. "I will see you tonight," she said. "Please try to not be late."

She knew I had little control over my clinical days, but I wasn't scheduled to work late, so most times I was home by six.

The anesthesia residents and I spent our morning on Labor and Delivery doing two Cesareans and three labor epidurals. Near the end of their monthlong rotation, the residents' procedural skills had improved. Most of my teaching was of the "What would you do if . . . ?" variety.

Watching happy parents greet their newborn is a job like no other, except when things don't go well; then it's still a job like no other, but in a uniquely devastating way. Today was all joyful tears, even from the sixteen-year-old having her second child, accompanied by her mother.

At sixteen, I was still an avowed tomboy. Becoming a parent might have been the furthest thing from my mind. I enjoyed being around boys, on the football field or softball diamond. Clearly. this young woman's childhood was not mine.

At noon, the charge nurse requested a lunch break for the scrub tech and OR nurse. Worked for me. I passed the food court and entered the Physician's Lounge where they served the same food as the main cafeteria, but in a room without lines and with one free piece of fruit per purchase. Not quite the free lunches offered at the private hospital across town.

Faculty members occupied a few small tables, sitting in twos and threes, deep in conversation. Rather than interrupt, I took my pre-made salad to one of the smaller tables, planning to catch up on email during the break. Soon after, though, Nikki Yarborough approached. "May I join you?" Her tray held her ever-present ice water, plus milk, a cup of soup, and a mountain of saltines. She looked pale and drawn.

"Of course." I put my phone facedown on the table. "Are you feeling okay?"

"I'm fine." Her tone and expression said the opposite.

I gave her my frown of skepticism. "Not buying it. You haven't been to the gym in weeks. What's up?" Months ago, we discovered a common interest in exercise, and she invited me to a boot-camp-type workout at her gym, SweatLife. It had taken a month of high-dose ibuprofen before I finally stopped hating her for the invitation, and it became part of my weekly routine. I had forgotten how enjoyable and motivating it could be to work out with a friend. Recently, it had been more hit-or-miss as our schedules seemed to align less often, even at five thirty in the morning.

She opened her carton of whole milk and drank half. I forced my expression to remain neutral. Whole milk seems disgusting after years of skim. Based on her grimace, she agreed and followed it with greedy gulps of water. Nikki guilted me into hydrating more when we worked out, and afterward. No matter how much she drank during the class, she chugged a whole glass of ice-cold water on the way to the car. It made my insides shiver.

Now, she looked around, as if checking for eavesdroppers. "Can I tell you something in confidence?"

"Of course."

"I'm pregnant."

I knew she and her husband, Ian, had been trying for years and had suffered at least two miscarriages. I had been her anesthesiologist for an operation to evacuate her uterus after one last year. "Congratulations. That's great news."

"Shhh."

I wiped the smile from my face. "Why the secrecy?"

"I don't want to jinx it. Last time, having to tell people I wasn't pregnant anymore, it was too sad."

That I understood only too well. "How many weeks are you?"

"Almost twenty."

"You're not showing." I thought back. I hadn't seen her in anything but flowing dresses or scrubs with a white coat or surgical gown recently. "Is that why you haven't been at the gym?"

"I'm sorry. I wanted to tell you. There's kind of a lot going on." She tore open a pack of saltines and bit off a corner of one.

"No problem. How are you feeling?"

"The nausea's better, mostly, except for today. I started to feel her move last night." She smiled, but it wasn't the shiny-eyed glow I'd come to expect when friends announce they're expecting. Too much fear there.

"I'm really happy for you."

"Thanks." She took another sip of milk, then wiped the white mustache.

"You're going to have to tell your chairman, you know. He'll need time to arrange coverage while you're on maternity leave." I didn't know Dr. Cantwell, but by reputation I didn't expect him to be particularly accommodating.

"Our division is a mess right now. Evelyn left again Monday on Family Leave at the same time Eduardo is on vacation so I've been covering every night this week." That explained the exhaustion in her face. She took a crunchy bite of another saltine and let the crumbs fall like snow on the table.

"You don't have to work extra to earn maternity leave, you know."

"Not technically, no. Until he hires more people, we're all working extra. It's sad to see the division imploding." Cardiology was one of the most respected departments at University. "I just hope Evelyn's back soon." Leaning forward, she lowered her voice conspiratorially. "I hate to sound insensitive, but she's been on a death watch for her dad for months now, taking leave at the drop of a hat, then he recovers again. Except he never really recovers. He's not even conscious, so why does she need to be there?" She leaned back and took another bite of cracker.

I tried to freeze my expression in "concerned friend" mode. This wasn't about me. She was simply overwhelmed and had forgotten about the year I spent with a comatose husband, visiting when I could, feeling guilty when I couldn't.

"Thanks for letting me get that off my chest. I couldn't say it to anyone else, but I know you won't judge me."

Exhausted-Nikki differed greatly from normal-Nikki. Always outspoken, apparently her filters required more energy than she had left. I couldn't hold it against her. Instead, I tried to be encouraging. "And you can't talk to Dr. Cantwell about your crazy hours?"

She shook her head.

"What's he going to do, fire you? Then who would take all the extra call?"

She smiled around another cracker.

"If not for yourself, how about me?" I said. "I need you pushing me at the gym."

She swallowed and said, "I can't take responsibility for you, lady. I led that horse to water."

"You know you can exercise while you're pregnant, right?"

"Yeah, I haven't really felt up to it. Maybe now that I'm halfway, I'll start feeling better. Except I'll look like I swallowed a bowling ball." I remembered that feeling fondly, in retrospect at least.

We ate in silence for several moments, then I recalled seeing her name in a recent faculty council email. "Hey, congrats on your paper."

"Yeah, thanks, finally. Can you believe it took a whole year to get it published?"

I could believe it, yes, if they had first submitted to leading journals and then worked their way down after rejections.

"The engineer wrote most of it. Cantwell's pushing me to write another one, about my experience with the Kadence so far, but with no non-clinical time . . . Hey, maybe I can use that to lobby for a day out of clinic."

"You absolutely should. But as an inventor, isn't it a conflict of interest for him to make you publish on his own device?"

"Yeah, feels a little incestuous, doesn't it? He calls it a unique opportunity to be the first to publish about a breakthrough technology."

"Of course he does. You do need publications for promotion and tenure, but you should never feel—"

"What if I don't care about promotion and tenure?"

That stopped me short.

"Publish or perish, give lectures to add lines on your CV, but give lectures to the right learners." She held up an index finger. "Medical students count more than residents. It's a bunch of . . ."

I waited, but she didn't finish the thought.

"Nikki, you sound a little stressed." Understatement. Though she'd never seemed driven, I chalked it up to being new on faculty and not yet clear on her academic goals. "You sure everything's okay?"

"Yeah." This time she didn't even try for convincing. "Have you ever questioned being a doctor?"

"Of course, everyone does, then you remind yourself why you chose to suffer through med school in the first place."

"What if you never wanted it?"

I couldn't formulate an answer to that.

"I never wanted to be a doctor. Did you know that? I went to med school for my mom because she had to drop out to have me after my dad abandoned her. She was never able to go back, so now I'm living her dream."

Not a good reason to go through medical training. "Did she know how you felt?" Nikki's mother died sometime during her training. I wasn't sure when.

Nikki wiped a single tear from the corner of each eye. "No. She died right after I graduated. By then I had too much med school debt to do anything else."

She'd suffered through eight more years of training. "What else would you do?"

Blinking back tears, she shook her head.

"Research?"

Her face screwed up in distaste. "God, no."

"What about private practice? Maybe getting away from academia would help."

She crumpled the cracker wrappers into a loose ball. "Yeah, maybe."

"Right now, it sounds like you need a break. When's the last time you and Ian took a vacation?"

"Ha. Our honeymoon five years ago." Her face cleared a bit, so I pushed her to relive the happy memory.

"Where'd you go?"

She made a sound somewhere between a chuckle and a scoff. "We didn't have any money, so we borrowed his uncle's fishing cabin in north Georgia. It rained the whole time and the driveway flooded and the power went out and we spent the week cold and starving."

Oops, wrong memory to relive.

"I'm sorry," she said. "I sound like an ungrateful whiner. With the pregnancy, I've been thinking a lot about my mom." I'd done the same, at the time. "Everything's fine, or it will be when my partners come back to work and I can catch up on some sleep."

"You sound burned out. How are you going to take good care of your patients if you're physically and emotionally exhausted?"

"We're doctors first, right? 'Place the needs of patients ahead of self-interest,'" she quoted.

All that was true, and at the moment I had my doubts Nikki could honor that pledge. "As long as you can do it safely," I said. "Once you get some rest, you should seriously consider leaving, or at least threatening to. It might put a fire under your chairman to hire you another partner. Even if you choose to stay, often the College will match another salary offer."

She didn't reject the idea outright; rather, she seemed too beat to even consider it. I'd be sorry to see her go. I enjoyed her company, blunt though she may be.

Her phone rang. She glanced at the screen and frowned. The frown deepened as she answered. "I'm on my way." She disconnected, pulled the napkin from her lap, and placed it beside her nearly full bowl of soup. "Gotta meet a patient in the ER. Thanks for listening, Kate. Sorry to be such a downer. I will be okay. Really."

I hoped that was true as she hurried from the room. If I had more Aunt Irm in me, I would have a chat with Nikki's chairman myself. But it wasn't my battle. I had to get better at recognizing that and then following through . . . or not following through.

Back on Labor and Delivery, we started another Cesarean. After delivery, I helped with some of the all-important first photos for the happy family until I was interrupted by a phone call from Tom Angley, Esq. I stepped from the OR, remaining just outside where I could watch through the warped window blinds.

He apologized again for blindsiding me at the cemetery. "I have a virtual meeting scheduled with Adam Downey and his attorney tomorrow afternoon. Would you be able to join us?"

"I can't make it before five." Even that would be a stretch.

He agreed to adjust the meeting time and a small rock formed in my stomach. An hour later, Nikki's text turned it into a boulder. "Another Kadence misfire."

CHAPTER FIVE

ON THE DRIVE home after work, I felt an interesting combination of anticipation and dread. A few months ago, Christian O'Donnell, Aunt Irm, and I uncovered a mercy-killer-for-hire scheme and helped stop the nurse anesthetist-turned-serial-killer. Through it all, Christian was helpful and resourceful and supportive. Too supportive. I came to rely on him and enjoy his company more than a married woman should, even one whose husband had been in a coma for almost a year.

Then Greg died, or finished dying as his brother claimed, and Christian left with a promise to return when I was ready.

But I wasn't ready. Was I? It was too soon to consider a relationship. Except I had. Deep down, in the lonely hours. And then chastised myself endlessly.

Before my head exploded from arguing with myself, I was home with Christian's SUV parked out front, and my heart clawing its way into my throat. I parked in the garage, then closed my eyes and took a slow, deep breath. *I can do this.*

Laptop bag in hand, I climbed from the car and opened the door into the house. Shadow greeted me, then ran back to Christian, excited to show me our company. And what company. Christian stood from his seat and looked . . . incredible. The gold flecks in his deep brown eyes sparkled as he approached, as if asking permission for the embrace that was coming anyway. Once I allowed myself to relax, it felt surprisingly comfortable, and maybe less wrong than before.

"Kate, it's really good to see you." He stepped back without breaking contact, his eyes locked on mine.

"You, too." I couldn't help but return his smile, then he released me and I went around the open counter to Aunt Irm. "How are you?"

"I am fine, kindchen." She kissed my cheeks. "Check the bread, please. Then pour yourself wine."

"I can handle that one." Christian reached for the bottle.

Ten minutes later, we sat around our small kitchen table, plates full of pork and rice and cooked carrots, and ate in relative silence for several minutes.

"How is your mother?" Aunt Irm asked him. "Why did she not join us?"

"She's really well, thanks. She's pouring her considerable energy into politics, believe it or not, lobbying for legislation on assisted suicide and the right to die. She had plans tonight or we would have invited you to the house. She'd love to see you."

Aunt Irm considered, then nodded. "I would like this as well."

"I saw Lieutenant Garner this afternoon," Christian said. "He asked how his local Holmes and Watson are doing." Christian's childhood friend Lieutenant Frank Garner headed the investigation last spring.

Aunt Irm smiled proudly and held up her fork. "Tell him we are available for consultation."

"No, we absolutely are not." My laugh was interrupted by Shadow's barks as headlights flashed through the front windows. "Are you expecting someone?" I asked my aunt.

She stood. "Sorry to leave you with the dishes. I have an appointment with Carmel."

"You didn't." I stared at her, embarrassed and a tiny bit irritated. Christian had the decency to look away, but he was grinning. I walked with her to the front door and whispered, "I can't believe you did this. I don't need you to set me up."

"Enjoy your evening, kindchen." She didn't whisper. "Wonderful to see you, Christian." And she was gone, outside and down the sidewalk. I closed the door behind her, confused and unsure.

Dishes clattered in the sink. "I'll go after I finish these, if you like," he said.

"You don't have to do these, you know."

"I know." He smiled and I joined him at the sink, taking the rinsed dishes from him and loading the dishwasher.

"Shadow and I could use the company on our walk, if you have time."

"I absolutely have time. Tell me what's been going on."

I did. I told him about work and Aunt Irm and Carmel's help and my recent failure teaching Shadow to heel. He told me about his work, including a recently successful merger he'd handled, and now the project that brought him to town. He'd taken over when his colleague was injured in a car accident.

The awkwardness melted away as he caught me up on his family, especially Michael, his eldest brother, who had followed their father's wishes and helped arrange his mercy killing. "He and Mom both knew it was illegal, but I believe Michael when he says he thought it was humane and the best option at the time. Now remorse is eating him up. I haven't seen him, but Mom says he's lost weight and looks awful. He's been living with her since Dad died, but he disappeared a few days ago and she's worried about him. He won't answer calls from any of us."

Shadow danced by the door as I took down his leash and clipped it to his collar. Christian held the door for us, closed it, then paused.

"We're just going around the block," I said.

He frowned but said nothing.

"Have you always been a security freak?"

"Freak? No. Appropriate safety measures though. I grew up with Garner, remember?"

"So he was a cop in grade school?" Shadow pulled and we headed down the street. "On the message, you said you had a question for me."

"Yes, I do. I wonder if I could borrow your expertise. My client is about to purchase a medical device company here. As I mentioned, I got involved at the tail end and feel like I need to conduct my own due diligence."

I don't know what I expected, but it wasn't this. "Sure, what's your question?"

"What kind of AICD did Aunt Irm get? This company makes one called the Kadence and claims it's going to become the industry standard."

"That's the one she has. Her cardiologist recommended it for the cloud-based communication, which I appreciate. I can check on her remotely any time." I pulled out my phone and showed him the app. It reported the date and time followed by: "Sinus rhythm, no events last 24h."

"That's good, right? Sinus rhythm?"

"Right."

"Do you think I could talk with her cardiologist? University Hospital is the only place inserting them so far, and it would help to interview someone with firsthand knowledge."

"You know the chairman of the department invented it, right?"

"I do. But I'd like the opinion of someone with slightly less to lose if the sale doesn't go through."

I promised to ask Nikki. "While we're trading expertise, I want to do something charitable in Greg's name. Something to help families of soldiers with head injuries. Though I've only just started the research, I know I'll need legal advice."

"I have a friend who can help with that."

"Isn't it great we both have helpful friends?" Shadow stopped for a particularly engrossing odor. "Speaking of which, I'm meeting with my mother-in-law's attorney tomorrow evening. She passed away and named me executor after Greg. Can you tell me what to expect?"

"First, I'm sorry about your mother-in-law. Were you close?" He looked in my eyes, as if assessing my sense of loss.

"No. She was suffering from early dementia by the time I met her."

"Second, will Adam be at the meeting?"

"Virtually, yes."

More assessing. I was okay. He couldn't hurt any of us over a video chat.

"Do you have a copy of her will?" he asked.

"Probably, somewhere." I hadn't even thought to look. I pulled on Shadow's lead to give another walker more space. My dog had a tough time understanding that not every human wanted to pet him.

Christian continued, "You should have someone review it, especially considering your history with Adam."

"I only found out about it yesterday. Any chance you'll still be in town tomorrow afternoon?"

"I will be. In exchange you have to join me for dinner."

My insides trembled a little. "I'd love to, but I have a dinner meeting tomorrow night. It's the county medical society and the governor is speaking about funding for indigent care."

"So he's campaigning."

"That, too. The dean of the medical school wants a good showing from the faculty."

"How about Saturday? Bring Aunt Irm and Shadow to the house and we can have a picnic and maybe get out on the kayaks." Christian's family owned what could only be called a compound on the other side of Paynes Prairie, south of town, complete with a small lake. A day relaxing near water was kinda tough to turn down.

"I'll have to check with Aunt Irm, but it sounds great." We walked on and I had an idea. "You know what? My cardiologist friend could use some time away. If she's not working, can I invite her? You could ask her about the Kadence."

"Great. Two birds with one stone."

"That's kind of morbid, don't you think?"

"You prefer the less efficient two birds with two stones? Then one has to watch its partner die first."

"I stand corrected. It's a well-thought-out idiom." It felt good to smile and laugh. Aunt Irm and I hadn't done enough of that lately. Though it had been weeks since her nearly fatal arrhythmia and Kadence placement, neither of us had fully recovered, always fearful of the next event. If I made a point of relaxing Saturday afternoon, it might help her do the same.

We finished the circuit of the neighborhood and made it back to the house. As I refreshed Shadow's water, my phone vibrated a text message. I apologized but had to check it. It could be Aunt Irm, or work, or Randi going into labor. "Aunt Irm says there's banana cream pie in the fridge."

"I love your aunt." Christian opened the refrigerator and pulled out the pie while I took down two small plates and opened the cutlery drawer.

"What do you think, forks or spoons?"

He jiggled the pan. "Forks." With the pie on the counter, he glanced at his own phone. "Aunt Irm says there's whipped cream in the door of the fridge."

"She texted you?"

"Only about the whipped cream. You got the pie."

"True. Whew."

"Worried about losing most-favored status?"

The knife glided through the soft pie, then I pressed harder to cut through the graham cracker crust. "Nah, it's okay if you're a close second."

"Your brother wouldn't mind?"

"Oh yeah, okay, third. You can be third favorite. Wait, Shadow. Fourth—would you take fourth?"

"You sure there's not a talented squirrel in the backyard, or a spider that spells German words in the corner of her room?"

"*Nein*," I said. "Shadow pretty much takes care of the squirrels and the bug man came yesterday, so you've got fourth place free and clear."

CHAPTER SIX

The next morning, I went without coffee. Aunt Irm had stayed the night with Carmel and I couldn't be bothered to make coffee for one. The house felt empty and quiet without her clanging in the kitchen, humming to herself.

After starting my OR cases, I returned to the clinical office to review notes on my patients from the day before. Sam Paulus, my colleague in charge of the daily schedule, sat at his NASA-worthy command center. On his desk was a computer with two large screens. Overhead, another massive screen displayed the real-time OR schedule in a rainbow of colors indicating patient locations and surgical status. To his left, he maintained a wall-size whiteboard with a handwritten copy of the same schedule in a taped-off grid where he wrote an abbreviated list of the scheduled operations, then added a labeled magnet indicating the assigned anesthesia staff. Like a conductor, he arranged cases and staff as emergencies were added or cases were canceled.

"Happy Friday, Professor," he said.

"Good morning, Sam."

"Any fun plans for the weekend?"

I was telling him about the meeting with Adam's attorney when the Code Blue alarm blared. "Charge nurse and anesthesia stat to the cath lab. Charge nurse and anesthesia stat to the cath lab." Over and over. Sam and I ran down the hall to the cardiac catheterization lab where a nurse held open the door and directed us into the preoperative holding area. A large man in scrubs rhythmically compressed the chest of an elderly male patient on a stretcher. The ECG showed v-fib.

Twice in one week? I hadn't participated in a code in months.

The patient's thin frame bounced with the compressions. I went to the head of the bed, applied a face mask over the man's nose and mouth, and tried to breathe for him, but his hollow cheeks created insurmountable leaks. Sam joined me and pulled up on the cheeks to form a seal.

Nikki Yarborough attached defibrillator patches to the patient's chest while the nurse gave a quick report. "He has critical aortic valve stenosis and was scheduled to have the valve ballooned open this morning by Dr. Patel. He started having chest pain during IV placement and lost consciousness."

"Clear." Nikki's finger lingered over the "Shock" button on the defibrillator. Compressions stopped and we released the patient's head. His chest muscles tensed with the ka-thunk of the shock, but after the square wave, the ECG remained in v-fib.

She called for chest compressions to resume, for doses of epinephrine to be given, and administered several more shocks while I inserted the breathing tube and continued ventilating him, but we knew it was futile. When the aortic valve won't open properly, the heart struggles to eject blood at the best of times. Trying to accomplish that by pushing on the chest was like squeezing an intact orange to get out the juice.

After ten minutes without a functional heart rhythm, Nikki called the code. The room fell silent as the team paused for a moment, most with heads bowed, then they moved off quietly. "Thanks for your help, everyone," Nikki said, dejection in her voice.

I waited while she spoke to the nurse. When he moved off to clean up the patient, I put an arm around her.

She took in a long, deep breath. "I'm okay. I finally got some sleep last night, but this is not how I wanted to start my Friday." She looked around. "Patel still isn't here so I have to go talk to his patient's wife." Again with the bitterness in her voice. She was having a tough week . . . or month, but this wasn't a good look for her.

"How about I talk to her?" *Ouch. Did I really just offer that?* "Breaking bad news" was one of my least favorite topics in medical school. Despite lectures and role-playing exercises, it wasn't a skill that came easily to anyone, and certainly not to me. Fortunately, it isn't one anesthesiologists often exercise. This patient and his family's Friday had started far worse than Nikki's, though, and they deserved more compassion than she might have in her tank at the moment.

"No. It's okay. It should come from a cardiologist," she said.

"I could come with you."

"No, Kate. I've got this. Don't worry." She pushed through the double wood doors.

I was about to return to the OR suites when an exam room door flew open and a middle-aged man in a tailored suit stopped me. He read my badge. "You're a doctor. Come in here, now."

Rude, but maybe someone needed medical attention, so I followed without argument. On the exam table, talking on a cellphone, sat another well-dressed man I vaguely recognized. Probably a VIP based on his companion, his own expensive suit, and—was that makeup? Though the man was not acutely ill, I hid my annoyance. "How can I help?"

The man who summoned me said, "Governor Michaelson was supposed to have his Kadence interrogated half an hour ago."

That would be why he looked vaguely familiar. He was our governor. I didn't much care for his underling.

"He has a schedule to keep."

On the phone, Governor Michaelson raised his voice. "Where the hell are you? If you tell me to come to the hospital, you damn well better be here."

Wow.

"A woman doctor came in and left without doing anything. Now another one is here." He listened for a moment while I considered my title, "another woman doctor." How sweet. He thrust the phone at me.

I took it with as much professionalism as I could muster, my face surely reddening. "This is Dr. Downey from anesthesia." Normally I used my first name. Not this time.

"Anesthesia, what are you doing there? This is Dr. Cantwell, chair of cardiology. Where is Nikki Yarborough?"

"Dr. Yarborough responded to an emergency in the cath lab and is now speaking with the family. She will be here as soon as she can."

"She was supposed to—"

"She was the only cardiologist present when a Code Blue was called and appropriately managed the event."

After a brief knock, the door opened. "I'm sorry for the delay," Nikki said, then gave me a quizzical look.

"Here she is now, Dr. Cantwell."

She reached out her hand for the phone, her lips a thin line. I handed it over. "Sorry," I whispered. In a weak effort to reduce the tension in the room, I said, "I look forward to hearing your speech tonight, Governor."

He looked at me for a long moment, maybe measuring my political affiliation, before he gave a curt nod. Nikki said something into the phone, then handed it back to the governor and reached for the interrogation computer on a small cart nearby.

I nodded to her in solidarity. "Call when you get a minute." The governor's health was none of my business. Maybe this was a routine interrogation or maybe Dr. Cantwell was worried about the two misfires. On my way back to check my ORs, I pulled up Aunt Irm's cloud report. No events. All's well . . . for now.

CHAPTER SEVEN

WHEN NIKKI DIDN'T call by late afternoon, I called her. "How are you doing?" I had to come up with a better question.

"I'm okay. No more sociopaths to deal with."

"Want to carpool to the Medical Society dinner tonight?"

"I'm exhausted and after this morning, I'm not especially interested in seeing the governor again."

"He won't notice us."

A long pause followed and I thought I'd lost her until she said, "Can we make rude remarks from the back row?"

"Absolutely."

"Okay. I'll meet you there." Good. Unexpected, but good. I wasn't sure, in her place, I could have been so easily convinced. My backup plan was to take her out to dinner somewhere else. After a patient death, it helped to talk with someone who understood, which, according to her, was not her engineer husband.

In the clinical office, Sam Paulus volunteered to take over my remaining operating room so I could attend the meeting with Adam and the attorneys. Sam knew Adam and most of the long, sad story. "Hang in there, Kate."

I thought about his words as I drove to the attorney's office. I missed Greg, worried about Aunt Irm, and stressed over work.

"Hanging in there" was about the best you could say about my life at the moment. And now I had to deal with Adam again. My fights with him began during his residency when I wouldn't support his efforts to get back into the program. Not that I had much influence on the department back then, but he'd diverted drugs from patients, become addicted, overdosed, and nearly died. Adam lied and begged and made crazy promises, but Greg and I agreed with the residency program director that anesthesia, with its ready access to powerful drugs, wasn't the field for him.

After Greg's accident, Adam and I fought over withdrawal of care. Then, as his mom succumbed to dementia, we fought over management of her estate. Finally, he nearly had me killed. I didn't trust Adam, then or now.

And yet, I still felt responsible for him. Aunt Irm had a point, Adam had gone too far. Would Greg want me to wash my hands of him? Maybe with bleach and sandpaper? No. Not yet. Waiting until his release from prison made more sense, though part of me wondered if I was just postponing a decision that would get no easier.

Arriving several minutes early, I took a moment to collect my thoughts. When I finally climbed out of my Honda, Christian stood by my back bumper in a very lawyerly suit, carrying a very lawyerly briefcase, but with a not-at-all-lawyerly smile. "You okay?" he asked.

Wow.

"Yeah, fine, sorry, I was . . . I really appreciate you being here." He grinned when I made a show of taking in his suit, then my khakis and collared shirt. "Looks like I missed the memo on appropriate dress."

He reached out an arm for a quick hug and my unease faded.

We walked together to the single-story brick building. Christian pulled open the door with the attorneys' names emblazoned on it. The receptionist looked up from her desk. "Dr. Downey?"

At my nod, she stood and invited us to follow her. Rather than the office where I'd met Mr. Angley before, she led us to a conference room with a large table of dark wood, paneled walls, and comfortable-looking leather chairs. On the table sat a massive screen filled with the larger-than-life face of my brother-in-law. When Christian and I passed in front of the camera, Adam's normal, irritatingly carefree smile morphed to something much darker. "What's he doing here?"

I introduced Christian to Mr. Angley and to the attorney whose face had appeared next to Adam's.

Mr. Angley stood and shook both our hands, then nodded toward the video feed from the prison in Starke. Adam's attorney, John Golanka, introduced himself.

"I'm sorry for your loss, Adam," Christian said.

Adam remained silent, sullen. I should have said the same. I didn't.

Mr. Angley opened a file on the table, passed some pages to us, and slipped on a pair of rimless glasses. Christian opened his briefcase on the table and pulled out his own folder, with copies of the same document.

At my questioning look, he said, "I read it this morning. It's pretty straightforward."

Mr. Angley summarized the will. Mrs. Downey left everything in equal shares to her two sons, but specified that Greg, or his wife in Greg's absence, control disbursements from the estate until such time as Adam was deemed "in the right state of mind" to manage on his own.

Adam seemed to look directly at me. In everything but the eyes, he'd always looked so much like Greg. Something was different now. His features had hardened over the last few months. It was a relief, really. For the first time, my heart didn't skip a beat with an instant of recognition. "My attorney has my account information," he said.

I thought of Greg, rescuing his brother, caring for him, trying to keep him out of trouble. "Once you've served your time, we'll reassess."

Adam's face changed again, back into that of an angry, bitter man. "I've been clean for years. You have no right to keep interfering in my life."

"You really think serving time is what your mom had in mind?" I said, maybe too sharply.

"You didn't know my mother enough to make that assessment."

"I seriously doubt manslaughter and accessory to attempted murder square with anyone's definition of 'right state of mind.'"

"I was helping my brother finish dying." Adam's voice rose.

"Repeating the words of a serial killer isn't better. There's no way Greg would consider you ready to handle this money after you tried to have me killed."

"You want an apology? Is that it? You're going to hold my money hostage?"

Wow.

My face burned. Christian pressed his leg against mine. I took a slow deep breath.

Adam's attorney said something and Adam slouched in his chair. Mr. Golanka then looked into the camera. "'Right state of mind' is a rather vague bar to set. Some specific goalposts would be helpful."

"This is the verbiage on which Mrs. Downey insisted," Mr. Angley said.

"She had dementia for God's sake," Adam said.

"At the time this will was written, she was of sound mind," Mr. Angley said.

"By whose assessment?" Adam said. "She'd been losing her mind for years."

"Be that as it may, this document is legal and binding."

Adam swore and his expression took my breath away—pure loathing. Christian stiffened beside me as Adam spoke in a low, menacing voice. "I never needed you to be responsible for me. I'm paying my debt, but you can never be absolved of your crimes against my brother. You and your boyfriend can go to hell." His arm reached toward the camera and the video feed vanished.

A pale Tom Angley stared at me.

I forced my jaw to relax. "Is there anything you need me to do?"

He gestured to the document. Christian reviewed the sections briefly with me and asked if I wanted more detail. I didn't. Honestly, Adam's words echoed in my head letting in little of Christian's explanation. I trusted him and signed, stood, thanked the attorney in a voice not my own, and led the way out. Seething, I ignored the secretary, ignored Mr. Angley's meaningless words of reassurance, and stormed down the steps to my car. My whole body tingled with heat, but why? Anger? Shame? I stopped at my car.

Christian watched me, concern in his eyes.

"I'm okay." But not okay enough to face Aunt Irm. Not yet. "Do you have a few minutes?"

We agreed to meet at a chain restaurant-bar a few blocks away.

Alone in my car, I leaned my head back and replayed the scene. Why did it upset me? Adam was in prison. He couldn't hurt me or Aunt Irm. Was it the boyfriend crack? He couldn't know anything about our relationship. There wasn't anything to know, for that matter. Had I expected an apology? I shouldn't need it from him. Or was it the accusation? The Greg I knew understood my choices. Was my anger just because Adam had the last word in our long-standing feud? Petty as it sounded, partly. I slammed my hands on the steering wheel. He deserved no more of my energy. He had power over me only if I allowed it.

If only it were that easy.

CHAPTER EIGHT

AT HOME, I greeted Aunt Irm and offered to help as she bustled in the kitchen.

"I need help only with Shadow." He stood by the door nudging his dangling leash so the hook clanged against the wall.

"Impatient brat." I patted his head. Leash attached, we went for a quick walk around the neighborhood. "We'll go longer tomorrow, I promise." Why was it I convinced Nikki to attend the dinner tonight? If it weren't for her, I might stay home with my dog and Aunt Irm. We had not yet discussed her disappearing act the night before.

I fed Shadow dinner and freshened his water.

"Sit and talk to me while I finish," Aunt Irm said. "Tell me about your day."

"Really? My day?" With a smile, I raised my eyebrows. "That's what you want to talk about?"

Her eyes twinkled. "Begin with yesterday evening." She covered a pot on the stove, dried her hands on the bottom of her apron, then sat on a stool beside me at the kitchen island.

"I can't believe you left us," I said.

"You need time alone together."

Inwardly I groaned, only inwardly. "We had a nice time, caught up, took Shadow for a walk." His head popped up. He would walk twelve times a day if given the chance, each time as if it were the first. "Christian offered to represent me at the meeting this afternoon about Greg's mom's estate." Shadow put his head back down between his paws with a soft groan. Poor, neglected dog.

Aunt Irm nodded sagely. In her mind, above-and-beyond was not unexpected when it came to Christian. "And did Christian agree for you to give everything to charity?"

I laughed. If she'd seen Adam's face . . . "It didn't come up, though I would have loved to do just that. I'm still in control of her estate until Adam gets his life in order. Maybe that will give him a purpose."

"Hmph. At best, he will fake this. At worst, he will find a way to gain control anyway."

That made my skin crawl.

"And tonight, will Christian join you?" That twinkle in her eye again.

I shook my head but couldn't help grinning at her tenacity. "No, he is not attending a meeting of the County Medical Society. I barely want to attend and I'm a member. I'm going with Nikki Yarborough."

"Oh."

"What do you mean, 'oh'?"

"I think only it would be more enjoyable with Christian."

"Medical Society meetings are never enjoyable, and Nikki's going through some tough stuff right now."

"Hmph." She stood.

Her attitude surprised me. Aunt Irm loved everyone. Well, not everyone, not Adam, or Christian's brother, Michael, or her sister-in-law, Martina. Ha, maybe time to rethink that assessment. "What do you have against Nikki?"

Back at the stove, she removed the pot from the burner and switched everything off. "Perhaps it is only that she is troubled as you say. She does not take time to talk to her patient. And when she was here for dinner with your friends, she did not take interest in you or the others." When I hosted a Women in Medicine and Science dinner several months before, I hadn't noticed anything off about Nikki, and she was a good doctor. Maybe her abrupt nature rubbed Aunt Irm the wrong way.

"If you like her, I will give her another chance," Aunt Irm said.

"Thank you. Christian invited all of us out to his mom's tomorrow for a picnic. What do you think?"

She didn't have to think. "I would like to visit Molly. I will call to see what we can bring."

As she lifted the phone, I went into my bedroom to dress for the dinner. With the governor on the program, I chose something more on the business end of "business-casual." Shopping-hater that I am, that meant my only pair of black dress pants and a blouse, with a sweater for the inevitable hyper-refrigeration of a hotel meeting room. I brushed my hair, put on earrings and a gold chain Greg gave me for our first anniversary, and a touch of mascara.

On my way out, Aunt Irm gave a nod of approval, and Shadow offered a coating of dog hair. Black pants, black dog, it worked. While I waited for the garage door to rise, I texted Nikki. "See you there in 15."

She replied before I'd backed down the driveway, "Yeah, yeah," and was waiting outside the glass doors when I arrived. Only she could make a shapeless dress look beautiful, likely chosen to hide any evidence of a baby bump. We joined the already packed hallway outside the meeting room.

I attended County Medical Society meetings only sporadically. Tonight, the governor attracted a larger crowd than usual, in part because the dean of the medical school had strongly encouraged junior faculty to attend. Nikki and I stood in line for our name tags, then went to the bar—soda for me, ice water for her.

"Let me know when you see your chairman so I can steer clear," I said.

"Chicken." Her smile was genuine, the first in a while, but it didn't last long. "He's out of town. That's why I had to deal with the governor this morning."

"Ah, how nice for him."

"Exactly." She lifted her glass in a toast. "Head down and power on." She gestured to the dean, who stood off to the side, surrounded by a throng of well-dressed physicians. "Do you think we have to kiss his ring to get credit for coming?"

"Ha." I touched my name-badge. "Hopefully picking this up counts for roll call."

The doors into the dining area opened and the crowd flowed inside. Unlike the rest, jockeying for seats near the stage, Nikki and I chose a back table. The other six chairs filled up slowly with private practice physicians from outside the university. We introduced ourselves, then spoke largely to each other.

At a lull in the conversation, I said, "I need to ask a favor. The company that makes the Kadence is about to be sold. Did you know that?"

She sipped her water. "I've heard rumors."

"My friend Christian O'Donnell is involved as a legal consultant for the buyer. He'd like to talk to a cardiologist familiar with the device. Who better than you?"

She paused longer than I expected. "Yes, of course, I'm happy to talk to him."

"He invited us to his family's property near Paynes Prairie tomorrow for a picnic. You can bring Ian and have some outside relaxing time while you help him out."

"That sounds nice, but I'm on call, and Ian is busy." Her husband never went out with us.

"Their house is less than thirty minutes from the hospital." While anesthesiology call was in-house, most other services took call from home, and thirty minutes was the generally accepted response time. "I'm on tomorrow night, too. We won't stay long."

Another long pause. "Let's see how morning rounds go, okay?"

I agreed, and the evening's program began with some words by the president of the society, followed by a brief business meeting, to which neither Nikki nor I paid any attention. At last he introduced the governor, "to talk about healthcare financing in the coming years." A frequent topic in an election year and always with promises of more of everything—more money to provide more care to more people, and all without raising taxes. If only basic economics were a required course. Still, I hoped to gauge his sincerity and level of understanding, despite his behavior that morning.

Behind us a number of people entered, at least two with large shoulder-mounted cameras labeled with local television station call letters. Nikki rolled her eyes.

The governor began with the obligatory gratitude for the invitation, "and for what you do as physicians on a daily basis."

"What a bunch of crap," Nikki whispered. "He has no respect for us."

"Maybe he meant every other daily basis. Today doesn't count."

Nikki put a hand over her mouth to smother a laugh.

"I have personally benefited from advances in medical technology made possible by physicians in this very society." He tapped a finger dramatically against the lectern with the last three words.

"Do I have to listen to this?" A few at our table glanced at her as Nikki's voice rose above a whisper. Then all heads swung back to the stage as shouts and a collective gasp seemed to suck the air from the room. The governor slumped against the lectern, then vanished behind it. Several people seated in the front row of tables leapt onto the stage. In a room jam-packed with physicians, Nikki pushed her way to the front and onto the stage. "He's my patient." Positioned too close to the microphone, her words projected above the din.

She called for the AED, the automatic external defibrillator. The governor had a Kadence, though. Had she disabled it to prevent a misfire and now it was unavailable when he needed it most? Maybe she wanted to view his ECG using the chest pads of the AED. A staff member ran along the side wall, bright yellow box in hand. With so many people on the stage now, it was handed bucket-brigade-style toward the lectern. Moments later, Nikki shouted, "Clear!"

I felt the pain in my own chest. Three codes in a week and two in one day. That couldn't be normal, even for a cardiologist. And, of course, it had to be the governor. In my futile and helpless musings, I wanted his collapse to be unrelated to the Kadence Nikki had interrogated just hours before and likely given a clean bill of health.

"Clear!" sounded again.

The first shock must not have converted his heart rhythm. A second shock followed. Someone said, "He's back in sinus," and the room let out a shared sigh of relief. A team of paramedics arrived and the sea of physicians parted. Many filtered to the back where awkward conversation ensued. Someone thought Nikki might be a cardiologist. Someone else questioned why the governor would withhold a cardiac condition from the public. I decided unexpected traumatic situations impair the logic of observers.

A reporter approached the group, microphone in hand, followed closely by a cameraman. "Excuse me, did you say the physician who responded is a cardiologist? What is her name, please?"

The group exchanged looks. No one spoke. Heads shook. The reporter let out a frustrated groan and turned toward our table. I grabbed Nikki's purse along with my own and headed away, to the far side of the room to wait. Ten minutes later, the paramedics lifted the stretcher from the stage, expanded the undercarriage, and wheeled the governor from the room, still breathing for him through an endotracheal tube. The monitor's steady beep sliced through the sudden silence in the room.

As the crowd filed out, I made my way to the side of the stage where Nikki stood looking toward our now vacant table, then scanning the room. She finally found me and descended the steps on shaky legs.

I led her to a chair and sat beside her.

"He was in v-tach. The Kadence didn't get him out." Her phone rang inside her purse.

"Leave it," I said. She needed a moment.

But she fished it out and answered. "Dr. Cantwell—"

From a foot away, I heard his raised voice. Not the words, but the tone. *What an ass.*

"Yes, sir. He's alive, although he was down for several minutes . . . by the time we got the AED, he was in v-tach . . . Yes, there were square waves from the Kadence, but he didn't convert until we used the external pads . . . Maybe the lead . . . Yes, sir." She disconnected, dropped the phone on the table, and put her head in her hands.

I looked around for someone to bring water and saw instead members of the press headed our way. "Brave face for the cameras," I muttered and pulled her to standing.

She opened her eyes and understood. "I have to get to the hospital." Back stiff, she walked toward the exit.

"I'll drive," I said. She didn't argue.

"Doctor, how is the governor?" "Are you his doctor?" "Does he have a heart condition?"

Nikki ignored them and together we pressed past, out the door, and to my car. She climbed in the passenger seat, and I pulled away.

"I cannot believe this is happening," she said. "This morning during the interrogation everything was fine except for the impedance of the lead. It wasn't out of range but was higher than before."

"What does that mean?"

"It can mean there's a problem with how it's implanted in the ventricle. If that happens, the shock won't get into the heart muscle. I wanted an X-ray to make sure it hadn't moved, but Cantwell was still on the phone and overruled me." She looked at me. "What if that's why the Kadence couldn't convert him?"

"The governor wouldn't have let you fix the lead anyway. He would have insisted on waiting for Cantwell to return. Nothing about tonight would have changed."

"I could have given him a LifeVest."

"You think he would have worn it?" Similar to the internal defibrillator, the LifeVest continuously analyzed the ECG and shocked the wearer when necessary, but it was cumbersome, uncomfortable, and the shocks significantly more painful.

"He would if Cantwell suggested it."

"And what are the odds of that?"

"I don't know." The frustration came through in her voice. "I wish he hadn't asked me to interrogate it this morning."

"Was it because of the two misfires?" My mind and heart leapt to Aunt Irm.

"I assume so. He insists they were coincidences, then he makes me check out the governor's device. It doesn't make sense."

"You think he knows something's wrong?"

"I think he's covering his ass."

"Or making you cover it"

"Ha, that is so true." She turned in her seat to face me. "I know you're worried about your aunt. I can order her a LifeVest until we figure this out if you want. Bring her to clinic first thing Monday morning."

"You'll disable her Kadence, so it can't misfire?"

"Just the defibrillator function. I'd keep the backup pacer going. Geez, what a cluster."

"You'll have to warn all the Kadence patients."

She stared straight ahead, lost. "I'll talk to Cantwell."

"He's conflicted, remember? You should ask someone else." Press vehicles surrounded the ER main entrance. I drove around to a side door and Nikki released her seat belt.

"Like who? He's the chairman. I'd have to go to the dean or the chief of staff. I can't do that and accuse my boss of conflict of interest. I'd lose my job."

"You hate your job."

"Cantwell knows everyone. He'd make getting a new job impossible."

I didn't want to believe that was true.

She climbed from the car before I could argue. "Thanks for the ride."

"I can wait for you." It was the right thing to do, though the need to be with Aunt Irm grew ever more intense.

"No. Thanks. I'll get a ride back to the hotel for my car. I might be a while."

"Call if you want to talk."

She wouldn't. Her sad smile was a keen reminder of life as a new attending—the lack of confidence, the constant questioning of every decision, the fear of being revealed as incompetent. It had a name, impostor syndrome, and the only treatment was time and experience. Unfortunately, her experience of late was more reinforcement than treatment.

CHAPTER NINE

EARLY THE NEXT morning, I greeted Aunt Irm, already busy in the kitchen, and immediately felt guilty. Standing there in my workout clothes with Shadow wagging furiously at my side, I had to disappoint one of them. Saturday mornings, SweatLife ran their workouts at the park, dogs welcome. Shadow ranked them right up there with belly rubs and rawhide bones, but I should help my aunt.

"Ah, good morning, kindchen." Aunt Irm poured a steaming pot of pasta into the sink, presumably through a colander. I went to help with the heavy pot, but she shooed me away. "You do your exercise, then come back to help."

"Is it Bereavement Committee baking day?"

Aunt Irm's church committee involvement often occupied her Saturdays, occasionally mine as well. Apparently not today, though, judging by her open-mouthed stare.

"It is for the O'Donnells' picnic."

I looked at the pots and pans scattered around the kitchen. "Do not the O'Donnells provide food at the O'Donnells' picnic?"

"You know it is polite to bring something when invited to dine."

"Something, yes, but not enough to feed . . . never mind, you're very kind, as always." I kissed her cheek, and Shadow and I left. On such a beautiful summer morning in Florida, the park's basketball courts, soccer fields, and play structures were all in use. Shadow and I joined ten others already beginning the warm-up.

"What's happened to Nikki?" Art, the trainer and chief of physical torture, asked. "She hasn't been here in weeks."

"She's been busy at work," I said.

"Let her know we're thinking about her."

I said I would, but when we started doing burpees, I figured she'd rather be most anywhere. Heck, I'd rather be most anywhere, too.

As the only dog today, Shadow stayed close. When we started running wind sprints between cones, he ran with me for the first couple, until he realized I wasn't going anywhere. Then he lay down in the shade and watched the crazy humans run back and forth without even fetching anything.

On the drive home, I told him we were going to visit Riley. He would remember Christian's yellow Lab, though maybe not by name. They'd bonded over dog treats the previous March.

At home I showered, dressed in shorts and a t-shirt, and reported to the kitchen feeling refreshed. "Put me to work."

"Thank you, kindchen. Check the cake in the oven, please."

I opened the door. "Yep, it's still there." Chuckling to myself, I slid a toothpick into the perfectly browned bundt cake of indeterminate contents. When it came out clean, I used thick mitts to pull the heavy pan from the oven and place it on the stove.

"Did you test it in the center?" Aunt Irm asked.

"Well, that would just be silly. It's a bundt cake." I held the toothpick over the hole in the center of the pan.

"Oh, posh." She took the toothpick and tested it herself. "Yes, done. It is good to see you cheerful."

"It's good to feel cheerful." I felt lighter than I had in . . . I didn't know when.

"Perhaps it is because you will spend the afternoon with—"

"Don't say it."

We packed up cookies and pasta salad and the cake and a container of homemade frosting and several other containers I didn't open.

She looked me up and down and up again. "It is time for you to dress."

"Um, I am dressed."

"For exercise, maybe. I thought you might wear the lovely sundress I've seen in your closet."

"I have a sundress?"

She moved toward my room.

"Christian said we might go out on the water. I can't kayak in a dress."

"Ah." Still, it was the disapproving version.

I took her hands. "This is not a date. I know you want it to be more, but I'm not—"

"Do not say you are not ready." She squeezed my hands. "You have been a widow for more than a year." When I tried to pull away, she tightened her grip. "You know this is true. Your Greg has been gone since the accident. You must not use him as an excuse not to live. You are young and have much left to do. Do not condemn yourself to a life of loneliness."

I could have argued that I wasn't alone, but it would serve no purpose. "Voice of experience? Do you wish you'd divorced and remarried?"

"Divorced? No. I am Catholic. It is not allowed." I waited while she stared into the past, then her lips formed a faint smile. "And no, I did not wish to remarry. After Heinrich left, I had my brother." Uncle Max, too, was separated, and the two siblings lived together for many years after my brother and I left for college. She took care of Uncle Max after his stroke, until his wife reappeared and arranged his death. "And now I have you and Carmel, but I am an old woman. You need to have a family and travel and entertain and do young people things."

"We'll see, Aunt Irm. Just, be patient." I pulled her into a hug to hide the tears welling in my eyes.

We loaded the ridiculous amount of food into two coolers and then into the trunk of my Honda. I drove, with Shadow in the back seat. Well, mostly in the back seat. Unless I rolled down a back window, he preferred to stand with his front paws on the console between the front seats, his attention on the road ahead, monitoring my driving. Except when he pressed his chin into my shoulder or squeezed his snout under my arm, then he was interfering more than monitoring.

"Shadow, you must lay down." Aunt Irm pushed on his chest.

He obeyed, briefly.

The drive took us south on US 301, a four-lane highway that parallels I-75 across Paynes Prairie. At over twenty thousand acres, the state park boasts loads of animals, none of which I'd ever seen from either highway.

"We still need to walk some of the trails here," I said to Aunt Irm.

"Yes. I would like to see the bison and the birds. I would not like to see the alligators. Perhaps we will see some animals from Molly's home. She told me they pass at times. The bison, not the alligators."

Probably both.

Twenty minutes later, we started down the long tree-lined drive to the O'Donnells' antebellum mansion. Two stories of white wood with black shutters, white columns, and a wraparound porch, the house still took my breath away. I passed the front entry on the circular drive and parked. Christian appeared even before I switched off the ignition. He took Aunt Irm's arm and walked with her up the stairs while I let Shadow leap down and start sniffing. His tail wagged, then his whole body joined in when Riley bounded from the porch and the two were off. Christian returned and we watched the happy dogs romp and chase and play in all their doggy glory. "Not many happier sights in the world," I said.

"Agreed."

I opened the trunk and lugged out the lighter of the two coolers. When Christian tried to take it from me, I said, "You get the heavy one."

He grunted as he lifted it from the trunk. "Wow, Mom's been cooking all morning, too."

"Apparently it's a competition."

"Happy to be a judge, as long as I don't have to actually rate anything."

I led the way through the grand foyer and down the hall to the kitchen where we hefted the coolers onto the old oak kitchen table. Aunt Irm and Mrs. O'Donnell were already chatting away as if no time had passed since they'd last spoken. I thanked Mrs. O'Donnell for the invitation while Christian and I unloaded the cold items into the refrigerator. When I pulled out the icing container, I offered to ice the cake.

"No," Aunt Irm said. "You and Christian go play in the water."

He and I both chuckled. "Better than inviting us to play in the street," he said as he escorted me out the back door and whistled for Riley.

I texted Nikki, "ETA?" as both dogs came running. "Handy," I said to Christian.

"I can teach you."

"But can you teach Shadow?"

He looked doubtfully at my dog. "Not today."

Which didn't mean it was impossible. How little he knew Shadow.

My phone buzzed a reply. "I can leave the hospital in thirty."

"Nikki will be here in about an hour."

We strolled across the recently mown lawn toward the lake. "That gives us time to kayak. There's something on the far side of the lake I want to show you." He stopped at a small, weathered boathouse by the dock. Unlike the immaculate mansion, the boathouse had fallen into disrepair. Strapped to the outside wall of peeling white paint were three kayaks. He ignored the tandem green one on the bottom in favor of two red singles above. "Grab the paddles and seats inside?"

The hinges squealed as I pulled open the door and found the paddles standing against a corner shared with cobwebs old and new. The black seats hung from rusted hooks against the wall, each with a small pack on the back. I grabbed two of each at random, then followed Christian's lead to attach one of the seats to a kayak by the numerous straps, buckles, and clips.

Shoes off and sunglasses on, we walked several steps into the cool water before climbing onto the kayaks. I braced one foot on each side and paddled from the shore, grateful for my clothing choice. Christian steered alongside. At an easy pace, we crossed the small lake, talking most of the time, about everything and nothing. Several white egrets passed close overhead and a couple of ducks landed nearby, their V-shaped wake marking the smooth surface. White puffy clouds reflected bright against the blue of the sky. Definitely a good day to be outside—with sunglasses.

Christian guided me to a cluster of trees on the far side and stopped paddling. We glided for a moment, then he pulled near enough to grab the side of my kayak. Leaning close, he pointed to a clump of tall pine trees. It took a moment, then I saw it, an enormous nest of sticks and twigs high in the tree at a fork near the trunk. On it I could just make out a dark shape with a white head. "Is that a bald eagle?"

He unzipped a pocket on the back of my seat and handed me a small pair of binoculars. After a few adjustments, the eagle came into focus with its yellow beak and bright white head. Goose flesh rose on my arms. "Wow," I whispered. "She's beautiful." There's something about bald eagles, whether patriotism or just awe at nature, who knew?

"Yeah. You think that's the female?" He looked through his own binoculars.

"I have no idea. The genders look pretty much the same, right?"

"Right. The same nesting pair was here for years. We used to come out to watch for chicks every spring, then two years ago, there was only one adult."

"Oh." Sad.

"Last year, there were two again. I spoke with the park ranger, who said it was almost certainly the same eagle who took a new mate. I'm hoping to see chicks again next year."

I watched him, peering through his binoculars. Was he trying to tell me something? The parallels with both our lives were unmistakable. "If I didn't know better, I'd think Aunt Irm put you up to this."

He lowered the binoculars. "I debated showing you this for that very reason. I really just wanted to show you something remarkable, something I thought you'd appreciate as much as I do. No hidden meaning, no pressure."

I believed him. "None taken. It's amazing. Thank you." I took one more long look at the eagle and handed the binoculars back to Christian. "Invite me back when the chicks appear?"

"I promise." His gaze held mine for what felt like a long time, then the corners of his mouth quirked up.

"Are you thinking about flipping my kayak?" I asked.

He laughed. "That obvious?"

"Only because I thought the same thing. Aunt Irm would never forgive me." I pushed against his boat, propelling myself toward the house and him toward the weeds. "Race you back."

CHAPTER TEN

IN THE KITCHEN, Aunt Irm and Mrs. O'Donnell were discussing the dramatic scene from last night's Medical Society dinner before an open laptop replaying the news clip. "You were there, kindchen. And Dr. Yarborough saved him."

"Please don't bring it up in front of her."

"Of course," Mrs. O'Donnell said. Aunt Irm gave a single nod. Maybe with new respect for her doctor.

Shadow alerted us to Nikki's arrival, and Christian and I met her in the front circle. She was reaching into the back seat of her Toyota sedan when I greeted her. "I told you not to bring anything. We have enough food for—"

She came out with a bouquet of summer flowers. "I'm not going to come empty-handed. My mother would strike me down."

"They're beautiful." I admired her outfit. "You've got the whole summer look going on—sundress, sandals, fun earrings." Large iridescent red flowers, they matched her dress perfectly. Aunt Irm would most definitely approve. She never understood why I wasn't a dangly earring, cute shoes kind of girl.

Christian held out his hand and introduced himself. "Thank you for coming."

She accepted his hand. "I'm Nikki. Thanks for the invite. This place is beautiful."

I led the way up the stairs. He held the door for us.

"How's the governor?" I whispered to Nikki.

"Same."

Once inside the two-story foyer with its sweeping staircase and enormous chandelier, she caught my eye. "Wow," she mouthed. Unsure whether she meant Christian or the house, I nodded. Both were accurate.

In the kitchen, she greeted Aunt Irm, who introduced her to Mrs. O'Donnell. The flowers were a hit and took pride-of-place in the center of the picnic table on the back patio. We filled plates from platters of no particular theme: Italian pasta with homemade sauce, Mexican casserole, Cuban arroz con pollo, and German pancakes. Not to mention all the dishes of unknown nationality.

Christian, Nikki, and I took seats at one end of the table set with bright yellow place mats. "Lemonade?" He held the pitcher over her glass.

"Nikki prefers her liquids flavor-free." I filled her glass with ice water.

"Thanks. The view is amazing," she said. "Ian and I talked about getting a lake house someday. He spent a lot of time at his uncle's fishing cabin when he was a kid. It's a shack compared to this." I wondered if it was the shack of their disastrous honeymoon.

"Might you and your husband find such a place near here?" practical Aunt Irm asked.

"We looked a while back, but it's not the right time."

After an appropriate amount of small talk and compliments to the chefs, Christian apologized to his mother and Aunt Irm, and started in on his questions. "How long have you been implanting the Kadence?"

"Almost two years. I worked on the project under Dr. Cantwell at Emory until he left. Then he recruited me to do my EP fellowship down here."

"EP?" Christian asked.

"Electrophysiology."

"Right, I knew that."

"When I finished, he asked me to stay, in part to conduct the final testing required by the FDA. By then, he had started MDI to market the device."

"They really couldn't come up with a more creative name than Medical Devices, Inc.?" I said.

Nikki grinned. "I'm guessing they didn't hire a marketing genius."

"Our consulting engineers were impressed with the FDA documentation," Christian said.

She beamed. "I can't take all the credit. Our study coordinator handled most of the paperwork while I did the doctor stuff. Can you tell us who the buyer is?"

"Unfortunately, no. Not until the sale is official."

"Really?" Not that it mattered, but now I was curious.

"Standard practice."

Yet another world I knew nothing about.

Christian asked her opinion of the advantages and disadvantages of the Kadence. Her answers echoed the ad copy from the brochure, sounding more like a sales pitch than a critical evaluation.

"It's okay," I told her. "Christian won't identify you. He's interested in your experience."

She took a long sip of water, put down her glass, and dabbed at her mouth with the cloth napkin. "Seeing as we're the only group implanting them so far, and our group is pretty much only me these days, it's not hard to identify me." Too true. "It really is a great device."

It wasn't my place to mention the recent misfire events, though it took all my self-control not to.

She answered a few more benign questions, all in the positive.

"How about battery life?" Christian asked. "I'm told several devices have required early replacement."

"That's true. They are using more battery than expected. Dr. Cantwell is aware and I'm sure he has MDI looking into it."

When Nikki stood to leave half an hour and twenty-plus questions later, I walked with her. "Was the governor another misfire?"

She glanced back to make sure we were alone. "It was. And then the Kadence fired multiple times but failed to convert him. On X-ray it's clear the lead is dislodged, probably from his fall against the lectern or maybe the chest compressions."

"You were worried about that lead. I'm sorry."

She nodded. "He's stable from a cardiac standpoint. We have to wait and see what sort of damage his brain suffered."

I wanted to reassure her. "CPR was started right away and you converted his rhythm quickly once the AED arrived." Unless he had disease in the vessels to his brain, he should recover, probably, maybe. In truth it was unpredictable, especially with older patients.

"That makes three misfires in less than a week," I said. "Are you warning the other patients with a Kadence?"

"Dr. Cantwell is coming back this evening to deal with it and the media about the governor." She opened her car door.

"And if he refuses to do the right thing?"

She looked past me, toward the tree-lined drive, but I doubted she saw it. "What would you do?"

Though tempted to give the obvious answer, I tried to put myself in her scrubs. "I . . ." An image popped into my mind, a beloved face with a tight German bun, and I said with confidence, "I'd push or go around him."

CHAPTER ELEVEN

CHRISTIAN AND I cleaned the dishes while the older women divided up the considerable leftovers. Aunt Irm set aside a large portion for me to share with my residents on call. After we'd put the kitchen in order, Aunt Irm and Mrs. O'Donnell drank iced tea on the porch while Christian and I walked the dogs. Actually, we walked. The dogs chased squirrels and each other.

"Tell me more about your friend Nikki."

"She and her husband moved here from Georgia three years ago. He's an engineer of some kind. She and I have been workout buddies for a while, and we hang out occasionally."

"Was it my imagination or did you want her to tell me something?" he said.

Wow, observant. I considered my answer. "I agree she didn't seem comfortable with some of the questions." It was the truth, as far as it went.

He didn't press and we walked on. After a moment, he said, "The man who killed my family will be released on parole next Thursday." His wife and daughter were killed by a drunk driver.

I stopped walking. "It's only been a few years."

"The minimum mandatory is only four. Garner says he must know people." As a big dog on the police force, Christian's friend would know.

"Wow. I'm sorry. That seems way too short."

"I think Mom's taking it harder than I am. We expected him to be in prison for ten, so it came as a bit of a surprise. I can't waste any more energy on him, though."

Hadn't I recently thought the same about Adam? We resumed our walk, slower now.

"Your turn," he said. "Tell me how you're doing."

"I'm fine. Like I said, work has been busy and Aunt Irm's 'ticker trouble' was a little stressful."

He stopped walking again and faced me, his eyes searching mine. "I think you know that's not what I'm asking."

I had to break eye contact. His were too warm, too inviting.

"Hey." His voice softened to the texture of the perfect melted chocolate on a peanut butter cookie. "I'm not asking if you're ready for a relationship. I'm asking, as one grieving spouse to another, how you're feeling. Are you talking to anyone? Aunt Irm? A friend? Maybe a professional?"

I forced my eyes back to his. "No, unless you count Greg at the cemetery. Aunt Irm has enough on her plate, Randi is about to have a baby, and Nikki never met Greg." Not to mention she wasn't up for such a conversation.

"I never met him, but I'd be happy to hear about him through your memories."

My turn to examine him. "Really?"

"Really. He meant the world to you."

That made me think, and I realized I felt the same about his family. Helen and their daughter, Caroline, were his life. Maybe that's why he'd shown me the eagles' nest. Not to convince me to consider a replacement partner but to share a fond memory. "You can't talk about your wife and daughter with anyone either, can you?"

"No. I can't put Mom through that again, thinking about them, or worrying about me." After the accident that took his family, Christian became obsessed with seeing the drunk driver, and anyone associated with him and the tragedy, punished. "If you'd like to talk about Greg, I'm happy to listen."

"Same," I said.

By the time we returned to the house with the dogs, Aunt Irm was packing for our departure. She and I thanked our hosts, and Christian helped load the car with coolers possibly heavier than when we arrived. An exhausted Shadow finally lay down across the back seat.

On the drive, Aunt Irm told me about her conversation with Mrs. O'Donnell. "She is worried about her son Michael. He lives with her but does not speak to others. She believes he has not recovered from his father's death."

And his role in it, I thought.

"He does not wish counseling and now has disappeared. Did Christian mention him? Perhaps the reassurance of a brother would be of help."

"You know they aren't close."

"Yes, I remember Michael said awful things about Christian, but now we know he was protecting his family. Trying to halt our investigation."

I fought a smile. She liked to refer to "our investigation" and recalled the period with pride. Classic selective memory. Fear and tragedy were an integral part of "our investigation" and not something I wanted either of us to revisit.

"Molly is quite worried about him and about Christian. I cannot believe the horrible man who killed his family will be set free so soon."

"I agree. Christian seemed surprisingly okay with it all. He's more worried about her."

"How is that possible? I will never forgive the man who killed my Max."

"I don't think forgiveness is likely. Christian said he doesn't want to waste any more energy on him."

She was still considering when I dropped her and Shadow off at home, grabbed my on-call bag, and headed to the hospital. After changing into scrubs and squeezing the picnic leftovers into the clinical office refrigerator, I took over the ongoing cases from the daytime attending—an orthopedic trauma, an appendectomy, and a Cesarean—then checked on the residents in each room and promised them dinner. With resident salaries and debt what they are, a little free food on call is much appreciated.

As each case ended, we started another. Mostly bread-and-butter weekend fare, but a horse-hoof to the face of a teenager made for a stressful anesthesia induction. Trying to put a breathing tube in around all the traumatic injuries without causing more damage took great caution and a little ingenuity. We succeeded and the reconstruction of her face would take most of the night.

I made it to the call room around two in the morning, but my phone rang before I could wet my toothbrush. I hit speaker without checking caller ID. "This is Kate."

"Kate, it's Nikki, do you have a minute?" Her voice shook.

"Of course."

"Can you come to the cardiac ICU stock room?"

"On my way." Strange place to meet and her voice worried me. I hurried through the empty halls and badged into the ICU. The stock room was in the middle core, accessible to the surrounding ICU pods. Nikki stood over a sink. Blood covered her hand at her right ear and coursed down her forearm as well as onto her cheek and green scrub top.

I reached for the blood-soaked cloth. "What happened?"

"Don't." She twisted away. "It's still bleeding. Can you find some suture?"

I stared for a moment too long, then scanned the labeled bins, eventually locating sterile packets of suture, chlorhexidine prep solution, and skin glue. "Let me get some lidocaine."

"Don't bother." She sat on a rolling stool.

"Are you sure?" At her nod, I took over compressing her earlobe with a clean cloth. During the brief moment it was uncovered and visible, I saw her earring had torn through.

I asked again what had happened while I applied pressure and assessed the best way to stitch the awkward area.

"Cantwell's flight got delayed. The governor woke up. I went to assess him and he was . . . less than happy to see me."

She winced as I pushed the tiny curved needle through her skin.

"Sorry," I said.

"It's fine."

I brought the needle back up, cut the suture, and tied a small knot. The bleeding slowed. "You should really have a plastic surgeon do this. I'd hate to leave you with a scar."

"I won't leave it in long."

I popped open the skin glue and rubbed it on both sides of the tear. "Finish the story."

"Rookie mistake. I left in those huge earrings while I listened to his heart. He ripped out my stethoscope and took the earring with it."

"The governor ripped out your stethoscope? That's battery, or assault, or something."

She stood, went back to the sink, and examined her ear in the mirror.

I wet another clean cloth and handed it to her. "I'll get you a new set of scrubs." In the back of the stock room, I pulled a new set for her from the dispenser.

A door banged open. "What were you thinking? How could you tell the governor's chief of staff we have concerns about the Kadence?" It was Cantwell.

I considered staying hidden, but the dispenser reset loudly when I closed its door. I walked around the shelving with the clean scrubs and handed them to a dispirited Nikki. "She's been through enough," I said to her chairman.

"Who are you?" His commanding voice boomed in the suddenly small room.

"Kate Downey, the anesthesia attending on call tonight. I just had to suture her ear."

With no apparent concern for Nikki, he looked instead at my badge. "Leave. This is none of your concern."

"Dr. Yarborough was assaulted by one of your patients. She needs Tylenol and a break." I grasped her arm, surprised by, and proud of, my audacity.

"No, it's okay." Nikki pulled away. "I'll talk to you later. Thanks for the stitches."

I turned to her, my back to Cantwell. "You don't have to—"

Her expression said back off. Because she was afraid of him? Or because she wanted to face him herself? *Dammit.* I wouldn't want someone fighting my battles. But then, I hoped I would actually fight. Would Nikki?

CHAPTER TWELVE

THE REST OF the night was steady. I missed Nikki's call when I was helping a resident place a labor epidural and was eager to speak to her the next morning. She didn't answer my texts or a call, so I decided to drop by her house. Seeing her face was the only way to be sure she was telling me the whole story. Besides, I needed to check my handiwork.

I arranged for Carmel to drive Aunt Irm to church and promised to meet them there. On the way to Nikki's house, I stopped by a drugstore for antibiotic ointment, then proceeded to the beautiful home she shared with her husband in the northwest part of town.

Though I'd met Ian a couple of times, generally Nikki and I went out somewhere rather than visiting at home. I drove slowly down the curving tree-lined streets, with people out exercising or working in the yard. I reached the house I thought was hers, but a For Sale sign in the front yard made me question. I double-checked the address in my Contacts. Right house. Yet another significant fact she'd opted not to share.

It was almost nine. She might be asleep, so I knocked rather than ring the doorbell. Ian answered.

"Can I help you?" No recognition.

"Hi, Ian, I'm Kate Downey. Is Nikki awake?"

His mouth formed a thin line. "I'm afraid I wouldn't know." I waited and he finally relented. "She moved out two weeks ago." He read the surprise on my face. "She hasn't told you. She needed time to sort some things out."

That was news. "I'm sorry to hear that. Can you tell me where she is? I need to talk to her."

He thought a moment, then said, "You'd better call her. I don't want to overstep." He closed the door, resigned.

Wow. Separated and pregnant. Her recent work hours would strain any relationship.

I texted her again. "Can I come by?"

This time she answered immediately. "I'm not home."

"Yep, got the not-so-subtle memo from Ian."

She apologized and provided an address near campus. I followed Google's directions to a new apartment complex less than a mile from the hospital. She'd sent me a code to access the main lobby and I found her apartment on the first floor. She answered my knock looking exhausted, her ear swollen and bruised. The sparse apartment could have been anyone's. She'd hung no pictures on the walls, placed no knickknacks on what looked like rental furniture. This was a temporary place to lay her head.

I handed her the antibiotic ointment. "How's the ear?"

"Thanks. A little sore, but fine." She unscrewed the tube and winced as she dabbed a small amount over the scab. Glancing in the mirror by the front door, she said, "God, I'm going to frighten my patients."

"And how are you going to put in a stethoscope? Cantwell should cover and give you a few days off."

"Right. That'll happen." She poured us each a coffee and we sat at a tiny kitchen table.

"I'm sorry about all you're going through."

"Yeah, not the best timing." *Understatement.* "Things with Ian are complicated. He wants me to leave University and go into private practice so I'll have more regular hours."

I nodded. He wasn't wrong.

"I can't quit right now with us so short-staffed." She put down her mug. "And I don't want him telling me what to do." She flopped back in her seat. "God, these hormones are making me crazy." A common refrain of pregnancy, if not a proven fact.

"Working a hundred hours a week is bad for anyone's health. Might Ian just be worried about you and the baby?"

She groaned. "I suppose. It's not fair, you know, that we have to change everything to have a baby and men don't."

Pros and cons, I thought. At the moment, she saw only the cons. "I'm worried about you."

"Ian made us an appointment with a counselor. I'll meet with her alone, too."

"And you'll tell her how you're feeling about the pregnancy?"

"I will. I'm not unhappy about the baby." Her hand strayed to her abdomen. "I'm just frustrated."

"Do you want to talk?"

"No. Not now. But thanks."

I waited, leaving her an opening, but she said nothing further. "What happened with Cantwell last night?" I asked. "What did you say to the governor's chief of staff that fired him up?"

"The guy accused me of messing up. Of causing the Kadence to fail. He got me flustered and I asked why he thought Dr. Cantwell wanted me to interrogate the device in the first place."

I waited for more. It didn't come. "That's not so bad, as long as he didn't—"

"He did. He put it together and figured out there had to be other patients with problems. I didn't admit anything, but he was pissed and apparently made some calls to Cantwell and the CEO of MDI."

"Maybe that'll force them to solve the problem before it kills someone."

"Agreed. Meanwhile, I've been ordered to stay out of it."

"And you're going to?"

"It's an impossible situation. I want to protect my patients, but he's tied my hands."

Despite my best efforts, I couldn't see her side on this one. "Your patients need to know so they can protect themselves."

"How? Until we know why it's misfiring, how are they supposed to protect themselves?"

"Bring them in for a LifeVest like you're doing for Aunt Irm tomorrow." If she didn't look so exhausted, I'd beg her to do it today.

"LifeVests aren't perfect either. They also misfire and hurt like . . . a lot, plus they're crazy expensive. And what will I say to insurance companies and Medicare? They already paid for the AICD and will demand an explanation I'm not allowed to give." She raised her face toward the ceiling and closed her eyes. "Same problem if we have to replace them."

Bile burned my throat. Aunt Irm barely survived the initial placement and suffered additional injury to her heart. Another operation so soon could cause irreparable damage, or worse.

"So what are you going to do?"

Nikki was silent for several moments. I waited her out, telepathically telling her to be strong. She wasn't, not today. "I don't know, Kate. I can't talk to anyone about this. My boss gave me a direct order."

"Since when did that stop you?"

The cowering version of Nikki reappeared. "I can't lose my job right now. Not with everything else that's going on."

Separating from her husband was big, being pregnant was big, together they were ginormous. All I knew of her financial situation was her frequent allusions to student debt. Regardless, it was none of my business. "I wish there were something I could do to help."

"Please, you've done plenty." She waved at her ear. "Trust me, you don't want to get involved in this. Cantwell will destroy anyone who gets in his way, or so I've heard."

"I appreciate that, but he's not my boss. I'm not comfortable keeping this a secret."

Her eyes rounded and filled with tears. "Kate, you can't say anything. He knows we're friends. He'll blame me."

"I'll figure out a way to keep you out of it. We have to keep the patients safe."

She rubbed her face with both hands. "You're right. If they haven't found a solution by tonight, I'll talk to him in the morning." Her earnest expression convinced me, even if her words did not. I could give her until tomorrow.

CHAPTER THIRTEEN

I MADE IT to church too late to join Aunt Irm in our usual pew. But then, she wasn't in our usual pew. I scanned the far side of the church where Carmel normally sat—not there either. Had they decided not to come? Impossible. Aunt Irm never missed Mass. Had something happened? I checked my phone—no texts. I checked her Kadence report. Clean.

"Hey, no texting in church," someone whispered and touched my arm.

Startled, I fumbled my phone.

A hand caught it and my arm. "Sorry." It was a smiling Christian. He nodded toward the middle pews. "Aunt Irm and her friend are sitting with Mom."

"Oh, thank God."

"Good place for it."

I grinned. We remained standing in the back until Father Jeff instructed the congregation to stand. Then Christian pressed me forward with a hand on the small of my back. We genuflected before sliding in. I squeezed Aunt Irm's hand and returned her nod, not quite sure whether she was pleased with my appearance or annoyed at my tardiness. Probably both.

When we knelt before Communion, I added Nikki to my usual prayers and asked God to give Dr. Cantwell and MDI the wisdom to fix the problem with the Kadence. Those kinds of prayers always felt suspect to me, but it couldn't hurt.

After Mass, Carmel invited us and the O'Donnells for brunch, which would sound lovely any other Sunday. Aunt Irm begged off for me. "I will go. Kate must sleep. She was up saving lives all night."

"Nothing so dramatic, but I do need a nap."

The O'Donnells also declined. Christian's sister was bringing the grandkids for a visit.

"Ah, how lucky for you," Carmel said. "We don't see the grandkids nearly enough. Another time then."

Aunt Irm went with Carmel, Christian with his mom, and I drove home blissfully alone feeling the fatigue unique to post-call days, a shaky burning in my stomach from continual rehashing of the night's medical decisions. Shadow recognized my look and, though happy to see me, didn't beg for a run. Instead, he followed me into the bedroom and curled up on Greg's side of the bed.

I fell in beside him and into a troubled sleep. I woke not at all refreshed, to Shadow's cold nose pressing to get under my arm for a pet. The key on post-call days is to sleep just enough to make it through the day, but not so much as to cause a persistent sleep disturbance. Call didn't bother me; the next two days did.

Feeling more agitated than normal, I brushed my teeth, then took Shadow for a run. More like he took me as I let him make the route decisions. By the time we reached home, I was fully awake, soaked with sweat, but still rattled deep down.

Aunt Irm had returned from brunch with a doggie bag for me, as if there weren't enough leftovers in the fridge already. I thanked her, took a quick shower, and ate heartily of the fruit and muffins.

It was when Aunt Irm asked about dinner that I realized the source of my unease wasn't post-call-ness; it was Nikki and the misfires.

With little coaxing, Aunt Irm agreed, and I called to invite Nikki to dinner. She was alone and needed support, but also encouragement to do the right thing—to protect Aunt Irm and all the other Kadence patients. I left a message on her voicemail and followed up with a text. The gnawing sensation in my gut remained.

"I need to run to the farmer's market for broccoli," Aunt Irm said.

I gave her a knowing smile. Though she always went to the market for something in particular, she never returned with less than three bags of produce. We drove the mostly empty streets to the closer of the two local farmers' markets. The other doubled as a flea market and would take all day to peruse. I parked in the lot nearest the open-air downtown market, and Aunt Irm walked with slow purpose to her favorite vegetable stand, where she spent several minutes selecting the perfect head of lush green broccoli that looked to me exactly like the fifteen rejected heads that came before. I waited for, and was rewarded with, Aunt Irm's signature, "As long as we're here . . ." And she proceeded to select a colorful mix of fruits and vegetables. Four bags' full in the end.

We spent the rest of the afternoon in the yard. Aunt Irm loved to garden and could kneel better than I could. One benefit of a lifetime without sports, maybe the only benefit. Soon after she moved in with me, I'd given her a kneeling pad with arm supports to help her get up and down, but she went without it much of the time. After an hour toiling in the dirt, I tried to convince her to take a break. She refused. "I wish you would stop worrying about me. When Dr. Yarborough comes, I will ask her to tell you I am fine."

Nikki still hadn't returned my call. Surely Dr. Cantwell had taken over care of the governor, but she was still on call and likely working. I texted again.

"You are concerned, kindchen. Why?"

"Oh, I'm overreacting. Nikki's been out of sorts lately and had a really tough night."

"You are also worried about me. Are the two related?"

I turned to look at my overly perceptive aunt. "Why would you ask that?"

"Because I know you. You do not often get your knickers in a wad."

A chuckle escaped at her mixed metaphor. I wondered sometimes if she did it on purpose. She looked cross, then thoughtful. "Is it twist? Knickers in a twist? What is it that is in a wad?"

"Panties," I said. "Don't get your panties in a wad."

She shifted from knee to knee on the grass. "That would not be comfortable."

I could only laugh. My phone vibrated a text. It was from Nikki. "Sorry, busy at work. I'm fine but I can't do dinner. See you in AM with your aunt."

My shoulders relaxed only a fraction, but at least my knickers un-wadded.

CHAPTER FOURTEEN

MONDAY MORNING, AUNT Irm was at the door ready to leave at seven fifteen, over-large handbag on her arm. I often wondered what she carried in it. So far, I knew it held tissues and mints and hairpins and hand cleanser and a compact and probably a compass and Swiss Army Knife.

"They don't open until eight," I said.

"It does not matter. Doctors are busy. We should arrive early, especially since you asked for this appointment."

Must be a generation thing, such patience and respect. Then I remembered the governor. Must be an Aunt Irm thing.

Despite my delay tactics, we still arrived at the clinic twenty minutes early. By the time an attractive woman in dark blue scrubs opened the glass doors and waved, there were two cars parked near us. Aunt Irm hurried from the car and had already registered by the time I caught up. We sat in adjoining chairs while she completed the same forms she filled out each visit.

"I wonder if I make up answers on this form, will anyone notice?" she said.

"Ha, I doubt it."

Once she finished, I returned the forms and clipboard to the receptionist. Before handing it over, one answer caught my eye.

Barely suppressing a laugh, I sat back down. "You are allergic to sinners and bad drivers?"

Her eyes twinkled with a mirth that always filled my heart.

A nurse called her name and escorted us to an exam room where she took Aunt Irm's blood pressure and pulse and checked her oxygen saturation. She entered all these in the computer. "What is the reason for your visit today? Has your device fired?"

"It has not. I have been fine. My niece is a mother chicken."

The nurse eyed me, both of us stifling a smile. When she left, I said, "Hen, a mother hen."

"A hen is a mother chicken. It is the same. Is not mother hen redundant?"

"I suppose it is." God, I loved this woman.

After a brief knock, Nikki entered with the interrogation computer.

"Oh my goodness," Aunt Irm said. "What has happened to you?"

Nikki's hand went to her dark, swollen earlobe. "Earring accident. Your Kate fixed me up the other night."

Aunt Irm looked from her to me and back again.

"How are you?" Nikki asked her, then repeated the same questions, thankfully not the one about allergies. I helped Aunt Irm onto the exam table while Nikki switched on the interrogation computer. She placed the receiver over Aunt Irm's AICD and invited me to watch the screen as she explained each straightforward step of the interrogation. "She's had a few PVCs, but no runs. Everything looks fine."

"Excuse me," Aunt Irm said. "What are PVCs?"

Without looking up, Nikki said, "Occasional abnormal beats; it's normal."

Aunt Irm raised an eyebrow. "Then why do you call them abnormal beats?"

I laughed. Nikki didn't seem to hear, so I explained. "It's normal for your heart to beat from the bottom up occasionally, as long as it doesn't make a habit of it."

Nikki looked at me. "What do you think?"

"I am the patient," Aunt Irm said in an unfamiliar demanding tone. "Tell me what is going on."

Nikki waited an uncomfortably long moment. "You know I put the Kadence in to fix your heart rhythm if it suddenly went wrong."

"Yes."

"Recently, in a few patients, it has fired when it wasn't supposed to and actually caused that bad rhythm. In each of those cases, it then recognized the rhythm and tried to shock them back to normal."

Aunt Irm's eyes flicked to me, then back. "Are these patients okay?"

"They are."

"So what is the problem?"

Nikki took too long to answer, so I did. "We don't know why the misfires are occurring, or why they're stopping patients' hearts. If it happened to you, you would faint and if you were driving, or climbing stairs, or in the shower, you could be seriously injured."

"On the other hand," Nikki said, "if I turn off the device and your heart goes into the bad rhythm on its own like it did before, there will be nothing to correct it."

Aunt Irm was silent a long moment, looking between us, but ending on Nikki. "What do you recommend, Doctor?"

"I can only give you the options. It's your job to choose."

It was all I could do not to interrupt. Of course, Nikki should make a recommendation. No patient had enough knowledge to choose on their own, not even another physician. I stayed silent, for now.

"Here are your options." She held up an index finger. "Turn off the AICD, the part that shocks your heart, and keep the pacemaker on, then wear a LifeVest until we figure it out. You know what that is, right?"

"This is the vest we spoke of before, where a shock would hurt so much." She pressed a hand to her chest.

Nikki nodded. "Right. It takes a lot more energy to go all the way through your skin than directly into your heart."

"Ida from my support group had that shock. She said it was agony and she screamed. It causes her nightmares." Aunt Irm pursed her lips. "What are the other options?"

Nikki added a finger. "Turn off the AICD and hope for the best. You haven't needed a shock since we placed it and hopefully that would continue."

"No. That's not a viable option," I said. Speaking of nightmares, Aunt Irm's ECG still appeared in mine, the runs of ventricular tachycardia soon after her episode. None lasted long enough to require a shock, but any of them could have. I knew she didn't want to take risks with her life, and the likelihoods and odds in this situation were beyond her comprehension. Beyond mine, too, for that matter.

"Or three, leave it as is and have you take precautions, like not driving or swimming," Nikki said.

"I am not driving now, and I could not wear the LifeVest while swimming anyway. I do not live a dangerous life."

I waited for Nikki to disagree, to insist on the LifeVest as we discussed. She didn't.

"Aunt Irm," I said, "the LifeVest is safer. The random shock can happen any time."

"Yes, kindchen, this is what random means. Do not LifeVests also misfire?" She directed the question to Nikki.

"They do, rarely."

"But they don't misfire at the exact wrong moment," I said, with absolutely no data to back up the claim. Nikki nodded, but not in the definitive way required to convince my aunt.

"I will be careful." She turned her eyes on me. "Thank you for respecting my decision."

Crap. She knew exactly what to say to shut me up.

"The manufacturer is working on a solution," Nikki said to Aunt Irm. "In the meantime, I must ask you not to mention it to your friends in the support group. We don't want to scare anyone unnecessarily."

Aunt Irm angled her head, and her eyes narrowed. "Are you not seeing all patients with this Kadence and offering the same options? Are we not all at the same risk?"

"We're not sure yet. You're a special case."

My aunt's cheeks reddened. "This is not right. Everyone deserves the same care. Is that not your oath?"

Now was not the time to explain that it actually isn't part of the Hippocratic Oath we recite at graduation. An age-old oversight. Besides, I agreed wholeheartedly with her on this one.

Nikki's mouth curved into a facsimile far short of a smile. "I will do my best."

I helped Aunt Irm from the table and, while she slipped back into her shoes, I followed Nikki into the hall. "When are you talking to your chairman?"

"This afternoon, Kate. I'll talk to him this afternoon, okay?"

I touched her arm. "I don't mean to upset you."

Some of the redness in her cheeks faded. "I know." She gave a grunt I recognized as utter frustration. "Sorry. I'll talk to him."

I felt sorry for her, and worried. Despite conflicting mandates, though, there was only one right decision—patients first. She had to see that.

CHAPTER FIFTEEN

OUTSIDE, THE MORNING air was already stifling. Many more cars had joined ours in the parking lot. An elderly couple trudged up the wheelchair ramp. The woman pushed a walker decorated with large felt daisies. Her husband followed behind.

"What lovely flowers," Aunt Irm said.

The woman stopped to catch her breath. "My grandchildren made them." Her face lit with a proud smile.

"That makes them even more lovely. Congratulations." Aunt Irm took my arm as we descended the two brick steps. Suddenly her grip tightened, and she made a sound somewhere between a groan of pain and a shriek of surprise. Her full weight collapsed against me.

I held on and lowered her to the ground. *Oh God.* "Get Dr. Yarborough," I yelled toward the door. Crisis training said to assign tasks to individuals rather than to bark orders. But an elderly couple hampered by a walker?

Time slowed. I seemed to be both there and observing from a distance. My practiced fingers went to her neck. No pulse. I started chest compressions, kneeling at her side. Meanwhile, my observing self stared on in disbelief. This couldn't be happening.

Frantically I scanned the area and saw a man at the end of the sidewalk. "Help, please. Go inside and ask for Dr. Yarborough."

He seemed to look at us, then moved off. Away. Toward the parking lot.

"She's coming," the elderly man said from the doorway. "What can I do?"

"Call 911."

Nikki flew from the building, a man in scrubs close on her heels carrying the bright yellow defibrillator. She dropped to her knees on Aunt Irm's other side and ripped open her blouse with such force buttons flew. I let the fabric pass beneath my hands between compressions. Nikki slapped on the defibrillator pads and powered up the machine. A normal ECG appeared, accompanied by welcome beeps. Had I been wrong?

"Pulse check," Nikki said. I stopped compressions but didn't move my hands. Didn't breathe while she checked Aunt Irm's pulse at her neck.

"Strong pulse."

I felt Aunt Irm's wrist. Nikki was right. Her pulse was strong and speeding up, though not nearly as fast as mine.

"What happened?" she asked.

"She collapsed. I couldn't find a pulse." Tears burned as I stared at my aunt's beautiful face. She hadn't moved, but maybe color was returning to her cheeks. She had to be okay. In my mind, I prayed unceasingly. *Please don't take Aunt Irm. Please let her be okay.*

"Get me the Kadence interrogation computer," Nikki said to the nurse.

Moments later, as sirens shrieked in the distance, Aunt Irm's eyes fluttered open. They locked on mine, then took in her surroundings. "Oh my goodness. What happened?"

The relief that flooded me was indescribable, like falling into a pool after a hot summer run. "You're okay." I leaned down and kissed her cheek, lingering to look into her eyes, to check her pupils. I pulled her shirt closed over the defibrillator pads.

Nikki placed the wand of the interrogation computer over Aunt Irm's left chest and we watched the stored tracing. Sinus rhythm, an inexplicable shock, then v-fib for much longer than I would have expected, followed by another shock from the AICD and return to sinus rhythm sometime during my chest compressions. Her Kadence had misfired immediately after the visit. I kept my expletives in my head. Aunt Irm would not approve.

The ambulance pulled close and the paramedics took over, checking vital signs, asking questions. Nikki gave them the summary. When they lifted Aunt Irm onto the stretcher, I moved to climb in the ambulance with her. "No," she said. "Bring the car so we can go home. I am fine." She looked more determined than scared, which was fine since I was terrified enough for the both of us. Though the ER was only blocks away, and I could easily walk back for the car, I didn't argue.

Instead, I stalked after Nikki back into the clinic and through to her office where I carefully closed the door behind us when I wanted to slam it.

"I'm so sorry." She slumped into her chair. "I should have turned it off. That's what we'd planned. I'm so so sorry." She pointed to a box on a shelf against the side wall. "That's the LifeVest. Take it. I'll have my fellow turn off her AICD in the Emergency Room." She looked near tears. I couldn't take out my anger and fear on her.

"It's not your fault. When Aunt Irm gets something in her head . . ." She'd not shared the story of Ida, her support group friend who suffered an external shock, with me before. It explained her reticence. Now she had no choice.

Nikki's phone vibrated once on the table. She picked it up, read the screen, then tossed it back where it slid before coming to rest. "Cantwell wants to see me. How could he possibly know already?"

"More likely about the governor, don't you think?"

"Dammit. Why'd he have to get me involved in all of this?"

Why indeed? "Since you are involved, you have to do something about it. You've seen what can happen." I gestured toward the front of the building.

"You're right. I'll tell him."

"Good. Meanwhile, I'm going to talk to my chairman."

"No—"

I cut her off. "I've witnessed three of the misfires. I have to report it. I won't mention you."

Shrinking before my eyes, she nodded.

I drove the two blocks to the hospital, adrenaline spiking again as I replayed the morning. I should have insisted Nikki turn off Aunt Irm's Kadence in the first place. None of this would have happened. But "regrets are not useful" and patient autonomy. Dammit, I'd never forgive support-group-Ida.

God, now I was blaming an old woman I'd never met. Aunt Irm made her own decision. She was alive and as long as her heart suffered no further injury . . . How could it not though? Her chest would certainly be sore. What if I broke one of her ribs? I was crying again. Tears of anger this time. Anger at Nikki for not telling my aunt what to do. Anger at myself for not insisting. Even more anger because I knew it was all misplaced. Anger at a situation is nonsensical. It changes nothing.

Once parked in the gated garage, I wiped my face, grabbed the heavy LifeVest, and hurried to the ER's side entrance. On the wall-mounted monitor by the nurses' station, I found Aunt Irm's name and located her room on the back hallway. Without my badge and dressed in street clothes, I was a little concerned no one stopped to ask who I was. The "act like you belong" adage at work.

I knocked twice and entered without waiting for a response. Aunt Irm lay on a gurney with her head elevated, a smile on her lovely face and a mischievous glint in her eye. Next to her stood a young man in scrubs, also smiling and maybe blushing. *Aunt Irm.* I introduced myself to him, put the LifeVest on the counter by the sink, then leaned over the stretcher to hug my dear aunt. Tears threatened again. "Are you okay?"

She broke the embrace. "I am fine. I wish people would stop asking me that." She tried for feisty, but I saw her fear and kept hold of her hand.

Dr. Annabelle Kessler, the electrophysiology fellow, joined us moments later. Nearly a year into her two-year fellowship, she seemed very competent.

"Dr. Annabelle, could you please tell my grand-niece that I am fine?"

She smiled. "I wish all my patients were as fine as Irm here."

"Did Dr. Yarborough reach you?" I asked.

"She did. I'm supposed to turn off the defibrillator functionality on the Kadence." She switched on the all-too-familiar interrogation computer. To Aunt Irm, she said, "Didn't it just save your life, though?"

Could she really not know what was going on? She'd been involved in at least two of the misfires now. It wasn't my place to educate her about the pattern, only about my aunt. "It misfired and caused the arrest. We're going to use the LifeVest for a while."

Aunt Irm didn't argue. Not that it would have done any good.

Annabelle clicked some buttons, then took the LifeVest out of the box, and I helped Aunt Irm fit it on her back, with the strap across her upper abdomen. Though she tried to hide her discomfort, the pain from my CPR was all too obvious and a knife to my heart.

Annabelle explained how the LifeVest worked to my surprisingly agreeable aunt, then left to complete the discharge orders.

Aunt Irm was unusually quiet.

Nikki called. "How is she?"

"I'll put you on speaker so she can tell you herself." I held the phone between us.

"I am fine and ready to go home."

"Did my fellow switch the Kadence mode?"

Aunt Irm looked at me, done with the conversation.

"She did. The LifeVest is on and capturing."

"We should monitor you overnight."

"I am fine and will not stay overnight. Kate will be my monitor." Aunt Irm hated the hospital. After the protracted deaths of both her parents in hospitals, and the weeks with Uncle Max after his stroke, it was a challenge to keep her hospitalized more than a night when the AICD was placed. I knew it would be a losing battle today.

"I'll borrow a monitor. We'll be okay." Who needs sleep? I pulled the phone back, leaving it on speaker. "How did it go with your chairman?"

"About as well as can be expected. The governor wants me fired."

"That's ridiculous."

"I have never liked that man," Aunt Irm said. "His eyes, they are shifty. I hope you both will not vote for him."

That's the first I'd heard of her dislike or his *shifty* eyes. No way he had either of our votes.

"Thank you, Irm," Nikki said. "Surprisingly, Cantwell came to my defense and is keeping me employed, for now at least."

He was likely defending his own work schedule more than his junior faculty member. "What about the misfires?"

"I don't think he has any idea what's causing them. Nothing he shared with me at least."

"So you will call in all the patients and give them this vest," Aunt Irm said.

"I will take care of it. Call if there's a problem." The abrupt end to the conversation proved her annoyance. It went both ways. Call *if* there's a problem? Of course there's a problem. Her patients' AICDs were indiscriminately stopping their hearts.

"We must get home." Aunt Irm pulled ECG stickers from her arms. "Christian and his mother will expect dinner when they arrive."

I'm pretty sure my mouth actually fell open. "What? You can't entertain tonight. You need to rest."

"I will rest while you cook. You heard Dr. Yarborough. They are not fixing this. We must inform Christian so he can add force." She raised a fist.

It wasn't a bad idea. The buyer could pressure MDI to do the right thing or lose the deal.

Aunt Irm sat up and pulled her blouse around her. "And if they will not, there is always the newspaper."

CHAPTER SIXTEEN

ON THE DRIVE home, Aunt Irm asked why Dr. Annabelle could not be her doctor.

"Annabelle is a fellow. She's still in training."

"Hmph," Aunt Irm said. "When she graduates, I will like to switch doctors."

"If she stays at University, we'll do that," I promised, though I didn't understand her aversion to Nikki.

As soon as we arrived home, Aunt Irm called the AICD Support Group coordinator and passed on the information she'd been instructed to keep quiet. From her end of the conversation, it wasn't well received. She hung up the phone without her usual, "Have a lovely day."

"He said he does not know what brand of device each person has and does not wish to frighten people. This is a lie. It was on the application form."

"And when you reminded him of that?"

"He said many people did not know and left it blank. He said he will call the company, but they will not tell the truth." Her face flushed in frustration and anger.

"You need to rest," I said. "I'll call my chairman and we'll figure out what to do."

She didn't argue. In her room, I helped her into bed, placed ECG stickers, and connected the borrowed monitor. Nathan Castle, the simulation center engineer and a friend, had gladly loaned us a transport monitor with an extra-long cable. With the monitor outside her door, I was reassured by the regular beat of Aunt Irm's beautiful, kind heart.

My chairman, Dr. James Worrell, answered my call.

"Have you heard what's happening with the Kadence AICD?" I asked.

"That a misfire caused the governor's collapse?"

"There have been four of those misfires in the last week, including my aunt this morning."

"Is she okay?"

"She is, thanks, and we disconnected the AICD and put her in a LifeVest. They have done nothing to warn patients."

"Have you spoken to Nikki Yarborough?"

"I have. She knows about all of them, but she's afraid of her chairman."

"Ah. Cantwell has a conflict of interest."

"Exactly. I think the chief of staff needs to know." I'd met the new chief only in passing, but James knew him. "I can call, but it would have more weight coming from you."

Silence.

"And more distance from Nikki. Cantwell knows we're acquainted."

He gave a sort of grunt I read as agreement. "Let me see what Cantwell has to say, then I'll take care of it. Send me the details."

Relieved, I wrote up a summary of each incident, including patient medical record numbers in case he needed more information.

I spent the afternoon answering email, completing resident evaluations, and editing a research paper. Meanwhile, Aunt Irm rested and her ECG behaved.

She slept much of the early afternoon and felt stronger, and pushier, a few hours later. Though we'd cooked together innumerable times since becoming housemates, today she was even more obsessive than usual. When she corrected my choice of stirring utensil, I simply complied. When she discarded half my chopped onion for lack of uniformity, I bit back a retort. But when she insisted I iron a tablecloth she'd ironed only the week before, I rebelled.

"What's going on?" I asked her.

She looked at me from her chair at the kitchen table with feigned innocence, then defiance, then melancholy. "Your mother died before she could teach you these things, God rest her soul. I have been remiss. You must learn. I will not always be here to prepare for visitors."

There it was. I leaned down and wrapped my arms around her. "This is about this morning. I'm so sorry. It scared me, too, but you're fine."

She wiped her eyes with the edge of the apron she made me wear. "Now you say I am fine. You must make up your mind, kindchen." Her wet chuckle might have been a sob. "I cannot leave you alone until I know you will be okay."

"Spoon, not spatula. I got it."

Her smack to my arm lacked the commitment of my adolescence. "You know that is not what I mean."

"I know." I retrieved the box of tissues for her.

"I need to know you have someone to share your life. That you will open your heart again."

"No pressure there." Before she could argue, I said, "First, I am not opposed to finding someone to share my life with, but neither am I searching at the moment. I'm happy with my life right now."

"Oh, posh."

"Second, you have many years to teach and worry and fill my dance card. You're not going anywhere any time soon. I won't let you, and you're too stubborn anyway."

Her nod was unconvincing

"And third, I owe you so much already. Even if I learn nothing more about domestic life, I'm going to be okay, and it's largely because of you. I don't know how I would have made it through the last eighteen months without you."

Now she stood and hugged me, and we both grabbed more tissues. "I must wash my face," she said as she withdrew toward her room. She returned seconds later with the iron. "Just touch up the folds, kindchen."

*   *   *

An hour later, Christian and his mother arrived. He helped me transport the roast, potatoes, broccoli, and bread to the table. It did look beautiful set with Aunt Irm's china, and not a wrinkle in sight.

Over dinner, we laughed as Aunt Irm and Mrs. O'Donnell out-did one another with childhood stories of both Christian and me. I'm pretty sure my aunt embellished her secondhand stories, heard from my parents when she still lived in Germany.

After clearing the table and serving dessert, a crazy complicated torte that had taken me almost an hour to construct, Aunt Irm decided it was time. "Christian, the MDI company is evil. You must not work with them."

He struggled to swallow his coffee.

"My Kadence misfired at me this morning. Kate saved my life. They do not even apologize."

"Oh my, Irm." Mrs. O'Donnell's face screwed up in concern as she placed a comforting hand on Aunt Irm's arm. I found the alarm on Christian's face endearing. He really did love my aunt.

"I am fine now. My doctor turned it off so it could not stop my heart again."

Christian turned to me. "A misfire?"

"They happen to all AICDs, usually without any major problem. Unfortunately, this one occurred at the worst possible instant in her ECG. It's such a tiny fraction of the total time—it almost never happens."

"So it was bad luck? I'm so sorry," Molly O'Donnell said.

"Four different patients have suffered the same bad luck in the last week," I said. "All with Kadences."

His wide eyes darted from me to Aunt Irm and back again. He held up his phone. "I don't mean to be rude. I need to check something."

"Of course, you may work on our case." Aunt Irm leaned nearer to him.

"It's not a case," I said. "So far it's a technical bug they haven't disclosed."

"Which is not legal, which makes them criminals we must stop," Aunt Irm said.

Though unsure about legality, the failure to warn patients was certainly wrong. I watched Christian as he continued to scan and scroll until he found what he was looking for.

"Our consultant engineer said the Kadence misfire rate is well within tolerances."

"It probably was when the data were collected," I said. "According to Nikki, these are the first significant misfires."

He returned his phone to the table. "Tell me what's going on."

"The Kadence is hurting people and they are keeping it a secret from the patients. This is not right," Aunt Irm said.

Christian waited for more. Aunt Irm deferred to me.

"If the misfires were random, the odds of hitting the T wave, the dangerous fraction of a second on the ECG, would be small. Multiply that times four in the span of a week."

"They're not random," he said.

"They can't be," I said. "According to Nikki, MDI is working on it."

"This is not enough. We must figure this out." Aunt Irm emphasized the "we."

I forced back a smile. "We don't know near enough about AICDs to figure out anything. My chairman is going through channels to see what we can do about the patients."

"We can compare the cases," Aunt Irm persisted. "What do the victims share in common?"

Though I hated to encourage her dramatic tendencies, it couldn't hurt to talk it through while my chairman worked his political magic. "Both you and the governor had your devices interrogated within hours of the misfire."

"Minutes for me," Aunt Irm said.

"And the other two?" Christian asked.

"The first one had been interrogated the day before." It was Mr. Abrams, my hernia patient. "I don't know about the other one." I called Nikki. When it went to voicemail, I texted instead. "Sorry to bother you, I have questions about one of the patients who had a misfire."

With no immediate response, I sent a follow-up text. "At least three out of the four misfires were interrogated within twenty-four hours. What about the fourth patient?"

"I'm waiting for Nikki to tell me about the other patient. Maybe there was an update to the interrogation computer software that introduced a bug into the Kadence."

"Who would do such a thing?" Aunt Irm asked.

"It was most likely an accident," I said.

My phone buzzed a reply. "Please leave me out of it. I'm begging you."

CHAPTER SEVENTEEN

DR. CANTWELL HAD gotten to Nikki.

"So Dr. Yarborough will not do the right thing." Aunt Irm sounded smug.

"Is there another way to find out whether the fourth victim had a recent interrogation?" Christian asked.

"Maybe." I called Annabelle Kessler. "Is Dr. Yarborough with you?"

"No. Dr. Cantwell took over."

Only an abundance of self-control kept me from saying, "It's about freaking time." Instead, I said, "She told me there have been four Kadence misfires. I know about Mr. Abrams in the recovery room, my aunt, and the governor. Can you remind me the name of the other one?" I hoped she wouldn't see through the white lie, though it approached gray.

Annabelle barely hesitated, which made me feel the tiniest bit guilty for taking advantage of her respect. Still, "needs must" as Aunt Irm might say. "Allison Woodson. She works at MDI, believe it or not."

"That's quite a coincidence." Or not. I thanked her and disconnected.

Christian followed me into my home office where I logged in via VPN to the medical record system and opened Allison Woodson's chart. The illegal action could bring the might of the privacy police down on me, if an audit revealed I had no documented medical relationship with the patient. The less time spent in the chart the better, so I went straight to the Discharge Summary and skimmed for information.

"It's the same. She collapsed in the cafeteria at work, lost consciousness, and recovered moments later. Her Kadence log showed the same pattern as Aunt Irm, an inappropriate shock at the worst possible time, followed by v tach, then another shock and a normal rhythm."

"When was her last interrogation?"

I looked back through the note. "Three months ago."

"So if we're thinking a new software bug, it doesn't fit."

It didn't. The misfires hadn't occurred at a consistent interval from the interrogation, making the link tenuous at best. Disappointing. Something was causing them. Something I couldn't fix. But I could protect the patients. If I could identify them. No convenient list of Kadence patients existed in the medical record system. At least not one I could access.

"I have to talk to Nikki."

But calls and texts went unanswered.

"Let's go," Christian said.

"Go?"

"She may not want to talk, but you need information, and so do I before this sale goes through."

Though unsure ganging up on her would help, I certainly preferred the company. "You don't think your mom would mind staying a little longer?"

"They're playing Rummikub. They'll be fine for at least an hour."

The women sat at the kitchen table, white tiles with colored numbers arrayed between them. Both seemed fine with our departure, Aunt Irm maybe a little too fine.

I drove to Nikki's apartment complex and found a spot on the second floor of the parking garage.

"Students sure drive nicer cars than I did in college," Christian said.

"No kidding. Most have nicer cars than I drive now." Granted, I still had student loans and would for the foreseeable future.

I used the code Nikki sent me Sunday to open the lobby doors. At her apartment, there was no answer to my knock and no ringing from inside when I dialed her cell.

"Where else might she be?" Christian asked.

The only other place I could think of was the house she shared with Ian. We drove there in relative silence. At night, the neighborhood looked quite different, but not to Google Maps. The house was dark and the garage door closed. A streetlight three houses away did little to illuminate the area on the moonless night. Guided by my phone's flashlight, I approached the front door and rang the doorbell. Nothing. I knocked, hard, and repeated Ian's name at increasing volume. Nothing.

I dialed Nikki's number once again. A sound, faint, but there, a ringtone. Christian heard it, too, and went to the garage door.

Lights came on across the street. A gruff voice yelled, "Who's there?"

I turned to face an intense beam shining directly in my eyes. With my arm up to block it and my eyes tightened into slits, I walked toward its source. "I'm a friend of the Yarboroughs. I'm looking for Nikki. We work together at University Hospital."

He switched off the beam and a shape in the doorway moved forward onto the patio and resolved into a fifty-something man in gym shorts and a t-shirt that couldn't quite cover his belly.

"It's not like her to be out of contact, especially from work. And when I call her cellphone, it rings in the garage." I showed him my phone with her name on the screen.

"Hang on a minute." He went inside his house and returned in flip-flops, carrying a single key and a flashlight, a cellphone at his ear.

"I hear another phone ringing." Christian moved toward the front windows again. "Sounds like a landline."

"Ian, this is Chuck from across the street. Call me back when you get this." He disconnected. "Yeah, that's the only number I have for him. I don't think Ian would mind if I take a peek in the garage."

Christian and I stayed on the driveway as Chuck went to the front door, knocked loudly, then disappeared inside. Lights came on, then the garage door opened. Nikki's Toyota occupied the right-hand side, with an empty space on the left. Chuck opened the driver's door and reached in, reappearing with a cellphone.

I dialed her number again and the phone in Chuck's hand lit up. "Kate Downey?"

I nodded and disconnected. He offered me the phone, which displayed alerts for multiple missed calls from me. It would have to be unlocked to see what came before.

I leaned into the car to return the phone and patted the floor mat where she usually left her keys when we exercised at the park. I palmed them, stood, and slipped my hands into my pockets.

"Should we call the police?" Chuck asked.

"Did everything look okay inside?" Christian said.

"You mean like an attack or something?" Chuck shook his head. "They probably won't consider adults missing, huh? Except she left her phone. Who does that these days?"

"Good point," I said.

"I have a friend on the force," Christian said to Chuck. "I'll give him a call."

"Do you know what kind of car Ian drives?" I nodded to the empty parking spot marked only by an oil stain.

"One of those small SUVs," Chuck said. "An Acura I think, dark blue or gray maybe."

We thanked him and exchanged contact information. Back in the car, Christian made a call. "Garner, hey, you're on speaker. I'm with Kate Downey."

"Kate, long time no see. How are you?"

We caught up briefly as Christian navigated back to the main road.

"How hard is it to track someone's cellphone?" Christian asked.

"Not hard at all if I have a warrant."

"And if you don't?" I said.

"Still possible in exigent circumstances," he said.

"Define *exigent*," Christian said.

"Why don't you just tell me what's going on?"

"Unofficially?" I said.

"Sure. Unofficially."

I described the misfires. As a police officer, he'd carried an automated external defibrillator in his patrol car. "I need a list of people with the Kadence so I can warn them."

"Wait, why you?" Garner asked.

My jaw tightened. "People are getting hurt and the company's doing nothing."

Christian reached for my hand. "Aunt Irm's misfired this morning."

"Ah, I'm sorry, Kate. Is she okay?"

"Yes, but the doctor who knows the most about the device and should be calling the patients has disappeared."

"Disappeared?" His skepticism, though warranted, annoyed me.

"She's not at work and we found her car and cellphone at the house she shared with her recently estranged husband."

"Tell me you didn't break in," Garner said.

"We didn't break in," Christian said. "A neighbor had a key."

"We didn't even go inside," I said.

"Did that neighbor find any evidence of a struggle?" Garner asked.

"No, but how do you explain her leaving her car and phone at a house where she no longer lives?" I said.

"I hear you, Kate, and I trust your instincts, but this isn't much to go on."

"Can't you ping Ian's phone or credit cards or something?"

"You watch too much TV." Garner asked for their names and address. "I'll see what I can do."

I thanked him, grudgingly, and we disconnected. "Agent Gibbs on *NCIS* could find them."

"Do not mention TV cops to Garner," Christian said.

"Why?"

"Because I care about you and don't want to clean up the blood."

CHAPTER EIGHTEEN

AFTER A RESTLESS night visiting dark places in my dreams and getting up to check on Aunt Irm, I made a decision. One that would not be popular.

I found her in the kitchen, her face half hidden behind a mug of steaming coffee. I breathed in the delicious aroma and greeted her with a kiss on both cheeks. She'd already filled my travel mug and placed it next to the borrowed monitor, its cable neatly coiled on top.

I thanked her for the coffee and took a fortifying sip of caffeinated courage. "I know you're not going to like this, but I need you to do me a huge favor."

"Of course, I will help you." Then her expression turned wary. "What is it that I will not like?"

"I don't want you alone today."

"Yes. I already spoke with Carmel. She will be done with her appointments at noon and will come here. We are going to make homemade pasta."

"Good. Have her pick you up at the hospital. You can come to work with me."

"To the hospital? I do not wish to watch you operate."

That I don't actually operate was beside the point. "You won't be in the operating room. You can sit with my assistant."

"Mary? Such a lovely woman." Mary kept my work life manageable, much as Aunt Irm did for my home life. I knew how blessed I was.

"Thank you for agreeing." Though she hadn't actually agreed, neither had she refused. Yesterday's misfire had frightened both of us. I could only hope Mary's day was such that Aunt Irm wouldn't be a bother. We'd "play it by ear" as my mother used to say, ignoring the fact I'm pretty much tone deaf.

Conference on Labor and Delivery began at seven thirty, before Mary would arrive, so Aunt Irm joined me on the third floor where I taught an interactive session with the three assigned anesthesia residents and one medical student. Though she said nothing, my aunt took in everything. Even if she understood little of the terminology, she could read people—their confidence, their fears, their insecurities, and their lies.

After conference, I called Mary. Residency interviews would have her occupied all morning. "I'm sorry. She's welcome to sit in the outer office with the other secretaries."

Instead, she sat with me in the OB office. When I had to leave, I would ask to have her sit at the nursing station.

I called Annabelle Kessler and learned Nikki was not expected at work today. "Have there been any more Kadence problems?" I asked.

"No, thank God."

"What do you think about warning patients with the device? Or disabling the AICDs like you did for Aunt Irm?"

"I think that decision is light-years above my pay grade."

I texted my chairman, eager to hear what progress he'd made. "Meeting with Cantwell at 2," he replied.

Frustrated by the delay and my impotence, I answered email while Aunt Irm read a paperback German crime novel. It occurred to me that might be a poor choice of genre for my conspiracy-prone aunt. Romance, however, would be infinitely worse for me.

Clinically, the morning was unusually quiet, something no one dared acknowledge out loud.

At nine, my colleague Sam Paulus took over Labor and Delivery so I could teach a simulator session, Aunt Irm in tow. I re-introduced her to Nathan, the simulator engineer. She remembered him from Greg's funeral, of course. She remembered everyone.

I placed the borrowed monitor on his desk in the observation room and thanked him again for loaning it to me.

"It helped?" he asked.

"Helped my peace of mind," I said.

The students arrived, and I moved into the lab that resembled an operating room complete with a full-size human manikin that breathed, had a pulse and blood pressure. From the other side of the one-way glass, Nathan created emergencies for the students to recognize and treat before they were faced with the real thing.

Each time we finished a scenario and I entered the observation room, Irm and Nathan were smiling, sometimes laughing. As two of my favorite people, it was no surprise they'd hit it off.

After the students left, Aunt Irm said, "Nathan has invited me to stay here until Carmel arrives."

"I have a few more sessions, so I won't be going anywhere," Nathan said. "She's welcome to keep me company."

"He knows defibrillators," Aunt Irm said with a small measure of awe.

"Really?"

Nathan had a biomedical engineering degree, so it wasn't all that surprising.

"I did my master's thesis on communication protocols for implantable devices. The model we used was an AICD."

Okay, that was surprising.

"Is it not a small world?" Aunt Irm said.

"Seriously small. Did you happen to work with Dr. Cantwell in cardiology?" I asked.

"Not directly. He was the medical advisor on the project. He'd developed some new hardware and Dr. Bennett, my advisor, handled the software."

"The MDI company should call this Dr. Bennett for help," Aunt Irm said. "They cannot fix their own device."

"He's gone," Nathan said. "He left a few weeks ago for the private sector."

My phone rang. Sam Paulus said, "I need to start a bring-back heart downstairs. Can you take over Labor and Delivery? They're about to start another C-section."

"I've got it. Thanks, Sam." I'd rather do fifty C-sections than one repeat heart operation.

"I will stay here with Nathan," Aunt Irm said, "and catch him up on our case."

My doubt must have shown, because she said, "I will not be a distraction. We will talk between classes."

Probably better to have her with Nathan than sitting at the nurses' station, both for her and the nurses. To Nathan, I said, "I'd like to talk more about the AICD."

"Sure. It's been a couple of years, but I remember a few things." His childlike enthusiasm made me smile.

Back on Labor and Delivery, the C-section went fine. Of course, it was a boy baby causing trouble. Right about half my patients undergoing an unplanned C-section are amazed when I correctly guess boy. The other half have girls.

Afterward, I went in search of Nikki's administrative assistant at the cardiology department and ended up in the chairman's office. *Hmmm.*

No. My chairman would talk to him. I was only looking for Nikki. "I need to speak with Dr. Yarborough," I told the secretary. "She's not at the hospital today. Would you know how I can reach her?"

"Have you tried her cellphone?"

"I have. She left it behind. Did she leave another number? Maybe her husband's cell?"

"If you left a message, she will call when she has time." She'd barely looked at me over her desk.

"I need to speak with her about a patient as soon as possible." It was kinda true.

"Dr. Cantwell is covering her patients for the time being."

Apparently, wheedling information was not a strength of mine. "Look, Nikki and I are friends. It's not like her to be out of contact. Can you at least tell me whether you spoke with her this morning?"

She relented, a little. "She left a message with the answering service. She requested time off for a family emergency."

Crap. I was about to leave when a door to my right opened and Cantwell emerged, trailed by a young man in a suit. They shook hands. "It was very nice to meet you, Dr. Cantwell."

"We'll be in touch next week."

Sounded like a job interview. Hopefully a partner for Nikki. The young man left via the main office door, and I knew I should follow him out, but I couldn't. "Dr. Cantwell, I need to speak with you about the Kadence."

He glanced at me with curiosity, disdain, and absolutely no recognition.

"Kate Downey from anesthesia."

Without a word, he led me into his large but remarkably bare office and closed the door. The blinds on a wall of windows were closed, leaving only harsh overhead fluorescent lighting.

"What's this about?" He moved behind a large, empty desk that would be perfect for paper football. I was channeling Nathan now.

"What are you and MDI doing about the Kadence misfires?"

He stared at me stonily, but his eyebrow twitched.

"You have to warn patients while you figure out how to fix the problem."

"That is not any of your concern."

"It is my concern." My cheeks warmed. "My aunt's Kadence put her into v-tach yesterday."

"And cardioverted her back," he said with absolutely no change in expression.

"After she collapsed in the parking lot." I forced my voice to remain calm. How could he possibly think that was okay? "Because of the misfire, Nikki Yarborough had the AICD function disabled and my aunt is now wearing a LifeVest."

Nothing. No grimace or apology or eye contact even.

"Four patients have suffered an arrest due to misfires of your device in less than a week."

His lips thinned. "Did Dr. Yarborough tell you that?"

"I was present for three of them. She didn't tell me anything."

"We are investigating." He enunciated each word, his rising anger clear. It was no match for mine.

"That's not enough and you know it. You have to warn patients." I was proud of my newfound boldness. Him, not so much. He returned to the door and gestured for me to leave.

I didn't move. "Have you reported the misfires to the FDA?" Manufacturers are required to report malfunctions of medical devices.

His expression and voice hardened. "We have made our manufacturer aware. That is our only obligation."

"But you're closely linked to them. Has MDI reported to the FDA?"

Cantwell opened the door and waited. In the secretary's office was James Worrell, my chairman. Though he had to be angry, he only nodded to me. "I was looking for Nikki Yarborough," I said to him.

He gave another nod. One of dismissal. Of, "we'll talk about this later." But he didn't chastise me in front of Cantwell or his secretary. For that, I was grateful.

"Thank you for fitting me in early," James said as he followed Cantwell.

Angry at myself for overstepping, I returned to a quiet Labor and Delivery. So nice of the babies to recognize today was too busy for a birthday.

James invited me to his office half an hour later.

"Dr. Cantwell is confident they will correct the problem with the Kadence in the next day or so," he said.

I realized too late that I'd rolled my eyes at my chairman.

His eyebrow rose.

"You don't believe him," I said. "He's saying what you want to hear."

Still with the eyebrow.

"What if he's wrong and more patients are injured?"

"I agree with you. We called the chief of staff from Cantwell's office. He agrees with you, too, and will investigate."

Wow. That was unexpected. "Did he insist they warn the patients?"

"Not yet, but I suspect he will."

"When?"

"I know you're worried about your aunt—"

"It's not just that. It's the principle of the thing. Putting fears over bad press above patient safety. It's wrong."

Light dawned in his eyes. "Like before, when the chief of staff wouldn't help chase down our serial killer."

I lowered my head, less defiant. Was I overreacting?

"I get it." His voice was kind, not at all angry. "You did the right thing bringing it to my attention. I'll follow up and let you know what he decides."

I thanked him but felt little better about the situation.

Aunt Irm texted her departure with Carmel. We finally had some work to do on Labor and Delivery, and in between cases, I read Nikki's paper on the Kadence. I needed to learn more about AICD technology so I downloaded one of the references, a paper by her engineer co-author, Dale Bennett.

Getting through the introduction required me to google a dozen terms. I called Nathan for help. It went to voicemail. I started highlighting what I didn't understand, to review with him later. I would have used less ink if I highlighted what I did understand.

Instead, I scrolled through Dr. Bennett's other papers on PubMed, the database of publications related to medicine in the last fifty years. He had several, a couple with Nathan's name on them, and another with Nikki. The abstract of that paper was so engineering-dense I was surprised she would be a co-author. Then I looked again at the author list. It wasn't N. Yarborough; it was I. Yarborough. Ian. Her husband.

I clicked on Author Affiliations. Ian Yarborough worked for MDI. Was that weird? Had Nikki kept it a secret for some reason? It might explain why she was so reticent to complain to Dr. Cantwell—both their jobs depended on him. The whole situation had suddenly become even more incestuous.

CHAPTER NINETEEN

AT FOUR O'CLOCK, an hour before I was supposed to hand off to the on-call attending, I asked if he could cover early, promising it was quiet. "Famous last words," he said, but agreed.

"I'll make it up to you." I changed out of scrubs, entered "MDI" into Google Maps, and drove north, toward the airport, then east several miles to a modern metal and glass structure that looked out of place in the long-depressed part of town.

I parked and entered through automatic glass doors. There was no receptionist so I went to a directory by the elevators. Engineering, fourth floor.

It wasn't hard to find. ENGINEERING was written in large blue letters across the wall. I opened the adjacent frosted glass door into an entryway that funneled into a large area filled with tables of equipment. Offices lined the perimeter of the space, all with identical closed doors.

Only two people occupied the common area. A man sat at a table with a laptop and several other monitors, all aglow. A woman standing at his side leaned in, pointing to his screen. They were deep in conversation.

I started around the outside, found Ian's office, and knocked. No answer.

"Can I help you?" It was the woman from the lab area. I took it as an invitation and approached.

"I'm looking for Ian Yarborough."

"He's not here." Up close, she looked much too young to have an engineering degree. "Is there something I can help you with?"

Change of plans. "Are you an engineer?"

"I am." She extended her hand. "Erin Stevens."

I shook it, introduced myself, and confirmed she worked on the Kadence. "Can I ask you a few questions?"

"Um." She looked at the other engineer.

"I promise it will only take a minute." She didn't refuse, so I pressed on. "You're aware of the recent misfires causing arrhythmias."

Her expression remained blank, except for her eyes. They told me everything.

"Sorry to blindside you. I resuscitated two of the patients and was there when the governor collapsed. I realized last night that three of the four misfires occurred in patients who had their device interrogated not long before the event." Nothing. "So I'm wondering if that could be related."

Her eyes avoided mine. "We are looking into it. I'm afraid I have to ask you—"

I put a hand gently on her arm. "One of the patients is my great-aunt. She might not survive another misfire."

Her face softened. "I'm sorry, but there's really nothing I can tell you."

"Have you been able to replicate the problem?"

She hesitated, glanced again at the other engineer, then said, "Not yet, but we're working on it."

"Is it possible the interrogation computer inadvertently introduced a bug? Was the software recently updated?"

She angled her head slightly, considering, then moved to a laptop on another table. She clicked some keys. "The last update to the interrogation software was six months ago."

I deflated. "So that's not it."

She shook her head. "Once we have a solution, we'll let your aunt's cardiologist know."

Though disappointed, I remained determined. "Would you have Ian's cell number?"

"He doesn't work here anymore."

Selling the house, quitting his job—this wasn't just a trial separation. "When did that happen?"

Her naturally full eyebrows came together.

"It's very important I get in touch with his wife, but she doesn't have her cellphone. I'm hoping Ian knows where she is."

Still, Erin Stevens hesitated. Whether mistrustful or respectful of privacy, it was getting in the way.

"How about you text him and ask him to call me." I found a pen and paper on the table, wrote my name and cell number, and handed it to her.

When she realized I wasn't leaving, she typed on her phone. "Today was supposed to be his last day, but he said there was a family emergency." She finished typing. "I hope you hear from him."

I thanked her and left. When I stepped onto the elevator, it went up instead of down. On the fifth floor, two people in suits waited for me to exit. Past them was a sign for the CEO's office, Edward Samuels. My internal debate lasted only an instant. I left the elevator.

The CEO didn't work at University. I wasn't going around the chain of command to talk to him. At least that was my rationalization as I approached his secretary. If possible, she was even more abrupt than Dr. Cantwell's. "No, I will not interrupt him with a message," "No, you cannot wait to see him," "No, you cannot have an appointment for later today."

"Can you tell me if he's even here?"

"No." She pushed over a pad and pen. "You may leave him a message."

Wow. Helpful. I wrote, "Mr. Samuels, If you won't report the Kadence misfires to the FDA, I will." I signed the note, included my cellphone number, and handed it to the secretary.

"I will see that he gets this," she said in dismissal.

I waited in the hallway, expecting her to read the note and interrupt him after all.

Framed patents lined the walls, along with a photo of a much younger Dr. Cantwell holding what must have been the original Kadence. All but one of the patents listed him as an inventor. That one, entitled "Method and System for Bidirectional Communication for Implanted Devices," listed Dale Bennett, PhD, and several others, including Nathan Castle. He said he worked on the project, but I hadn't realized he was so involved. Good for him.

One of the diagrams mentioned a chip capable of two kinds of Bluetooth, as well as FM radio and GPS. I'd have to ask Nathan about that. Aunt Irm "accidentally" switched off our shared mapping app with some frequency. Maybe I could still track her location. Big Brother wasn't always a bad thing.

The elevator dinged and a man in dark pants and a black collared shirt approached me. "I'm sorry. The building is closing soon. I must ask you to leave."

A security escort? Must be courtesy of the secretary. Had she shared my message with her boss?

He held the elevator door and accompanied me all the way to the first floor and out the front door without a word. It felt formal and threatening at the same time.

As I slumped into the driver's seat, my phone rang. Unknown number. I answered anyway. I wouldn't risk letting any call go unanswered now. "This is Kate Downey."

"Kate, it's Nikki."

I sat up. "Are you okay? Where are you?" The background hum sounded like a car.

"Listen, I haven't got much time. Someone is triggering the Kadence on purpose. I don't know who or why. He threatened me and my patients so I'm leaving town for a while. Sorry. Please let the police handle it or he might go after you, too."

"Wait, Nikki, where are you going? Are you safe? Is Ian with you?" The words spilled out. She'd already disconnected.

CHAPTER TWENTY

HOLY CRAP. I stared out the windshield at MDI, too shocked to start the car. Aunt Irm was right. These were attacks, not random events from a software bug.

I called Christian, frustrated when it went immediately to voicemail. "Nikki says someone is triggering the Kadence. She's in hiding."

I called Aunt Irm.

"I am fine, kindchen. Carmel is here. Whatever is wrong? You sound upset."

"I'm on my way home. I'll tell you when I get there."

Christian texted back. "With Samuels and Cantwell. Emergency?"

Was he here at MDI now? There were several dark SUVs dotting the parking lot. More likely, they met Cantwell at University.

"Listen to voicemail," I replied and started the car, still trying to get my head around the idea that someone could fire an AICD on purpose. And not just fire it but stop the heart.

Fear for my aunt turned to outrage as I drove. Why would someone trigger the Kadence? First thought: to damage the reputation of MDI or its owners. But why? The temporal relationship to the sale couldn't be a coincidence. If the goal was to interfere, though, why not just go public with the hacking and cover-up?

Nikki said that she was also threatened. These were her patients, her career. Her marriage was in trouble. Could Ian do such a thing? He was an engineer and had access to the device. Could he possibly be that evil? Was she with him now? But she'd called. If he was doing this, why would he let her call?

I was getting a headache.

Another option struck me. Someone could blackmail the patients directly or their family members. "Pay or I'll stop your heart." Maybe the triggers so far were just proof he could do it.

But neither Aunt Irm nor I had received such a threat. My skin prickled. Adam. He would pay to hurt Aunt Irm to get back at me. As I thought it through, though, it didn't make sense. There couldn't be more than a hundred devices implanted, so advertising Kadence shocks as a service-for-hire was a limited business model.

No, if it was blackmail, the most likely targets were Cantwell or Samuels or both. They had the most to lose if the Kadence failed. In which case, they'd known what was going on the whole time and Cantwell had lied to my face.

I passed Carmel's car in the driveway and parked in the garage. Inside, I was immediately enveloped in the warmth of Irm, Shadow, Carmel, the scent of Italian food, and something else. Fish. I screwed up my nose. Even gallons of tomato sauce couldn't cover that unwelcome odor. I kissed my aunt on both cheeks.

"We are almost done, kindchen. You take Shadow for some exercise, and we will talk."

Grateful for the opportunity to clear my mind, and nose, I changed and took Shadow for a run, not a jog, a real run. He soon realized slowing to sniff caused a literal pain in his neck and ran at my side.

By the time we returned, Carmel had packed up her pristine metal pasta maker. "Are you sure you don't want to keep some of the fresh bass?" she asked me. "Richard caught it yesterday at Lake Alto. He calls it his alto-bass." She pronounced it like the vocal range rather than the fish. Who could resist her infectious laughter?

Aunt Irm joined in, shaking her head. "Your Richard. He is something."

Carmel had six kids, all of them successful. If Richard was the son I was thinking of, he *was* something, a PhD in neuroscience, a trained chef, and now a fisherman. Quite the Renaissance man.

"Thank Richard for me, but no. I'm not much for seafood." It was another thing Greg and I agreed on, except maybe tuna salad on occasion. I helped Carmel load her car, then took a cool shower.

Afterward, I couldn't find my blow dryer, again. Aunt Irm borrowed it on occasion for something she did in the kitchen. Wrapped in a towel, I stepped from my bedroom. "Aunt Irm—" I froze. Two aproned figures stared back. One should not have been there, should not have been wearing an apron, and definitely should not be staring at me in only a towel.

"I think she might want her blow dryer back," Christian said with an adorable crooked grin.

"I am sorry, kindchen." She unplugged it and brought it to me. Even with her between us, I felt Christian's eyes.

Back in the bathroom, my red face betrayed my embarrassment. Except that wasn't all that heated my face. Christian's expression was more than amusement. There was a hunger there, apparently a hunger shared.

I turned from the mirror, unable to face my own shame. *Get over it. Greg is gone. You're a grown woman. You're allowed to feel.*

Acting on those feelings was another story, and one for another chapter. Tonight was about some crazy idiot attacking people with heart problems.

I dried my hair, applied no makeup, dressed in shorts and a t-shirt, and exited the bathroom looking pretty much the opposite of "hot."

Christian's grin remained and my face heated all over again.

Aunt Irm took one look at me and said, "Oh, kindchen, do not be embarrassed. That towel covered more of you than your bikini."

Christian's eyes widened.

"When's the last time you saw me in a bikini?"

"Oh, posh." She waved a dishtowel at me.

"Because it's kind of different when you're twelve."

Christian laughed. I did, too. Even Aunt Irm joined in eventually.

"Dinner is ready," she said. "Sit."

"I just came by to talk about your voicemail," Christian said to me. "Sorry to surprise you like that." He wasn't sorry.

"Nonsense." Aunt Irm set another place at the table. "I insist you stay."

"You don't want to cross her." I pulled out my usual chair across from my aunt. She'd positioned Christian beside me, what a surprise.

Once we'd passed the dishes and served ourselves vegetable lasagna, salad, and bread, she said, "First, Christian, have you heard from Michael?"

"We haven't. It's driving Mom crazy."

"Please tell us how Kate and I can assist with the search."

"I wish I knew. We've run out of places to look, and he's an adult so we can't interest the police." He drizzled balsamic dressing over his salad. "He'll come home when he's ready."

"Hmph," she said. "Young men should not frighten their mothers."

"You tell him that when he gets back," Christian said.

She turned to me. "What so frightened you today?"

"Nikki said they're not misfires. Someone is triggering the Kadence." I watched for a response from my aunt—shock, anger, disbelief. Nope. None of the above.

"Of course this must be true," she said. "It is too much coincidence. We must find the purpose." She'd been a target of this madman, yet she remained dispassionate. Well, not dispassionate exactly, she was always passionate, but clearheaded. She amazed me.

"Did you ask Cantwell and Samuels?" I asked Christian.

"Who is Samuels?" Aunt Irm asked.

"He's the CEO of MDI, the company that makes the Kadence," Christian said. "They claim it's not possible to trigger it remotely."

"Of course they did," I said. "Did they even admit to the misfires?"

"They didn't offer the information, but when I asked, they didn't hide it. Mr. Samuels said his engineers are working on a solution."

"They aren't even close," I said. "They haven't been able to replicate the problem."

My dinner companions stared at me.

"After work, I went to MDI and met with an engineer."

"How did you swing that?" Christian asked.

"Our Kate can be very persuasive." Aunt Irm had returned to her meal, taking bird-size bites of lasagna.

"Turns out Nikki's husband, Ian, works for MDI. I went looking for him, but he wasn't there. Instead, I spoke with another engineer, Erin Stevens. She's investigating the misfires and told me how little progress they'd made. I told her I really needed to talk to Nikki, and she agreed to text my number to Ian. Soon after, Nikki called from an unknown number. I assume it was Ian's."

Both Christian and Irm leaned a little closer, dinner forgotten.

"It sounded like she was in a car. She said that someone is intentionally triggering the devices. She didn't know any more but said whoever it is threatened her and her patients."

"Who would do such a thing?" Aunt Irm said. "Christian, you must call your Lieutenant Garner. This man must be stopped."

With a glance, he confirmed with me and lifted his phone.

"Invite him here. We have more pasta." Aunt Irm was already headed to the kitchen for another plate, certain no one could resist a home-cooked meal.

The call was brief. "He's at dinner now and will stop by on his way home."

Aunt Irm returned with the new place setting. Declining a meal, even a second meal, was not something she understood.

"How involved is Cantwell with MDI?" I asked. "I asked him whether he was warning patients about the misfires or reporting them to the FDA. He said it was up to the manufacturer, but that's him, too, right?"

"He owns a forty-nine percent stake," Christian said. "Samuels has the other fifty-one. They're both on the board. As far as the FDA goes, unless the device causes a death, they have thirty days to report any problems. If they have a solution by that time, it looks much better."

"And if someone dies in the meantime, it will look much worse." I shouldn't have stated it so bluntly, but Aunt Irm took it in stride.

"What does your client company think of this?" she asked.

"They are requesting more information before we complete the deal."

She nodded. "This is good. They should not wish to work with this MDI company." She saw things in such black and white, definitely not in green, the only language of business.

I tore a piece from my baguette and wiped it through the remaining sauce on my plate. As I lifted it to my mouth, I met Aunt Irm's disapproving glare. Oops. "She can't take me anywhere."

Christian laughed, then copied me, except he used a fork.

"Show-off."

"After that look? No way I'm following your lead."

Aunt Irm scoffed. "My father, rest his soul, would take you outside with a switch for those table manners."

Rest his soul, indeed. "What else did you do to earn the switch?" She never talked about her family, and I was always curious.

The corners of her mouth turned up in a mischievous grin. "I will never tell."

"Not fair. You told stories about me last night."

"It was Max who got the switch, for performing poorly in school, or not completing his chores, or talking back to our mother."

"Uncle Max told us stories about his misguided youth. I want to hear about you."

"I might have misbehaved on occasion, but nothing like you and your brother." She shook her head in mock dismay. "My poor Max." It could have been real dismay.

"He never once spanked me."

She raised an eyebrow almost all the way to her hairline. "That is not to say that you did not deserve it. He did not know how to discipline a young lady."

"Ha. No one accused me of being that."

Christian laughed.

"She is not being funny, Christian. I visited the Christmas she turned sixteen and do you know she owned not one dress? Nothing for Christmas Mass."

"We were talking about you, Aunt Irm, and my life marches along quite nicely with only one or two dresses." Actually I could do without the black one. It had seen enough funerals.

Shadow leapt up from the floor and ran for the front door, barking and wagging in equal measure. The fun was over.

CHAPTER TWENTY-ONE

IT TOOK LITTLE time to update Lieutenant Garner. With Aunt Irm, there was no building to the punch line. "I was attacked," she said. "Someone caused my ticker minder to shock me when we left the clinic." She pressed her sternum. "My Kate saved my life."

"I'm very glad you're okay." Garner turned to me. "Attacked? You said it was a misfire."

"This is why we have called you." Aunt Irm put her arm in his and led him to the table. He knew better than to turn down lasagna.

"As I mentioned yesterday," I said, "several Kadence AICDs have fired unexpectedly in the last week, each occurring at the fraction of a second in the ECG that stops the heart until another shock converts it back into a normal rhythm. It's too much to be random. An engineer at MDI told me they've been unable to replicate the misfires, which means they're nowhere near correcting the problem."

"Because they are not *misfires*," Aunt Irm said.

Garner put down his fork, pulled out his ever-present notebook, and looked at me for an explanation.

"Nikki Yarborough, the person we were looking for last night, called and said she and her patients were threatened by someone claiming to be able to trigger the Kadence at will."

He paused to absorb that. "What else did she say?"

"That's it. She hung up before I could ask any questions."

"How did she sound?"

I tried to remember. "If I say 'terrified' can you track the number?"

"Nice try." He took another bite of lasagna.

"She wasn't whispering or screaming, but she hung up awfully fast. It sounded like she was in a car."

He took down the number she'd called from, though he made no promises.

"Kate discovered another clue," Aunt Irm said. "Ian Yarborough works for MDI."

Aunt Irm and her clues. "Today was supposed to be his last day," I said. "He called out this morning for a family emergency."

Garner wrote more. I felt like I should apologize for the convoluted story. He looked over his notes and shook his head. "Someone is shocking people and stopping their hearts. What is it with you finding all the wackos trying to kill people in crazy ways?"

"It is not her fault. She is only observant." Aunt Irm tapped her temple with an index finger.

To Aunt Irm, Garner said, "Tell me more about your misfire."

"It was an attack." She nodded to me. "I was not awake. Kate must tell what happened."

"I went with her to her clinic appointment that morning."

"An appointment Kate made for me because she was concerned about this very thing." She nodded for me to continue.

"Dr. Yarborough checked out her Kadence and everything was fine. Soon after we stepped outside, though—"

"We were on the stairs," Aunt Irm said. "It would have been dangerous if my Kate had not caught me." I hid my smile at the piecemeal story and waited until she nodded again.

"I yelled for someone to get Dr. Yarborough."

"So there were witnesses?" Garner said.

"The woman with the lovely grandchildren flowers," Aunt Irm said.

Garner looked at me. This would be so much easier if I could just tell the whole story.

"She and her husband were pushing her walker up the wheelchair ramp."

"Ah, anyone else?"

I pictured the scene. My helplessness despite a decade of training. "There was someone else, a man in a baseball cap. He was at the end of the sidewalk, near the corner of the building. I yelled to him, and I swear he looked right at me, then walked away, out into the parking lot." I'd forgotten about that.

"A man?" Aunt Irm looked into the middle distance with her "searching my brain" expression. "I do not recall him."

"I only saw him after you collapsed." Gooseflesh rose on my arms. *It could have been him.* Eyes closed, I tried to picture him. "All I remember is the red baseball cap. Maybe jeans and a t-shirt?" So much for being observant.

"Maybe there are cameras outside the clinic," Christian said.

Garner wrote down the clinic's address. "Could this man have triggered the device?"

"I . . . don't know," I said.

"Would he have to be that close?" Christian asked.

"It depends on how it's triggered, I guess." I thought of the other victims. "If it requires line of sight, it wouldn't have been hard at the governor's speech, or maybe at MDI where the other misfire occurred, but the first one was in the recovery room at the hospital. An outsider can't get in there."

Garner grunted. "Where there's a will, there's a way." His skepticism gave me pause. Considering the number of people in a hospital at any one time, from support staff to patients to families, he was right. Heck, I was allowed to navigate the ER in street clothes.

"That's encouraging."

"What happened next?" Garner said.

"Aunt Irm's Kadence finally converted her back to a normal rhythm. Dr. Yarborough confirmed it was a misfire, and we decided to switch it off for now."

Aunt Irm surprised me when she pulled out the neck of her blouse, revealing the white LifeVest. "Now I must wear this. It is not comfortable."

"It's an external defibrillator," I said.

"Everyone with a Kadence needs this," Aunt Irm said. "We must be protected."

Garner gave her a sharp nod. "Is that happening? Are they getting vests?"

"The people running MDI are convinced they'll have a solution soon," Christian said.

"The people running MDI don't acknowledge they're being attacked," I said.

"They do not care about their patients. Even the leader of our support group would not let me warn everyone. He does not believe us." Aunt Irm folded her arms over her chest.

"You know he can't give you that information," I said. "We'll find another way."

"I met with MDI's CEO, Edward Samuels, and Dr. Cantwell today," Christian said. Garner wrote furiously. "MDI makes the Kadence. Cantwell invented it and owns just under half the company. They deny it can be purposely triggered and insist more harm than good would come from turning them all off."

"They care only for money," Aunt Irm said. "This news would hurt their reputation."

"She makes a good point," Christian said. "The timing couldn't be worse, right when they're trying to sell the company."

Aunt Irm beamed.

"Do you have any idea how they might trigger the device?" Garner asked.

It would require sending data to the device remotely, without the interrogation computer. I shook my head.

Christian put his fork on his empty plate. "Our engineering consultants mentioned a patent on bidirectional communication bundled with the others as part of the purchase agreement. That technology isn't incorporated in the current model because the FDA doesn't like remote control of implanted devices."

"I saw that patent at MDI," I said. "Nathan, our simulator engineer, was on it."

"But, Kate, you watch me from the cloud." Aunt Irm pointed upward, presumably to the cloud. I wondered if she understood it wasn't an actual cloud.

"That's right," Christian said. "Communication goes in only a one-way direction, though, from the device to your cellphone, and then to the cloud through Wi-Fi or the cellular network. It can't go the other way. The FDA required penetration testing before they would grant clearance. The only way to send a signal to the Kadence is through the interrogation computer and the proprietary wand that has to be within six inches of your device."

"Someone found a way in," I said. "And a way to trigger it at exactly the wrong millisecond." Which would be incredibly difficult. Even if the psycho could watch Aunt Irm's ECG real-time, there's no way he could hit a button that triggered a shock at the same instant. It had to be automated in some way. Funny that I assumed a *he*. Maybe because of the guy in the ball cap. Or maybe just because.

"What about Dr. Yarborough's Ian?" Aunt Irm said. "Is it not suspicious he left today?"

"He should certainly be high on the list," I said.

"You mentioned a threat, Kate," Garner said. "To Dr. Yarborough and her patients."

"That's what she said. That someone is triggering the device. She didn't know who or why, but he threatened her in addition to her patients so she was leaving town."

"Threatened with what?" Garner asked.

My shoulders were growing tired of shrugging. "She hung up before I could ask. I assumed more shocks." Maybe worse, but I didn't say that. If he could trigger a shock, he could probably stop it from rescuing the patient afterward, too.

"And according to you there was no evidence of a struggle at her home." Garner softened his evident disapproval with a slight grin.

"I do not believe she had to be forced," Aunt Irm said. "Her Ian worked on the Kadence and now they have run away."

"That doesn't make her part of this. She's the one who told me about it." I wondered again what my aunt had against Nikki. She'd been pleasant at the picnic and appropriate during the appointment the day before. She'd followed Aunt Irm's wishes over mine, for heaven's sake.

"Her Ian had means and opportunity. We must find his motive." Aunt Irm jabbed the table on the last word.

Christian grinned.

To Garner, I said, "I blame you for this," and nodded toward my aunt.

He chuckled. "She's not wrong." He flipped back a page in his notebook. "Could the person you saw outside the clinic have been Ian?"

Ian? I tried to put his face under the baseball cap, but the man had been too far away. "It was only a second."

My cell rang. It was Sam Paulus at the hospital and not likely to be a social call. I apologized, stood, and stepped away from the table. "Hi, Sam, what's up?"

"Sorry to bother you. There's a big accident on the interstate and we're activating the disaster call list. How soon can you be here?"

"Twenty minutes."

He thanked me and disconnected to make the next call.

I turned back to our guests. "I need to go to the hospital." I couldn't leave Aunt Irm alone, not with her new LifeVest and a maniac on the loose. Though we'd disconnected the shock capability, what if he could reactivate it remotely?

"I will call Carmel," Aunt Irm said at the same time Christian said, "Aunt Irm can come to our house."

"We will handle it, kindchen. You go save lives."

I kissed her on the cheek, patted Shadow, and said goodbye to Christian and Garner as I hurried out the door. Google Maps showed wide black lines where the interstate should be. Bad. Many of the surface streets were also red, especially those near on- and off-ramps. I chose a route many blocks from the gridlock and still took twice the promised twenty minutes to reach the hospital.

After changing into scrubs, I reported to the clinical office where Sam was distributing faculty, residents, and anesthetists throughout the hospital towers. Everywhere, staff in scrubs strode with purpose, faces resolute.

"At least one of the victims is pregnant," Sam said to me. "She's on her way to Labor and Delivery. I'll send Mariel to join you."

I took the stairs two at a time.

A C-section was underway in one operating room, the labor rooms were full, and the few available nurses were rushing to prepare for the new arrival.

"What do we know?" I asked the charge nurse.

"Only that she's close to term."

Mariel arrived. In only her first year of training, she had no obstetric anesthesia experience, but beggars can't be choosers. Trial by fire came to mind. Clichés abound in the calm before the storm.

And then came the storm. The double doors slammed open, and a gurney flew through guided by two paramedics in blue flight suits. The writhing patient, covered in blood, screamed only three words, over and over: "Save my baby."

We ran straight back to an open operating room, where I introduced myself to the patient and promised to take good care of her and her baby. We moved her to the operating table and applied monitors while the attending obstetrician examined her abdomen with ultrasound.

One of the paramedics gave report in rapid, clipped speech. "Jolene Holloway is twenty-six-years old, thirty-six weeks pregnant, unrestrained passenger in an MVA. Her vehicle was sandwiched between two others. Unknown whether she had loss of consciousness at the scene. Extraction required Jaws of Life. She has a closed fracture of her left lower extremity, a scalp laceration that has bled heavily, as well as vaginal bleeding. BP ninety over fifty, heart rate one-forty." More softly he added, "We cannot confirm fetal heart tones. And her husband didn't make it."

Oh God. I turned my attention to Jolene.

"My baby. You have to save him."

I understood her desperation only too well. She would see through an empty promise.

"Section," the attending obstetrician said loudly over the din, replacing the ultrasound probe on the machine. "She's abrupting."

The rapid deceleration of a car accident can cause the placenta to shear off of the uterine wall, resulting in maternal bleeding and loss of blood flow to the baby. The child's survival depends on how much flow is left and how quickly we deliver him.

The obstetrician came to the head of the bed. "I'm Dr. Ross. We're going to have to do a C-section right now." She asked about allergies and a couple other questions. Jolene answered through her tears, repeating her mantra to save her baby.

"Order cryo and FFP," I said to the charge nurse as Dr. Ross and her resident stepped out to scrub and the OR nurse prepped Jolene's abdomen. Mariel applied a mask of oxygen to Jolene's face, and when everyone was poised and ready, I tried to sound reassuring as I injected the propofol that would put her to sleep.

"I just lost my husband. If my baby is dead, please don't wake me up." As her eyes closed, tears overflowed, dripping down her temples, pooling by the bridge of her nose.

I blinked back tears of my own as Mariel inserted the breathing tube and confirmed its location. "Cut," I said and started work on a second IV while Mariel secured the breathing tube.

The teamwork achieved in disasters never ceases to amaze me. Nurses and techs anticipate every need of the surgeons and of us at the head of the bed. We worked in concert, and in under a minute, the surgeon handed off a motionless baby boy to the waiting neo-natologists. I couldn't watch their resuscitation, partly because I couldn't bear it, but mostly because Jolene hemorrhaged. An inability to form blood clots is common after abruption. The only cure is replacement of the factors that were consumed.

"I need those blood products," I said to the charge nurse. The cryo and FFP would stop her bleeding.

"I don't want to do a hysterectomy," Dr. Ross said to me.

"She's only twenty-six," the OB resident said. "This was her first baby."

"And her husband died in the accident," a nurse added.

Obstetricians never take lightly eliminating a woman's fertility, but if the alternative is bleeding to death . . .

The charge nurse held out the phone to me. "It's the blood bank."

I took it. "I need that cryo and plasma right away."

"We're out of cryo and very low on plasma," said a frustrated someone. Away from the phone, he said, "Director."

A new voice came on the line. "I'm sorry, Doctor, the multi-trauma has drained our blood bank, as well as that of the surrounding institutions. More is on its way, but it will be at least an hour."

"My patient doesn't have an hour."

"I'm hearing that a lot this evening."

With an ache in my soul, I made eye contact with Dr. Ross and shook my head. She immediately switched gears, barking orders for the new instruments required to remove a uterus instead of sewing it up. "Dammit," she said. "How does a Level One trauma center run out of blood products?"

"Too much simultaneous demand," I said.

Mariel nudged me and gestured to the computer screen where she'd pulled up the current operating room schedule. Nearly every OR was full, in all three towers. Lots of orthopedic cases, but also general surgery and neurosurgery. She pointed to the pediatric ORs downstairs. Children. At least a dozen. Some in the OR, some in preoperative holding, all scheduled for trauma-type cases. "It's going to be a long night," she said. Then added, "But I guess longer for those families."

I liked Mariel.

CHAPTER TWENTY-TWO

"I NEED SUCTION," Dr. Ross said.

The three-liter suction canister had filled. I switched the tubing to a second canister. We were losing the battle. Blood slicked the floor around the OR table, including the head of the table where we had stitched up her scalp wound as best we could and applied a pressure dressing to staunch the flow. Someone threw blankets down for us to stand on. All the blood salvage machines, which enabled us to return blood suctioned from the surgical field back to the patient, were in use in other ORs.

As we emptied unit after unit of blood into Jolene's IVs, we tossed the bags on the floor to keep count. The OR phone rang. "It's for you, Dr. Downey," the nurse said.

I stepped around the power cord for the rapid infuser and took the phone. "This is Dr. Downey."

"Dr. Henderson from the blood bank. I have four units of FFP. Are you certain it will make a difference if it's all you get?"

"I am," I said immediately. Fresh Frozen Plasma would replace the clotting factors she lacked.

"Dr. Downey, do you hear what I'm asking you? Half a dozen of your colleagues are asking for these units. I need to know it will—"

"It will save her life."

He paused a moment, likely weighing my trustworthiness. What doctor would decline in this situation? At last, he said, "Okay. On its way."

It made sense to ration blood products, to administer something in limited supply only to those who would benefit. That is, not to a patient who will die without more than the four units on offer. But it was not something I'd faced practicing medicine in the U.S. While I could make no guarantee of her survival, Jolene would surely die without the plasma. Now it was my job to ensure it was enough.

I turned off an infusion of pressors meant to keep the blood pressure stable. Mariel's eyes rounded. "We have to slow down her blood loss." To the surgeon I said, "What do you think about clamping the aorta?"

She looked at me. "I think I've never done it before."

"Have someone press it closed until you get control of the bleeders. We're getting some plasma. I have to make sure it doesn't end up in the suction cannister."

She reached behind the uterus, then took the hand of the resident assisting her and showed her how to press down on the pulsing aorta at the back of the abdomen. Though it was an awkward position for the resident, she complied without comment. Immediately, Jolene's blood pressure increased.

"Good call," Dr. Ross said. "I can see. Clamping the uterine arteries, now."

I should have thought of it earlier.

As soon as the cooler arrived from the blood bank, Mariel spiked the first bag.

"Wait until we're sure they have control." Then over the drapes, I said, "We have to release the aorta soon or the kidneys will take a hit." Though life with poorly functioning kidneys beat bleeding to death. Jolene's words rang in my ears. I wouldn't honor them, couldn't honor them, whether or not her baby survived. I'd felt the same way not so long ago. They were not words of reason, however passionately felt.

"Just one more . . ." Dr. Ross tied a knot in the suture. "Okay."

The resident compressing the aorta slowly removed her hand, bleeding resumed, but slower now, not rapidly filling the abdomen as it had before.

"Start the plasma," I said.

Mariel opened the clamp. After two units, we checked labs. Better, but she needed the other two units as well.

My phone rang. Sam.

"You guys are using only the one OR now. We'll leave you one for OB emergencies, but we have people dying down here. I'm sending you a ruptured spleen."

"Of course."

Over the night and the following morning, Mariel, another resident, and I took care of four more trauma cases. They sent us the less specialized ones, since Labor and Delivery is remote from the OR and lacks much of the equipment surgeons would expect. I worked with Dr. Stone, a gynecologist I'd known since medical school, who had stopped operating the year before. It was no surprise to see him volunteer. He'd been a military surgeon and worked with Doctors Without Borders in Sierra Leone. He'd once popped my dislocated finger back into place between plays as we stood on the base path between first and second during a "Storks" softball game.

"This is as bad as anything I saw in a war zone," Dr. Stone said with his permanent crooked grin.

I learned later that other physicians and nurses in the community came out of retirement to volunteer. Medical and nursing students converged to donate blood, then help in any way they could. Hundreds of people showed up at blood donation stations set up all around town and in the surrounding communities.

I learned more about the accident, too. A dense fog contributed to the interstate pileup, which, according to traffic cameras, began when a single car in the northbound lane lost control.

At last, around noon, ORs finished and remained empty. Sam ordered me home. "I'm non-clinical tomorrow. Let me know if you need me." Major traumas were about more than the stabilizing initial operations. There were bring-backs for bleeding or other injuries. Sometimes numerous repeat operations for burns or serious orthopedic trauma. The hospital would feel this multi-trauma for weeks to come.

I went to check on Jolene. Her room was empty. I found her in the Neonatal Intensive Care Unit. She sat in a wheelchair, her casted left leg supported straight out in front. Her hand rested on her small son's enclosed bassinet, a rosary in her other hand. A monitor displayed vital signs while a ventilator breathed for him. I introduced myself.

"You're the one who stayed with me. Thank you." She looked at the baby. "They're cooling him. Something about limiting damage to his brain while he starts to heal. I'll love him no matter what. He's all I have left." Her body shook with sobs.

I squatted next to her and placed a hand on her uninjured knee, knowing there could be no comfort. "I'll pray for him, and more importantly, my aunt's prayer chain will get to work. We have a priest on call to baptize him if you'd like."

Her eyes brightened a fraction and she thanked me again.

"Do you have any questions about the surgery or anesthesia?"

I felt her crushing sadness. "No. They said the hysterectomy was the only way. It doesn't matter anyway, now."

I stayed for several moments, then left her alone with her son. I hoped her words weren't true—that the hysterectomy didn't matter. She could adopt or use a surrogate. She was too young to give up on having more children.

She's not much younger than you, kindchen. Aunt Irm was in my head now. Great.

I checked my watch—nearly one. Time for a shower and a nap. I trudged to the locker room. Before I could change, my phone rang. I answered without checking the screen.

"Dr. Downey? It's Annabelle Kessler, the cardiology fellow. We met when your aunt was in the ER."

"Yes." Foreboding tightened my throat. "Is she okay?"

"She's fine. Sorry. But can you possibly meet me in the morgue?"

My sleep-deprived brain must have misheard. "The morgue?"

"Yes, please." Her voice trembled.

Then it struck me. "Is it Nikki? Dr. Yarborough?"

"No. No. This is different. Can you come?"

"Of course, I'm on my way." I'd not been to the morgue since my less-than-collegial interactions with the head pathologist months before. I could only hope someone other than Dr. Ramsey had been called in.

No such luck, though his distaste for me seemed to have faded. He led me to a white-faced Annabelle, cheeks streaked with mascara. She held a Kadence interrogation wand by a partially covered cadaver with an open Y incision on his chest. "His name is Mr. McCann," she said.

"Now tell me what's going on," Dr. Ramsey said. "Why do you need an anesthesiologist to interrogate a pacer?"

Holy hell. I stood next to Annabelle and stared at the now demonic-looking square wave on the interrogation computer monitor.

"It's just like your aunt. It fired for no reason, right on the T wave."

"The AICD?" he said.

I nodded. "He was the driver, wasn't he? The one who lost control and caused . . ."

"Yes," Dr. Ramsey said. "His device fired? He had an arrhythmia?"

Neither of us spoke.

"Wait, did you say it fired for no reason?" he said.

"We should have turned them all off," Annabelle said.

"Dammit, I need to know what's going on," Dr. Ramsey said.

"This is our fault," Annabelle continued, as if she hadn't heard. "Dr. Yarborough—"

"Hey, it's okay," I said. "You did the right thing calling me. Now we need to tell your chairman."

She nodded absently.

I led her to a nearby sink and handed her a damp paper towel. "We need to call from your phone. He might not answer an unknown number." Or me.

She tapped her screen several times, then handed me the phone. I stepped away from both her and an impatient Dr. Ramsey. Cantwell answered on the third ring.

"This is Kate Downey from anesthesia. We spoke yesterday." I didn't give him a chance to interrupt. "The massive accident on the interstate last night appears to have been caused by a Kadence misfire." I paused a second to let that sink in. "I'm here with your fellow, Dr. Kessler, in the morgue."

Silence.

"Dr. Cantwell?"

"I heard you." His voice was gruff.

"Dr. Kessler is understandably shaken up, and the pathologist needs answers for his autopsy report."

In the ensuing silence I could almost hear the gears in his insincere brain churning.

"Shall I explain things to Dr. Ramsey? Or would you like to come to the morgue?" I couldn't keep the irritation from my voice. I didn't try all that hard.

"No," he said quickly. "I'll be right down."

I'd struck a nerve. Finally. I handed the phone back to Annabelle and relayed the message to Dr. Ramsey. I debated whether to stay. Cantwell wouldn't want me there; Annabelle would.

Her phone rang, a consult in the ER for a patient with an apparent heart attack. I followed her out into the main hallway to offer reassurance. We found the opposite—an out-of-breath and red-faced Dr. Cantwell.

"We have to warn everyone with a Kadence." She spoke with calm assertion. Impressive. "We have to tell them not to drive."

"I will take care of it." He continued past into the autopsy suite.

"Great job, Annabelle," I said.

"For all the good it did. Should I call them myself?"

Even more impressed, I said, "What are the pros and cons?"

"The pros are obvious. The cons are I could lose my job and maybe my career."

I waited. This was not a decision I could make for her. Then she asked the dreaded question, "What would you do?"

"I would call them, but I'm in a very different position, and he's not my boss. I can make the calls instead, if you like."

Undeterred, she went on. "What would you tell the patients?"

"That there might be a problem with the Kadence. If it were to misfire, they could become incapacitated for several seconds, which would be dangerous if they were driving or swimming. I would reassure them that the manufacturer is working on a solution and they should expect an update soon."

She nodded slowly.

"One more thing you deserve to know. I heard from Dr. Yarborough yesterday. She said these aren't random firings. Someone is triggering them on purpose."

She stared at me, mouth slightly open. "Someone intentionally caused that accident?"

I hadn't thought of it that way. "He might not have known where Mr. McCann was at the time." I recalled the mystery man from the clinic when Irm was attacked. Line of sight couldn't be required.

Annabelle's phone rang again. She answered. "I'm on my way." To me, she said, "You're sure?"

I held her gaze.

"I can't even think about that right now. I have to get to the ER. Thanks for your help."

Shoulders hunched, she walked away.

"Annabelle."

She turned.

"We're going to figure this out."

She nodded and left, her posture maybe a little straighter.

I returned to Autopsy. The suite was empty, of living people anyway. I knocked on all five hallway doors. No answer. My input was not desired. Shocking. Desired or not, both Cantwell and Ramsey were going to hear it. Later, after I slept.

CHAPTER TWENTY-THREE

I DROVE HOME on autopilot. Aunt Irm had spent the night at Carmel's and it wasn't until I opened the door and found only a very excited Shadow that I realized I forgot to pick her up. On the table was a note, in Christian's handwriting. "Aunt Irm is with Carmel. I fed and walked Shadow. I'll come back this afternoon unless I hear from you." He signed it "C."

Aunt Irm didn't answer her phone so I followed up with a text and climbed in the shower. The hot water drained what was left of my energy. Every limb felt heavy and I wanted nothing more than to lie down with Shadow and sleep for days. But I couldn't do that until I knew my aunt was safe, and she hadn't responded. I called Carmel's house. "This is Kate Downey. Is Aunt Irm still there?"

"Oh, hello, Kate. Are you home from that awful accident?"

"I am, and I thought Aunt Irm was with you."

"She was. A young man called and picked her up several hours ago."

A young man? "Did she say where they were going?"

"I'm sorry, dear. No. I was on the phone with my daughter when she left. Might she have left you a message?"

I thanked her and checked. No voicemail. I dropped onto my bed. Irrationally, I wanted to cry. Aunt Irm was fine—of course she was. She'd never leave with a stranger, but I hadn't slept in more than thirty hours and the night had been horrific and I couldn't take another setback.

Shadow scratched at the back door. I let him out and refilled his water bowl. The answering machine light was blinking. Water splashed as I jabbed the button. "Kindchen, this is Aunt Irm. I did not wish to bother you at work. Nathan has an idea and wants me to go to the hospital. He will pick me up at Carmel's. I hope you will be able to rest soon. Oh, I called the prayer chain as you asked. We are very busy with your patient and the others from the accident. I will be home when I have finished helping Nathan."

Nathan. Definitely a young man. I dialed his number, which also went to voicemail. Why have a cellphone if you aren't going to answer it? I needed sleep.

I set an alarm for two hours and snuggled into Shadow's soft back. Jolene and her baby boy haunted my thoughts and I squeezed my eyes tightly closed. What seemed like moments later, I woke to my alarm, certain I'd mis-set it for minutes instead of hours. Nope. Another shower to wake up was definitely in order, and caffeine . . . lots of caffeine.

Before I'd taken the first sip of my freshly brewed coffee, Christian texted: "Headed your way with pizza."

Pizza sounded heavenly. I couldn't remember the last meal I'd eaten.

Shadow ran past me to the front door, barking and wagging his tail. The lock turned before I could reach over my crazy dog. Though Aunt Irm patted him on the head, he was more interested in her companion. "That's Shadow," I told Nathan. "He won't bite, but he also won't leave you alone."

"No problem." He leaned down to rub whatever body part Shadow decided to put under his hand.

"Christian's on his way with pizza," I said to Aunt Irm as she kissed both my cheeks.

"Yes, we placed our order." She held me at arm's length. "You did not rest enough."

"I saw video of the accident," Nathan said. "Even through the fog, it looked awful."

I made a mental note to avoid said video. "Coffee?"

Nathan declined. "I need my beauty sleep."

Aunt Irm opted for red wine. "Nathan has figured it out, kindchen. You must give him a raise."

"Wow, will you be my agent?" he said.

"Sadly, I have zero pull in the finance department, or any other department for that matter," I said.

Nathan declined the red wine Aunt Irm offered. "I haven't figured it all out, but I think we're close. The thing Aunt Irm mentioned about the low battery life gave me the idea."

Shadow's barking drowned him out. Christian had arrived, bearing pizza, followed closely by Lieutenant Garner, bearing beer. Shadow was delirious, as was Nathan. It was high quality beer.

After introductions, Christian followed me into the kitchen. "Hey, are you okay?"

"Yeah, fine." But my eyes started to fill. *What the hell?*

He came closer. "Kate?"

"I can't talk about it right now." I pulled a stack of paper plates from the cupboard, and for once, Aunt Irm didn't argue.

With pizza and drinks all around, we sat at the kitchen table. "Start with your background with AICDs," I said to Nathan.

"During my master's, I worked in Dr. Dale Bennett's lab in biomedical engineering. We were designing a communications protocol for implantable devices. The model we worked on was an AICD, on a grant through Dr. Cantwell at the medical school."

The coincidence was almost too much to believe, except all of our simulator engineers to date had come from the school's relatively small biomedical engineering program.

"Normal AICDs can receive signals sent from a wand placed near the device. The wand and the protocol are proprietary and very secure. What we added to the Kadence was the ability to communicate with a normal cellphone via Bluetooth. We can't transfer as much information, just a quick update, but it's practically realtime, so a big advance over existing technology." Nathan washed down an enormous bite of pizza with half a bottle of beer, then continued. "Back when I worked on it, our goal was the ability to communicate both directions, so a doctor could ping the device to ask how it was doing, and it would answer. Instead of having to wait for an update at whatever interval was programmed. They could also ask for more frequent reports for a period of time, things like that."

"Sounds like a big project," Christian said. "What was your role?"

"The security protocol. Making sure no one could hack the device or read information from it without authorization." He finished both the piece of pizza and beer in one more bite and gulp while we waited. It didn't take long. "As you can imagine, security is a big deal with any medical device that communicates, and especially one that's implanted. We researched a bunch of existing protocols and came up with one that required a crazy complicated handshake to connect."

"It is not an actual handshake," Aunt Irm said, helpfully. "It is a secret code the two computers must each emit." She raised her arms, apparently emitting.

Nathan smiled at her, a teacher's pride in his star pupil. "But to get that approved, the FDA insisted the company go through a long, drawn-out process, so instead they submitted a version of the

Kadence without the two-way communication. It can send signals to the cellphone, but not receive anything over Bluetooth."

Christian nodded. "Dr. Cantwell says they're hoping for a federal policy change before the next version, rather than having to go through that approval process. It would be costly and far from a sure thing."

"Dale Bennett was pis—" Nathan looked at Aunt Irm. "Angry that MDI gave up so easy. I heard the company also reneged on a job they offered him, so Dr. Bennett decided to start his own medical device company with his technology."

"Your technology, too, right?" I said, "I saw your name on the patent."

His cheeks colored a little. "Yeah, he put all our names on it—all the students who worked on it. We would have shared in the royalties if MDI used the technology in the Kadence. Since they didn't, Dr. Bennett offered each of us a job in his new company."

"His patent is bundled with a couple of Cantwell's that are also owned by the university," Christian said. "They're all part of the sale. Bennett can't develop anything with that technology."

"He cannot build his own invention?" Aunt Irm said.

"I know it doesn't sound fair," Christian said, "but intellectual property, like a patent, always belongs to the employer where the work occurred. Unless Bennett can prove he invented it on his own time and without any university resources."

"Nope," Nathan said. "We definitely did the work on campus."

"You cannot leave to work with him anyway," Aunt Irm said to Nathan. "Our Kate could not teach without you."

Her words made him blush even more.

"Nathan runs our patient simulator," I explained to a confused Garner. "He gives the manikin different medical problems so the students can practice saving him."

"Or not," Nathan said.

"Funny." I fake frowned at him. "Tell us what you figured out today."

He swallowed the last of his second beer and began. "First, when Irm told me someone was claiming to trigger the device, I knew the receptive capability had to still be in there. It fits with the battery life being less than expected. An always-on receiver uses a lot of power. That part of the code was supposed to have been removed. So, I decided to test it."

"You had access to a Kadence?" Christian asked.

Aunt Irm straightened and pointed to her chest. "He had access to me."

Nathan cringed.

"You tested it on my aunt?" Clearly, she'd survived, but who experiments on an eighty-year-old woman?

"See why I did not wish you to ask her permission?" Aunt Irm said.

Uneasy laughs died away. "I'm sorry," Nathan said. "I did take precautions. Since the communication almost certainly came through her phone using Bluetooth, we went into the simulator's gas storage room. It used to be part of radiology, so the walls are lead-lined. No cell signal can get through. With the interrogation computer—"

"Dr. Annabelle was happy to let us borrow it," Aunt Irm interrupted.

"Your aunt could charm the scales off a trout," Nathan said. They shared an admiring grin. It was kind of cute. "Anyway, I put the Kadence back into its normal mode, then disabled the lead so no signal could actually affect her heart."

"Why didn't we do that in the first place?" I asked.

"It disables the pacer function as well," he said, sheepish.

"I was fine," Aunt Irm said. "Go on, Nathan."

"Anyway, I started with our original password design and planned to use a random text generator."

"He cracked it open on the second try," Aunt Irm interrupted yet again.

"It wasn't exactly the same handshake but really close. I was able to change the pacer mode." I must have looked a little horrified, because he quickly followed with, "I changed it back."

I decided not to argue. "So somehow the original software stayed in the device instead of the version approved by the FDA."

"Maybe," Nathan said. "Without looking at the code, I can't say it's definitely the same as what we worked on. The security access is virtually identical, though."

"Can you not read this code from my Kadence?" Aunt Irm asked.

"It's compiled," Nathan said, "translated into an unreadable computer language. I have to find the original program and read that."

"Why can you not translate it back?"

He smiled at her. "Unfortunately, much is lost in translation, especially twice."

"Ah, with this I am familiar." She held up her wineglass, satisfied. Christian chuckled.

"Who could substitute the software and get it past the FDA?" Garner asked.

"Scary as it sounds, the FDA only knows what the company submits to them," I said. "For the most part, no one goes back to see if what they're selling is what was approved."

"Until there's a problem," Christian said.

"Right." Surely this qualified, yet the FDA remained in the dark.

"Even then, if their investigator doesn't know the handshake design, it would be tough to crack." Nathan seemed proud of that.

We were silent for several moments. "Wait, how did you leave Aunt Irm's Kadence?" I asked.

"It is as before. Dr. Annabelle turned the defibrillator off and I am wearing this awful vest." Aunt Irm raised her shoulders as if weighed down, which they were.

Garner took over. "Take me through the steps of the software getting into the finished device."

Nathan swallowed another enormous bite of pizza and wiped his hands on a napkin. "MDI farmed out most of the software coding to Dr. Bennett's lab. By the time they needed to remove part of the code, I had graduated. He probably assigned one of the students to remove it, re-compile the software, and repeat the bench testing. Then Dr. Bennett would send the compiled code to MDI for more tests before they incorporated it in the device."

"So somewhere in there they ended up with the wrong code," Garner said.

"Right. It might have been an accident, except they changed the password, so probably not," Nathan said.

"Whether on purpose or by mistake, it does not matter," Aunt Irm said. "Someone is using it for harm."

"You're right, Aunt Irm," Christian said. "Who knows about the handshake, Nathan?"

He considered. "Everyone in our lab that worked on the project."

"How many people is that?" Garner asked.

"Besides me and Dale Bennett, there were several undergrads and grad students. Maybe more after I left. Also some of the engineers at MDI and probably Dr. Cantwell, though I don't know to what level of detail."

Garner wrote in his notebook. I'd have to buy him another one.

"What I don't get is why someone would switch the software and trigger the Kadence." Nathan sat up straighter, his speech quickened. "Unless they planned to blackmail someone at the company."

Garner looked at Christian, eyebrows raised.

"Not that they've mentioned it to me," he said.

"Might have slipped their minds," Garner said. "Tell me more about the owners."

"There are only two," Christian said. "Victor Cantwell, the cardiologist who invented the device, owns forty-nine percent. Edward Samuels owns the rest and runs the company."

"What did this Dr. Samuels invent to own more of the company?" Aunt Irm asked.

"He's not a doctor," Christian said. "Or an engineer. He's a serial entrepreneur. Someone who looks for new technology, starts companies based on it, then sells them off in a few years for a profit. This is his fourth such venture and by far the biggest."

Aunt Irm's eyebrows remained furrowed. "I do not understand this. Surely the inventor deserves more than the businessperson."

"Money." Nathan rubbed his fingers together. "Right? Samuels put up the money to get the company going."

Christian nodded, impressed.

"My A in Entrepreneurship for Engineers wasn't for attendance, you know."

Aunt Irm patted his arm. "Of course not, Nathan."

I went to the kitchen to replenish drinks. "So, A-student Nathan, how do we stop it? How do we disable the handshake?"

"In the short term, we don't have to actually disable it," he said. "The signal comes through Bluetooth, so if patients with the device avoid that, the signal can't reach the Kadence."

"Don't you have to specifically pair Bluetooth devices?" Christian asked.

"You do," I said. "The MDI rep set up Aunt Irm's Bluetooth right after the procedure and spent almost an hour explaining how to use it and what to do if it stopped communicating."

"So we could disable the pairing, or to be safe, disable Bluetooth on their phone completely," Nathan said.

Aunt Irm retrieved her cellphone from her purse by the garage. "How do I do this? I do not want to wear this vest another moment." She placed her phone on the table, fingers poised to click buttons.

Nathan held his hands up. "Whoa, slow down. First, we need to talk with Dr. Kessler, then we have to test it with everything enabled and make sure I'm right."

Aunt Irm sat back down heavily. Bad as it sounds, I was relieved to let Nathan be the one to disappoint her for a change.

He looked up at me. "I didn't want to do that without you there."

"I know how insistent my aunt can be, so thank you."

Aunt Irm rebounded quickly. "We can do this tomorrow and then call all the patients and talk them through each step."

I didn't bother pointing out we had neither patient names nor contact information.

"The more permanent solution is to fix the software and update all the devices," Nathan said. "We have to do that through MDI."

"We cannot trust them," Aunt Irm said. "They do not even admit the problem."

"They wouldn't sabotage their own device," I said. "Especially not now, when they're about to sell."

Christian put down his glass without taking a drink. "Maybe someone is trying to prevent the sale."

"Who would benefit from this?" Aunt Irm needed a curved pipe and Sherlock Holmes deer-hunter hat. "Does someone else wish to purchase this awful company instead?"

Christian considered for a moment. "None that I know of, and even if there were other suitors for MDI, they wouldn't benefit from device problems and an FDA investigation. Neither would anyone inside the company who preferred to remain independent."

"What about a competing technology?" I asked.

"Another company that wants to discredit MDI? Or wants my client to purchase them instead? It's possible. I'm not aware of any, but I got involved late in the game."

"How would another company know about the communication protocol?" Nathan said.

"You mentioned undergrads in the lab," Garner said. "They always need money."

"Not the ones living in Nikki's apartment complex." Christian stacked the paper plates, and I followed him into the kitchen.

"We need to talk to someone inside the company," Garner said.

"I met an engineer there yesterday," I said. "She was working on the misfire problem and seemed reasonable."

"We cannot trust her," my increasingly suspicious aunt said. "What if she is involved? She might have even caused the problem."

Possible, but as Aunt Irm herself had pointed out, how could the engineer benefit? "What will happen to the engineers after the sale goes through? Will any lose their jobs?"

"Good question," Christian said. "Part of the agreement is that no one is fired or has a reduction in salary or benefits for at least one year."

One year wasn't that long. I pulled the ice cream from the freezer, handed it and the scooper to Christian, and carried dishes and spoons to the table. While we served, Garner said, "Okay, let's summarize. Someone with knowledge of a supposedly disabled communication protocol is using it to trigger devices and cause harm. The doctor who identified the problem has been threatened and disappeared, maybe with her estranged husband. That husband is an engineer who used to work for the company that makes the device. Meanwhile, that company is about to be sold. Am I missing anything?"

"What about the man outside the clinic?" I asked.

Garner shook his head. "The only camera is directly above the door."

So that was a dead end. "Nikki Yarborough's chairman invented the device and isn't cooperating," I said. "He hasn't done anything to protect patients or reported the misfires to the FDA."

"Is that illegal?" Garner asked.

"Now that someone died, maybe."

Aunt Irm's face lost all color. "Someone died from the Kadence?"

Crap. No one knew the cause of the interstate accident. "Indirectly." I left it at that for now and forced thoughts of Jolene and last night to the back of my brain, to be dealt with later.

Garner flipped a page in his notebook and started writing. "So our suspect list includes Nikki and her husband, Ian Yarborough—"

"I don't think Nikki is likely," I said. "She installs the devices and is dealing with all the complications. She wouldn't have any reason to cause them."

"Hmph," Aunt Irm said. "This does not rule her out."

Christian and I exchanged a grin at her choice of words.

"I agree," Garner said. "It's better to have an inclusive list for now. Does she have any role at MDI or Bennett's lab?"

Christian scrolled on his phone. "She's not listed as an employee of MDI."

"She wrote a paper with Dr. Bennett about the Kadence, so they're at least acquainted." I returned the ice cream to the freezer.

Garner made a note and moved on. "Other engineers at MDI, Dale Bennett and members of his lab."

"Except me," Nathan said.

Garner appeared ready to argue, then deferred to Aunt Irm. "What do you think?"

She narrowed her eyes at Nathan, then grunted, but couldn't hide her smile. "Unless he is a very fine actor, Nathan cannot be our suspect. He was very surprised to find the handshake this morning."

Garner wrote with a flourish and held up the page that read EXCEPT NATHAN in all caps. Then he continued with his list. "Dr. Cantwell and Mr. Samuels. Anyone else?"

We looked at one another, heads shaking.

He scanned his list. "Who looks best for it?"

"I don't know about best, but Ian has information about the software that we need." Not to mention I suspected he had Nikki and I wanted to confirm she was okay.

"To track him I'd need a warrant." Garner held up the notebook. "And this won't get one. I will visit with MDI's CEO tomorrow, though."

That was something. And I wasn't out of options either. Nikki's keys beckoned from my laptop bag.

CHAPTER TWENTY-FOUR

NATHAN AND GARNER left soon after. Christian helped me clean up from dinner while Aunt Irm finished her wine.

"After Nathan fixes my Kadence, we will need a list of the other patients," she said.

"Annabelle will call them."

"From her you can get the list so we can help." She handed me her empty glass.

"She isn't allowed to share it with me," I said. "Or you, so don't ask."

"Is this the hippo thing?"

"HIPAA, yes, privacy."

"We are saving people. This is more important than their secret Kadence."

"I couldn't agree more, but that's not how our lawmakers see it." I handed the clean glass to Christian to dry.

"You said someone has died?" Aunt Irm persisted.

The events of the previous night flooded back. Jolene, widowed and holding onto hope for a son clinging to life. Suddenly the weight of it all, looming just out of view all evening, slammed into my soul. I remained facing the sink, my back to my aunt. "I can't talk about it."

With disappointment in her voice, she said goodnight without our usual embrace.

I stopped her and apologized. "I wish I could do more."

She hugged me and nodded. "You will."

Once her bedroom door clicked shut, Christian's hands gripped my shoulders and he gently turned me to face him, his eyes examining mine. "What's happened?"

Jolene happened, and the corpse with the Y incision whose Kadence caused the accident, and all the others whose lives were irrevocably changed. We could have prevented it. I could have prevented it. A tear slipped through, then another. Christian pulled me into an embrace, and I let the tears soak his shoulder. I hadn't let myself cry since Greg's funeral. Now it seemed I would make up for it all at once. He held me and said nothing, just let me cry until my sobs subsided. Then he led me to the couch and we sat, his arm around me, comforting.

I knew I shouldn't, but I told him, about all of it. Once begun, the words flowed. His expression alternated between anger and sorrow, regret and compassion.

"Aunt Irm's right. This is more important than privacy. If Annabelle and the chief of staff won't make sure all the patients are contacted, I'll do it." It felt good to make a decision, even if it could get me fired. "If Nathan's right, Annabelle won't have to turn them all off." Though safe from attack, it also meant the devices would be unable to report problems. Pros and cons. The pros far outweighed the cons.

"Thank you, Christian. Sorry for the mini-meltdown."

He angled himself to look at me, his shoulder shifting away, but his knee pressed firmly against mine. With Shadow on my other side, I couldn't pull away, and, if I was honest, I didn't want to.

"Someday we'll spend time together talking about things other than murder and serial killers." The gold flecks in his eyes caught the

lamplight as I drowned in the deep brown beneath. I didn't want
to talk about those either.

"I'm really glad you're here."

He dried my cheek with a slow swipe of his thumb, a caress that
sparked a long-extinguished flame in my chest.

His voice was tender and low. "Full disclosure, I jumped at the
chance to take over this project. To be here. I stayed away as long as
I could." The intensity of his gaze, the depth of emotion his words
stirred in me, overwhelmed my senses. I lifted my face toward his,
just a fraction. It was enough. He pressed his lips to mine, soft and
warm, and my insides pooled. I slid my hand around his neck and
pulled him closer. We deepened the kiss and my mind went completely and blissfully blank for the first time in years.

When he pulled gently away, his eyes locked on mine. We stayed
like that for a long moment. I pressed my face against his hand as
his thumb grazed my cheek.

"You are so beautiful."

My eyelids drifted closed at his touch, his voice, expecting
another kiss. Instead, he said, "And you need sleep."

I wanted to argue, but he was right. I had work in the morning.
Though I wasn't scheduled in the OR, "too tired" still wasn't an
option.

He stood and pulled me to my feet. At the door, he pressed
another soft kiss on my lips and left.

For the first time since I'd started dating Greg in residency, I'd
kissed another man. And the world hadn't ended, my heart hadn't
stopped, my head hadn't rebelled . . . yet.

I slept. I don't know if I dreamed but was very glad not to remember them, guilt-ridden as they likely were, between the deaths I
might have prevented, and Jolene whose fertility I might have saved,
and Christian.

As I dressed for work, I pushed thoughts of him away. Today was about protecting patients and finding Nikki.

Though I needed to spend my non-clinical day preparing a lecture and reviewing grant applications, there were more pressing matters. First, I checked on Jolene and her baby. He'd had no seizures, which was a good sign. The neonatologists would start the warming process tomorrow. Until then, we could only wait and hope.

Annabelle Kessler agreed to meet me at the coffee cart in the lobby. I invited Nathan to join us and bought three overly sweet caffeine vehicles. We stood at the round, bar-height table farthest from the doors. "Do you know of any more misfires?" I asked Annabelle.

"Attacks you mean?" She wiped the foam from her mouth. "No, but every time my phone rings, I'm terrified. I started calling patients yesterday evening and warned them not to drive or swim. I told them there might be a minor glitch, and out of an abundance of caution, blah blah blah . . . Eventually it will get back to Dr. Cantwell, but I don't even care anymore."

"You're doing the right thing," I assured her. "Nathan has another idea we need to look into."

As she put down her cup, the surface of the liquid rippled. She was trembling. "Is this about what you were doing yesterday?" she asked Nathan. "I'm sorry I couldn't meet with you after."

He described the receptive communication capability. "Somehow it was left in the Kadence software and someone knows how to get in and trigger the device."

She shook her head slowly. "Unbelievable."

I concurred.

"It means that if your patients disable the connection on their phone, the signal shouldn't be able to get through."

"Are you sure the Kadence can't receive it some other way?" I asked.

"Like what?" Nathan said.

"I saw something yesterday on the patent. The chip they used also handles GPS and FM radio signals."

"Aren't you the little engineer wannabe," he said.

"Or capable of reading text on a diagram."

He laughed. "That, too. Pretty much all commercial communication chips have multiple capabilities these days. They're less expensive that way, but we only activated the Bluetooth."

"So I can't use the GPS signal to track my aunt?"

"Sorry, and shame on you." He finished his coffee.

"Without Bluetooth, I won't receive warnings from the Kadence if something is wrong. I'll be blind to everything." Annabelle closed her eyes and whispered something I assumed was a swear word. "They would have been better off with a traditional AICD where at least I could get a report when they connected at home. Can't we fix the software on the device instead?"

"Eventually," Nathan said.

"How many people have a Kadence?" I asked.

"Fifty-seven." Her face fell. "Fifty-six."

That brought a contemplative silence, then Nathan said, "I'm going to find a way to replace the code with the right version, without the receptive capability, but turning off Bluetooth should keep them safe in the meantime, at least from triggered attacks. Irm offered to come in at eleven to test it." One glance at my face and he said, "She didn't tell you. I'm sorry."

I turned to Annabelle. "What are you doing at eleven?"

"Um." She looked between us. "I have a study patient at noon."

"Perfect. You can join us in the simulator room before that." Too bossy. "Please?" I added.

"I'll be there." Her smile was rueful, but there. "I guess I shouldn't call the rest of the patients until after we test your theory. What if something happens between now and then?" Tears filled her eyes. "Being a doctor wasn't supposed to be like this."

I tried to reassure her with the rarity of such events, ignoring the fact this was the second psycho I'd dealt with in less than a year.

CHAPTER TWENTY-FIVE

NATHAN HAD A class to set up for, Annabelle had a consult to see, and I had work to do.

"Do not do anything with my aunt until I'm there," I said to Nathan.

"Of course." He crumpled his coffee cup and tossed it into a nearby trash can, where it bounced off other trash and landed on the floor. "Rejected." He stooped to pick it up.

"Hey." I waited for him to make eye contact. "I mean it. Don't let her talk you into anything."

He chuckled. "It's as if you two are related."

I scrutinized his face.

He held up his hand, making a V between his third and fourth fingers. "Scout's honor."

"That's Spock."

He looked at his hand. "Yeah, whatever, they both work under the circumstances."

Live long and prosper? Sure. I'd be satisfied with that. I texted our plan to Christian. He replied several minutes later. "Sorry I can't be there. I have to go to Jacksonville. I'll tell you about it later. Keep me posted."

Nathan's call interrupted my extremely boring ten o'clock meeting. I answered and said, "I'm on my way." The other attendees might have interpreted it as a clinical emergency. It kind of was.

Rather than the small storage room where he'd experimented on my aunt last time, I found them in one of the Simulation Center's windowless classrooms. Aunt Irm reclined on a gurney normally reserved for a manikin. The well-lit room, presence of others, and my aunt's broad smile kept me from dwelling on the resemblance to another day, another simulator room.

Annabelle had already prepared Aunt Irm. Her LifeVest lay on a nearby table. The wires from defibrillator pads snaked up from the collar of her blouse and into the machine where her ECG traced across the small screen. Annabelle extended the wand of the interrogation computer.

Nathan entered carrying a laptop. "You're here. Good."

As the only person with no real role, I stood by the gurney and held my aunt's hand. My chest tightened uncomfortably. Helpless was a feeling I hated more than most. I could handle sadness, even grief, but helpless felt so . . . helpless.

"Do not ask if I want to change my mind, kindchen," Aunt Irm said.

"I wasn't going to." But she raised her do-not-lie-to-me eyebrow. I kissed her cheek. "You're very brave."

"Okay, first thing, phones out, except yours." Nathan nodded to Aunt Irm. "Also, anything else you have that sends or receives Bluetooth—smart watches, whatever."

I handed him my phone and watch. "Thank you for this, Nathan."

He gave a curt nod. Clearly focused. Good. With our devices deposited outside the room, he took Aunt Irm's unlocked phone and confirmed her Bluetooth was disabled. To Annabelle he said,

"Switch on the Kadence. I'm going to send a command to change the pacing mode just like yesterday. It should ignore me."

Annabelle held the wand near Aunt Irm's chest and clicked some buttons on the interrogation computer. I watched the ECG tracing. Normal, though the rate had increased several beats. I added a second hand to monitor the pulse at her wrist. On rare occasions, ECGs can lie, report a trace when the heart isn't actually beating.

"Anything?" Nathan asked Annabelle.

She shook her head. "No. Nothing changed."

"Okay, now the real test." Nathan began typing again.

Suddenly my pulse pounded in my neck. What were we doing? Aunt Irm's heart was already damaged. If Nathan's test caused her Kadence to fire, she might not recover. "Are you sure—"

"He's sure," Aunt Irm interrupted.

Nathan gave me a questioning look.

I exhaled. "Go ahead, before that maniac decides to attack her again."

Aunt Irm held my eyes. "I love you," she whispered.

Tears burned. "I love you, too." I couldn't let her do this. We'd find someone else. "Wait!"

"Uh, too late. It's done." Nathan smiled sheepishly. "I sent all the handshake passwords along with a shock command and nothing happened." He clicked some more keys on his computer, his smile growing.

I looked to Annabelle for confirmation. "He's right. No signal came through."

Aunt Irm's eyes closed, her smile serene. "You did it. You have saved us. We must now tell everyone how to turn off this Bluetooth."

Annabelle ran a complete interrogation of Aunt Irm's Kadence. "It's functioning normally, except for the Bluetooth connection."

"This is wonderful," Aunt Irm said. "May I help with the phone calls? I will recite your words precisely. I can call my support group friends."

Annabelle's eyes darted to me. "That's kind of you. It's probably better coming from me, though."

"Hmph, perhaps, as long as they are all protected."

"I'd be happy to hear it from you, Aunt Irm." Nathan gave her phone back, along with instructions not to touch the Bluetooth icon.

I helped her sit up.

"Now, I can go home, alone." Emphasis on the last word. "And without that ridiculous vest." She clicked buttons on her phone and watched the screen. "Carmel will be here in five minutes." Aunt Irm's friend had gone to a nearby coffee shop to wait. I really had to think of some way to thank her.

"I want you to text me every hour, okay?" I said to my aunt.

"Yes, dear."

"If you don't, I'm going to call."

"Yes, dear."

"Don't 'yes, dear' me." I hugged her tightly. "Give me a minute and I'll walk you out."

"It is only down the elevator. I am now light like a feather. You do your work."

I watched her leave with more than a little trepidation.

As Annabelle packed up her equipment, I spoke to Nathan. "What do you need to fix the software?"

"I'd like to see what was installed, but all we really need is the final version of code and I can remove the communication part."

"Any chance there's a copy still in your old lab?"

He shrugged. "Even if there was, there's no guarantee it's the final version."

"Do either of you know anyone at MDI?" I also texted Christian. He knew all the major players at the company.

"I can look at the list of engineers and see if I recognize any from before," Nathan said. "But I doubt it."

"Doesn't Dr. Yarborough's husband work there?" Annabelle asked.

"He quit recently. I met an engineer yesterday named Erin Stevens. Either of you know her?"

They both shook their heads.

Annabelle groaned. "All those patients I called and told not to drive. Now I'm calling them back. I sound incompetent."

"Not you, the device," I said.

"They'll be happy they can drive," Nathan said. "You're doing them a favor."

"I wish Dr. Yarborough was here."

"Me, too," I said.

Annabelle's gait was more of a shuffle as she wheeled her cart from the room.

"Your aunt is right. How do we know we can trust this engineer?" Nathan asked.

"We don't. Can you think of another way to get access to the software?" I checked my phone—no response from Christian.

Nathan shook his head. "If she's involved, she'll just refuse to give it to us, or claim she doesn't have it."

"And alert others that we're fishing."

"They'll figure it out soon enough. I don't have any more classes today if you want to give her a call now."

I dialed and put the phone on speaker. She answered on the first ring. "Ms. Stevens, this is Kate Downey. We met yesterday about the Kadence misfires. I'm here with an engineering colleague, Nathan Castle. He was part of the university team that wrote the software and has an idea that might solve the problem. Can he meet you at MDI and look at the code with you?"

"I don't have the authority for that."

"I wrote the security protocol," Nathan said. "I can fix it."

"We don't know it's a software problem."

"I do," he said, "and you need to let me correct the problem before any more people die."

Ouch.

"Die? What are you talking about?"

Nathan was on a roll. "The massive accident the other night? The dozen people who died and counting? It was a triggered shock like all the others."

"A misfire caused the accident?"

"No, a triggered shock," he said.

"Easy," I whispered. "It's not her fault." At least I hoped it wasn't.

"Well, she needs to know what's going on," he said.

"So tell me," she said.

And we did.

She whispered something after.

"So you see why I need the code," Nathan said. "I wrote that section and I can tell what needs to be removed."

"I have to check with my boss." The words came slowly.

"No, you don't." Nathan's words weren't slow. "Twelve people are dead and your boss didn't even see fit to tell you."

This was a new side of Nathan. I muted the microphone. "We need her on our side."

He backed away and paced a small circle in the center of the room. "Sorry."

"Wait, you think someone here might be involved?" Erin asked.

I clicked the microphone icon and said, "We can't rule it out. Someone is triggering patients on purpose, and the list of capable suspects is pretty short."

"Allie," she said.

I put a hand up to stop Nathan. We waited.

"Allison Woodson, one of the misfires, she's my friend. It happened right in front of me. Why would anyone attack her? She's about the nicest person on the planet."

"Sounds a lot like my aunt," I said softly. "We have to stop this person. Nathan's not going to tamper with anything. He'll help you remove the receptive capability, then you can take over and do all the appropriate testing and get it into the Kadence as soon as possible."

She was silent a long moment, then said, "I can't access the code. I've been looking for it all morning. Ian Yarborough has it somewhere, but I can't get onto his drive on the server, and he's not answering his phone or email."

My eyes closed. "I'll find him. In the meantime, if you find another way, please call Nathan." They exchanged contact information and I ended the call. "Why can't anything be easy?"

"Because then it wouldn't be any fun." Calm Nathan had returned. "Has your cop friend pinged Ian's phone?"

I groaned. "Of course not, that would fall under 'too easy.'"

CHAPTER TWENTY-SIX

IN MY OFFICE, I pulled Nikki's key ring from my bag and fingered the three keys on a car fob. She was gone, likely with Ian. Meanwhile her patients were being attacked. Had she been led to believe leaving town would protect them? She needed to know the attacks hadn't stopped. And handling patient communication was too much to put on a fellow. Annabelle needed her help.

Garner didn't have enough to track her down. Maybe I could find something to either locate her or convince Garner she was in danger. Maybe. I couldn't sit at the hospital doing nothing.

I had no meetings scheduled and everything else could wait. I drove to Nikki's apartment complex and was pleased to find the corridor empty of curious onlookers when I unlocked her door and slipped inside.

The apartment looked much as it had when I'd visited on Sunday. Sparse, clean, and totally anonymous. No mail on the counter or even in the trash. No blinking answering machine, no pad of paper with the hint of a message. Her bedside table held no books, not even a lamp. I half-expected to find a hotel-size Gideon's Bible in the drawer. Instead, there was a small photo album. The old kind with slots full of 4x6 prints.

The photos started with Nikki as an infant and progressed. All the milestones were there—kindergarten graduation, Halloween costumes, Christmas mornings—only two people, her and the woman who must be her mother. No grandparents or other relatives or friends. Maybe those were in another album. I hoped so. Someone had to have taken at least a few of the photos, though the later ones appeared to be selfies, including the last, a photo of Nikki in graduation regalia hugging her mother in a wheelchair.

When I reached the end, peeking out of a well-worn slot in the back cover was another photo. It slid out easily.

The image was a candid shot of Nikki's mother in probably her mid-twenties with a man's arm wrapped around her. A tingling began at the back of my neck and spread to my scalp. I'd seen that man before. Victor Cantwell.

Holy hell.

Questions whirled. Was Cantwell Nikki's father? How long had she known? Did he know? Did he know that she knew? All unanswerable and giving me vertigo.

I replaced the photo, returned the book to the drawer, and finished the search quickly. The vanity in her bathroom, cluttered with makeup, a toothbrush, moisturizer, might have represented the first evidence of foul play. If she'd planned a trip, she would have taken those items. In the closet were clothes, hanging and neatly stacked on shelves. No way to tell how many were missing, if any. No hint of where she might be.

I drove to Ian's house and passed slowly. Chuck-the-nosy-neighbor's driveway was empty, the doors of his three-car garage all closed. I continued down the street of large brick and Arocrete homes, with high peaked roofs and well-maintained lawns. At the cul-de-sac I turned and headed back.

It couldn't be breaking and entering if I had a key. Entering maybe, but not breaking. I was getting good at this rationalization stuff.

I left my car on the adjacent side street. No point highlighting my presence at a house that should be empty. As I made my way toward the front door, trying not to look furtive, Chuck's garage door began to rise. *Crap.* He would recognize me. A large viburnum hedge lined the side road. In my eagerness to disappear, I searched for a break between bushes. Finding none, I considered plowing through, nothing suspicious about that, then decided instead to turn back toward my car as if I forgot something.

The BMW drove past without slowing. With my face averted, I couldn't tell whether the driver investigated the misplaced car at all. I waited to be sure they were out of sight, then strode to Ian's front door, unlocked it, and entered, closing and locking it behind me. Only then did I breathe.

I'd been inside once before. The grand entryway looked just as grand, with expensive furniture in the living room. Greg and I agreed never to have a living room—a formal space that required expensive furniture but no warmth. We were a "great room" couple. Now I was a "great room" person. I wondered fleetingly how Christian felt about living rooms, then chastised myself for the thought. It had only been one kiss, after all, one memorable, distracting, kiss.

A huge wedding portrait hung in an ornate frame. Maybe the realtor had recommended leaving it in place. As expected, the living room furniture looked unused and uncomfortable—no sense searching there. I moved into the family room. On the bookshelves that surrounded the massive television were other photos. Mostly of the two of them, a few of other people who looked a lot like them.

The books looked more like a decorator's idea of the books one should be seen to collect, rather than anything I thought would interest Nikki. Though I didn't know him well, Ian didn't strike me as a reader of *Meditations* by Marcus Aurelius or *Confessions* by Saint Augustine.

Inside the cabinets beneath the bookshelves, I found a pile of old DVDs next to a player, a complicated stereo system, and several neatly folded blankets. Unsure what I was looking for, I checked the kitchen, the master bedroom, and the master bath. These all appeared more lived in than the formal living room. Not dirty, but messy, except the king-size bed, which was made, including a ridiculous number of decorative pillows arranged against the head-board. Still, I found no convenient printouts of hotel reservations or driving instructions or flight numbers.

In the home office, the desktop computer demanded a password, of course, and the drawers held only office supplies. With waning optimism, I moved on for a cursory search of the guest room and bath. To my surprise, the queen bed was unmade with the sheets crumpled on one side and the comforter pushed to the foot. On the bedside table was a lamp and two framed photos, both selfies of Nikki and Ian. One was taken in front of a log cabin with azaleas blooming on either side of the porch steps, the other on a dock at a lake. They looked so happy. Nikki's hair was different, longer, but neither photo could have been more than a few years old. She'd mentioned a lake where they'd spent weekends during her residency, and their ill-fated honeymoon. I examined the background. The lake wasn't huge, though larger than Christian's. On its far side was another dock and what looked like a man-made beach with white sand that appeared out of place. Thick evergreens obscured any buildings, but there was something on the dock.

With my phone, I took a picture of the photo and sent it to Christian. Maybe his photo-editing genius friend could make something of it. I tried zooming with two fingers on my phone, but it became too distorted. Then I had a better idea, an old-school idea. Frame in hand, I returned to the home office and searched the desk drawers for the magnifying glass I'd seen earlier. With some adjusting I was able to optimize the focal length and read the sign: GUESTS OF HAMILTON LAKEVIEW RESORT ONLY.

Feeling like quite the investigator, I opened Google Maps on my phone and searched. There were several Hamilton Lakes around the country, but only one Hamilton LakeView Resort anywhere near Atlanta, where she'd lived at the time. It was in north Georgia.

I checked my phone—no response from Christian to either of my last two texts. Time to go. I returned everything where I'd found it, peered through the peephole in the front door, and left, locking the door behind me. I tried to look casual walking around the side of the house while dialing Lieutenant Garner. "I understand you can't track Ian's phone directly, but I've heard you can pick an area and ID any phones that have been there over a certain time frame."

"To find witnesses to a crime, yes." His voice was wary again. He must hate my calls.

"So if I gave you an area, could you check to see whether Ian Yarborough's phone has been there recently?"

"Kate . . ."

It had been a long shot. "Never mind. I don't want to get you in trouble." I climbed in my car and pressed the ignition. *Road trip it is.*

He hesitated. "I wish I could . . ."

"No, it's fine. Did you learn anything from Mr. Samuels?"

"He pushed off our meeting to tomorrow."

"Shocker. Have you talked to Christian by any chance?"

"Why do you ask?"

"I know he went to Jacksonville this morning and . . . oh my God, it's Thursday. The man who killed his family is being released today. You don't think he . . ."

"I don't know, Kate. He's in a much different place now than back then, but I'm worried about him, too."

Crap.

CHAPTER TWENTY-SEVEN

WHILE I GASSED up my Honda, I downloaded the latest Louise Penny book I'd been meaning to read. Google Maps predicted the trip to Hamilton LakeView Resort at a little over six hours, so I stocked up on Diet Mountain Dew and sunflower seeds.

Heading north on I75, I called Aunt Irm. Her bridge club met on Thursday evenings and she was already at Carmel's preparing. They cooked enough food for each participant to take home another meal's worth, from which I benefited regularly. With less argument than I expected, she agreed to stay the night.

Hopefully, I would make it back in time to cover Labor and Delivery at seven thirty Friday morning. If not, I had enough sick and vacation days to cover several months. The old me would have considered it irresponsible. The new me did, too, but now I appreciated the bigger picture.

Louise Penny's Three Pines characters kept my mind occupied and off of Christian, mostly. I couldn't help but wonder what drew him to Jacksonville and why he wasn't answering texts. The timing suggested it was related to Johnny Barillo's parole. Garner said Christian was in a better place emotionally now, but knowing the man who killed your wife and daughter was going free had to have an impact. Really, the trip could just as easily be work-related. Either way, why the radio silence?

I made it around Atlanta without any major traffic delays and was heading north again when he called. "I'm so sorry to disappear on you, Kate." At the sound of his voice, I felt immediately lighter, warmer, and a little juvenile for worrying.

"Is everything okay?"

"Not exactly. Megan Barillo—the wife of the man who killed Helen—asked for my help. Johnny's making threats about taking the kids. I handled their divorce while he was in prison. I'm helping her obtain a restraining order."

"That's kind of you." I tried not to think about the fact there were any number of attorneys in Jacksonville he could have asked to handle it. It was none of my business. This was the man who killed his family, who tore Christian's life apart. Who wouldn't jump at the chance to actively interfere with the man's undeserved freedom?

"Hopefully I'll be back in the morning. Where are you?"

"I'm going to try to see Nikki and Ian. Don't bother with the photo I sent. I figured it out."

"Sorry, I've been distracted all day. Wait, Ian? Where?"

"North of Atlanta. I'm almost there."

"Not alone, I hope." He paused a moment, then, "Shoot, I'm getting another call. I have to take this."

"No problem, Christian. I'll see you tomorrow." He had issues to deal with, and so did I.

The GPS led me north past Canton and off the interstate into rural north Georgia where streetlights vanished and other cars were few and far between. As I neared the lake, I paused at a fork in the road. The resort was to the right. The cabin in the photo sat on the opposite shore of the lake, so I turned left and headed around the small lake. Driveways appeared at intervals, with the

occasional rustic cabin or double-wide barely visible through the
dark trees.

The road narrowed. The rumble of my tires kicking up gravel
grew too loud to hear the audiobook, and I switched it off right at
a good part.

At first, I glimpsed an occasional reflection of the moon off water
to my right, then nothing. Pitch blackness interrupted occasionally
by dark gray where a driveway or lane intersected. The road curved
left, away from the lake. I glanced at the map as I drove, impressed
the road had made it on Google at all.

When the resort was directly across the lake, the driveway I
needed had to be close. I slowed to a crunchy crawl until I found
an opening to the right, a dirt path barely wide enough for the car.
I turned and drove slowly. Heavy shrubs whined against the doors
as I passed, more racing stripes for my poor car. Due to the constant
curves, even with the high beams, my headlights illuminated only
feet ahead. To the right and left was only blackness. Sadly, only then
did I wonder what the hell I was doing. I stopped the car.

It was a B-grade horror plot. Dark night in the middle of
nowhere, going after a friend in distress, who might be held against
her will. Hmmm. What could possibly go wrong? At least I hadn't
told anyone where I was. I nearly laughed out loud at my stupidity
but sobered quickly when I discovered there was no cell signal.
Perfect.

Grumbling, I knew the right answer was to go back and let someone know where I was. But when I looked over my shoulder, there
was no way to back down the mile-long excuse for a driveway. The
only way was forward. I gripped the steering wheel, pressed the
gas, and moved ahead slowly, scanning for a place to turn around,
preferably before I could be spotted from the cabin that had to be
up ahead.

The woods began to thin, allowing more moonlight to penetrate. I switched off my headlights to only the running lights and proceeded with my foot tapping the brake rather than the gas. A small log cabin resolved from the darkness. Maybe the same one from the springtime photo on Ian's nightstand. No lights were on, but in the moonlight, I could make out a front porch Laura Ingalls's family might have built. An SUV of indeterminate color sat off to the right.

I stopped again and considered what to do next. Ian and Nikki might be gone; they might never have been here in the first place; it might not even be the right cabin. It was too dark to walk around the back and check the dock view to be certain.

Nikki could be inside right now, tied up or injured. I couldn't leave without checking, though what would I do if Ian was there? I didn't have a gun and couldn't call the police.

A year before, I'd considered driving to very near here to check on Jenn, a very special medical student caught up in our investigation of hospital deaths. That time, I didn't go, and she was murdered. I could have prevented it. Regrets may not be useful, but they are a harsh teacher. I would help Nikki.

Opening my door quietly, I remembered too late to switch off the overhead light. Which reminded me what a bad criminal I was. I closed the door softly behind me and tried to walk lightly, heel to toe on the hard-packed dirt.

Something cold and hard touched the back of my neck and a deep male voice said, "Stop."

My hands flew up. "I'm sorry. I mean no harm." Terror apparently makes for strange phrasing, and stranger thoughts.

"Why are you here?" The words were a snarl. It might have been Ian; I didn't know his voice well enough.

My mouth turned so dry my tongue felt stuck. "I'm looking for Nikki and Ian Yarborough."

"Why?"

"I need their help. Nikki's patients are dying." I tried, unsuccessfully, to swallow. "Is she here?"

Noise came from the cabin, a raised voice, a woman's. A door slammed, and a shape came running toward me. "Kate? Kate. Let her be, Ian." Nikki's voice eventually materialized into Nikki as she ran into me, arms wrapping around me as the metal pressed into my neck disappeared. "I'm so sorry. We're still afraid he'll come after us." She took a step back. "Did you say my patients are dying? He promised it would stop if I left."

"He triggered someone who was driving on the interstate. It caused a huge accident. Twelve people died." I didn't add "so far." Though she might have prevented it, the accident wasn't her fault, not really.

"The driver?"

I nodded. "His name was Oliver McCann."

Even in the dim light I could see her face crumple. "Mr. McCann?" She wavered and I grabbed her arm to steady her. We walked to the porch steps where she sat heavily.

In an instant, Ian had flicked on a light and was beside her. She buried her face in his shoulder.

"It's not your fault," he said.

"I should have . . ." Sobs replaced words.

"There's nothing you could have done," he said, rubbing her back.

In a role reversal, I wanted to argue that point. Ian didn't know what she could have done. I kept quiet.

A moment later, she sat up and wiped her face with her sleeve. "I should have insisted all the Kadences be turned off, like we did with your aunt. At the very least, I could have told them not to drive."

"And then this crazy idiot would have come after you," Ian said.

I watched him closely. Did he know *this crazy idiot*? Ian was in charge of the software. He had means and opportunity. I just wasn't clear on a motive yet. That thought led to the next. The threat to Nikki got her away from town, out in the country, completely dependent on him.

"Let the police and MDI figure this out." Ian's voice was nauseatingly saccharin. "You're safe here."

"But my patients aren't."

"Let's go inside." Ian helped her up, then held the door. Once she passed, the look he gave me was nearly as chilling as the gun to my neck had been. I ignored him.

Nikki switched on an overhead light, and I had a good view of my friend for the first time. She wore sweatpants and a baggy long-sleeved shirt. There were no bruises, healing or otherwise, visible on her hands or face. She appeared clean and healthy, despite the austere environment. The cabin, too, looked clean if claustrophobic with its dark wood floors and paneling.

She stepped into a kitchen too small for two and returned with three glasses of ice water.

The dining table had only two spartan wood chairs. Ian pulled an end table close to Nikki and sat.

She took a long sip of water, then set the glass down slowly. "When I was threatened, Ian brought me here." She gave him an adoring smile with a tinge of sadness. Such a strange time to rekindle romance. But then, who was I to talk?

"Where did the threat come from?" I asked. "Was it by text? A phone call?"

"Dr. Cantwell told us. Someone emailed him and said they could trigger a misfire for any patient, any time." She blinked back tears. "He's being blackmailed, and this monster is threatening our patients and . . ." She paused a long time. I waited. "And his family." Her eyes met mine then. "He's my father, Kate."

I opened my mouth, hoping to signal surprise. Add actor to my list of nonexistent skills.

"He and my mom agreed never to tell me. He put money aside for us, but Mom never touched it." This she said with pride. "He's been looking out for me all these years."

Wow, a self-absorbed, misogynistic, egotistical guardian angel. Lucky her.

"Trying to help me be successful. I couldn't see that before."

It wasn't for me to burst her rainbow-colored bubble. "How did you find out?"

"With the pregnancy, I started missing my mom. I went back through her things and found a picture of her with my dad. I couldn't believe it at first."

Neither could I. The odds of her ending up in his department, or even in his field, had to be astronomical. Unless he'd been quietly nudging her along somehow throughout her life, which would be creepy. The other option, of course, was that she was lying. But why? Again, not for me to bring up now. "What did Cantwell say when you told him you knew?"

"I didn't get to. When he received the threat to his family, he called me to his office and told me the truth. I pretended not to know. It was surreal, Kate. He sat me down and said he had to tell me something very difficult. I thought he was going to fire me." She rubbed the condensation on her glass. "Then he said, 'I knew your mother in medical school. . . . Well. I knew her very well.'" She'd lowered her voice in imitation. "Isn't that funny? Then he just looked at me, like he wanted me to figure it out. I pretended not to understand. He deserved to squirm after abandoning my mom."

She paused a moment, then said, "He explained that he loved her, but was engaged to someone else. That he wished he had made a different choice. That he always wanted to be part of my life but respected her decision. That he set aside the money in hopes she would go back to medical school. He knew how smart she was and said he felt terrible that her dreams were ruined."

Basically, he said everything Nikki wanted to hear. So why didn't I feel happy for the reunited family?

"He begged me to leave town so I would be safe. We called Ian, and he agreed to protect me and the baby."

I just bet he did. How did Nikki manage to surround herself with suspicious men?

Ian took her empty glass into the kitchen for a refill. Nikki watched him. "When I first found the photo, I was confused and scared. I'd always imagined my dad as some awful person. He had to be to leave my mom."

Bingo.

"Ian and I argued over confronting him. I needed time to think." Ian placed her water on the table and resumed his seat. "Now that missing piece of my life is filled in. I know where I came from." She reached for Ian's hand, and they shared a look. "We're going to make it work."

"That's great news." I forced a smile. "Did Dr. Cantwell say anything more about the blackmail? Is he going to the police?"

She shook her head. "He just told us to get away."

Ian released her hand and turned his attention to me. "How did you find us?"

I chose not to admit my misdemeanor breaking and entering. "Nikki mentioned visiting a lake house during training."

Ian's head tilted, his eyes narrowed. "There are lots of lake houses."

"I saw a photo of you here. In the background is a sign for the resort on the other side." I hoped he wouldn't ask where I found said photo, or when.

Instead, he said, "Who else knows?"

How to answer? If I was in danger, my response would be quite different. "No one." I ignored Ian's obvious skepticism, preferring not to expound on my lunacy.

"I'm glad you came," Nikki said. "If I'd known the attacks wouldn't stop..."

"I came for another reason, too. We need the original software installed in the Kadence." Ian stared at me. "The code isn't on MDI's main server, only the compiled version. We need access to your directory."

"Who is *we*?" he asked.

"Erin Stevens said she's been trying to reach you. The other person is an engineer who worked with Dale Bennett on the original software." Did he flinch at the name? I told them what Nathan had found.

Ian shook his head. "There is no receptive capability over Bluetooth."

"Actually, there is, with the appropriate handshake." I watched his expression closely. Did he already know? I'd read about microexpressions, those instantaneous "tells" on people's faces before they could cover them up. But reading about them, and trusting myself to read them, were completely different.

"No. We removed that from the software."

"Who removed it?" I asked.

"We did penetration tests. The handshake no longer worked."

"Who did the tests?"

"I did them myself."

"It was changed slightly, but it still works," I said. "Was Dale Bennett's lab involved?"

Something might have crossed his face, but the light wasn't great, and I really needed to take a detecting class. "We worked with them. Why?"

Tired and hungry and running out of patience, I said, "Someone left in an access handshake. If it wasn't you, then it must have been someone in that lab."

"No. They fixed the software and we tested it. It was secure."

Clearly not. "Where is the code?"

Nothing.

"Ian," Nikki said. "They're trying to help. We have to protect my patients."

"I'll email Erin the password." His grudging agreement rubbed me the wrong way. This whole thing rubbed me the wrong way.

I glanced at my phone again. "There's no signal here. Give it to me and I'll call her on my way back."

"You're going back tonight?" Nikki asked.

"I have work tomorrow."

"Do it, Ian," Nikki said. "Please. The quicker they get the software, the sooner they can end this."

Face grim, he gave me the password.

"How long will it take to fix?" Nikki asked.

"He's using Bluetooth to trigger the devices. If your patients turn off their phone's Bluetooth, they should be safe." Ian had to know that, yet he hadn't offered the solution. Why? Confronting him now, here, alone, was probably unwise.

"So I could call and have them unpair the Kadence from their phone," Nikki said.

I nodded. "Annabelle's already started, but it will take a while to talk them through the steps."

"Dr. Cantwell is okay with that?"

I shrugged. "She made her own decision."

With a determined nod, she said, "I'll call her and coordinate."

"So you'll come back?"

She looked at Ian. "I'm sorry. I have to. Once the software is fixed, I'll need to bring in all the patients to update their device."

He gave a curt nod. The opposite of his expression.

"The police can keep you safe," I said.

Ian stood. "No. I will protect my family."

"We'll close up the cabin and head down in the morning," Nikki said.

Relieved, I stood, too. "Walk me out?" Had Ian followed, I would have asked him for a moment's privacy. He didn't. Once the door closed, I whispered, "Are you sure you're okay? He's not holding you here? You could come with me now."

"No, Kate, I'm fine. We're fine. I agreed to leave because the maniac said he'd stop attacking my patients if I did. He lied, so I'm going back until this is resolved."

I pulled her farther from the door. "I hate to ask, but are you sure Ian's not involved? He should have known about the Bluetooth connection."

"Ian?" She shook her head slowly, considering. "No. No, Ian could never hurt anyone." The right words said without confidence were not reassuring.

Her hand rested on her abdomen, emphasizing the baby bump largely hidden by her bulky shirt. "We're going to be a family, Kate."

A day ago, they were separated, now they were a family. Did the threat bring that about? Was it designed to?

By the time I reached my car, outside the small circle of light from the porch, Ian had come outside and put his arm around Nikki. She waved as I made a slow U-turn and headed back into the inky blackness. Ian didn't.

CHAPTER TWENTY-EIGHT

SOON AFTER REACHING the main road, my phone pinged multiple message alerts. When I stopped to pick up dinner and fill the tank again, I texted Ian's password to Nathan and Erin Stevens, then scrolled through the list of messages and was more disappointed than I should have been to find none from Christian. My phone rang as I accelerated up the on-ramp back to the interstate and I answered with the button on the steering wheel.

"You're fast, Nathan, did you get in?"

"Kate, it's Garner." Oops, caller ID was there for a reason. "What are you talking about, 'getting in'?"

"Nathan is trying to work on the Kadence software and he needed a password."

"Which you obtained how?"

"From Ian." I winced as if expecting a blow across state lines.

"Where are you?"

"Atlanta. I'll be home tonight."

"You wouldn't happen to be north of Atlanta by any chance, like near Canton?"

Busted. "Um. Not anymore."

"Why did I bother getting a warrant to track the phone? At your request, I might add."

"Because a young woman was missing and the authorities needed to ensure she wasn't kidnapped."

"Was she?"

"No."

He groaned. "So I should call off the welfare check at his uncle's cabin."

"Right. Sorry. They're coming back tomorrow so she can contact her patients."

"I guess that's good, but I wish you would keep me updated when you're going after a potential kidnapper."

"I told Christian." *Sort of.*

"He doesn't have a badge, Kate."

"You're right. And to be honest, I did regret it, but it was too late by then."

"Okay." And like that, I was forgiven. "What else did you learn?"

"Two big things. Ian claims the receptive capability was removed by Dale Bennett's lab. He also said they did penetration testing and the handshake access didn't work."

"I'm no engineer, but shouldn't they have tested other handshakes or passwords or whatever?"

"You'd think. Also, he should have known turning off Bluetooth might solve the problem."

"Good point. Did you ask him?"

"Believe it or not, I thought antagonizing him might be a bad idea."

"Wow, Kate, I'm so proud. So you think he's involved?"

Generally, I thought I read people fairly well and hadn't really suspected Ian. Then again, I once thought Greg's brother redeemable. "I don't know. How would it help him? He worked for the company, and his wife implants the devices."

"Maybe he didn't like his wife."

"That's a little far-fetched, don't you think?"

"I've seen farther-fetched. Or he has a beef with MDI. They were going to fire him in a year if he hadn't quit."

"I don't think he knew that at the time he installed the software. And he had a job already lined up when he quit. What if his new job is with Dale Bennett?" Nathan had been offered a position, why not Ian?

"My thought exactly. I spoke with someone in HR at the university about good Doctor Bennett." I heard pages flipping in his notebook. "He was faculty in biomedical engineering for more than ten years, was promoted to Associate Professor six years ago, and was about to go up for professor when he resigned last month with little warning and apparently not on the best of terms."

I slowed to pass an emergency vehicle stopped on the outside shoulder. "Interesting. Do you know where he is now?"

"You think I'd tell you after what you just pulled?"

I rolled my eyes from the safety of my car. "Nikki is a friend. I had to make sure she was safe. It was her and her husband. I wouldn't go after a murderer."

"Turning over a new leaf, are you?"

That stung. I'd had no choice before—the guy was actively murdering people I loved.

"Sorry, that was uncalled for," he said.

"I'll forgive you if you tell me where Dale Bennett is."

"Nice try. What was the second thing?"

Second thing?

"You said you learned two big things."

"Oh, yeah, Cantwell is Nikki's father. He's being blackmailed and besides targeting the patients, the guy threatened his family."

"Huh, that's . . . unexpected. I'll have to think about that one some more."

"Me, too." The interconnections were becoming a knotted mess.

We ended the call and I instructed my phone to play my voice-mails. The first was from Aunt Irm, asking whether I'd arranged for someone to feed Shadow dinner. *Crap.* The second was also from her. She assumed I would have asked Christian and since he wasn't answering his phone, she went home and fed my dog. I called her.

"Sorry about Shadow. I completely forgot to make arrangements for him." *Again.*

"It is okay, kindchen. He is fine. Carmel and I took him for a walk and he behaved. We did not pick up after him, though. I can tell you where he did his business if you wish to get it tomorrow."

"Thanks, it's probably okay." The self-appointed neighborhood police might send a note, but they couldn't prove it was Shadow, probably.

"Did you find Dr. Yarborough?"

"I did. She's fine. She's coming home tomorrow to help Annabelle call all the patients and have them disconnect their Bluetooth."

"Ah, this is good. I am pleased you convinced her to do the right thing. And Nathan? Has he fixed the problem?"

"He's my next call. I'll let you know. I won't be home until late. Are you staying with Carmel?"

"I am not. I asked Dr. Annabelle and she said I would be fine to stay alone."

And she was probably right. I had definitely become the mother chicken Aunt Irm accused me of. "Okay. Don't wait up."

We said goodnight and I called Nathan.

"Your MDI engineering friend isn't answering my calls," he said.

I glanced at the clock. "It's after ten, maybe she goes to bed early." Wishful thinking.

"I've been calling for hours. More likely she got cold feet."

"Ian Yarborough is coming back tomorrow. He can help."

"He doesn't work there anymore, remember?"

"This is probably not for public consumption, but it turns out Dr. Cantwell is Nikki's father."

"No shit," he said.

"None at all. She should be able to get Ian into MDI if it will fix the problem."

I disconnected and drove on, hoping Erin Stevens hadn't mentioned our concerns to anyone. It was classic catastrophizing—the farther I drove, the more disastrous the imagined consequences for someone who only wanted to help. I called Garner. "Sorry to wake you. Can I transfer that welfare check to Erin Stevens?"

He waited, an invitation to explain.

"She's an engineer at MDI. Nathan and I talked with her this morning and told her what was going on. She agreed to help us and now isn't answering her phone."

"She's probably asleep," Garner said. "We humans like to do that on occasion."

"It's a known weakness of your species."

"You really think she's in danger?"

Did I? "I really think that if she told the wrong person she was helping us, there's a possibility she could be in danger. Can you check on her? She doesn't know what we've dragged her into."

"*We* don't know what you've dragged her into."

"Good point."

He made no promises, but I knew Garner took my crazy hunches seriously. Whether that was a good or bad thing remained to be seen. Despite the hour, I called Christian. It went to voicemail. I left a message that I was headed home and looked forward to catching up the next day, assuming he made it back. And I realized that I really hoped he made it back.

As I crossed the state border, Garner called. "I did a drive-by. It's dark. No cars in the driveway, and the garage door is down. I can't justify knocking on her door in the middle of the night. I'll check back in the morning if you still can't reach her."

I thanked him and promised to call. He was probably right. She was probably fine. But not answering Nathan's calls worried me. That she had silenced or switched off her phone seemed highly unlikely. Either she'd decided on her own to back away, or someone decided for her.

CHAPTER TWENTY-NINE

IT WAS AFTER two in the morning when I pulled into the garage. Shadow greeted me with the doggie affection I loved. I'd completely neglected him for two days, yet all was forgotten in an instant. When at last my head hit the pillow, exhaustion won out over my troubled mind and I slept.

Aunt Irm woke me just before seven. I'd slept through my alarm. "You must call in sick today. You need rest."

I jumped from bed and turned on the shower. "I can't do that."

"Hmph. You tell me to rest. You do not prescribe your own medicine."

I let that one go, apologized without conviction, and got ready for work. On the way to the hospital, I tried Erin Stevens' number. When there was no answer, I called Garner and left a message.

At work, I took caffeine pills with my coffee and stayed focused. Once I finished conference and we'd started our first case, I checked my email. I'd received one from "Anonymous" at a nonsense address that included two attachments: Latest Code and Latest Compiled. I called Nathan. "I think Erin Stevens sent me the files."

"On my way."

Ten minutes later, he'd taken over the computer. "She used a Virtual Private Network to hide the originating computer. Smart.

Just in case, let's not open these on the network." He pulled a USB drive from his pocket, copied over the email and attachments, then opened them on his laptop in airplane mode.

I watched as he scrolled through the main body of the software's code and then through various subroutines. When he reached the bottom, he scrolled back up. "This is pretty much the same as what we gave them from the lab." He stopped on a subroutine in a light gray font set off with slash marks. "Here. This is the routine that accepts the handshake via Bluetooth and enables incoming communication. It's commented out. It shouldn't run."

"Commented out rather than deleted?"

He raised his shoulders. "Turning the lines of code into comments is quicker and makes it easier to debug."

"Does it also run the risk of getting un-commented out?" Probably not a word, but he understood.

"No, it would have to be purposely switched back." He resumed scrolling. "And I don't see any section that was added.

"So this can't be the code they compiled and installed in the Kadence."

He minimized the editing screen and looked at the file details of the compiled version Erin Stevens had sent. On the office computer, he opened his directory. "I pulled this code from your aunt's Kadence. It's the same compile date."

"Even I can fake that," I said.

"Even you?" He looked back at the file on his laptop. "They're not the same size."

"So not the same file." We were right. I tried Erin Stevens' cell again, then called MDI's main number and asked to be connected to her. Her office phone went to voicemail. I tamped down my frustration and called Garner again. More voicemail. *Dammit!* I tried Ian's number and finally got an answer.

"Kate, hi, it's Nikki. We just got home."

The answered phone, and her words, came as a great relief. "You must have left before dawn."

"Neither of us could sleep, so we packed up and hit the road."

"Can you put me on speaker so we can talk to Ian as well?" I did the same for Nathan's benefit.

"Okay." Nikki sounded farther away.

"Ian, this is Kate and Nathan, the engineer from Dale Bennett's lab I mentioned last night."

He said something we couldn't make out, maybe a greeting, pretty sure not a happy one.

"I sent Erin Stevens your password last night and today received a file. But it's not the code that's actually installed on the Kadence, and we can't reach her. I'm afraid someone scared her off."

Nathan tapped mute on my phone. "Or she didn't want to commit a felony by sharing proprietary software."

I gave him what I hoped was an admonishing glare. He grinned as he reactivated the microphone.

"My access is disabled," Ian said. "I can't log onto the server to find the original code."

"Since we have the version that should have been installed," I said, "can you compile it and then replace the software on all the devices? That should prevent the attacks."

Nathan nodded, his head arcing farther than necessary, as if trying to convince Ian by telepathy.

"Not me," Ian said. "Erin would have to compile it and run the safety tests."

"Assuming she's out of the picture, who else can do it?" I asked.

"At this point, don't you think we should go directly to the head of the company?" Nathan said. "Or maybe Dr. Cantwell?"

When Ian said nothing, I asked, "What do you think, Ian? Would either of them listen to you?"

"I don't know. My departure was a little . . . abrupt. I'll try to find Erin first. If that doesn't work, I'll reach out to Mr. Samuels and Dr. Cantwell."

"If we explain it to him, I'm sure my dad can help," Nikki said. How weird that must sound to someone raised without knowing his identity.

"How long will it take to update the Kadences?" I asked.

"Not long, but it will require the interrogation computer, so each patient will have to come in," Ian said.

To see fifty-plus patients, even for a brief appointment, in between all the others scheduled, would take days. Meanwhile the device wasn't operating as designed. If it went into a failure mode now, without Bluetooth, Nikki had no way of knowing. Switching off Bluetooth was a stopgap measure. We had to replace the software and find the psychopath who was messing with the devices. And if anything happened to my aunt in the meantime . . .

I asked Ian to let us know what happened. Nathan left my office while I went to check on my OR. The surgeon was closing so I stepped back into the hallway and called Garner. This time he answered.

"Any luck with Erin Stevens?" I asked. "She's still not answering her mobile or her work phone. If you can't go by, can you give me her address or do I have to find it some other way?" It came out more threatening than I'd intended.

"We can discuss that request." He sounded strangely formal. "I'm in Dr. Cantwell's office. Can you join us?"

CHAPTER THIRTY

I CHECKED WITH the Labor and Delivery charge nurse, who was holding the next Cesarean while another patient on the ward delivered, so I took the stairs to the Cardiology Division. That Garner was meeting with Cantwell came as no surprise. The surprise was the invitation. It surely hadn't originated with Cantwell. Had I earned involvement from Garner's standpoint? More likely, I'd beaten him down to the point he'd rather control my involvement.

This time, Dr. Cantwell's secretary showed me directly into his office. The chairman and Garner faced each other across the pristine desk. Garner stood at my entrance. "Thank you for coming, Dr. Downey. Dr. Cantwell has information regarding the Kadence misfires."

I wanted to correct the term—attacks, not misfires—but I let it go. As I sat next to Garner, Cantwell looked not at me, but at him, and in the instant before he spoke, I knew what he was going to say. "We're being blackmailed. It started two weeks ago."

Garner handed me a printout of an email: *I have hacked your Kadence device. You pay me 1,000,000 $ in Bitcoin and patients will not die.*

A "btc" address followed—a long string of random letters and numbers.

"I don't suppose it's traceable."

Garner shook his head.

"The phrasing is a little off."

"I agree," he said. "If I had to guess, though, I'd say it's faked to look that way. To make us think it's Russian hackers or another foreign agent."

Cantwell's lip curled. "Russian hackers did not access the Kadence."

He was obnoxious, but he was also right. We already knew it had to be an inside job.

"Mr. Samuels at MDI received the same message," Garner said.

Cantwell stared at his desk. "He convinced me to ignore it. He said companies receive empty threats all the time. Several hours later, I received another note with the name of a patient this person claimed to have attacked."

"Mr. Abrams," I said. I recalled the scene in the recovery room. His v-fib had converted back to sinus before I could charge the defibrillator. "He was the first attacked. Proof this guy could do it."

Cantwell nodded, still avoiding my gaze. "The price doubled. I told him I didn't have that kind of money, and I don't, not until the sale goes through." His bloodless hands were clasped together on the desk. I almost felt sorry for him. Almost. Except that he'd hidden this information, allowing others to be attacked, including my aunt, and then lied. "I pulled together what money I could, but he refused to give me more time."

"What about Samuels?" I asked.

"Same problem. We both invested everything in the company."

"And neither of you contacted the police?"

He ignored the question. The answer was obvious. Fear of publicity was a disturbingly common refrain. "He attacked another patient and sent another message."

Garner handed me another printout. More rhetoric about paying up. The last line read, *Next will be very public. Transfer the 2,000,000 $ now.*

Cantwell sat stone-faced. I waited him out, my eyes taking in the credenza behind him, and I finally realized what looked so odd. He had no photos at all. Not of family or famous acquaintances. None.

"I told him I needed no further proof. I bought and transferred as much Bitcoin as I could, but it was only a fraction of his demand. Samuels did the same. It didn't matter. He attacked the governor."

"You knew," I said. "That's why you had Nikki interrogate his pacer."

"No." Cantwell's face reddened under my glare. "If I'd known about the speaking engagement, I might have put it together."

"So why the emergency interrogation then?" I asked.

"Because of the other two misfires. I still thought they could be coincidental."

"You can't be serious. Twice someone threatens to fire a Kadence, does, takes credit for it after, including the victims' names, and you convince yourself it was coincidental?"

"You have to admit it's unlikely," Garner said as I added, "inconceivable."

"I didn't want to take any chances." His arrogant chin dropped slightly.

"What about all the other Kadence patients?" I asked. "You took chances with them."

Cantwell sat sullen as my stomach twisted. This man knew his patients were at risk and did nothing.

Garner's foot pressed mine under the edge of the desk. Grudgingly, I had to admit he was right, not the time or place.

At last, Cantwell spoke. "I thought we could finish the sale and I would have the money to transfer. It took longer than it was supposed to. On Monday, he attacked your aunt without another warning, at least not to me. Afterward, I received a note that he'd give me twenty-four hours, but the price had gone up another million dollars. It's ridiculous. If I couldn't come up with two million, how was I going to come up with more?"

"Maybe it's not about the money." I said it without thinking. Why ask for more than the victim had? Unless . . . "Do you have money hidden away somewhere? Someplace you think no one knows about?"

"No." Cantwell shook his head hard, defensively. "I don't. All my money is tied up in MDI. I have nothing liquid."

"What is your relationship with Ian Yarborough?" Garner asked.

He leaned back in his chair, distancing himself. "He's an engineer. He worked in my lab at Emory, then came here when we started MDI. He's good at his job."

"Which he'll lose in a year, right?" And then it occurred to me. "Wow, putting your own son-in-law out of work."

Cantwell winced. "I asked the buyer to give him a longer contract or to make exceptions for key employees. They insisted one-year guarantees are standard. There's a chance they'd keep him on." Even he seemed to think that a long shot. "Why are you asking about Ian?"

He directed the question to Garner, but I answered. "The software in the Kadence is the wrong version. Someone switched it. Ian was in charge at the time."

At last Cantwell looked directly at me, his mouth slightly open. "What are you talking about?"

I waited.

"Ian wouldn't . . ." He hesitated, wheels spinning.

"How about Dale Bennett?" Garner asked.

"Dale . . ." Cantwell trailed off again.

"MDI offered him a job and then withdrew it," Garner said. "That had to make him mad."

Cantwell opened his mouth, closed it, then started over. "He asked for a job with us. He was tired of academia and wanted to pursue more applications of bidirectional communication technology for medical devices. It was a win-win. We would gain an experienced engineer with ideas, and he would have financial backing for his commercial projects without continually having to publish and write grants."

It was a common enough reason to leave academics, along with the salary differential.

"We offered him a position, but then Samuels came to me with the purchase offer. It was more than either of us dreamed. During due diligence, we had to keep everything confidential and freeze all personnel changes. Regardless, Dale Bennett wouldn't be satisfied with only a one-year guarantee, so we withdrew our job offer. He was angry, of course, but angry enough to tamper with his own software? I can't believe that."

"I just came from the Office of Technology Licensing on campus," Garner said. "Dale Bennett tried to get them to withdraw his patent from the licensing deal."

"He can't do that," Cantwell said. "We funded the work that went into that patent."

"So he can't develop any products based on his own patent." Garner made it sound inconceivable.

"It's how universities always work," Cantwell said. "I'm in the same position with my patents."

"But you'll benefit from the exclusive license," I said. "You'll get a portion of the royalties. What does Dale Bennett get?"

"He'll receive royalties when his technology is incorporated in the next generation of devices."

"That could be years," I said. "Maybe never. You can't think that's fair." Though from how he treated his own daughter, his fairness meter needed calibration.

No surprise, he said nothing.

"Seems like a motive to me," Garner said.

"No doubt." So why was the blackmailer demanding money instead of the patent? "Have you seen the blackmail notes Mr. Samuels is receiving?" I asked Garner.

He shook his head, then referred the question to Cantwell.

"I assumed they were the same. Once the deal is complete, we'll have the money."

"What if his are different?" I said. "What if they aren't just about money?"

"Call him," Garner said to Cantwell.

He pulled his phone from his pocket, tapped the screen, and held it to his ear for a long moment. "It's Victor. Call me back right away."

"I'm headed there after this," Garner said.

"If you're right about the software, we can fix it," Cantwell said.

"Who can? Ian left the company," I said.

"There are other engineers."

"Any luck finding Erin Stevens?" I asked Garner.

At last Cantwell looked less assured.

"She is not at home or at MDI," Garner said. "According to my officer, it appears she left in a hurry, though without evidence of a struggle. Her cellphone was left at the house." He looked at me with that last sentence, warding off my incessant request for tracking, presumably. To Cantwell, he said, "She was helping provide access to the software, then she disappeared."

With his elbows on the desk, Cantwell's head dropped into his hands.

"Ian has the correct version of the software that needs to be compiled and tested," I said. "He's willing to help, but since he was involved in the original failure, it makes sense to have another party observe. I know an engineer who wrote much of the code in question. He can monitor the tests."

"Ian can't do it," he said behind his hands. "He has to stay with Nikki."

"They're here," I said.

Cantwell's face came up, eyes wide.

"She is going to do what you should have done from the very beginning—warn all the patients. Meanwhile, you and Mr. Samuels have to give Ian and Nathan Castle access to MDI's server so they can fix the Kadence and stop the attacks."

His face reddened. "Nikki can't—" He reached for his phone again. "You don't know what you've done."

"I do. Unlike you, Nikki is willing to put herself at risk to do the right thing." I stood to leave. "Any other father would be proud."

CHAPTER THIRTY-ONE

IN THE HALLWAY outside Dr. Cantwell's office, I accompanied Lieutenant Garner to the elevators.

"So what comes next?" I asked.

"For you, nothing. You did good in there. Now let me do my job and we'll figure this out."

"Has someone spoken with Dale Bennett?"

"What a great idea. I'll add it to my list."

My phone rang. "Sorry." I answered the call.

"Kate? It's Randi. The baby has decided Monday isn't soon enough."

"Are you okay?"

"Mostly. Except every few minutes. Then not so much."

"I'll meet you on Labor and Delivery."

"We're here." With a loud groan, she disconnected.

"Duty calls," I said.

"One more thing, Kate." He cleared his throat. "Christian is in the emergency room in Jacksonville with a concussion."

My throat tightened. "What happened?"

"Apparently Johnny Barillo took exception to Christian helping out his ex-wife."

Christian in a fight? The kind, gentle man I knew, throwing punches? Or, more accurately, receiving them.

"The guy showed up at her house this morning, and he and Christian got into a . . . disagreement." Somewhere in the back, my brain registered the part about Christian being at her house in the morning. "A neighbor called 911, but by the time the police arrived, Barillo was gone. They insisted Christian go to the hospital because he'd lost consciousness."

"Lost consciousness—Are they sure it's just a concussion? Did they do a CT scan?"

"I don't know."

"Can I talk to his doctor? Why isn't Christian answering his phone?"

"I only spoke with him briefly. The responding officer called me as a courtesy. Christian assured me he's fine."

Part of me wanted to demand that he call him back, another part wanted to drive to Jacksonville immediately, and a third, more insecure part that I tried to keep buried wanted to know why Christian had been beaten up by a jealous ex-husband this morning while ignoring my calls. That part needed to stay buried. This was about him. Not me.

"I didn't want you to read about it somewhere," Garner said. Pre-internet, such a fight wouldn't approach the bar of newsworthiness. No longer. "I'll have him call you if I talk to him." The Christian of two nights ago, the one who kissed me so passionately, wouldn't need a reminder. God, I belonged in high school.

"Does his mom know?" She'd been worried about Michael, now Christian. Poor woman.

"I'll call her on my way to MDI."

"While you're there, why don't you plant a bug or something? You know both these guys are hiding something."

"If only it were that easy."

"They're tiny, aren't they? You could accidentally on purpose drop one." My phone rang again, Labor and Delivery's main number. "I have to go. Thanks for telling me and good luck with Samuels." I pushed open the double doors as I answered my phone and assured the clerk I'd be there soon.

I couldn't wrap my head around the idea of Christian in a fight. Not the Christian I knew. But his brother Michael told me Christian decompensated after the accident that killed his family. He lost his job, his house, and his savings in his efforts to punish the bars who had served Johnny Barillo, as well as the friends who hadn't stopped him.

At the doors to Labor and Delivery, I shook Christian from my mind. Randi Sinclair and my other patients deserved all my attention.

I found Randi in a triage room, breathing hard through a contraction, her husband Craig's fingers white in her grip. "This little one doesn't want to wait," I said.

"Nope," she said through gritted teeth. Once the contraction passed, she added, "Since I started labor spontaneously, Dr. Ross asked again about me trying for a vaginal delivery." We'd talked about this several times in the last few months. The online calculator gave her a sixty percent chance of success, offset by the small possibility of the scar on her uterus rupturing, which could be disastrous. It was a tough decision for any woman and not helped by the excruciating pain she felt every few minutes.

"How about I go ahead and place an epidural, then you and Craig can talk about it? Once you're comfortable, we could also wait a few hours and see what happens."

"I don't want to make you stay."

"Oh, for God's sake, that should be the furthest thing from your mind right now. You know me. What in the world could I have to do on a Friday night?"

She laughed, until another contraction hit. I stepped out to get the epidural supply cart. Ruby, her labor nurse, helped with positioning and a few minutes later Randi relaxed in bed. Color had returned to her husband's hand—and face for that matter.

"Wow, you have a great job," she said.

"I do. Wish I could say the same for you."

Ruby adjusted the monitor recording the baby's heart rate. "What do you do?"

"I teach middle school math."

"Oh," Ruby said, "tough job."

"I love it."

"And you're amazing at it," Craig said, his face adoring. The look they shared warmed my heart and also pierced it a little. Love like that happens once in a lifetime, if you're lucky. I'd had mine.

At the bedside computer, I caught up the medical record while we chatted about how their not-yet-two-year-old, Robbie, was going to deal with the invader. Eventually, I was called away for another case. When I returned a couple of hours later, Randi was seven centimeters dilated, further than she'd made it with Robbie. "I guess we're doing this," she said.

At five o'clock, the on-call attending took over the rest of the patients with labor epidurals, and I went to my office to catch up on work until Randi delivered. If all went well, she wouldn't need me. If something happened and she required a C-section, though, I wanted to be there.

Less than an hour later, Ruby texted: "She's starting to push."

That was Randi, overachiever. Back on Labor and Delivery, she pushed like a champ and declined an epidural top-up dose. "I don't want to feel nothing, just close to nothing."

I offered to step outside to give them a modicum of privacy, but both Randi and Craig asked me to stay. Randi grabbed my hand. "If you don't mind."

"Of course."

"You know what I mean. If it won't make you sad."

And that was why she was my dearest friend. At a time like this, she's worried about me. When I went into preterm labor with Emily soon after Greg's accident, she stayed with me through the whole ordeal, despite having a newborn at home. Aunt Irm had not yet moved down, and Randi was my savior during that painful time. After, I'd become distant, convincing myself a new mother didn't need a grieving not-quite-widow hanging around. Over the next year of Greg's coma, Randi tried to maintain our relationship, but I failed her. I wouldn't do that now. If she wanted me there for her delivery, I would be there.

"How about I take the camera so you can focus on each other." Craig looked questioningly at Randi. "I'll only take tasteful shots, I promise."

Dr. Ross came in. At barely over four feet tall, she was a dynamo of energy and humor, even when things became tense, which I vowed they would not. I stayed on Randi's right side and supported her leg while she pushed. Ten minutes later, a beautiful baby girl arrived, wailing and healthy. Dr. Ross placed the baby on Randi's chest where she and Craig counted fingers and toes and oohed and aahed. Grateful for something to do, I blinked back happy tears and captured photos of the joyful family.

"Her name is Carol," Randi said, "after my mom."

"She'll be thrilled."

After several minutes, Ruby took baby Carol to the warmer for an assessment and I got my first good look. "She's beautiful." I wasn't even lying. Most newborns squeezing through the birth canal have a cone head or a squished face, but Randi's relatively short labor left baby Carol round-headed and perfect. I waited for the clean bill of health from the pediatricians, then took some more family photos and left for home after many thanks and congratulations.

I called to let Aunt Irm know to expect me. "Perfect timing," she said. "We'll meet you in the driveway."

CHAPTER THIRTY-TWO

I DROVE THE fifteen minutes home curious what my aunt meant. Perfect timing for what? As promised, she waited in the driveway holding a paper bag and a thermos with a duffel at her feet, and she wasn't alone. Molly O'Donnell stood by her side, an immense purse on her arm and another, smaller, bag on the ground beside her. Only one purpose came to mind, and I felt strangely ambivalent. Torn between wanting to see Christian and fearing what I might find. The man I'd become close to, the man I'd kissed, might not be the same man in a fistfight defending a woman whose husband killed the love of Christian's life. Rationally, I'd recently dealt with Greg's inheritance, and it hadn't changed how I felt about Christian. So why the insecurity?

I stopped in the driveway next to Molly O'Donnell's Lexus, put the car in park, and stepped out without turning off the ignition.

Aunt Irm came around to the passenger side. "I have your dinner. Shadow ate and did his business. We need to be there by nine."

"Dare I ask where we'll be by nine?" I opened the back door and leaned in to unhook the dog-fur-covered blanket from over the headrest. Aunt Irm did the same from the other side. "You could have warned me," I whispered.

She gave me her innocent "who-me?" look. "I knew you would wish to go."

I tossed the dog blanket into the trunk, along with the overnight bags, presumably one of which held clothes for me.

Molly O'Donnell thanked me and insisted on the back seat while Aunt Irm sat beside me. She pulled my phone from the cup holder and handed it to me. "We're going to the Hyatt in downtown Jacksonville. Molly has the address for you to put into your mappy thing."

My mappy thing accepted the address. Ninety minutes.

"Thank you for agreeing to accompany me," Mrs. O'Donnell said. "I couldn't face this alone, and Christian will be so pleased to see you."

"Of course," I said under my aunt's warning gaze. Was this another ploy to push the two of us together?

She opened the paper bag and began withdrawing contents—a napkin for my lap, a sandwich pulled from its plastic bag and placed carefully on the napkin, and a small bag of carrots in the cup holder behind my water bottle. "Would you like coffee or water?"

"Water's fine for now." I thanked her for the meal and nibbled as I navigated through town and north to the highway.

"How does Christian sound?" I asked his mother.

"I haven't spoken with him. Frank says he's doing as well as can be expected. He's with him now at the hotel but has to leave by nine, so we're taking over."

So Frank Garner had finished his business in Newberry and driven to Jacksonville that afternoon. "Does Christian know this?" I asked.

"That does not matter, whether he knows or not," Aunt Irm said. "He needs us and we go. That is how family works."

"He may prefer to be alone."

"A man needs his mother, no matter the age. Max was more dev-astated than even I when our mother passed." Another nugget from Aunt Irm's past that I couldn't explore at the moment.

Mrs. O'Donnell spoke then, with unexpected intensity. "This man destroyed my son's life, murdered his wife, and took his beau-tiful daughter from us. We lost Christian himself for a time and now we are so worried he will . . ." She trailed off.

"We won't let him," I said.

In the rearview mirror, she wiped a tear. "Thank you."

Aunt Irm changed the subject and the women talked about church and bridge and their arthritis. My attention drifted, to Jolene, to Randi, to Nikki, and back to Christian.

I dropped the women at the front doors of the sparkling Hyatt. It had to be at least fifteen stories, a skyscraper by my standards. Through the two-story glass front, a chandelier hung far above the wood and glass lobby. I declined valet parking and drove slowly into the garage, looping upward in search of an open spot.

By the time I made my way back to the lobby carrying the bags, Aunt Irm was nowhere in sight. I texted her. No response. Finally, I called Lieutenant Garner. When he failed to answer, anxiety flut-tered in my stomach. I should have paid the ridiculous valet fee. I shouldn't have left two elderly women . . . Aunt Irm would not approve of that thought process.

At last, she and Mrs. O'Donnell emerged from the shiny gold ele-vator bay and my heart slowed back toward normal. Until I saw the looks on their faces, that is. "He's not there," Mrs. O'Donnell said.

"At least he is not answering our knock," Aunt Irm added.

"Did you try calling him?" I asked.

"He hasn't answered his phone all day," his mother said. "I don't think he has it. And Frank's phone went to voicemail. I left a message."

"How about ringing his room from the front desk?" I said.

She walked to the counter, still with the erect posture I'd come to expect, no matter the situation. The clerk smiled solicitously, picked up the phone, dialed, and stood looking past Mrs. O'Donnell, one hand holding the receiver, the other toying with the old-fashioned coiled cord. She stood that way for at least a minute, then shook her head and replaced the receiver. Mrs. O'Donnell's perfect makeup couldn't hide the pallor of her concern.

"Mom?" The glass doors closed behind Christian as he strode toward her. From his right side, he looked normal, if determined. Only after he folded his mother into his arms, after decorum trumped relief and his mother pulled away, after she nodded our way and he turned, only then did I see his gaunt, haunted, exhausted expression. His darkened left eye was swollen nearly closed. A bruise extended down his cheek bone. With an arm around his mother, he made his way to us. We greeted each other with only uncomfortable nods.

"Have you eaten?" Aunt Irm asked. It was after nine. Some might think it an awkward icebreaker, unless they knew Aunt Irm.

"I'm fine, but we can go into the bar if you're hungry," Christian said.

We walked together, in silence, Aunt Irm and I in the lead. She chose a corner booth, signaled to a waiter, and ordered appetizers, white wine for herself, and gestured for the rest of us to order drinks.

After the waiter left, Mrs. O'Donnell asked Christian, "Where were you when we arrived?"

"I needed a walk." He gave his mother a meaningful look. She bowed her head and nodded. I didn't ask.

"Where was Lieutenant Garner?" Aunt Irm said.

"Did he call you?" Christian asked his mother.

She met his gaze without a flinch. "He did, and I promised to sit with you when he had to return to work."

Christian closed his eyes and shook his head. "I'm not seventeen, Mom."

"You've had a concussion. We must keep you awake."

I bit my lip to avoid contradicting her medical mythology. My phone rang. Garner. "Hey, we found him."

"Found who?"

"Christian. He'd just gone out for a walk. Mrs. O'Donnell said she left you a message."

Garner swore loud enough for Aunt Irm to raise her eyebrows beside me. "The police are on their way to the hotel to question him."

"Again?" I kept my face impassive. "Why?"

"Johnny Barillo is dead, Kate. He was shot an hour ago not two miles from the Hyatt."

My eyes flew to Christian. He stared back. "It wasn't him," I said with complete and unwarranted confidence. It couldn't have been him. Not only could he not kill anyone, he certainly couldn't walk calmly into a hotel immediately afterward and hug his mother. No way.

"We're shorthanded," Garner said. "That's why I had to leave early. I can't get back there until tomorrow. Don't let Christian say anything." He provided the name and contact information for Christian's attorney, then said, "Let me talk to him."

Christian accepted the phone. Soon after, he closed his eyes, agreed to something, then handed the phone back. Garner had hung up. Christian took his mother's hand. "Someone killed Johnny Barillo. I had nothing to do with it, but the police want to question me."

Mrs. O'Donnell's free hand flew to her mouth and she let out a small cry.

"They'll be here soon. I'm sorry you drove all this way."

Aunt Irm consoled Mrs. O'Donnell as I got Christian's attention and said quietly, "Tell me what's going on."

He stood and gestured for me to follow to the alcove near the restrooms. "I got the restraining order for Megan and her kids, but she was scared so I slept on her couch last night. Johnny showed up this morning, found me there, and went ballistic." He touched his cheek. "He's a better fighter than I am."

Of course he was, after several years in prison, if not before.

"When I woke up on her floor, he was gone, and the police were there." He grasped my shoulders, his eyes boring into mine. "I have not seen him since. You have to believe that. I did not kill him. No matter what you hear."

The last words sent a chill down my back. "What does that mean?"

"I think someone is setting me up."

I waited.

"Yesterday, Megan Barillo received a text from an unknown number advising her to call me for protection. Early this morning, the same number texted Johnny a photo of her and me meeting last night on her doorstep." He shifted uncomfortably. "We were hugging." He followed quickly with an unnecessary explanation. "It was just a friendly hug. We haven't seen each other in years."

"It's fine, Christian. Finish the story."

"After he knocked me out, Johnny confronted Megan about our relationship. He showed her the photo. She's the one who noticed the numbers were the same. The police are trying to track it."

"Christian O'Donnell?" Though expected, the authoritative voice startled me. A uniformed officer stood in the alcove entrance.

Christian nodded to her, then looked back at me. "You believe me." It wasn't a question, which filled the pit in my stomach a little.

"Of course." I stared after him as two officers escorted Christian from the room. His mother gave a small moan but otherwise maintained her composure.

As instructed by Garner, I called Christian's attorney, who promised to meet him at the police station. Another officer separated me, Aunt Irm, and Molly O'Donnell, and spoke with us individually. It took more than an hour. At long last, we were allowed to go to our hotel rooms. They had reserved two. Aunt Irm and I bunked together but kept the adjoining door open to Christian's mother. "In case she needs us," Aunt Irm explained. "She has had a shock today." My aunt would have been such an amazing mother.

She used the restroom first while I texted Randi and apologized that I couldn't drop by in the morning.

She called immediately. "Is everything okay?"

I must wear my emotions on my proverbial sleeve, even in a text. "Yes, fine. I had to run to Jacksonville to take care of something. You just focus on your little angel. Did Robbie meet her yet?"

"He did. He was so excited. He didn't even try to push her off my lap . . . yet. The whole ward heard it when he had to leave though." I, too, had experienced the volume capacity of Robbie's well-developed lungs.

"Now he has someone to give him a run for his screaming title."

"I hate you," Randi said.

I laughed, told her to call if there were any problems, and disconnected. My next call was to Garner. I wasn't laughing anymore.

CHAPTER THIRTY-THREE

OVER THE PHONE, the growl in Lieutenant Garner's voice made it nearly unrecognizable. "What the hell was Christian thinking? How are we going to find him an alibi for the time of the murder if he was out walking?" He made walking sound like an inexplicable activity in which to engage. "Did you reach his attorney?"

"I did, and for what it's worth, I don't think Christian was planning to need an alibi."

He grunted, though I'm not sure it was in agreement.

"Christian told me about the texts Megan and Johnny Barillo received. Any luck tracing the number?"

"It's almost certainly a burner phone," Garner said.

"I thought that was just on TV."

"Unfortunately, no. Hollywood got that part right."

"So someone is screwing with all their lives."

"The Barillos were going to be a mess either way," Garner said. "Why bring Christian into it?"

Why indeed? Without the text, Megan Barillo might have called another attorney or the police if she thought she needed protection. Without the photo sent to her husband, Johnny Barillo might have followed visitation rules to see his children and not attacked

Christian. The pot-stirrer here used the couple to go after Christian. Two possibilities came immediately to mind—Adam Downey and whoever was trying to ruin MDI.

"Is there any chance Johnny Barillo and my brother-in-law were acquainted in prison?"

"You think Adam would target Christian?"

"I wouldn't put it past him. He was furious that Christian helped me with my mother-in-law's estate last week." Even without that, he despised me. Everything bad in Adam's life, he found a way to blame on me. What better way to ruin my life than to target the man he perceived as Greg's replacement? "On the other hand, distracting Christian from completing the MDI sale bought the blackmailer time."

"Has Adam specifically threatened you or Christian recently?"

I recalled his look of loathing. "Not in so many words."

"I'll check with the warden."

"Christian said he took over the MDI sale late in the process. Do you know what happened to his predecessor?"

"Huh. Good question. I'll have to look into that, too. I do know it pissed off Mr. Samuels."

"How did that meeting go?"

"He insists the company has the misfires under control and categorically denies that someone could be causing them."

"Despite all evidence to the contrary," I said.

"He wants this deal done yesterday."

"And now Christian will be otherwise engaged. Does his law firm have someone else who can take over?"

"Hell if I know."

"Did Samuels admit to being blackmailed?"

"He did, and after much coaxing, he handed over the notes. In addition to money, the blackmailer demands the sale be canceled."

"The whole sale, not just the one patent." As I said it, though, I knew it meant nothing. "If he named the patent, it would narrow down the suspect pool."

"You know it's not too late to change careers," Garner said.

"Why not go to the buyer instead?"

"Their identity is confidential. One of the few well-kept secrets, I'm told."

It was a secret from me. "But this guy could inform everyone in the industry with a few well-placed public reports." News that smacked of evil corporate cover-ups would go instantly viral. "I suppose that would burn a bridge if he wants to use the technology later."

"You don't really need me, do you?"

"Not for your search warrants, that's for sure."

He chuckled. "There's a reason we do things the way we do."

"To annoy the innocent and falsely accused?"

"Not exactly."

"What about Samuels' family? Were they threatened?"

"In a later note, yes, but his wife left him months ago, and he's not worried about her."

"How sweet. How about Erin Stevens?"

"Sorry, I meant to tell you earlier. She and her young daughter are safe at her parents' home out of state and not interested in communicating with us in any capacity."

Someone must have threatened her. With a young child, I couldn't blame her for running away. At least she sent the files.

"You'll keep an eye on Molly?" Garner said.

"I'll try."

"Yeah, doesn't seem necessary, I know."

"What's going to happen with Christian?"

"I don't know yet. I'm in contact with the detective. So far there's no physical evidence against him."

"Of course not. When will he be released?"

"Unless something comes up, tomorrow some time."

"And then what? Can he go back to his mom's house?"

"He can, but I have no idea what's going through his head right now."

"Probably a lot." The man who killed Helen and Caroline was dead. His ex-wife and kids were safe, which should absolve Christian of his misplaced responsibility for them. But maybe there was more to it. Maybe he wasn't prepared for this last link to be severed. It might sound like psychobabble, but I understood like few others. With my thumb, I spun the plain gold wedding band still on my ring finger. Holding on is what we do, because once we stop, they're well and truly gone.

Aunt Irm emerged from the bathroom and went to check on our neighbor.

"I haven't heard from Nathan lately," I said to Garner. "Do you know what's going on with the Kadence software?"

"Samuels gave them access, believe it or not."

"That's good at least. Hopefully they're making progress."

"I'll let you know if I hear anything about Christian."

Aunt Irm and Mrs. O'Donnell stood in the doorway connecting our rooms. Both women wore old-lady cotton nightgowns printed with tiny flowers and rimmed in a small amount of lace. Aunt Irm's I was used to, but someone as sophisticated and wealthy as Molly O'Donnell wore the same? Note to self, find somewhere else to buy nightwear in fifty years.

I invited the women to take the two chairs around the small table by the window. From the fifth floor, lights of downtown Jacksonville sparkled, while headlights and taillights passed on the interstate. People living their lives, one day flowing into the next. I missed that—the gradual passage of unhurried, uneventful time. Instead, we sat in a hotel room and I told two elderly women that someone they loved had been manipulated into becoming a murder suspect.

"Someone has caused this?" Aunt Irm said when I finished. "They have set up our Christian?"

"It looks that way," I said.

She tapped her chin in thought. "The man attacking my Kadence will gain from trouble for Christian." She'd gone straight there, no energy wasted on other possibilities. Not even on Adam, whom she despised even more than bad drivers and sinners.

"Lieutenant Garner and I both agree with you, Aunt Irm."

Mrs. O'Donnell stared straight ahead, silent, stoic.

"We must stop him," Aunt Irm said. "We must watch Dr. Yarborough."

"Why do you say that?"

"She claims to have been threatened by him." Her word choice made obvious what she thought of the threat. "Either he will go after her, or she is part of it. Watching her will help, whichever is true."

I stared at her. "You are brilliant." I kissed her cheeks, then called Garner back, but midway through my recitation, I knew what his answer would be.

"Although it's a great idea, unless she requests our protection or we have sufficient evidence for a warrant, we can't watch her. It's an invasion of privacy."

Aunt Irm waited to voice her frustration until we'd disconnected. She continued to grumble even after we'd switched off the lights.

Both of us suffered disturbed dreams, and it sounded like Mrs. O'Donnell did as well. By morning, I felt not at all refreshed for a Saturday that would be anything but relaxing. The women made coffee in our room while I went for a run in the early morning fog, grateful to Aunt Irm for her packing consideration. I couldn't remember my last run without Shadow. He was home in the care of a neighbor kid who adored him. Though it wouldn't be enough exercise, it would suffice for a day. I, on the other hand, would go stir crazy without a run this morning.

Before leaving, I checked the local headlines. There was nothing new about the murder. I mapped the location on my phone and ran in that direction. It was less than two miles from the hotel down a busy road. I opted for side streets and a less direct route that left me a block south of my destination. A cemetery lay in between. I'm ashamed to say the convenience of being murdered near a cemetery occurred to me. I forced the thought from my mind.

The entry gate read, "Our Lady of Mercy Catholic Cemetery." I wasn't aware Catholic cemeteries were a thing. Then I remembered the exchange between Christian and his mother the night before, regarding his walk. Could he have visited this cemetery? Near the entrance, a sign provided a code for my cellphone that opened a directory. Helen and Caroline O'Donnell were there. After a quick check of the map, I paused my running music and walked across the cemetery to their plot on the far side.

Christian's wife and daughter shared a beautiful granite gravestone with Helen's name carved in relief on the right half and Caroline's centered below. The left half remained glaringly empty, waiting for Christian. I had wanted to do the same for Greg and Emily. To switch out her small headstone for a family one, but Aunt Irm refused to allow it, and I was too emotionally spent after Greg's death to argue. She considered it too morbid. As I stood looking at the blank space waiting to be filled, I knew she was right.

On the ground before the headstone was a small bouquet of red roses. Not fresh but less than twenty-four hours old. Unfortunately, I had experience with such things.

Christian's walk the night before had been to visit his family's grave. I checked the map on my phone. The murder occurred on the other side of a stand of trees, not more than a hundred yards away.

The flowers suddenly felt wrong, an accusation against Christian. I glanced around at the surrounding gravestones, most without adornment, and considered a simple donation of the flowers. Pros and cons warred within me. Each time the pros won out, my limbs wouldn't cooperate.

My phone rang. I clicked to answer on my headphones and stepped away from temptation, headed for the exit and the site of the murder.

"Kate?"

"Hey, Garner."

"He'll be released in an hour."

"Thank God."

"Is his mother with you?"

"No. She's at the hotel. I'm on a run."

There was a long pause. "Either you need to run faster or you're in incredible shape."

"Yeah, I took a break." I turned right after exiting the cemetery and saw yellow crime scene tape twenty yards ahead. A car had pulled off the road, partially blocking the sidewalk.

"Kate. Dammit." The car door opened and Garner stepped out. His look of disapproval was almost comical.

"I feel for your future kids," I said. "With that look, they'll put themselves in time-out."

He disconnected our call and raised his voice. "What are you doing here, Kate?"

"Did you know Christian's family is buried on the other side of those trees?" I pointed.

"I do. You didn't answer my question."

"Did you know flowers were left there yesterday some time?"

His lips formed a grim line, which morphed into a silent swear word.

"I could move them . . ."

"No." He looked through the trees toward the gravesite. I wondered if he was considering moving them himself, or maybe hoping his laser vision could incinerate the evidence. "I'll pick him up and bring him to the hotel."

"Can I ride along?"

He screwed up his nose.

"I don't smell that bad."

He moved a little closer, breathing deeply through his nose. "We'll keep the windows down."

CHAPTER THIRTY-FOUR

GARNER PARKED AT the Jacksonville police station. "You should probably wait in the car."

"Because I forgot my suit and badge?"

"Something like that."

Granted, I was under-dressed for pretty much anything other than a gym, but what did one wear to the release of a prime murder suspect? While Garner took the steps to the brownstone building two at a time, I called Aunt Irm and let her know I'd be back soon, with company.

"We are just finishing breakfast. Shall I order you something?"

"I don't know how long this will take."

Climbing out of the car, it felt good to stretch. Too much sitting too soon after running, even if the run had been cut short. I called Nathan. Ian had installed the correct software in a Kadence that was not Aunt Irm's. He said that part several times. They were testing it now.

"Is he letting you observe?" I asked.

"He hasn't tried to kick me out."

"I appreciate it, Nathan." Another person I would never be able to adequately thank. I asked him to keep Annabelle Kessler updated as well, since Nikki had a lot on her mind. He agreed. I could only hope his knowledge and experience was sufficient to identify any major lapses in Ian's testing procedures. Maybe just the threat of detection would suffice.

Leaning against the car, I tried not to stare too intently at the building's entrance. Each time someone appeared at the top of the steps, my heart gave a little extra thump. By the time Christian emerged from the station, my heart had run another mile. Who knew police stations were such busy places? Police officers, obviously.

With his wrinkled shirt, disheveled hair, and bruised face, Christian looked beat in every sense of the word. His eyes found mine in the parking lot and he smiled. Not a big smile, but enough. We embraced.

"You okay?" I asked, stupidly.

"Yeah. After a shower I'll be good as new."

"New from the bruised and battered shelf," Garner said as he climbed into the driver's seat. "Does that mean you're deeply discounted?"

"Nope, one of a kind." Christian opened the car door.

"Thank God for that," Garner said.

I declined the front seat, so Christian and Garner could strategize. As I listened, I texted Aunt Irm to expect our arrival. Christian had been questioned on and off for most of the night, mostly off, and sat in an interrogation room alone and bored.

"Do you cops special order the most uncomfortable chairs on the market?" Christian asked.

Garner chuckled. "One of our many secret weapons. Did it break you?"

"Maybe if I'd been guilty. Or is that part optional?"

Garner stopped laughing.

Christian apologized.

"No problem," Garner said. "You're sleep-deprived."

Back at the hotel, Christian earned a number of stares as the three of us made our way through the lobby to the elevator bay. He was going to have a time resuming his lawyer duties. If only I knew something about makeup.

We stopped at his mother's room, where her stiff demeanor cracked ever so slightly as she fell into his arms. Then he and Garner went upstairs to finish their conversation and let Christian clean up.

In the meantime, I showered and we waited together in Mrs. O'Donnell's room. The women sat, murmuring softly, while I paced. I trusted Christian. He couldn't kill anyone. Still, a tiny part of me questioned his proximity to the crime scene near the key moment. I ignored that part. Wrong place, wrong time, that's all it was. God, I hoped that's all it was.

A man from Room Service delivered three trays with covered plates. He placed them on the small table and left with a tip from Mrs. O'Donnell. Actual cash. Our nearly cashless society must be hard on hotel staff dependent on tips. They must prefer to serve older patrons who still carry purses and cash.

Christian arrived, looking somewhat better in clean clothes, with his hair still damp from the shower. He'd shaved, making the bruise around his eye appear darker and more swollen.

While we ate—pancakes, bacon, and hash browns for Christian and Garner, an omelet for me—Christian caught us up on his night. They'd repeatedly questioned him about his whereabouts between his discharge from the hospital and the time of the murder, and were repeatedly dissatisfied with his answers.

"Can they not track your phone to prove where you went?" Aunt Irm asked. "If you agree, perhaps Lieutenant Garner need not seek the very impossible warrant. I am told it works even if you turn the phone off."

I nearly choked on my omelet. She was told by TV cops on *NCIS*.

"I didn't have my phone with me," Christian said.

That part of me I was ignoring might have found his actions a tad suspicious, if I were paying attention.

We ate quickly, then Garner gave Christian strict instructions to keep his phone on him and to answer immediately if Garner called or texted. He had work to do.

Aunt Irm and I returned to our room to finish packing. I called Randi; she was napping. Her husband assured me mom and baby were well. I called our neighbor to check on Shadow and promised to be home by the afternoon. My phone beeped an incoming call as I was disconnecting, and I switched to it.

"Kate? It's Nikki."

"Everything okay?"

"It's good. Annabelle and I have contacted all the patients. I'm still worried something will happen to them while I can't monitor so I hope this will be over soon. Ian says they're making progress."

"That's great news. How about you? Are you safe?"

Aunt Irm stopped folding her nightie to stare at me.

"We are. Thank you. Listen, I need to see you. I can't talk about this over the phone."

"Sure, of course. I'm just leaving Jacksonville. I'll go by your house as soon as I drop off Aunt Irm."

"Actually, we're staying on Lake Santa Fe. Ian decided the house wasn't safe."

"Safe from whom, Nikki? Who is doing this?"

Aunt Irm's stare intensified.

"When you get here." She gave me an address and I promised to be there as soon as I could.

Mrs. O'Donnell overheard from the adjoining doorway and offered to give Aunt Irm a ride. "I was going to ask if you both might be willing to stay at the house with me. Michael has disappeared and if Christian has to leave again, I could use the company."

"Of course, we will," Aunt Irm said. "Kate will take Christian with her to meet Dr. Yarborough, then they will pick up Shadow and we will stay with you."

Good to be informed of my plans. It wasn't a bad plan, though Nikki might be less forthcoming with Christian there. Also, neither Aunt Irm nor Mrs. O'Donnell liked driving on the interstate. "How about Christian and I drive you two to Waldo, and you take it from there while we go visit Nikki?"

Aunt Irm nodded. "This will work. The drive is not so far from there and not on very fast roads."

"Thank you for agreeing to disrupt your life for me." Mrs. O'Donnell's eyes glistened.

Though unsure whether a hug was appropriate, I gave her one anyway.

Christian appeared then, just ending a phone call. His mother informed him of the plan and he agreed, though it wasn't clear he really thought about it. He seemed distracted, and rightfully so. He and I carried the luggage to the cars while his mother and Aunt Irm checked out at reception. Both still preferred to hand in a key and receive an itemized receipt.

As soon as we exited the lobby, Christian said, "Do you know what Nikki wants to talk about?"

"No, but at this point, I'll take any information I can get."

"Agreed."

At my car, I loaded the bag Aunt Irm and I shared in the trunk. Christian put down his own luggage, slid his hands in his front jeans pockets, and bounced on his toes like a nervous adolescent. It was sort of adorable. "I owe you an apology. The way we left things the other night, it was so . . . and then I just . . . left."

"You did what you had to do."

He touched his bruised face. "Not very well."

Even his pained smile was endearing, but one thing still bothered me. "Why didn't you call from the Emergency Room?"

"I didn't have my phone." He looked away then back again. "Garner's is the only number I have memorized, besides Mom."

Made sense. Come to think of it, I couldn't recite his number, either. "Did you leave it behind on purpose?"

"I did. A little something I picked up from my friendly neighborhood detective." The corners of his mouth turned up. "For all the good it did me."

"Complicates the whole alibi thing. The flowers might be a problem."

He cocked his head to the right. "Flowers?"

"At Helen's grave."

"I didn't leave any flowers."

"The red roses." Had the concussion been more serious than recognized?

His look darkened. "I've never left red roses for her, always white, and lilies for Caroline. Are you sure it was her grave?"

I called Garner and put it on speaker. "Christian didn't leave the flowers."

"Are you sure?"

"Of course, I'm sure," Christian said. "Who would leave red roses at my wife's grave?" He sounded more dubious than angry.

"The detective is picking them up for prints," Garner said.

"How about video in the cemetery?" I said.

"I'm checking. Meanwhile you guys need to get out of there before the press shows up."

"We're leaving now," I said.

We stood awkwardly for a moment, then he moved closer so we were very nearly touching. "I'm sorry I couldn't keep you updated."

"It's okay." I wrapped my arms around him and pressed my cheek to his chest until a car pulled in and parked nearby. We stepped apart. "Are you sure you're okay to drive?" One-eyed and exhausted, he might be more dangerous than Aunt Irm and his mom.

"With Mom as co-pilot, we'll be fine."

CHAPTER THIRTY-FIVE

WITH A LITTLE help from Google Maps, I found I10 West and we left Jacksonville behind.

"Who gains from trouble for Christian?" Aunt Irm asked.

Adam came to mind; I ignored it. "Whoever doesn't want MDI sold will benefit from the delay."

She made a call and put it on speaker. "Christian, this is Aunt Irm. Kate and I wish to know what happened to the person for whom you had to finish this sale."

"He was injured in a car accident."

"We think, perhaps, it was not an accident."

"He was driving drunk and plowed into a tree." Seconds later he caught up to Aunt Irm. "You think someone was trying to interfere with the sale even then."

"It fits like a mitten."

"Glove," Christian and I said in unison.

Aunt Irm looked at her hand. "Yes, better."

"Garner and I talked about it yesterday," I said. "He's going to look into it."

"Huh, I should have thought of that." He sounded a little impressed, which made Aunt Irm sit up taller.

"This is why we are a good team," she said.

Soon after we ended the call, I turned south on US 301 and reached tiny Waldo, Florida, forty minutes later. In a fast-food restaurant's parking lot, we switched passengers. Mrs. O'Donnell drove Christian's car, and I followed Aunt Irm to the passenger side of his SUV.

"You both be careful," she said.

"I promise."

"And do not forget food for Shadow."

I promised again and closed her door.

Christian joined me in my car, and I followed the GPS directions, crossing over railroad tracks, then turning left toward Lake Santa Fe and eventually to a lakefront lot with a sun-bleached For Sale by Owner sign and a phone number too faded to read. Unlike the cozy lived-in wood cabin in north Georgia, this double-wide trailer had suffered in the relentless Florida heat. Ian's SUV was nowhere to be seen.

I tried to text Nikki our arrival, but had no cell service. A common theme with her lately.

A formerly bright blue tarp covered the flat roof. The yard was sand and tree roots and weeds covered with dead leaves that crunched underfoot as we approached the door. She answered my knock and pulled me into a hug. "Thank you for coming."

"I'm glad you're safe."

Her eyes widened at the sight of Christian. "Oh my goodness, what happened to you?"

"A misunderstanding," he said.

She invited us inside the well-worn trailer. "Can I get you something to drink? We have water and coffee." We declined and joined her at the scarred Formica table. "Ian and I looked at this property a year or so ago. We wanted to build a cabin like the one up north, but the county is a permitting nightmare." Ice clinked in her glass as she took a sip.

"Where's Ian?" I asked.

"He's at MDI fixing the Kadence." She adjusted her position on the hard chair and eyed Christian.

"I can wait outside if you would feel more comfortable," he said.

"No, it's fine. She's going to tell you everything I say anyway." Her smile was meager. "Ian lied to me. To both of us. He's part of the attacks."

I forced my expression to remain impassive. "In what way?"

"To begin with, he let the software through without completing all the penetration tests. By the time Dale Bennett sent him the final version, there wasn't time, so he only tested the previous access codes."

Convenient.

"When the sale came up, Bennett convinced him MDI wouldn't protect his job. I knew Ian was angry about something, but he wouldn't tell me what. Then he suddenly had a new job opportunity out of state, but I couldn't leave with our department such a mess."

"Was the job with Dale Bennett?" I asked.

She nodded, frowning. "He was manipulating Ian. He said he was starting a new company to develop other medical devices and invited Ian to join him. But first, he had to help get the rights to Bennett's patent back."

Pretty much what we had guessed—Dale Bennett drove the whole thing, but I didn't buy Ian as the unwitting accomplice.

"Ian stole my Epic login," she said. A login to our medical records system is sacrosanct. The passwords have ridiculous requirements and have to be changed at regular intervals. "He used it to identify my patients with a Kadence and gave that information to Bennett." Her voice cracked as tears rolled down her cheeks. "I can't believe he'd do such a thing. He betrayed my trust and Mr. McCann died and . . ." She covered her face with her hands and sobbed.

I put a hand on her back but had no words of comfort. Christian looked as helpless as I felt. Eventually, she wiped her face and said, "I'm sorry. I just feel somehow responsible."

"It's not your fault, Nikki." I stood and refilled her water. When I returned, she'd calmed considerably. "I'm sorry you're going through this, but I have to ask—how did they choose the victims?"

"Ian claims they chose people they knew could be resuscitated, like Mr. Abrams having scheduled surgery, and the governor in front of a bunch of doctors, and the MDI employee in the cafeteria where they have an AED." She looked up at me. "And your aunt right there at the clinic."

"Generous of him to want his victims resuscitated," I said with maybe too much sarcasm.

Nikki grimaced.

"Why did he choose her?"

"He didn't know you were related. He never met Irm. He felt so awful about it, he told Bennett he was done."

"Was he at the clinic when it fired?"

Her eyebrows came together.

"There was someone there, in a baseball cap," I said. "He walked away and I didn't get a good look. Was it Ian?"

She shrugged. "I don't know. Maybe. Maybe he wanted to make sure she would be okay." Nikki gave him way too much credit.

"Then he should have done it before she walked outside."

Irony of ironies, having Aunt Irm scheduled for an appointment with Nikki caused her to be targeted. Best-laid plans . . .

"What about the last victim, the driver?" I asked.

"Ian didn't trigger him. We'd already left town. Mr. McCann wasn't supposed to be shocked until the next day when he had a doctor's appointment. When Ian refused to be part of the attacks anymore, Bennett got angry and triggered the next patient early."

I wondered if either man had considered the possibility of the carnage that followed.

"How do they trigger the device?" I asked.

"It's Bluetooth, like you said. Ian showed me an app on his mobile. They contact the patient's phone and use its connection to the Kadence. I can't believe this was happening right under my nose and I didn't suspect a thing."

"You'd moved out by the time they started," I reminded her.

"You're right. What if that's what made Ian do it? What if me leaving him is why he started targeting my patients?"

"They were blackmailing both Dr. Cantwell and Mr. Samuels at MDI," I said. "Besides money, they demanded the company not be sold. This is about money and control, not your marriage."

She nodded. Hopeful if not convinced.

"What about the threat against you?" I asked.

"That was all Dale Bennett. He was angry the blackmail hadn't worked. Ian said threatening family members was never part of the plan." She was thoughtful a moment. "Huh, Ian must have told him Dr. Cantwell is my dad." She seemed neither surprised nor angry, just strangely intrigued.

"Does Ian know where Bennett is now? What he's doing? Have they been in contact?"

Her eyes rounded. "No, we're hiding from him."

"The police need a way to find him." Tracing his emails to Cantwell and Samuels had led nowhere. "Ian must have his number."

She nodded. "I'll ask when he comes home."

I checked my phone. Still no bars. "Does your phone have signal out here?"

"No, you have to head back toward town. I called my patients from the parking lot of the barbecue place in Waldo."

I would call Ian myself after we left. "How about Cantwell? Does he know you're here?"

She shook her head. "No one knows about this place. We came with a realtor like eighteen months ago. It's been on the market for years."

They were squatting. Maybe safe enough. "Has Bennett contacted Cantwell again?"

"I don't know. He told me not to worry." She gave a wistful smile—her lifelong dream of a father, finally fulfilled. "He said he would take care of everything. He wanted us to stay away, but I had to come back."

"He didn't know about Ian's involvement, though," I said. He'd sent his daughter away with the very man triggering his device.

"Ian's not involved anymore." It seemed unlike Nikki to be so trusting and forgiving. "He didn't know anyone would get hurt. He was angry that MDI wasn't going to protect him in the sale." She looked at Christian. "Is that true?"

"Not really," Christian said. "MDI couldn't protect anyone. A year was all the buyer offered."

Nikki frowned. "Well, Bennett's the villain here, not Ian."

That remained to be seen.

"So they haven't found Dale Bennett?" Nikki asked.

"How well do you know him?" I asked her.

"We wrote that one paper together, mostly by emailing edits back and forth. I've met him only a few times."

"Would Ian have any idea where he might go?"

She shook her head. "I can ask, but I doubt it . . . wait, what am I saying? I obviously don't know anything about my husband. They could be best friends, fishing buddies." She blinked several times, fighting back tears.

"If Ian helps the police, it will go better for him." That was a guess, based on television and movies, and logic. I looked to Christian to back me up.

"I know a detective working on the case, Lieutenant Garner," he said. "He's a good guy. Can I have him come by to talk to you and Ian?"

She thought for a long moment, too long, but finally nodded. "I don't know when he'll make it back—but sure, we need this to end."

Christian and I stood. "I really am sorry you're going through all this," I said.

She joined us, her hand on her round belly. "This will make quite the story for her baby book."

I smiled. "A girl?"

She nodded.

"Anything else we can do? Grocery store run?"

"I'm fine, Kate. I'm safe here and my patients are safe. That's enough for now."

And yet I was not the least bit reassured.

CHAPTER THIRTY-SIX

Driving back toward Waldo, Christian and I rehashed Ian's role and how much faith to put in his claims. When we finally had a cell signal, I called Ian and left a message. Christian called Garner. It, too, went to voicemail. "Hey, Garner, it's Christian. Call me back. We have news."

"Hopefully he's busy reviewing video from the cemetery that proves your innocence."

"I can't get past the roses. Who would leave red roses at my wife's grave?"

"Her family maybe?" Still, an odd choice, red implied the passionate kind of love—not that of a parent or sibling. Weird.

He shook his head.

"I suppose a mistake is far-fetched, that someone left them on the wrong grave."

"Nice try," he said with a grim half-smile. Outside, country turned to outskirts and then to city. "I wonder if they leave flowers often." He turned toward me. "Since I moved to south Florida, I don't visit their graves often. Only when I'm in Jacksonville for work."

I waited, ignoring the easy answers on the tip of my tongue. The answers Nikki and others gave when I said the same about Greg's grave. Except I didn't have the proximity excuse.

"I tell myself she wouldn't mind. That she wouldn't want me to spend money on flowers she couldn't enjoy, or to spend time at the cemetery when she isn't there. It still feels wrong. Like I'm letting them down somehow."

I reached for his hand. "Yeah, I know."

Several moments passed, then he said, "I need to update my client about all this. Do you mind?"

I released his hand and focused on driving, though I couldn't help hearing his side of the conversation. He told the client—whose identity I still didn't know—about the intentional misfires. "This person is blackmailing Dr. Cantwell and Edward Samuels and threatening their families." After a pause, Christian continued, "They're demanding money but also for the sale to be canceled. We think it might all come down to the patent on bidirectional communication." Another pause. "There are options. One would be to withdraw the offer until things are resolved."

Please take that option. If this was really about Dale Bennett getting his patent back, then ending the sale could solve everything. Well, other than Dale Bennett ending up in prison, and possibly Ian, too. Not much of an exit strategy.

"We could renegotiate once things are resolved, likely for a lower price." As he listened, Christian scanned the horizon, his eyes in constant motion as the world flew past at forty-five miles an hour. The conversation continued for several more minutes. Christian disconnected and let out a long, frustrated breath. "God, I hate my job sometimes."

I waited.

"I don't know why it still surprises me." He pressed back against the headrest. "It's all about money for them. He wasn't appalled. He didn't ask about the patients. All he wants to do is find a way to reduce the offer."

"That's cold."

"Iceberg." He thought a minute. "No, icebergs have depth."

"How about dry ice? It's colder and barely solid."

"Perfect." He took my hand. "Camden Health, by the way, that's who's buying MDI."

I'd never heard of them.

"They're a group of investors that acquire medical tech startups all over the country. Their model is to install one of their own as CEO, monitor the employees for a year, then keep on a few with the skills they need, and let everyone else go."

"Seems harsh."

"They're doing well by their investors, which is their only metric. They went after MDI because they want to break into the implantable device market."

A new thought struck me. "Is there any chance the buyer could be behind this? If it gives them a better deal and they're that cold?"

He stared out the window for several seconds. "It's a good thought, but they're just businessmen. They hire firms like ours to vet the company and we hire engineering consultants."

"Could Camden go around you and make a separate deal with the consultants?"

"Anything's possible, but we've worked with these consultants before and they have an excellent reputation."

"Does Garner know who the buyer is?"

"Samuels told him, so I'm sure he's looking into them."

"What about using the press to scare them off?" Aunt Irm had threatened that already. I was a little surprised she hadn't followed through.

He chuckled. "Have a reporter on speed dial, do you?"

"Not me, but surely you have a fraternity brother who runs a television network." Christian always had friends in the most surprisingly useful places.

"Not that I know of. Let's wait on that for now."

"Are you saying that because of your lawyerly duty to your client?"

"The one whose nondisclosure I just violated by disclosing their name to you?"

"Yep, that one."

He gave a half-hearted shrug, clearly torn.

"We wouldn't have to mention Camden Health by name." The conversation ended as I pulled into my garage. Shadow greeted us with all the energy of a fully loaded freight train. Christian offered to take him for a short walk while I packed. With Aunt Irm's texted list, I gathered a few things for each of us, as well as dog food. Garner called while I was loading the car. "Is Christian with you?"

"Yes. We stopped at the house to pick up Shadow. What's up?"

"I'm sending you the link to the video from the cemetery. Can you watch it now, with him?"

"Sure, as soon as he gets back from walking the dog." I took my laptop bag back inside. "Meanwhile, we have news."

"Figures. Do I want to hear it?"

I ignored him. "Nikki and Ian are staying at a trailer on Lake Santa Fe. He admitted to her that he's played a significant role in all of this. Not only did he let the software through without proper testing, he stole Nikki's access to the electronic medical records system to identify Kadence patients. He and Dale Bennett used that information to choose their targets. Ian triggered the device for the first three by remotely accessing their cellphones. Nikki thinks she can convince him to talk to you."

"So you didn't talk to him directly?"

"No, he was still at MDI with Nathan." I gave him the trailer's address. Then came the hard part. "I did say that if he cooperated, things might go better for him. I hope that wasn't wrong."

I felt more than heard his groan. "It's not wrong. It's not for you to say, but it's not wrong."

"Yeah, but I had to convince her."

"I get it. I'm on my way back from Jacksonville so I'll stop there on the way, then meet you at the O'Donnells'"

I didn't ask him to go easy on the Yarboroughs, though it nearly cost me my tongue to keep quiet.

"Have you received the link yet?"

I checked my laptop screen. "Clicking on it now."

"Call me back after you watch it."

In the comments, Garner directed us to watch the beginning, then to skip ahead to thirty-two minutes.

Christian returned. Shadow noisily lapped from his water bowl, probably relieved to finally have an empty bladder. Poor dog.

"Garner sent the video from the cemetery."

Christian stood beside me at the kitchen counter as I clicked *Play*. The black-and-white image showed a path and several head-stones lighter or darker than the surroundings. Only the movement of leaves suggested video rather than a still photo.

Christian pointed at a grave on the far left. "That's Helen and Caroline's."

There were no flowers.

A figure walked in from the left. I recognized Christian immediately. He stood before the graves. Feeling like a voyeur invading his private grief, I was about to hit fast-forward when something moved on the far left, in the trees, only visible for an instant. I paused the video, rewound, and replayed. "It looks like there's someone in the trees." I pointed, but it was too far away and the lighting too poor amongst the branches.

"Good eyes. Maybe Garner can get it enhanced." He noted the time stamp and sent a text.

I tapped *Fast Forward* and on-screen-Christian's head moved side to side repeatedly. At one point, his head jerked to the left. I rewound and played it again at normal speed.

He leaned toward the laptop. "There was a sound. I forgot about that."

"Like a gunshot?" How would he forget about that?

"No—or I didn't think so. I don't know. I had my earbuds in."

"Really?" It seemed somehow odd at a cemetery.

His cheeks reddened. "I always listen to the same song when I visit their graves, 'Find Your Wings' by Mark Harris. It was Helen's favorite. About giving your child roots so they can fly." He cleared his throat. "She would turn it up loud and dance with Caroline. Sometimes I joined them, not often enough." My heart broke for the sadness in his voice.

"I'm so sorry, Christian."

He leaned forward against the counter. "It was a long time ago. The song has become a tradition, or a habit. Anyway, even over the music, I heard something." He texted Garner again, then nodded to the screen and I hit *Play*.

The Christian on-screen remained at the gravesite another minute, touched the headstone, and walked to the left, off the screen. Still no roses at the grave.

Had he heard the shot that killed Johnny Barillo? If so, this cleared him.

The video continued with nothing happening. I slid the scroll bar to thirty-two minutes. A man approached from the top of the screen. Christian made a strangled sound. He stared wide-eyed as the man placed a small clutch of gray flowers on the base of the headstone, then knelt, his shoulders shaking with grief. Leaning forward, he placed his hands and forehead against the headstone and stayed there for some time.

Beside me, Christian's breathing became heavy and loud. He swallowed, then whispered, "Michael."

Michael who? Christian's brother? The man stood and walked slowly, to the right this time. The clip ended.

"It's Michael," Christian said, more strongly. With his elbows on the counter, he put his face in his hands. "How did I not see it?"

I dialed Garner and handed the phone to Christian. He put it on speaker and said, "It's Michael."

"Yeah," Garner said. "Did you know?"

"No."

"Me neither. They're sending security footage from businesses surrounding the cemetery."

The unbruised half of Christian's face was pale, the muscles around his eye tight, as if trying to make out words blurry in the dark.

"I'm sorry, Christian," Garner said.

"Yeah. Talk soon." The words sounded distracted, robotic.

I disconnected the call, closed my laptop, and waited for a signal from Christian. He took several aimless steps around the kitchen. "I never knew. How could I not know my brother was in love with my wife?"

I went to him, wrapped my arms around his waist, and rested my head on his chest. We stood there, leaning on each other, silent in our thoughts. Mine drifted to the one visit Michael made to our house. He came to warn me away from Christian. He told me Christian had caused the deaths of his wife and daughter. That he'd nearly lost his own life out of grief and regret. Michael claimed to be protecting his brother from another breakdown.

When I learned he'd lied about their deaths, that it wasn't Christian's fault, I wondered only vaguely why, chalking it up to an effort to subvert an investigation that would eventually implicate him. The sad truth was, he may have believed his own story. Michael suffered the intense jealousy of loving his brother's wife, with a subsequent grief he couldn't share.

Shadow pressed his snout between us, wanting in on the affection. Christian released me. "Shadow's right, we'd better go."

Nathan called as I set the alarm. "We're done. We can update the software. I talked to Annabelle Kessler. She's going to get your aunt in first thing Monday morning."

"Thanks, Nathan. You're a rock star."

Christian said little on the drive, and I didn't interrupt his rumination. He had much to assimilate, including what to tell his mother. Traffic was light across the prairie, bathed in gold and red as the sun set. We reached the long tree-lined drive in record time. Shadow's tail thumped against the door as he recognized "Tara," as Christian called his parents' home.

"I'd let you out here if I could trust you not to play chicken with the car," I told Shadow. He pressed his nose against my cheek and I petted his muzzle. "What have you decided to tell your mom?" I asked Christian.

"Nothing for now. She might be relieved to know Michael's alive, but not collapsing at Helen's grave."

The image had been heartbreaking.

Christian opened the back door for Shadow's escape even before I switched off the ignition. While he reached into the trunk for our bags, I watched Shadow run around the house in search of Riley.

We climbed the stairs and Christian let his dog out to join Shadow. In the kitchen, Molly O'Donnell and Aunt Irm carried platters of food to the table set for four.

"You can tell us about Dr. Yarborough while we eat," Aunt Irm said as I kissed her cheek.

Perfect. We could focus on Nikki rather than Michael.

After passing around plates of chicken, potatoes, and green beans, I told them about our conversation with Nikki, and Ian's betrayal of her trust.

"This does not sound right. Can you not tell if someone uses your medical computer system?" Aunt Irm asked.

"I don't think so. Why do you ask?"

"Dr. Yarborough is smart." Aunt Irm tapped to her temple, apparently where smarts reside. "She lived with this evil man. She would have suspected."

"First, I don't think he's actually evil—"

"He killed people," she said, shocked at my generosity, or naivety.

"No, he didn't, at least not intentionally. He'd stopped collaborating with Bennett before the highway accident."

"And the attack on me? Did he stop before that?"

I reached across the table for her hand. "You're right. I stand corrected. He is most definitely evil. He was angry with MDI for selling out and eliminating his job and he let Bennett manipulate him."

"Dale Bennett may be the chief evil person, but Ian Yarborough is his minion and his wife must have known." Her eyes shone wet. "She is my doctor. She is supposed to protect her patients."

Mrs. O'Donnell put an arm around her shoulder. "You are right, Irm. She should have known, even if she didn't." Solidarity, if slightly less an indictment. These women were not to be crossed.

My phone rang. Garner. "Hey, can I put you on speaker?"

He agreed and I placed the phone on the table between the salt shaker and gravy boat.

"Have you heard from Dr. Yarborough since we last talked?"

"No. Why?"

"I'm at the address, an old trailer, but there doesn't seem to be anyone here."

My insides quivered. "That's not right. Something must have happened."

"Okay. I'll call you back," he said, and hung up.

Not there? Had they chickened out of talking to Garner? Had Ian become angry that she'd shared his role with me? A weight hit my stomach. What if Dale Bennett had found them?

CHAPTER THIRTY-SEVEN

CONVERSATION WAS SUBDUED over dinner at the O'Donnells'. We didn't hear back from Garner, and neither he nor Nikki returned my texts. After a half-hearted game of spades won by Aunt Irm and Molly O'Donnell, both women retired for the night. Aunt Irm went to her room just off the kitchen, and Molly O'Donnell toward the front of the house. Though I'd not seen the master bedroom, judging by the rest of the home, it must be grand. Heck, the guest rooms were grander than the master in any place I'd ever lived.

Dad made decent money as an engineer, but not mansion money. Besides, he was a farmer wannabe. Anything extra went into land and passable crops and pretty much whatever Mom wanted. She had to be careful what she admired in an ad or store window, or it was liable to end up under the Christmas tree. Not the original name-brand version, a homemade replica of occasionally dubious quality, but full of love. Dad enlisted our help when we were old enough. Her reaction to that gift was my favorite part of Christmas morning. No matter how wonky it looked, how crooked the hem, how squeaky the hinges, whatever we made was the greatest thing she'd ever seen. And she used it, or wore it, or displayed it, with pride. Every time.

"Quarter for your thoughts," Christian said softly.

I blinked back to the present. "A quarter?"

"I figured with inflation . . ."

"Ah. I was just thinking about my parents for some reason." I couldn't remember what had triggered it. He waited for me to go on. "Another time. Do you want to talk about Michael?"

Christian took my hand and led me to his father's office. Books lined the walls on dark wood shelves. Leather chairs sat before a fireplace. On the small table between them was a lamp that looked like an antique—not that I knew anything about antiques. The room appeared just as I would imagine for a former university president— deep red and hunter green in the rugs and window coverings with a ceiling of rich wood. Though a little dark by modern standards, I could definitely get lost in a book there.

He directed me to a love seat and sat opposite in a dark leather chair, leaning toward me. He seemed unsure where to start.

"Did Michael know about Johnny Barillo's release?" I asked.

He shrugged, as if he didn't see the relevance.

"He was there, Christian. He was at the cemetery where Barillo was shot, and he looked . . ." How to put it? Out of control? Bereft?

"You think he shot Barillo?" Christian shook his head. "No. He couldn't. Michael is weak. I know that sounds mean, but he is. Always has been. He could never pull a trigger even at the shooting range." He stared into space for a moment. "He was in love with my wife for years and said nothing. He was too kind or thoughtful, or weak, to interfere with our marriage. He wouldn't kill Johnny Barillo."

I'd witnessed Michael's grief. Even in grainy black-and-white, the depth of his sorrow was heartbreaking. I wouldn't have imagined Christian in a fistfight before yesterday, though. Maybe Johnny Barillo brought out the worst in people. He'd killed the woman both men loved and then was released from prison early. Where was the justice in that? Was it so hard to believe Michael chose to claim his own justice? He might be stronger than Christian realized. Still, there were alternatives.

"What if Aunt Irm is right, and this whole thing was to disrupt the sale of MDI? Dale Bennett could have sent the texts to you and the Barillos to keep you from finishing the deal. Maybe he shot Barillo and set you up."

Christian mulled the possibility, his eyes brightening briefly, then dulling again. "I suppose it's possible."

I pressed the point. "He's already responsible for several deaths. What's one more?"

Christian's phone vibrated a text. "Garner's on his way." He typed a message back, then stood and walked around the desk to the French doors. He reached behind the curtain framing the doorway, and lights illuminated a small deck and sitting area.

"I'll take Shadow outside so he doesn't wake anyone." I started for his leash, but Christian opened the French doors and both dogs disappeared into the night.

"They'll be okay," he said. We followed onto the patio.

Headlight beams cut through the trees along the driveway and Christian whistled for the dogs. Both appeared, running full speed toward us. We met them on the driveway. Christian gave Riley a gesture and the dog sat. I had to hold Shadow's collar and bent to his ear. "It's okay. No barking. He's a friend."

He behaved—mostly—just a few growls and a lot of pulling until I released him. Once he recognized Garner, he calmed, if calm is pressing his body against Garner's legs, spinning, and whining. All the while Riley observed from beside Christian. I really am a crappy dog trainer.

When Garner barely acknowledged the dog, I knew the news was not good.

We returned to the office. Christian pulled bottled water from the small refrigerator, and Garner drained half of his.

"I'm not sure where to start," he said, his expression grim.

With a hand on the small of my back, Christian directed me to the love seat where we sat side by side. Garner sat across from us.

"It's not good news," he said.

"How about start with the least bad news," I suggested.

"Okay." He seemed to like the idea—or the fact he didn't have to decide. The anticipation might be worse than what he had to say . . . or not. "I asked the detective in Jacksonville to look into your predecessor's accident," he said to Christian. "It wasn't a DUI."

Christian stopped with his water bottle halfway to his mouth.

"The accident did happen as he left a bar, but he had had only one beer, and his blood alcohol level wasn't even a point-oh-three. Forensics got the car back. They're looking at it now." He let that sink in, then turned his attention to me. "According to the warden, there's no evidence your brother-in-law and Johnny Barillo interacted. They were in different wings."

I nodded. Set on Dale Bennett now, I hadn't thought more about Adam.

Garner took a deep breath. "We found Ian. He's dead, Kate. Shot at close range there in the trailer."

Dead? Ian was dead? "Nikki?" I asked.

He shook his head. "She wasn't there."

Ian was dead. Nikki was gone. Bennett had found them. He had Nikki. "Has he contacted Cantwell?" Why else would he take her?

"I sent an officer to Cantwell's home, but he's not there and he's not answering calls."

Dammit. "Of course not, that would be too easy."

"His last cellphone location we can track is the hospital this afternoon."

If he was still the attending in charge at the hospital, Annabelle Kessler would have to be able to reach him. Fellows aren't supposed to make decisions without attending approval. I called her, only noticing the time after I'd dialed. Though it was after ten, she answered on the first ring.

"Annabelle, it's Kate Downey. Is Dr. Cantwell still your attending?"

"Yes, why?"

"When's the last time you saw him?"

"He staffed rounds this morning. Is there a problem?"

"I don't know. Can you try to call him?" He might have her number selectively forwarded to wherever he was.

She called back moments later. "It went straight to voicemail. That's bad, right? He wouldn't turn his phone off when he's on call." She'd answered her own question.

"If he calls you, please give him my number and tell him it's urgent that I speak with him."

"What's wrong? Is it Dr. Yarborough?"

"I don't really know yet." I hated lying.

"I'm scared."

Patients were being attacked, and both of her recent attendings had disappeared. Of course she was scared. "Can you stay at the hospital for the next couple of days? I don't think you're in any danger, but it would be safest."

"Um, yes, sure, if you think I should."

"It would help to have one less person to worry about." Though she wasn't likely to be a target, who knew with this lunatic?

We disconnected. "Cantwell's on call and not answering his phone. What if he received another threat this afternoon? Can you trace his last call?"

"Seriously?" Garner's tone was sharp. I deserved it.

"Sorry."

"The last contact came from the same number that called both Johnny Barillo and his wife," he said. "It originated near Waldo late this afternoon."

"After he took Nikki and killed Ian."

"It looks that way. We'll track it once the signal comes back online."

He drained his water, then pulled his laptop from the bag at his feet and opened it on the table between us. "I have the security tapes from the bank across the street from the murder scene."

Christian's jaw tightened.

Garner angled the laptop so we could see, and with the video queued to Christian's approach to the cemetery, he pressed *Play*. The on-screen Christian walked up the sidewalk on the far side of the four-lane road and turned right into the cemetery where he disappeared from view. His hands were empty.

A moment later, a figure crossed the street toward the cemetery, jaywalking quickly between passing cars. Rather than enter the cemetery, he disappeared into the woods farther up. Near where I knew Christian would be, at his family's grave. "That must be the person we saw on the other video."

"Probably," Garner said.

Another figure followed into the woods.

"Wait, where did he come from?" I'd been so busy watching the first man, I hadn't noticed the second.

"Is that Michael?" Christian asked.

Garner rewound and played the segment several more times. There was no clear view of either man's face. "The second one is Michael," Christian said. "I can tell by the way he walks."

"The first one has to be Barillo," Garner said.

"He was following Christian? And Michael was following him?" I said.

I felt Garner's eyes on me, willing me to understand. And then I did. "Barillo had a gun, didn't he? He was going to shoot Christian." *Oh God.* Nausea welled at the thought. *Christian.*

"I suspect he followed us from the hospital to the hotel and hung around until you came out alone," Garner said to Christian. "Then he waited for an opportunity."

Christian closed his eyes. "Michael was protecting me."

This man who had never been close to his brother, who had rejected his offers of help, who had secretly loved his wife, had, in the end, risked his life to protect him.

"Go on." Christian nodded toward the laptop.

Garner fast-forwarded through several minutes of nothing, then returned to normal speed. A man emerged from the trees farther up the road and ran away from the camera. Christian and Garner were so quiet, I looked up. They stared at one another, a silent exchange, but somehow unbearably tense. Michael—not Christian—had killed Johnny Barillo.

Garner closed the laptop and returned it to his briefcase. "The charges against you should be dropped. The Jacksonville detectives will question the flower vendors in the morning. Meanwhile they're accessing more security video from the area and are searching for Michael's car."

Christian stared, speechless.

"There's one more thing," Garner said, earnest, apologetic. "Barillo's gun hadn't been fired."

Robotically, Christian stood, went to the desk, and opened a drawer. He withdrew a key and walked purposefully to a cabinet on the side wall behind the love seat. Garner followed. I stood but hung back. An onlooker to their silent conversation.

Christian inserted the key, paused a moment, then opened the door. Three rifles stood sentry on the right side, while on the left hung two handguns. Christian reached toward an empty hanger in the middle. Garner put an arm around his shoulder. "I'm sorry, Christian."

Garner waited until Christian had locked the gun cabinet and returned the key before he left, giving me a one-armed hug on his way out the office door.

Christian stood motionless, looking lost. I went to him and wrapped my arms around his waist.

He pulled me close and said, "He took one of Dad's guns. How am I going to tell Mom?"

"Maybe wait until we have more information."

I felt his body shrink in my arms. "I'm not sure I can take any more information tonight."

CHAPTER THIRTY-EIGHT

IN THE MORNING, we attended early Mass together. I watched Molly O'Donnell on the kneeler, hands folded before her, back straight. Her world would soon be rocked again. Did she have any idea?

Afterward, we drove the women back to the O'Donnells'. With apologies, Christian and I declined brunch and left to run errands together. Though less efficient, I decided Christian could use the company after last night's bombshells. Plus, I enjoyed his company.

We stopped first at Randi's house to drop off a gift I'd been carrying around in my trunk for days. Christian's black eye took a little explaining, but they didn't press. "Would you like to hold her?" Randi asked me. I accepted the bundle of blankets with a tiny perfect face peeking out. Beside me, Christian looked on.

I felt strangely detached. No thoughts of what might have been with my own baby, only of what might be happening now, to Nikki and her baby. We stayed a few minutes, then left for the hospital where Christian dropped me off so I could say goodbye to Jolene and her son. She had called and asked to see me.

I found her in her room, sitting in bed in normal street clothes. "You look so good," I said. So much better than the other times I'd seen her. She held out her arms and we embraced.

"Thank you for saving us." She looked lovingly at her baby in the clear plastic bassinet at the bedside. He'd been upgraded from the NICU and so far seemed healthy.

"It was a team effort."

She handed me a smooth wooden cross, too large for a necklace, pocket-size. The rounded edges showed off the grain. "I had it blessed by the priest when he baptized Joey. For your baby someday."

My eyes filled and I thanked her. I didn't trust my voice with much else. She promised to send updates and I departed via the restroom where I wiped my eyes in private.

In the car, Christian was on a call over the vehicle's Bluetooth. He pressed his finger to his lips and mouthed "Buyer." I pulled the door closed as quietly as I could.

"I don't know what's worse for the press to report," the male voice said over the car's speakers, "a bug in the device or that someone was able to hack it." Was the press involved, I wondered?

Christian offered no opinion. It wasn't clear one was requested. My hand drifted into my pocket and explored the smooth cross.

"And this is all over that one patent?" the voice said.

This? What this? Surely, he wasn't referring to the deaths of more than a dozen people.

"Almost certainly. If we eliminate it from the licensing agreement, the sale can move forward. We can make that one patent either non-exclusive, or return it to the university entirely and drop the offering price accordingly."

Christian handed me his open laptop and gestured to the screen, an email from Cantwell dated early that morning. It had already been forwarded to Garner. "Mr. O'Donnell," it read, "Dale Bennett is behind all this. He wants his patent. Take it out of the sale until he releases Nikki."

"That's the technology that caused the misfire problem," the buyer said.

Attacks.

"It is, and it's not incorporated into the current device as approved by the FDA," Christian said, "but it may have value moving forward."

"Figure out that value and we'll drop the offer by twice that. I want this finished." The line disconnected.

"Are all your clients so friendly?" I asked.

He groaned and put the car into drive. "There's no way they'll withdraw the whole offer now that they see blood in the water."

"Why did you mention the potential future value?" I asked.

"Because they're still my client and it's the truth."

"Yeah, sorry." Ethics get murky in business. In everything, really. I gestured to his laptop. "Did Cantwell figure it out or did Bennett contact him again?"

"That email is all I have. Cantwell won't answer my calls, so who knows?" Frustrated, and with good reason. "Let's get some breakfast while I make a few more calls." He drove to a coffee shop with a ridiculously long line at the drive-thru. I went inside to order for both of us.

When I returned, he mouthed a thank you for the coffee and muffin as he concluded his conversation. "Now for Samuels." First, he took a large bite of blueberry muffin and washed it down with coffee. I stayed silent, checking email on my phone and unapologetically eavesdropping.

Mr. Samuels answered on the third ring. It wasn't a friendly greeting.

"Can I stop by to discuss something with you?" Christian asked.

"Is this about the patent?"

Christian winced at the shouted words and lowered the volume with a button on the steering wheel.

"I told Cantwell no," Samuels said. "The buyer won't agree to losing that IP." Though I knew little about business, I knew intellectual property was the lifeblood of tech firms. Patent protection was the only way to ensure they'd recoup development costs before others incorporated the technology in competing products. But people were dying. How could he not see that? Instead, he went on, "What's he thinking? We're hanging on by our short and curlies, and he's stirring the pot."

Grinning, I now recognized a faint British accent.

"We are not renegotiating," he continued. "It took months and we are out of time. The patent is part of the deal."

"I'd still like to talk with you, if you have a few moments."

He grudgingly agreed and gave an address, which I entered into my phone's map.

"Wow, quite the bad personality parade," I said after he disconnected. "Why the rush for Samuels?"

"They were delayed several weeks because of my partner's accident and the need to free me up to take over the sale. Plus, the time it took me to get up to speed."

"Still, is he afraid it won't go through? Could he be hiding something that might complicate the sale?" As if it could get more complicated.

"Now you sound like your aunt. Our accountants went over everything and were satisfied. Same with the engineering firm we consulted."

"Except they missed the whole backdoor hack thing."

"Except for that."

He left a message for the accountant about the patent's individual value, then put his phone on the console.

"What do you think it's worth?" I asked.

"Millions probably, maybe more."

Millions? "Even without FDA approval?"

"Europe and other markets aren't so strict." He picked his phone back up. "One more call. I want to see if Garner's learned any more about Michael."

He hadn't. Nothing on Bennett or Nikki or Cantwell either. Wow, a lot of people were missing. "Kate and I are headed to Ed Samuels' house."

"For what?" Garner's words sounded like an accusation.

"For work." Christian grinned at me. "It has nothing to do with Michael, and Kate's just along for the ride."

"Of course she is."

"One other thing, we were talking about Camden Health, and it occurred to us that all of this might end up in a discounted price for MDI."

"Now you think the buyer's involved?"

"Only if you think so." Christian's crooked grin made me laugh.

"I heard that, Kate. We've ruled out no one, not even Nathan, but don't tell him that."

Moments after the call ended, we reached a massive gate anchored by brownstone columns. A large camera on the left seemed almost threatening. Christian keyed in the code Samuels had provided and the gates swung open.

"1-2-3-4, really?" I said.

His smile was brief, replaced by, "Wow," as we entered the vast grounds of mostly grass with a few stands of trees. Pasture, minus the cows. A paved drive led to a multi-tier fountain in a stone-tiled roundabout before a massive Italian-style villa. Though very different from the O'Donnell mansion, it was no less grand. Theirs was old South with white wood and columns. This was old Italy with natural-looking stone and a terra-cotta roof. Christian parked behind a red Jaguar sports car.

"Have fun," I said.

He left the keys in the ignition. I rolled down the windows to enjoy a slight breeze that smelled of newly mown grass. Christian mounted the steps to enormous front doors. He pressed a doorbell, then looked around as he waited. A moment later, he knocked and then angled his head toward the door as if listening. He tried the door, and it opened. With a quick glance back at me, he disappeared inside.

My phone rang. It was him. I could hear raised voices in the background. "Just in case," he whispered. The voices grew louder, though I couldn't make out the words.

"Samuels, put down the gun." Those words were clear, and in Christian's voice.

A gun. Holy hell.

As I jumped from the car, I texted Garner, including the address and gate code. It took several attempts, my fingers fumbling on the tiny keyboard.

"STAY OUT," he texted back.

"Put down the gun and let's talk about this," Christian said.

I silenced my phone and vaulted up the steps two at a time. The front door swung open at my touch into a two-story foyer of dark tile and plain white walls.

"He's going to kill my daughter." Cantwell's voice was higher than normal, plaintive.

Samuels' was the opposite, low and commanding. "The sale has to go through."

Heart racing, I followed the voices to the right through what was probably called a sitting room, except it had nowhere to sit.

"We can find another buyer," Cantwell pleaded.

"No, we can't." Samuels' voice was hard, final.

It came from a room on the left, with twin dark wood doors, one partially open. Staying out of the line of sight, I approached the doorway with my back to the wall.

"I spoke with the buyer," Christian said evenly. "Returning the patent to the university doesn't have to scuttle the deal. He's willing to negotiate." Through the opening, I could see Christian, hands raised in a placating gesture. Though Samuels had no reason to shoot Christian, my heart pounded in my throat. "I'm waiting on the accountant to help me with the numbers," he added.

"No!" Samuels yelled. "No more accountants. We need to close the deal."

"Ed? What's going on?" Cantwell said. "You and I can keep running things until we find another buyer."

"No, we can't." Samuels sounded as if his teeth were clenched. "We can't make payroll."

That was a surprise, to Christian, too, apparently, and Cantwell.

"Look around," Samuels said. "Eloise insisted we build this house. I did it for her. There were overruns the loan didn't cover. I borrowed from the wrong people. Then she left and took everything but the mortgage. Payments were due." He paused a long time. "I borrowed against the company just until the sale goes through."

"You stole from our company?"

"Borrowed. I'll pay it all back. The sale should have been done weeks ago. If it hadn't been for your firm slowing things down, none of this would have happened." This he'd obviously directed at Christian, who was slowly advancing. I adjusted my angle to keep him in view through the partially open door.

"It's only money," Cantwell said. "It's not worth my daughter's life."

"It is worth my life," Samuels said. "These people like to make examples. I can't risk it. I'm sorry, Victor."

Christian lunged from view. A gun fired. I bent low and slammed the door open, hoping to create a distraction. The door hit something, or someone. Glass shattered. I rolled behind a chair. Another gunshot. Bodies thudded, men grunted, and then there was silence. Horrible, terrifying silence. "Christian?" My only thought was him. He had to be okay.

"I'm fine. You?" He sounded as desperate as I felt.

"Fine." I couldn't breathe, but I was fine. "Where's the gun?"

"I have it. It's safe."

I peered around the chair. Christian stood pointing a gun down at Samuels, on his back on the floor, one hand raised toward Christian.

I said a silent prayer of thanks and looked to my left. "Cantwell's down." He lay motionless on his side. I rushed to him, back in doctor mode. He had a pulse, fast and strong. There was blood, from a head wound. It wasn't a bullet, though. His head had struck a table as he fell, probably dodging the bullet. His eyes opened, glassy and confused.

"Dr. Cantwell, it's Kate Downey."

"He has Nikki." His clarity of mind and voice surprised me. They didn't last.

"Where?"

His eyes drifted closed.

"Victor, open your eyes." The lids fluttered. "How were you supposed to contact Dale Bennett?"

"Phone. Nineteen-eighty-eight..." His eyes closed again. I felt his pulse. Still strong. He surely had a concussion, maybe more. I pulled a blanket from the overturned couch and pressed it against his bleeding scalp. His hair was too short to tie over the wound.

When the paramedics arrived, I slipped Cantwell's phone from his pocket and stepped back. Christian stood nearby, his forehead bleeding again. With gauze and a dressing from the paramedics, I cleaned him up.

They loaded Cantwell onto a gurney and departed for the hospital. Meanwhile, the officers questioned us until Garner arrived. The bullets had been fired by the homeowner with a registered gun. No one had been shot and no charges would be filed against Samuels. Christian and I were free to go.

When Garner pulled us aside, I gave him Cantwell's cellphone, a cheap plastic one. "He said Dale Bennett's contact information is in there."

Garner activated the phone. "I'll have to get it unlocked."

"Try nineteen-eighty-eight," I said.

He looked at me, then tried it. "Hmph." He pressed some buttons. On his own phone, Garner called someone to trace a number he read from Cantwell's screen.

Garner allowed us to read over his shoulder as he scrolled through Cantwell's text messages. The most recent one, presumably from Dale Bennett, had given an ultimatum—back out of the sale by six p.m. or his daughter and grandchild would be killed.

My skin prickled. It was two p.m. "He won't kill her, right? She's his only leverage."

"Desperate men do desperate things," Garner said.

No doubt. The proof was all around us, overturned furniture and blood, and the smell of gunpowder. The odor took me back to the farm and Dad teaching me to shoot soda cans off the fence. Anything my brother did, I wanted to do better. I must have been an insufferable younger sister.

Garner ended a call. "We have a last location." He eyed Christian and me. "I'd rather you with me than showing up."

Worked for us.

CHAPTER THIRTY-NINE

GARNER LED US outside and gave strict orders. "You follow in your car. You stay behind me at all times. You stop when I tell you to. You go only where instructed. And you remain in the vehicle unless I tell you otherwise."

We agreed, of course.

"Wow, bossy," I said as we climbed into Christian's SUV.

"Always has been. I don't see how our accountants missed all the money Samuels took from MDI."

"Maybe he took it after their analysis."

He nodded, thoughtful. We drove fast. Traffic in medium-sized Florida towns is minimal on Sundays. Churchgoers and farmers market shoppers and DIYers on the way to Home Depot, and not much else. We made it across and east of town, back to Waldo and Lake Santa Fe, in half an hour. Half the time it would normally take. Apparently, Bennett hadn't taken Nikki far.

Garner turned right on a dirt road north of the lake and pulled to the side. We stopped behind him, as ordered, and he motioned us out of the car. "This was the last place we have his phone."

"What's out here?" I asked.

"A whole lotta nothing." Garner looked around at the thick pine forest. "Plenty of places to hide."

"Could we use drones?" I'd read of someone finding a lost dog in the woods up north using a drone.

"In Florida, we need a warrant. I'm working on it."

I thought of Bennett, of where he might hide, of who knew him. I checked my phone. "Nathan might have an idea. I need to go back where I have a cell signal."

Garner nodded. We drove less than five minutes, and I had enough bars to make a call. "Nathan, it's Kate and Christian. We need to know more about Dale Bennett."

Christian pulled to the side of the road.

"We're up near Lake Santa Fe looking for him. Didn't you have a party up here with your old lab?" It had been over Christmas break a couple of years before. He'd returned to work with his arm in a cast from some kind of shooting game.

"Yeah, he hosted a laser tag party. It was cool, until I broke my wrist."

"Does he have property up here?"

"He does. We had a cookout there before the game."

My skin tingled. "Can you tell me where, Nathan? It's important."

"Hang on, I'm texting Jacob, he drove." Moments later, he read the address, a number on a State Road.

"What do you remember about the place?" Christian asked.

"It wasn't much, just a trailer. He only went out there to hunt and fish. He showed us plans for the house he wanted to build, with a theater and gym. He said he would start construction as soon as the Kadence started selling." He paused a moment. "Wait. Why are you looking for him? You think he's the one who hacked it?"

"We do, and he also took Nikki Yarborough hostage and killed her husband."

Silence.

"No way. I can't believe he'd do any of that."

"Since he can no longer attack patients, he needed another way to blackmail Cantwell," I said.

"Blackmail I can believe. He posted some pretty angry stuff on our group chat when they cut us out of the royalties. But then he was starting his own company to make other devices and...wait, he can't do that, can he? If the sale goes through. That would definitely piss him off, but enough to kill someone? Accidentally maybe, but I don't see it."

I wanted to tell him people can surprise us, but not in front of Christian. Not then.

"How about the property itself?" Christian said. "Can you describe it?"

"You mean like if he's hiding out there?" Nathan paused. "Besides the trailer there was a little boathouse by the swamp. He could drop in his fishing boat and go south toward the lake. Some of the guys went down there and saw a couple alligators. They threw them leftover hamburgers if you can believe it. I stayed up near the trailer."

Garner tapped on my window; I rolled it down. "Lieutenant Garner's here." I gestured to my phone. "Nathan is telling us about some property Bennett has nearby." Christian passed a note across to Garner on which he'd written the address.

"Treed? Cleared?" Christian asked Nathan.

"Are you planning an assault on the place?"

"Just tell us about it, Nathan," I said. "We need to see if Nikki is there."

"Sorry. Tall pine trees, lots of scrub brush. Around the trailer it's cleared for about fifty feet in all directions. You'll have a tough time sneaking up on him."

I thanked him, swore him to secrecy, and promised to let him know what happened.

Garner stepped away to make a call of his own. It was three o'clock. He gestured for us to follow. We climbed out of the car as he said into his phone, "We can't wait for that. It's too late." He tossed the phone into the front seat, pulled out his laptop, and opened it on the roof. Holding up the note Christian had given him, he typed in the address. "The images for this area are at least a year old." On the satellite view, the trailer stood out in the center of a forest, and I could barely make out the swamp-side shack and a dock with a covered area at the end.

"Backup's on the way," Garner said.

We waited there on the side of the dusty road while the minutes dragged. At last, sirens approached and, while they were still some distance away, Garner nodded and climbed back in his car. Christian and I followed in his. We drove even faster than before, despite the road conditions. The speed and jostling did nothing to calm my nerves.

When the back end of Garner's vehicle fishtailed around a corner onto another dirt road, Christian slowed a little. Still, my shoulder pressed into the door as we made the turn, and we caught up again on the straightaway. I fingered the wooden cross and said a prayer for Nikki as the clearing came into view. We parked behind Garner far from the lonely trailer in the center of the unkempt property. No landscaping. No trees. As Nathan had warned, no way to approach with stealth or protection. An older-model pickup was parked near the house, to the left of the sagging front porch.

Behind us, the sirens quieted as two police cars and a van hurtled into the clearing. Garner ordered Christian to drive back up the road. He complied-ish, backing down the driveway but keeping the scene within view. We rolled down the windows so we could hear.

Nothing happened for long, uneasy minutes. We heard amplified speech, too garbled to understand. I shifted in my seat, desperate for Garner to break down the door, and terrified of what might happen if he did. My right foot pressed into the floor, willing the car forward.

"New resolution," Christian said. "Only one shootout per day."

"How about per year?"

"Per decade works for me."

At last, officers in tactical gear surrounded the trailer. For the second time that day, my heart pounded in my throat. Christian gripped my hand. "They know what they're doing."

I nodded, my mouth too dry to form words. Two officers sprinted to the front door. They pounded and yelled, then forced their way in. The door offered little resistance. Garner followed soon after. No shots, no screams, nothing. He emerged moments later and signaled us to return. Christian reclaimed his spot behind Garner's car, and we followed him into the musty trailer. Dirty dishes filled the sink and spilled over onto the counter—some looked relatively fresh. Still, the odor of disuse and decay permeated everything. There was a single photo on the fake-paneled wall. A man proudly holding up a large fish. It had to be Dale Bennett.

"Anything here look like it belongs to Dr. Yarborough?" Garner asked.

Moving slowly through the small trailer, I tried to imagine Nikki in it. Where she would sit and sleep and eat. On the tiny kitchen table was a Jacksonville Jaguars plastic cup. Without thinking, I reached for it.

"Don't." Garner stopped my hand.

"Nikki drinks lots of ice water," I said.

He nodded to an officer with gloves on. She lifted the cup and poured a small amount into a clear glass. Water, with ice.

Garner directed us back out the door as he ordered the surrounding woods searched.

"He has a boat," I said.

He spoke into his radio. Someone spoke back. "No boat. I need you and Christian to go back and call Nathan. See what he knows about Bennett's boat. Model, color, anything."

I hoped that meant they had boats and maybe a helicopter on the way.

Christian drove until I had enough signal to call Nathan. "They were there," I said, "but now they're gone, and so is the boat. Do you remember what it looked like?"

"I only saw it from a distance. It was gray and had a small outboard motor. Let me call Jacob back. He's been fishing with Dr. Bennett."

"Don't tell him any more than you have to."

"Got it."

I thanked him and disconnected.

"Not very distinctive," Christian said. "There are probably dozens of gray fishing boats in the area."

Back at the property, we relayed the information to Garner whose, "We'll take it from here," was both a send-off and a warning.

CHAPTER FORTY

As CHRISTIAN DROVE toward town, I pulled up a map of the area on my phone. Virtually surrounded by homes, Lake Santa Fe was really two lakes connected by a narrow opening. No single road circumnavigated the whole thing, and the swampy area to the north was protected wetland near the lake, with no homes or roads. It was impossible to tell from the map, and even the satellite images, what parts of the swamp between Bennett's trailer and the lake were navigable. If he'd made it to the lake, he could access one of the three public boat launches, but with no vehicle and an unwilling companion, I thought it unlikely. Other than floating in the swamp or the middle of the lake waiting to be discovered, the only other option was to borrow the dock of a property he knew to be unoccupied and hope the neighbors didn't notice.

Christian paused at the intersection where we would join the main road south. He confirmed there were no cars coming up behind us and asked to see the map. "Garner and his dad used to fish up here. I came once, and he and I took kayaks down a canal and into another lake." He scrolled on the map and found the other lake. A tiny blue line, unnaturally straight, connected Lake Santa Fe to Lake Alto, and a road crossed over near its midpoint.

"Let's go look," I said.

While Christian drove, I searched the internet. "A canal was dredged in the late nineteenth century to facilitate transport of citrus to the train station in Waldo." He found it easily enough, a small bridge with a break in the forest on either side. Christian pulled off the road and we walked back to the cement structure, barely wider than the deserted two-lane road. From the center of the bridge, we could see several hundred yards in either direction. Trees ended abruptly at a steep sandy edge that dropped fifteen feet to a level green floor. "Has it run dry?" I asked. It didn't look like grass, though.

"Let's see." He went first, holding onto the bridge support as he slid down the embankment. I followed, with far less grace. The ground was rutted with tree roots, littered with branches, and slick with dead leaves. I stepped on a branch that moved under my weight. When I stepped off, the other end caused a splash. The green floor was a continuous mass of tiny floating leaves. Once the branch came to rest, the onslaught of green soon covered the water's surface. "There must be a blockage up ahead preventing surface flow," Christian said.

"So they didn't come this way," I said.

"Not likely, unless they could portage around the blockage in this muck." His shoe made a slurping sound as he raised it from the mud. I opted to step back on the branch as we made our way back. He climbed out first and helped me up. After scraping the mud from his shoe on the grass, he climbed back in the car and made a U-turn.

Seconds after we reached the main road, Garner called. Christian answered.

"Where are you?" Garner sounded angry.

"We made a quick stop." Christian glanced at me, eyebrows raised. "We're headed home now."

"I need to put a GPS tracker on both of you. Where are you right now?"

"Jeez, Garner, we're five minutes south of Waldo," Christian said.

"There's a gas station on the right before you get back to town. Stop there and wait for me."

Christian did as instructed without argument. While we waited, he gassed up the car and I went inside for bottled waters. Ten minutes later, Garner arrived. Parked next to each other in the few spots in front of the store, we stood on the sidewalk near the ice cooler. For the first time since I'd known him, Garner looked beat. Not just exhausted, though that was part of it, he looked beaten, overwhelmed.

"What is it?" Christian said, his voice wary. "Something's happened. Is it Michael?"

Garner breathed in deeply and finally looked at him. "It is. He's dead, Christian. He . . . took his own life."

A lump formed in my throat, blocking words, nearly blocking breath.

"His body was found in his car at a beach access parking lot at Anastasia State Park."

Christian closed his eyes for a long moment. "Does Mom know?"

Garner shook his head.

"Are you sure it's—"

Garner interrupted me. "He left a note."

"Can you give me the highlights?" Christian asked.

"He mentions guilt over your dad's death." Garner said it as if that were the whole of the note.

"Go on." Christian cleared his throat.

Garner looked at me, pleading, I thought.

"Please," Christian said.

In halting words, Garner said, "He apologized to you for being in love with Helen, for blaming you for her death, and for trying to come between you and Kate." My heart ached for Christian. "He said he didn't want to put your family through a trial for what he'd done and admitted to killing Johnny Barillo for both you and Helen."

Christian blinked several times. "How?" His voice cracked.

"He used a gun." Garner put a hand on Christian's shoulder. "I have to go back. I can send someone to the house."

"No, I'll tell Mom." Christian turned to walk back to the car.

I stopped him, wrapping my arms around him once again. It seemed all our embraces were out of sadness and loss. "Take a breath." He did, and after a few seconds, I felt his body relax. "Let me drive."

He handed me the keys. I adjusted the driver's seat, a lot, then pulled back onto the road. We were quiet for a while, hands clasped across the console between us, Christian lost in his thoughts, me simply lost. So much sadness and death. The world felt a very cruel place.

"I knew he was hurting," Christian said at last. "I tried to get him to talk to me or to someone." He shook his head. "He was so . . . obstinate. Mom and Dad put too much on him, asking him to arrange Dad's death. I don't know what I would have done if they'd asked me. Of all of us, Michael was probably the only one who would follow their wishes, and it destroyed him."

He was silent for several miles. I debated whether to leave him in his head, possibly brooding and inventing reasons to feel guilty. While that could just be a Kate-ism, I decided to intervene. "What was he like before?"

"We were never close." The words came slowly at first, then faster, as if he needed to say them. "When we were kids, he was a pain in the ass, always bossing the rest of us around. Typical firstborn stuff. He hated for any of us to be better than him at anything. When each of us started to excel at different things, he gave them up. Eventually he found his own niche in writing. He was really good. Won some awards for short stories and had several articles published online. In college, he decided he couldn't make a living at it and switched from journalism to business. I don't think he ever loved his job, though by then we didn't talk much. I guess now I know why he avoided us."

After a pause, he continued. "When Dad got sick, Michael quit work and moved back home to help take care of him. He said it was his duty as the eldest, but we all figured he preferred it over his job." Christian's right hand gripped the back of his neck and his head rocked back. "Luke and the girls—I'll have to call them all."

I squeezed his hand. "We could call Luke now. Get it over with. Maybe he could call your sisters." I liked Christian's physician brother. We'd met several times via video call and in person.

Christian debated. Brother or mother first, I imagined.

"It's okay to just take a few more breaths you know. Nothing changes if you wait."

"They get a few more moments of normal life."

I hadn't thought of it that way. The "before" shocking news and the "after." Once in the "after," you could never go back. "Then again," I said, "'grief shared is supposedly grief diminished.'"

He frowned. "You know as well as I do that's crap."

We were quiet as the sun began to set on our strange new reality—a dead brother and a kidnapped friend and her murdered husband. After several moments, Christian rested his head back and closed his eyes. I wondered where he went, then. To childhood memories? To upcoming conversations? To the litany

of horrible things he'd witnessed in the last year? Heck, the last
few days.

At last, we passed through Paynes Prairie, my second sunset on
the prairie in as many days. When would there be one I could enjoy?
As I started down his drive, Christian visibly tensed. "God, I hate
to do this to her."

CHAPTER FORTY-ONE

CHRISTIAN HELD MY hand as we climbed the stairs to his home, his anxiety palpable in his tight grip and in the slowing of his gait, as if he hoped the stairs would go on forever.

"Your mom is strong. It's going to be okay. She has you and the others."

The door swung open before we reached the porch. I recognized Jackie, Christian's oldest sister. She lived an hour south with her husband and two children. Though I'd seen her at her father's funeral and seen photos around the mansion, we'd never met.

Pale-faced, her words came quickly. "Have you heard from Michael?"

"Jackie, what—"

"Mom called me. She's worried about Michael, and you for that matter. Where have you been?" Her eyes widened as we reached the pool of light on the porch. "Geez, Christian. I hope the other guy looks worse." She stuttered. "Oh, that's terrible. I shouldn't have said that."

Christian introduced me.

"Hi, Kate. I'm sorry to meet you under these circumstances." I concurred. And the circumstances were about to become much worse. "What's going on?" Her eyes filled as realization dawned. "Oh God."

"Let's go inside."

I released Christian's hand so he could wrap an arm around his sister. I followed into the cold and dark foyer. It had never felt that way before.

"They're in the kitchen." Jackie wiped under her eyes and took a deep breath, then led the way.

Aunt Irm and Mrs. O'Donnell sat at one end of the large kitchen table, both cradling coffee mugs. My aunt extended an arm toward me, and I went to her, kissed her cheeks, and sat beside her.

I watched as Mrs. O'Donnell took in Christian's expression. "He's gone," she said. "Did he . . . ?"

She knew. Without a word, she knew.

Hand to her mouth, Jackie stumbled to her mother and wrapped her arms around the older woman. After a moment, Mrs. O'Donnell broke the embrace and guided Jackie to the seat beside her. "Tell us," she said to Christian, her voice strong.

"They found his body in his car near the beach."

"Anastasia State Park," she said.

That surprised me.

"It's where I introduced Helen to the family," Christian said quietly.

"Helen?" Jackie said.

"Michael suffered a secret and unrequited love for her," Mrs. O'Donnell said.

"You knew?" Christian said.

"A mother knows, but we never spoke of it."

"He admits it in his note."

"He left a note?" Jackie asked.

"It's with the Medical Examiner," Christian said.

Mrs. O'Donnell's expression remained one of benign interest. "I knew he was unhappy," she said. "We asked too much of him."

Aunt Irm nudged me and whispered, "We must leave them to grieve as a family."

We slipped out to pack up, then made our quiet goodbyes as the family huddled in front of a laptop. Voices came over the speaker. Greetings that quickly morphed to "What's wrong?" Mrs. O'Donnell remained stoic. I declined Christian's offer to walk us out.

I updated Garner by text. Before we'd reached the main road, he called. "How is Molly?"

"She is much too strong," Aunt Irm said. "Jackie is there with her, and Christian."

"I'll go by tomorrow."

"How well did you know Michael?" I asked.

"Not well. He was around when we were kids and I practically lived at their house. He was the brooding older brother and mostly kept to himself. Since then, I've only seen him at family events, where he acted the same. It turns out he was a very troubled man. I'm sorry we didn't realize how troubled."

Aunt Irm wiped a tear.

"Any news about Nikki?" I asked.

"No. They'll resume the search at first light."

We made it home in record time on the dark, empty streets. Aunt Irm bustled into the kitchen where she proceeded to wipe down the spotless counters.

"Talk to me," I said.

"Molly knew. She had already started speaking of him in the past tense. It must be a mother thing. When she saw him withdrawing, she asked her doctor to do something. He said he could not unless Michael became a danger to himself or others, which he most definitely was."

"In hindsight, yes. Unfortunately, maternal intuition isn't enough to get someone committed."

"It should be enough. Molly knew of his love for Helen from the first time Christian brought her to meet the family. She never confronted Michael, and he never got over Helen. When she died, everyone worried about Christian. Michael was left alone to ruminate and lay blame upon his brother. Only Molly knew his torment, but he shut her away."

"Christian had no idea."

"We do not see what we do not wish to see." She dabbed at her eyes with a tissue. "I am sorry for Molly. She has lost her sister and her husband and her son in little more than a year. Worse, she blames herself. Michael was not strong enough to bear the burden of his father's death. The senior Michael would consider no one but the eldest son. Molly regrets that she did not insist to do it herself."

"Regrets are not useful," I muttered. A refrain of both Greg and Christian. We sat, silent in our own thoughts for several moments.

"Has Lieutenant Garner found any leads?" She knew nothing of the events of the day.

"They tracked Dale Bennett to a place up near Lake Santa Fe, but he got away."

"And Dr. Yarborough, she is still with him?"

I nodded. "It looks like Bennett escaped with Nikki in his boat."

"They will not still be there. Whether or not she is with him, a man this evil has a plan two."

"B," I said. "A plan B." And, of course, as always, she was right.

CHAPTER FORTY-TWO

SLEEP DID NOT come easily. What was Bennett's plan B? Assuming we had it right, his original intent was to regain control of his patent by preventing the sale of MDI. When injuring patients didn't work, he threatened the families of MDI's owners.

Part of me wondered why Christian didn't just blow up the deal on his own. Surely, he had that power. The more rational part of me recognized I knew nothing about the sale or his role, and maybe crushing the deal would destroy his career. His world was as foreign to me as mine to him.

In the morning, I arrived early to the hospital. Nathan waited for me on Labor and Delivery. "So what happened?"

I rubbed my eyes. "Sorry, I should have texted you last night."

"By the looks of it, I forgive you. Rough night?"

"And then some."

"Um, I may have screwed up." He rubbed his hands together. Fidgety Nathan was new. "Jacob, the guy I called to get the address last night? I kind of told him who wanted it."

"You told him about the police?"

So much for swearing him to secrecy.

"Turns out when Jacob visits him out there, they smoke pot." Nathan made brief eye contact, seeming to want me to finish his thought. I didn't. "He warned Dr. Bennett, in case he was smoking then."

That explained the rapid departure.

"I'm sorry. I shouldn't have said anything. After he gave me the address, he asked why I needed it and I stupidly started to answer. Then I remembered you said not to talk about it, so I didn't mention Dr. Yarborough . . . and I'm an idiot."

"It's okay, Nathan." It wasn't, but accidents happen. "We'll find them."

He handed me his phone. "When he heard the news this morning, Jacob sent me this picture with the boat in the background."

A gray boat hung from the rafters over the ramshackle dock. "What news this morning?" I sent the image to my phone and then on to Garner.

"About the manhunt," Nathan said.

I stopped mid-text and stared. He typed on his phone and handed it back—now displaying a news report with photos of both Nikki and Dale Bennett, probably from their University IDs. He looked younger and more clean-cut than in the fishing photo at his trailer. "Former University Professor Sought for Questioning in Physician's Disappearance." I skimmed the article. Nothing about the Kadence or misfires or Ian Yarborough's death for that matter.

"Jacob recognized Dr. Yarborough," Nathan said.

"From where?"

"She'd been to the lab."

"She and Bennett wrote a paper together a year ago."

He nodded. "Why hasn't the press linked the Kadence to the accident the other night?"

"I don't know."

"Maybe someone should call in a tip."

So far, Aunt Irm had demonstrated surprising restraint with the press. I couldn't bring myself to encourage Nathan to go against Christian's wishes, so I changed the subject. "They're resuming the search for Nikki this morning. The picture of the boat will help. Thank you."

Still, he looked miserable.

"It's okay, Nathan. It was one mistake against all the good you did stopping the attacks."

As the residents arrived for conference, he turned to leave. "Aunt Irm thought I was a superhero."

"Ninety-five percent superhero," I said. "But if it makes you feel better, I won't tell her."

*　*　*

The day dragged. The only bright spot was when Aunt Irm came in and had her Kadence software updated. I could once again see reports on the cloud, which gave me immeasurable reassurance. Though exhausted, Annabelle Kessler seemed similarly relieved. "I'm calling in patients and seeing them as fast as I can. It's a little strange doing it without having a faculty member sign off, but it's the right thing to do."

"I'm impressed, Annabelle. You're absolutely right, and I'll defend your choice if it comes to that."

Hoping to head off such trouble, I illegally looked up Dr. Cantwell's room number and went to visit him. Still on pain meds, his words slurred. "Do you have news about Nikki?"

"I'm sorry, no. How are you?"

He ignored my question. "We have to find her." His glassy eyes were unfocused. "She's my only chance."

"Your only chance for what?"

"My legacy." He winced as he adjusted his position. "My ex-wife was barren." Harsh, but not the time to correct him. "I should have married Nikki's mother instead. You know the woman never touched the money I gave her? When she refused the abortion, I kept paying her."

He'd wanted her to abort. I hoped Nikki didn't know.

"I'm going to be a grandfather. Did you know?" His thoughts were so jumbled it was hard to keep up.

"I did. Congratulations."

"You have to find her."

"The police are trying."

"You're her friend." *Yeah, tell that to Garner.*

"You should rest."

"What about Samuels?" he asked.

"I don't know."

"I need my phone."

"The police are monitoring it in case Dale Bennett contacts you again."

"Not that one, my normal phone."

"They probably have that one, too."

He nodded, his eyelids drooping. With effort, he forced them open and glared at his IV pump. "Turn that damn thing off. I need to be alert."

I promised to inform the nurse of his request and she agreed to check with his doctor.

On my way back to Labor and Delivery, I heard from Christian. While his mom and sister made funeral arrangements, he made multiple trips to the airport for arriving family. From their home south of town, it would be an hour and a half round trip. And he had lots of family. "I take it you haven't seen the news," he said.

"About Bennett kidnapping Nikki? Nathan showed me."

"No, about the accident being triggered by the Kadence."

"Seriously?" I quickened my pace to check the computer.

"Someone with knowledge talked to them."

"Good."

A pause followed that became uncomfortably long. "Was it you, Kate?"

"It was not."

"Thank you." I found his relief a little disappointing. That he didn't trust me. Maybe the leak came from Nathan-the-loose-lipped-superhero, or one of the police officers, or Annabelle, or any number of people who crossed paths with the autopsy report.

"Do they at least say that the vulnerability has been fixed?"

"They do."

I wondered how inconsistent Annabelle's story was with what the news was reporting. It was so much for a young doctor to handle. For any doctor to handle.

I texted Garner to request an update. He called back. "I won't bother telling you yet again to leave this to us."

"Thank you," I said. "Cantwell wants his phone back."

"And you know this how?"

"I just saw him."

Garner groaned.

"I didn't tell him anything about yesterday. Has he received another call?"

"Another ultimatum for tonight."

When he didn't continue, I did. "And?"

"We're dealing with it, Kate."

"Did Samuels receive a call as well?"

"Kate." His voice reminded me of Dad when he wanted me to shut up. I did. "This is not our first kidnapping. You have to trust me."

My face heated. "I'm sorry, you're right. It's just—"

"I get it. She's your friend."

Slow, deep breaths.

"You're used to being in control. That's why you're good at your job. This is my job, and I'm good at it, too."

"I didn't mean to imply—"

"I know. It's okay, and I will keep you posted."

Chastised, I thanked him and disconnected. That he might hear an implication of incompetence hadn't occurred to me. Of course he was good at his job, or at least I assumed he was. What evidence did I really have? The halo effect is human nature—to assume people we like are also competent.

Stop. They're doing everything they can.

I resolved to check on Aunt Irm, then go find a patient I could help, or a student I could teach. She answered my call but was mid-conversation with someone else. "It's her. I'll put it on speaker." The background noise grew louder. "Kate? It's Aunt Irm." In case I'd forgotten who I called. "I'm here with Carmel and she has an idea."

"Kate, hello. Irm was telling me about your friend and Lake Santa Fe. When the kids were small, we used to fish out there. There is a canal that connects to Lake Alto."

"Yes. Christian and I looked at it yesterday. It's blocked."

"But that's where Richard caught the fish we cleaned the other night." The alto-bass. I remembered.

"Are you sure they went down the canal?" My heart beat a little faster.

"I am. They parked at the Keystone Heights boat ramp on Little Lake Santa Fe because the one at Lake Alto was closed. Why don't you give him a call?" She gave me his number.

If there were some way around the blockage, the police might be looking in the wrong place. I considered calling Garner, but in light of our recent conversation, decided to wait. He knew the area or had people with him who knew the area. Finding Nikki was not my job. Still, I called Carmel's son.

I explained the reason for my call.

He said, "The Santa Fe Canal was blocked after the last hurricane. My son and I took tools out there in hopes of clearing it a couple of months ago. We cut a path through the smaller limbs, but a downed tree needs a chainsaw so instead, we found a way around that section through the swampy area to the north. Some clearing was still required, and at one point we still have to raise the motor and paddle, but we make it past without getting out of the boat."

"Do other people know about this?"

"Probably. It's not a secret."

"How about Lake Alto? If this person got through, any idea where they might go?"

"It's mostly woods. There are far fewer homes relative to Lake Santa Fe, and parts are quite swampy. They may have accessed the boat ramp on the north side. It was closed for repaving last week, but should be open again now."

I heard my pulse in my ears, faster than it should be. Might this actually be a lead?

"If you would like to take a look, we could meet at the ramp and take a trip around Lake Alto. Mom's been wanting to go for a cruise on the pontoon boat."

"That sounds great. I could probably make it by five thirty, if that's not too late."

"Perfect, a sunset cruise."

I very nearly called to invite Christian, then remembered. He needed to be with his family, not on a sunset cruise that likely would come to nothing.

If we found something, I would call Garner. Meanwhile, I looked forward to a nice evening out with friends. Or that's what I told myself.

CHAPTER FORTY-THREE

As usual, the afternoon was feast or famine in terms of work. Two patients requested epidurals at the same time the obstetricians called for an urgent Cesarean. Afterward, it was quiet for more than an hour. A totally unpredictable service. I hoped they wouldn't call an emergency when it was time for me to leave. *Wow, how self-absorbed am I?*

Fortunately, it remained fairly quiet so I signed the patients over to the on-call attending on time and left for the boat ramp southeast of Waldo. I texted Aunt Irm and tried to get in the right frame of mind. This was a sunset cruise with good food and good company.

I found the ramp without difficulty and greeted Aunt Irm, Carmel, and Richard. A thumping from inside his van demanded my attention. They'd brought Shadow.

I opened the sliding door and he leapt over the seat and flew out into me.

Richard reached under Shadow and lifted him over the side and into the trailered boat, then took his mother's hand as she climbed a makeshift set of stairs. Irm followed, placing her hand in his. "Your turn," he said to me.

"You don't need help with the boat?"

He declined, even without learning that backing up a trailer was a skill I'd never mastered. Not even close. When I would try, and repeatedly fail, to maneuver our riding lawn mower with a trailer of yard waste onto the compost pile, my brother would tease me mercilessly. Inevitably, he would have to adjust the trailer's position by hand. Richard, though, was a master. My only role was to keep the boat from floating away while he parked the van. I helped Aunt Irm and Carmel into bright orange life vests, and Shadow into one of his own. Richard had thought of everything.

Moments later, he steered us down the narrow channel and onto the beautiful lake. It was at least three times the size of the one by Christian's house. Was it only a week ago we'd kayaked there? We puttered around the perimeter to the left. Docks extended over the water at intervals, but the homes hid amongst cypress and oak trees. Shadow stood at the bow, my hand gripping his collar. Life vest or no, I didn't want to dive in after him.

With covered docks rather than boathouses, we could view each boat. None was gray. These were pleasure craft with larger motors for skiing or pulling kids on tubes. We cruised around the lake slowly. Three-quarters of it had no homes, just dense trees reaching the waterline and beyond. Cypress knees jutted, threatening an unwary boater.

Carmel opened a cooler and served dinner—Italian subs and German potato salad. "Both your nationalities in one meal," I said. After several bites I added, "They go together well."

"Like World War II," Richard said around a mouthful of food. "Just need some sushi."

I had to cover my full mouth as I laughed. Aunt Irm and Carmel did not join in. A vague sense of something missing struck me. Only later, when Richard opened the wine, did I register what it was. Christian. He should be there. That I felt his absence so keenly was something I needed to explore, but not with Aunt Irm, at least not now.

Completing the circuit and nearing the boat ramp again, a few more homes dotted the shore. Still no gray boats. I'd kept my expectations low, but disappointment weighed all the same. Then I watched my beautiful aunt laughing with Carmel. I'd nearly lost her, twice. A pleasant evening with her would never be time wasted.

Richard idled the boat near the center of the lake as the sky turned pink on the horizon and jet contrails shone bright white overhead in long, intersecting lines. Carmel served more wine and I relaxed. Shadow helped, leaning heavily against me while the women told stories from their childhoods, Carmel's in an Italian neighborhood near Youngstown, Ohio, and Aunt Irm's in a small town in Germany. Theirs were so different from my own, and yet not so different from each other's. It seemed for each story one told, the other had a close parallel that was equally hilarious or touching or unbelievable.

Too soon, the sky lost its color, and Richard guided the boat back down the channel toward the ramp. I sat forward at the bow with Shadow, who seemed eager to be on dry land. "Hang on, buddy. Almost there." Something glinted to my left. The glint vanished, but I focused where it had been.

"Wait." I got Richard's attention at the helm. "Can you back up a little?"

He complied, turning to look over his shoulder as he reversed.

"There." I pointed into the darkness to our left.

Richard put the boat briefly back in gear so we came to a stop. "I see it." He opened a storage bin and withdrew a large flashlight. In its beam, a small boat appeared, tied to a tree. He maneuvered forward. "We can walk to it from shore." At the ramp, he jumped out in his water shoes and splashed onto shore. As he backed the trailer into the water, I stared at where the boat lay hidden amongst the trees, invisible from the current angle. It might be gray; I couldn't be sure. Aunt Irm and Carmel murmured about kidnapping and murder while he and I trailered the boat. Once Richard had pulled us onto shore, and everyone had carefully disembarked, I coaxed Shadow into the back of the van with a window down. Aunt Irm stayed near to reassure him.

Richard offered me his son's water shoes. They were too big but better than nothing. I rolled up my jeans and followed as he picked his way amongst the cypress knees and underwater debris. The boat was not far from shore and most definitely gray. In the beam of Richard's flashlight, it was just as Nathan had described, if generic. Richard sloshed to the back. "Take a picture of this," he said as he shone the light on an out-of-date license sticker near the motor. I sent the photo along with a note to Garner. "Sunset cruise on Lake Alto with friends. Found gray boat hidden near ramp." I followed with another text: "Don't be mad."

We waded back to shore.

"It is his boat, yes?" Aunt Irm said. Shadow whined from the van behind her.

"I don't know," I said. "We'll let Garner take it from here."

Her eyes twinkled. "We have found it when they did not, thanks to Richard."

My phone rang. I prepared myself for Garner's wrath.

"A sunset cruise that just happened to be on the lake near where Nikki Yarborough disappeared?"

"There are only so many lakes. And it wasn't Lake Santa Fe."

He groaned. He was doing that a lot lately. "The canal between is impassable."

"Actually, a friend knows of a way through."

"And you thought you'd go looking for the boat in Lake Alto."

"No, I . . . okay, yes, but after this morning I didn't dare call you."

"Because I would tell you to leave it alone."

"Because I didn't want to bother you until I knew it was worth it."

He groaned again, more of a growl this time. "I'll send someone out."

"And the sticker?"

"We're running it." In the background, I heard another voice, distorted. Then Garner said, "It's expired, but belonged to Dale Bennett."

I nodded to Aunt Irm. We'd found the boat.

"Tell me exactly where you are," he said.

"The Lake Alto boat ramp."

More conversation away from the phone, then Garner said, "They're on their way. Once you point out the boat to my officers, will you please go home?"

"I will."

"And, Kate. Thank you. That was good work. But please, if you think of anything else, tell me. I won't get angry."

"Yes, you will."

"Okay, but I'll be less angry than if you go off on your own. Christian has had enough pain in his life."

I disconnected the call, his final words ringing in my ear.

"Kindchen, what did he say?"

"He's grateful we found the boat. He said we did good work."

"This is true. We pieced together the clues with logic."

"And friends." I thanked Richard.

"Our team has grown," Aunt Irm said.

Richard insisted on waiting with me, and Carmel and Aunt Irm preferred to stay rather than drive home in the dark, so the four of us sat in Richard's van with Shadow in the back. As full dark set in in this remote area, I felt grateful for the company.

When the police arrived, I pointed through the trees where the beams of their flashlights barely illuminated the tip of the bow.

"That explains the car from last night," the younger of the two officers said.

"Car?" I asked.

Frowning, his partner said, "Thank you for your help. We'll take it from here."

I'd been dismissed. Though curious about the *car*, I couldn't very well ask Garner and get his officers in trouble. My guess was Dale Bennett stole a nearby car to escape. If so, maybe they could trace it.

Aunt Irm, Shadow, and I climbed into my Honda and headed toward home. As the excitement of finding the boat waned, my cruise-induced relaxation returned. Aunt Irm felt it too and dozed in the passenger seat. I opened my window to stay alert. Between the wind and Shadow's muzzle sniffing nearby, problem solved.

CHAPTER FORTY-FOUR

As I DROVE down ruler-straight Waldo Road, Christian's call woke Aunt Irm. He told us about the funeral plans for Saturday. "I know it's a lot to ask," he said, "but would you both be willing to come?"

"We will be there, Christian," Aunt Irm said. "I will discuss with your mother the plans for the reception. You are family." She meant it. Family to her meant the people you love, the ones you can count on. Relatives by blood or marriage didn't always qualify.

"Kate, are you sure you're up for another funeral?" he asked.

"Wherever you want me to be, I'll be there, Christian."

"Thank you. I'm going to hold you to that." Something in my abdomen shuddered.

"Tell him what we found, kindchen."

"He needs to get back to his family." I gave her an admonishing look.

"Tell me, please. I've been drowning in grief-ville all day."

"We found the boat in Lake Alto," she said. "They have stolen a car and Lieutenant Garner will find them now."

Silence followed, Christian likely trying to fill in all the missing pieces of Aunt Irm's declaration. I spared him the struggle. "It turns out there is a way to bypass the blockage in the canal. Carmel's son took us on a cruise around Lake Alto, and we found a boat registered to Bennett hidden near the ramp. It sounds like a car nearby might have been stolen, so now they have something to search for."

"And you called Garner."

"Of course."

"And he thanked you for being an indispensable member of the team."

"Have you met Garner?"

He laughed.

"More like 'leave it alone and let the professionals handle things,'" I said.

"And will you?"

Aunt Irm harrumphed. "They would be looking in the wrong place still if we did not help. It was a lovely evening, Christian. Next time you and your mother must join us."

Unphased by the abrupt change in topic, he said, "I'll look forward to it."

"What's happening on your end?" I asked. Besides funeral planning and grieving, of course.

"Camden still wants to close the deal on Wednesday, including Bennett's patent, and for less money."

"Even after the Kadence link to the accident made it into the news?" The report blamed a Kadence malfunction for the accident, but didn't call it an attack or mention the other misfires. Only Cantwell and Samuels' names appeared in the article, and nothing tied the event to Nikki's disappearance, or even to Camden Health and MDI's impending sale.

"They're dropping the purchase price by twenty-five percent but proceeding. I don't know how much Samuels owes, but I'll be surprised if he doesn't accept."

"But Dr. Cantwell cannot agree while his daughter is still missing," Aunt Irm said.

"He doesn't have to. In MDI's bylaws, a simple majority is sufficient and Samuels holds fifty-one percent of the company. Cantwell should never have agreed to that."

"Your client is not a good person to do business with that company," Aunt Irm said. "I wish I did not have their Kadence."

"That makes two of us," I said.

"Corporations aren't people," Christian said. "Only money and growth matter, and MDI is a valuable entity, regardless of the morals of its CEO. Unlike the others, Samuels will be replaced immediately."

"Does he know that?" I asked.

"It's in the contract."

"So he gets a truckload of money, out of the loan shark's cross-hairs, and retirement."

"This is not fair," Aunt Irm said.

A win-win-win for a man who refused to warn patients when he knew they were in danger. "What if the accident victims sue?"

"The buyer is indemnified for anything that happened before the purchase goes through."

"So Samuels and Cantwell would be responsible."

"They are and have insurance to cover it."

Of course they do. "What about Bennett? He could still go after your client as the new owner of his patent." Now I sounded petulant.

"Kate, I know it seems cold—"

"But it's business, and your job, and not mine. I'm hearing that a lot lately." In the background, voices called Christian's name. "You need to go."

He thanked us for the distraction and rejoined his family.

At home, I got ready for bed and tried to clear my mind. Not for the first time, I thought meditation skills would be helpful. After starting and abandoning multiple online apps and courses, I'd given up. Ever helpful, Randi suggested I meditate on my failure to meditate. I failed that, too. Curled around my cuddly dog, though, I slept.

The next morning, I had a non-clinical day. Since I wouldn't be changing into scrubs, I had to wear actual grown-up clothes. In the kitchen, Aunt Irm sliced an onion. "Molly wishes us to meet her family. Can you join us for lunch, kindchen?"

"No, I'm sorry, I have several meetings today." I went to the stove; minestrone soup simmered. My favorite. "You know she has a full-time housekeeper and plenty of family around. I seriously doubt she intended for you to cook." Before she could argue, I added, "I know, never go empty-handed, but that doesn't mean armloads either."

"They are grieving. It is the least I can do. You go to work. I will see you tonight."

It felt as if I hadn't spent a weeknight at home in ages. I missed our relaxing evenings of cribbage, or *NCIS*, or reading together. Though my life of a week ago had some rough edges, I missed its comfortable rhythm.

CHAPTER FORTY-FIVE

WITH MEETINGS INTERSPERSED throughout the morning, I had difficulty concentrating long enough to prepare an upcoming lecture for the cardiology fellows on the anesthetic implications of the pregnant cardiac patient. Though an interesting topic, it required more than fifteen-minute blocks of time to make any headway. Not to mention the other issues vying for bandwidth in my brain at the moment. I went by Dr. Cantwell's hospital room only to find he'd been discharged.

Christian texted at eleven o'clock. "Why does your aunt insist on cooking for my family?"

I grinned. "She's nuts, I mean generous. Enjoy her soup. It's amazing. Meanwhile I'll be eating Subway . . . again."

"But that's our restaurant," he typed back, followed by a smiley emoji, which caused the now familiar ripple in my stomach again. We'd run into each other at the hospital's Subway after his father's death. It's where our investigatory partnership began. "Would it be too weird if I met you there?"

The ripple intensified. "And reject Aunt Irm's famous minestrone soup?"

"I could use a break from the chaos factory," he said, "and I want to see you."

No longer a ripple, a full-blown flutter rose to my chest.

"How about I bring you lunch?" he texted. "I have to try and get Cantwell's signature anyway."

"He's been discharged."

"Ah, no matter. I don't need an excuse."

My responsible-doctor reflex said to decline. It was a workday. I'd already blown off one afternoon recently. But I reread his texts. "I want to see you." He needed a grief break. He was my friend. Before I could recognize my rationalization for what it was, I typed, "That would be great. I have a meeting at noon. I can meet you around one."

He agreed and the clock immediately slowed. The noon meeting of the OR Committee dragged as we discussed staffing numbers, again. The unsolvable question. How many cases would be scheduled each day? How many emergencies would come in? How many staff did we need? I should have skipped it in favor of an early lunch.

I met Christian in the front circle of the hospital. He pulled out and turned right, then right again toward campus. "How long do you have?"

I glanced at my watch, though I knew exactly what time it was. "Ninety minutes before my next meeting."

"How about up by Lake Alex?"

I agreed. The campus lake was home to many alligators but a lovely place for a walk, or a picnic. He drove slowly, obeying the twenty-mile-per-hour speed limit, then waited to turn left on Lakeview Road as students with backpacks slung over their shoulders crossed against the light. He found a parking spot across the road from the lake.

I helped unload a small cooler, a blanket, and a bag of food and utensils that clanked as we walked. No picnic plasticware for the O'Donnells.

Christian led the way past two cement picnic tables, then off the paved path into a wooded area closer to the water.

He chose a clearing amongst the trees and helped me spread the blanket, then pulled sandwiches and a plastic container of coleslaw from the cooler. "Mom decided soup was too difficult for a picnic. Aunt Irm will bring some home for your lunch tomorrow."

"They were okay with you leaving?"

He grinned. "Luke wanted to come, but his wife wouldn't let him."

"Ha. I look forward to seeing him."

"It will be nice when you can visit my family outside of attending funerals."

"It will be nice to stop having funerals to attend."

We talked about other things as we ate. The sun peeked in and out of high clouds keeping the temperature just about right with the faint breeze. From our little clearing, we could barely hear passing cars and were shielded from the occasional joggers and bicyclists on the path. Despite everything going on in our lives at that moment, Christian and I talked like normal people having a normal day in a normal world. It was wonderful.

It was also temporary. My watch dinged a reminder of my afternoon meeting. I flopped back on the blanket, raised my face to the warm sun, closed my eyes, and sighed.

"Play hooky." He lay beside me, our arms barely touching.

"I wish I could."

"Is the meeting about a patient?"

"No."

"Are you chairing the meeting?"

"I am not." In fact, I'd handed over the reins of this particular committee several months before.

"Are you presenting vital material essential to the conduct of the meeting?"

I smiled at the formality and turned my head to face him. "I am not."

His fingers interlaced with mine on the blanket. "Then what's the worst that can happen if you don't attend?"

"Um." I couldn't think. His thumb caressed my hand in a way that sent warm chills into my chest, if those are a thing. Before today, it had never occurred to me to skip a meeting just because. I was a rule follower.

He rose onto his elbow, pulling my hand to his lips. "Live a little, Kate." His breath felt hot on the back of my hand. "We both need to." He kissed my hand and the heat shot up my arm to my neck, my face.

"Don't you need to get back to your family?" My mouth had grown so dry I had to moisten my lips. His eyes darkened and he leaned slowly forward.

"Nope." His lips touched mine, gently at first, his eyes open, asking permission. I reached around his neck with my free hand and pulled him closer. The kiss deepened, then softened again as he pulled away.

"What, exactly, does hooky entail?"

"Seriously? Boy, do I have some corrupting to do." He bounced to his feet and reached down to pull me up. "First, ice cream."

I laughed, and it felt incredibly good. We packed up, walked out of the trees with our somewhat lighter bundles, and loaded them in the car. Once inside, he started the car, put it in reverse, then back into park. He leaned across the console between us and kissed me again. "I've been wanting to do that for a very long time."

Unsure how long constituted a "long time," I wasn't sure how to answer. Was "Me, too" a betrayal of Greg? But to not answer would be unkind, not to mention a lie.

"I understand," Christian said while I wrestled with a response, and I realized that he did. At a nearby ice cream shop, we chose two very boring flavors in sugar cones and shared them at a wobbly postage-stamp-sized metal table out front. I swallowed a delicious mouthful of cookies and cream. "I think I like playing hooky."

The corners of his mouth curved behind the strawberry cone. "You ain't seen nothing yet."

"I have another meeting at four thirty. That one I can't miss."

He glanced at his watch. "Perfect." He drove to the duck pond near our competing hospital and pulled leftover bread from our picnic cooler. Walking hand in hand, we circled the small pond, feeding ducks along the way and trying to avoid attacks by greedy swans.

He described childhood trips there with his mother and brothers. The boys would feed the ducks and chase each other in the grassy field behind the lake. "Once Luke and I got fast enough to catch him, Michael refused to play. He hated to lose. We all do, but for him it rose to another level, with temper tantrums and aggressive behavior toward all of us, even Dad."

"I assume he eventually grew out of that," I said.

"Somewhat. I didn't notice how he felt about Helen, and she never mentioned undue attention from him. None of the others noticed anything either. In hindsight, he did try to talk me out of marrying her, and I learned yesterday that he told the others I was making a mistake. They figured it was because he wanted to be the first to marry, not because he wanted my fiancée."

We continued walking along the cypress mulch path just wide enough for the two of us. "It must bother you."

He slowed our pace. "Mostly I can't get the image of him at her grave out of my head. I wonder how different his life would have been if he'd met someone of his own to love."

I pictured it, too, the depth of his emotions at Helen's grave invested in someone who reciprocated. How sad.

"Mom blames herself, but all of us should have reached out to help him."

"It's tough when he didn't want help."

"Yeah." He picked up the pace. "Let's talk about something other than my family problems."

"You mentioned you needed to work on 'living a little,'" I said with some trepidation. "What did you mean?"

He tossed the remaining breadcrumbs into the lake. "All this has me reassessing. I go to work, I go home, that's it."

"Yeah." I knew what he meant.

"I've been offered a promotion if this sale goes through."

A knot formed in my stomach. A promotion in south Florida. "That's great."

"Is it?"

"Something new anyway."

"Not really. Bigger clients, bigger mergers. I'm not sure it's what I want to do. I help companies grow, but I don't make anything useful, I don't help anyone who needs it. In fact, jobs are almost always lost in the mergers."

"Have you considered other options?"

We talked about other forms of law and even going back to school for an MBA.

As we returned to the car, I said, "My dad told me it's a blessing to have many career choices but a curse to have to choose. When I asked how to be sure I picked the right one, he said, 'You make it the right one.'"

As he drove me back to the hospital, Christian's mom called. I was invited to join the O'Donnell clan for dinner, which worked since I needed to pick up Aunt Irm and Shadow anyway.

He stopped again in the front circle. I unbuckled my seat belt. "Thanks for a really great afternoon."

"You needed the break as much as I did. Now the challenge is not feeling guilty about it."

He knew me surprisingly well. "That, I'll have to work on."

CHAPTER FORTY-SIX

THE CLINICAL COMPETENCY Committee took all my focus for the next couple of hours. With eighty-eight residents in the program, a few trainees inevitably struggled with some aspect. Usually the same few, month after month. Discussion went on for far too long and as chair, I did a poor job managing the meeting, something that was usually a source of pride.

Afterward, Sam Paulus, a longtime colleague and friend of both Greg's and mine, asked for a moment in private. I assumed he had information on a resident he preferred not to share with the committee as a whole. I was wrong.

We sat together at the conference table until everyone else filed out, then he said, "Are you okay? You seem distracted."

I went with the easy answer. "I'm worried about my aunt."

He nodded. "I heard about the Kadence issues."

"Hers misfired last Monday."

"I'm sorry." He waited, clearly expecting more. And he deserved more.

"Do you remember Christian O'Donnell?"

With his signature gap-toothed smile, he said, "I do."

"He lost his older brother this week."

The smile vanished, leaving a gap-toothed "O." "That family's had a rough go."

"They have."

"I hoped you had a different story for me concerning Christian O'Donnell."

Suddenly interested in my water bottle on the table, I avoided eye contact.

"You are a wonderful young woman who should not spend the rest of her life as a single widow."

"Is a married widow a thing?" Why did this conversation make me so uncomfortable?

"Probably not. What I'm trying to say is, don't rule out marrying again. I saw something in Christian O'Donnell I liked last year. I know it's none of my business, but you guys seemed like a good match."

Unreasonably, tears burned the back of my nose.

"Kate, it's okay. I know it's hard. You have no reason to feel guilty. Greg would want you to go on with your life and be happy."

"It's too soon." My voice croaked, and I cleared my throat.

"There are no rules in a situation like yours. And who cares if there are? If you are lucky enough to find love twice, be thankful. Don't punish yourself. The world has done that enough, don't you think?"

I let his words sink in. Though I doubted the world kept a scorecard on punishment, the sentiment was genuine. Many people never find someone to love. I found Greg and now maybe another. "Thanks, Sam. I'll keep that in mind."

And I did, until my phone rang with an unknown number. "Dr. Downey? It's Victor Cantwell. I need your help. Can you meet me in the cardiac ICU?"

Weird. I texted Christian, "I found Dr. Cantwell."

Cantwell waited for me at the ICU entrance. Despite his white coat, he looked nothing like the in-control chairman I'd dealt with before. He paced, his head on a swivel, seemingly searching for threats. He led me into the storage room where I had stitched Nikki's ear.

Weird times two.

"Nikki is bleeding. She may be having a miscarriage."

"Oh no." I pulled my phone out to call Labor and Delivery.

He snatched it from my hand. "No. We can't call anyone or he'll kill her."

I stared at my phone in his hand as it buzzed a text message. Then his words sunk in. "Where is she?"

"I don't know yet. All I know is she's bleeding and we have to save her." His voice quavered.

"If she's miscarrying, she needs to come to the hospital. She might need a D&C. He has to bring her here."

"I've tried to convince him of that. We have to keep her alive until he agrees."

"We?"

"I can't do this alone. I need you. She needs you."

"She needs a hospital and an obstetrician." I gave the words gravity, trying to make him understand.

Instead, he pulled something from the pocket of his white coat. Something that didn't belong in a white coat or a hospital. A gun.

I stared into his starkly white face. "You can't be serious."

"I'm sorry. She's everything to me. I have to save her."

Which meant I had to save her. I would have gone, probably, but this was crazy. My cellphone buzzed again in his hand.

"Get what you need." He slipped the gun back into his pocket; his hand remained there, too.

I started collecting supplies. He couldn't shoot me in the storage room of the ICU, could he? He'd be caught immediately. In his current state, he might shoot anyone who came to my rescue. I filled two bags meant for patient belongings with gloves, IV fluids, a few IV placement kits, and IV catheters of various sizes. Along the way I grabbed other things that might come in handy—a bladder catheter, sterile prep solution, suture.

What would come in handy was an obstetrician and an ultrasound machine and an operating room. She was twenty-one weeks pregnant and had a history of uterine surgery. That put her at risk for uterine rupture and other complications. I wasn't prepared for a routine delivery outside a hospital, much less this.

From the drug cabinet I withdrew medications to improve blood clotting and treat low blood pressure. I searched for drugs to make the uterus contract, like Pitocin and Methergine and Hemabate, but they were stocked only on the OB floor. I told Cantwell, "I can't get blood products without an order cleared by the Blood Bank."

He tilted his head like Shadow at a foreign sound.

A door opened behind me. He adjusted his hand in his pocket, and I shifted to stand between him and the new arrival.

"Dr. Downey?"

I spun to see Annabelle Kessler. She looked from me to Dr. Cantwell and back. "Is everything okay?"

I mouthed, "No" as Cantwell said, "Fine. We were just leaving."

If she was trying to hide her shock, she was a worse actress than even me. It didn't matter; Cantwell was beyond reason. He grabbed my arm and steered me out through the opposite door. "Keep up," he said through gritted teeth as he released my arm. We left the hospital by the staff door. He tossed my cellphone into a garbage can near the parking garage. Strangely, only then did my heart begin to race.

CHAPTER FORTY-SEVEN

CANTWELL MADE ME drive his red Porsche as he made a call. "I'm on my way. Tell me where." He listened for a moment, then put his phone down and said, "Go south on 441."

In other circumstances, it would be funny. I was headed toward my original destination. Thirty minutes later, I looked with longing at the O'Donnells' driveway as we sped by. Few cars passed in the other direction. With Cantwell next to me, watching, there was no way to signal them. There were no billboards or mile markers or numbered emergency call boxes, just the occasional radio or cellphone tower and miles and miles of power lines.

We passed tiny Micanopy and he ordered me to slow and turn left down an unlabeled, rutted road. A radio tower loomed, its light flashing a warning, to planes, and to me. Otherwise, there were only trees. The road ended at a single-story white box of a building—cinder block construction with a black door and broken windows in the front. Half a sign remained over the door that started with "WK" and ended with "radio." Something niggled. I parked in the center of the small parking lot, away from tree cover, trying to be visible in case Annabelle called someone, and they knew what car to look for, and they flew over with a helicopter. Yeah, grasping at ever-shrinking straws.

In my pocket, I gripped Jolene's wooden cross and said a prayer for survival, for Nikki, for courage. My prayers were more of the "what can it hurt" variety rather than certain they would help. Still, it calmed me.

Cantwell ordered me to get out of the car and carry the supplies. I pulled them from the back seat while he made another call, said a few words, winced, then spoke with more force. "I can't save her myself. I had to bring help." An argument about me. Perfect.

We stood in front of his car. Cantwell held the gun up by the barrel, displaying it to someone inside, then tossed it underhand toward the door. It skittered on the cement stoop and came to a stop. A decent toss, considering. The door opened, a hand reached out, and the gun disappeared. Cantwell grabbed my arm again and we walked slowly forward and through the door.

My eyes took a moment to adjust to the sudden darkness as the door slammed closed behind me. The lock snicked definitively. I winced at the odor of mold and desperation. The only way forward was a narrow hallway next to an opening that might have been the radio station's reception desk.

Bennett stood to my right, gun in hand, eyes wide and unblinking. He ordered me to drop the supplies and proceeded to give me a pat-down that made my skin crawl. Yanking on the collar of my shirt, he peered inside, either looking for a wire or just being a pervert. I turned my head from his greasy hair, the dankness of the room overpowered by his intense body odor.

"Where is she?" I tried to sound demanding rather than terrified.

He jerked his chin toward the hall. I reached for the supplies.

"Not yet." He opened the first bag.

I went in search of my patient, past a couple of closed wooden doors on either side, to the single open one at the back where the smell of mildew lost out to blood. A half-height wall split the large windowless room in two. By the light of a battery-operated lantern, I saw a large panel of electronic equipment in the area to my right, like a sound mixing board at a concert. And to the left was blood, lots of it. Nikki lay on the floor in the center of a large oval of deep crimson.

"Oh my God," Cantwell said from the doorway. He stood there, immobile.

Right, no way he was placing an IV.

I knelt beside her and pressed two fingers to her wrist. Cool to the touch, her pulse was weak and much too fast. "Nikki?"

Her eyes fluttered open. "Kate?" Her colorless lips formed the nearly inaudible word.

Bennett started pulling items from the bag, checking for contraband, I presumed.

Rather than ask a shell-shocked Cantwell, I gathered IV supplies, unwrapped everything, spiked a bag of saline with tubing, and let the fluid run through. "I need something to hang the fluids on, at least a few feet high."

Cantwell remained frozen as I wrapped the tourniquet around Nikki's arm. "Go!"

He startled and finally moved. Bennett took several steps back to watch both of us.

Nikki had bled so much, the tourniquet did little to make her veins visible, so I trusted anatomy. Unlike veins of the hand, which vary greatly from patient to patient, two large-ish veins are always found in the antecubital fossa, the inside of the elbow. Though I couldn't feel either, I went with the odds and inserted the needle where the basilic vein should be. It took a small amount of adjustment, which would have hurt if Nikki weren't beyond noticing. I secured the catheter in place, attached the IV fluids, and then squeezed the bag between my arm and side to speed the flow while preparing for a second IV in the other arm.

Cantwell returned with a crooked coatrack. He trembled so much it clanged on the hard floor.

I handed him the bag of fluid with instructions to hang it as high as possible. Meanwhile, I placed a second IV and ran fluid for that. "She needs blood. We have to get her to the hospital."

"No," Bennett said. "Get her stable enough so we can go."

"The only place she can go is a hospital. Why don't you go? We'll give you a head start before we call 911."

He ignored me.

"Give her my blood." Cantwell offered his arm, still in his white coat. The man was losing it.

"Are you the same blood type?"

"I . . . I don't know." I wanted to tell him I could have looked up both their blood types if he hadn't tossed my phone, but what was the point? "We need O-negative."

"Please," Cantwell said to Bennett. "Take me instead. I'm a valuable hostage."

I hoped Nikki heard his words, even if subconsciously. She finally had a father who cared about her.

"She's not going to the hospital." Bennett waved his gun. "You're doctors. Save her."

"We're not the right kind of doctors," I said.

He blinked and his eyes looked slightly less wild for an instant. Then it was gone. "Just . . . take care of her."

"Leave us alone so I can examine her." Both men disappeared around the half-wall into the adjoining room.

I glanced over as I pulled on gloves. It was the broadcast booth of the radio station. The soundproof glass that must have once separated the rooms was long gone. I knelt and pressed on Nikki's lower abdomen. She moaned softly. Blood gushed between her legs. Her uterus should be a tight ball. It wasn't. Even with massage, it failed to firm up. Likely a piece of placenta remained, and she would continue to bleed until it was removed.

Judging by the slickness of the floor and lack of dark red globs, her blood was not able to clot either. I could solve neither problem in a filthy room in the middle of nowhere. I took a slow breath and focused on the situation, on what I had, rather than what I didn't. I'd read an article about dealing with postpartum hemorrhage in sub-Saharan Africa and decided to follow their lead and play MacGyver.

I opened what I would need, then traded my gloves for a sterile pair and attached another sterile glove to a catheter meant to be placed in the bladder. With Nikki's knees spread, I fished the glove up into her uterus with some difficulty. Praying it had passed through the cervix, I filled the glove with water until it was under pressure, then clamped the catheter so the water would remain inside, hopefully pressing on the uterine walls and stopping the bleeding, at least temporarily. I replaced the blanket underneath Nikki so I could monitor the ongoing blood loss.

Over the next ten minutes, I switched bags of IV fluids as they emptied and checked her pulse every few minutes. I imagined it becoming stronger and maybe slowing a little from its unsustainable racing at my arrival.

Cantwell stood in the corner of the room, shaking uncontrollably. Was he really that attached to Nikki? To his "legacy" as he called her?

"She needs a hospital, Bennett." Down to the last bag of fluid, I stood to make eye contact across the half-height wall. I had to make him understand. "I've done everything I can."

Dale Bennett kept working on the electronic equipment. With no electricity, I wondered why—and then I knew what had niggled. He had a plan B. Radio. Nathan was wrong. The Kadence chip could receive radio waves. It was the only thing that made sense, the only reason he would have come here. Bypassing Bluetooth, he might be able to trigger all the Kadences at once, or all the ones within range of the radio tower. Could he time the shocks to stop their hearts? I couldn't risk it. I couldn't risk Aunt Irm.

He looked over at Nikki on the new clean sheet. "She's not bleeding anymore."

"She'll start again if we move her. The balloon in her uterus is a Band-Aid, not a treatment."

"Balloon?" He screwed up his nose. Cantwell gagged. *Men.*

"No choice," Bennett said. "We have to go."

"Are you listening to me?" I raised my voice. "If you move her, she will die. Do you want another death on your conscience?"

His expression changed. Remorse? Was that possible? Then his attention shifted and it was gone.

There was a sound. A car? He shouted an expletive as he ran toward the front room of the building, leaving us alone.

"She's going to die," Cantwell said. "We're all going to die."

"What the hell is wrong with you?" I said. "She needs us. You have to get yourself under control." It occurred to me he hadn't done much patient care in a long time. Being a chairman heavy into research, it may have been years since he was in a critical situation. Good thing, too. He sucked at it.

An artificially amplified voice said words I couldn't make out but imagined to be *come out with your hands up.* Or maybe that was just TV.

Most of me felt relieved; the rest concerned about Bennett's plan B. I considered trying to destroy the console in his absence, but he reappeared with a walkie-talkie-like device extended toward me. "Tell them what you need."

When I reached for it, he pulled it away. "Just talk."

"This is Dr. Kate Downey," I said into the device. "I have a patient with a postpartum hemorrhage who is still bleeding. Are you a paramedic?"

"Police. Paramedics are on their way." The voice over the walkie-talkie was strong, confident, but not Garner.

"Is Lieutenant Garner here?" I asked him.

"Garner?" he said.

Bennett raised the gun in his other hand, pointing it toward me. "Tell them what you need."

I rattled off a list, mostly blood products and more fluids, as well as drugs to contract Nikki's uterus. As I finished the list, as fast as I could, I added, "Tell Nathan Castle where we are."

Bennett pulled the walkie-talkie back and swung the back of his gun hand across my face. I stumbled, nearly tripping over Nikki. It had happened so fast I could only hope the police heard. Hope somehow Nathan got the message we were at a radio station and put twelve and twelve together. It was a long shot, a thousand yards into a headwind.

Bennett yanked me, hard, against him. "How did they find us?"

I tried to pull away. He was too strong. "I don't know."

Bennett attached the walkie-talkie to his belt and patted me down again, more thoroughly this time, like slime oozing over my skin. My jaw hurt too much to clench.

Nikki moaned.

"Let her go," Cantwell said, his eyes on his daughter. "She has to save Nikki."

Bennett did, and I knelt at her side and checked her pulse. It might actually be slower than mine at the moment. "If you were smart, you would have been gone already," I said to Bennett.

"Don't antagonize him," Cantwell said.

"It's not the smartest or the most deserving who get the breaks, is it, Dr. Cantwell?" Bennett said. "I worked for years perfecting that communication system. It's fail-safe. You could have convinced the FDA and gotten it approved. It could be in this version of the Kadence."

I probably should have listened to Cantwell, but adrenaline took over. "I'm pretty sure your backdoor stunt proved them right."

"I was forced," Bennett said.

"Right. Were you forced to kill Mr. McCann and all the others on the road that night?" Jolene's tear-streaked face came to mind, begging to die with her baby.

"Collateral damage is inevitable."

"I don't think your victims' families would agree." I adjusted the rolled blanket under Nikki's head. "Why didn't you just take your technology to China where American patents don't matter?"

In an instant, he stood inches away, the gun pressed against my forehead. His eyes crazed and voice feral. "Because I don't speak Chinese."

"Stop." It came from Nikki. Her eyes were open to slits. Her lips held maybe the faintest hint of color. To my surprise, Bennett took a step back. The walkie-talkie beeped and he left the room.

"If I'd pushed for the extra FDA trials, none of this would have happened. Ian would be alive. You wouldn't have lost your baby." Cantwell looked impossibly grief-stricken for the completely self-absorbed ass I knew.

Bennett returned with a duffel and a red Igloo cooler labeled *BLOOD*. He dropped both on the floor.

I moved toward them and the gun appeared yet again.

"I will check these first," he said.

Hands in the air, I backed away. "Start with the cooler."

He opened it, moved around the contents, then slid it over to me and started on the duffel.

I hung a unit of blood on each IV. "I need hot water to warm this or she'll never clot."

Bennett appeared ready to argue, then made the call instead. He returned moments later with two steaming cups with lids. I showed Cantwell how to coil the IV tubing into the hot water so the blood would be warmed before it reached Nikki. He trembled so much he spilled much of the water, and I took over. "You have got to focus," I muttered to him. "Think about getting us out of here."

From the supplies strewn across the floor, I found a clear bag containing the medications I'd requested—Methergine, Hemabate, and Pitocin. I administered all three.

After the units of blood were infused, I hung clotting factors on one IV and platelets on the other. We had a lot of catching up to do. Cantwell remained strangely distant from his daughter, his back against the wall, mumbling to himself. From the few words I heard, it sounded like a litany of life's regrets.

Nikki lay quietly. When she did open her eyes, she didn't reach for Cantwell, or ask him to sit with her, but stared at him with an odd smile. What a strange relationship these two would have—if we survived.

Bennett also stared oddly at times—at Nikki, at the blood on the floor, even at a pile of blankets. I thought he looked despondent, but that would assign him too much humanity credit.

Since I was finding everyone's expression confounding, I decided it was probably me.

Every few minutes, Bennett was on the walkie-talkie, demanding transport.

I debated examining Nikki's uterus again, but feared dislodging the makeshift balloon I'd inserted. I replaced the bloody sheet beneath her again. This time she helped lift her hips. "It was a girl," she whispered. "A perfect baby girl."

"I'm so sorry, Nikki." I'd been there, exactly there, with a perfect baby girl.

"Kate." I moved closer to hear. "Can you get Dale Bennett out of here? I want to talk to my father. He looks so sad."

He did. No doubt. The IV bags wouldn't need to be swapped for several more minutes. "I'll try." I stood and walked toward the door.

"Where do you think you're going?" Bennett said.

My pulse skipped several beats as I neared the wrong end of his gun. "To see if there's anything else I can scavenge around here. Tag along if you want."

He did, and I led him into one of the side offices. An old wooden desk sat in the center. I rifled through the empty drawers, taking as much time as I could without being obvious. Then I led him across to the other office and repeated the procedure.

A gunshot pierced the relative silence. Nikki screamed, "No!"

Bennett grabbed me from behind, pressed his gun to my back, and yelled into the walkie-talkie. "Do not enter or they're all dead." He pushed me ahead of him into the hallway and faced the front door. Nothing happened. The only sound was Nikki's sobs. "Why, Daddy?"

After a long moment, we turned around. Nikki knelt on the floor, crying, her hands on Cantwell's face despite the dark hole in his forehead. Blood pooled under his head, as well as around her. She was bleeding again.

Bennett finally released me.

"Nikki, I'm so sorry, but you have to lie down." As I helped her onto her back, she pulled a small bundle along with her. Out of a fold in the blanket, I saw an impossibly tiny foot. I looked away.

"I tried to stop him," she said through her sobs.

Bennett stood sideways, his head moving from the scene to the front door and back.

I grabbed a sheet and covered Dr. Cantwell's lifeless body, hoping to find the gun. It was gone. Bennett must have collected it already.

"Leave," I said to him. "I have to examine her." He closed the door, shoved Cantwell's body against it, and retreated around the half-wall.

"We just found each other. Why?" Nikki said.

I murmured words of comfort that I doubted she heard. Near as I could tell, the glove was still in place. I removed the clamp and instilled more water, but it accepted little.

"He blamed himself," she said.

I cleaned her up and sat next to her, back against the wall.

She continued to cry. "He insisted on seeing his grand-child . . . and then he apologized . . . and then he . . ."

Cantwell had a gun. Where had he gotten it? He'd been forced to give up the one he brought before we entered, and had been searched as well. The police might have sent one in with the supplies, but Bennett went through them. And why not shoot Dale Bennett instead of himself?

I looked at Nikki. "Give me the gun."

CHAPTER FORTY-EIGHT

NIKKI BLINKED, TEARS glistening on her lashes. "Bennett must have taken it."

"Where did it come from?"

"I don't know." She sobbed some more. This time, I didn't put an arm around her. My mind spun, trying to reconcile the information. Bennett stood across the wall, his gun pointed in our direction, but his focus was on the electronic panel.

Aunt Irm.

I had to end this. I searched the duffel for other helpful surprises, then expanded the search to the blankets and supplies that littered the room. Garner had to be outside by now. It occurred to me he might have hidden a listening device in the supplies. I described the room in a whisper, mentioned the possibility of a radio attack against the Kadence, told them Nikki was bleeding, then asked Garner to protect Aunt Irm.

Under the corner of a bloody blanket was an empty foil pill pack I hadn't noticed earlier. Misoprostol. A drug that causes uterine contraction and would be an appropriate treatment for Nikki, except I hadn't requested any. Had Cantwell found it and given it to her? He'd been decompensating. Maybe she found it herself?

Before I could ask, Dale Bennett returned with a smile that struck me as the picture of evil. "Car's here. It's time to go."

Nikki stirred.

"You can't move her," I said again, but with less conviction this time.

"She did fine getting over to her father. Get what you need. We leave in ten." He disappeared into the adjoining room followed almost immediately by the deafening rumble of a generator. *Holy hell*. He was going to trigger the Kadences. In a crouch, I peeked over the wall. He wasn't looking my way, but his gun was. God, I hated that thing.

I dropped out of view. Nikki's eyes were open. I leaned down, my mouth to her ear, and said, "He's trying to trigger the Kadences by radio. I have to stop him."

She pulled me toward her. "I'm sorry, Kate."

I saw hardness rather than sorrow in her eyes. Misoprostol. Cantwell's gun. Thoughts swirled, much too fast, too much to put together, and too much uncertainty. But that was my job, to make decisions on imperfect data. Anesthesiologists do it every day. I reached across as if to check the balloon in her uterus, as I had every fifteen minutes or so. This time I released the clamp. Nausea welled at what I'd done, but an image of Aunt Irm in my mind pushed me onward. I had to stop Dale Bennett.

In a crouch, I moved to the end of the half-wall and peered around the corner. He stood with his back to me. His left arm aimed the gun at roughly where I'd been with Nikki. He adjusted the station controls mounted on a shelf against the back wall. In an instant, I weighed my two options: generator or him. It had to be both.

The generator's red power switch was on the front. I took a deep breath, then crept forward unseen. I smacked the off button, spun, and plowed my left shoulder just below his hip with all the force I could generate. He crashed to the floor. I depressed the talk button on the walkie-talkie still on his hip and yelled, "Come now!"

During my invincible teen years, with no mother to instruct otherwise, I played tackle football with my brother and his friends. I was one of the guys, if the smallest by far. The key to taking down a larger opponent, I learned, is to stay low, hold tight, and not let go. With Bennett on his left side and my weight on his legs, I braced my right foot against the wall and my left as far out as I could reach and resisted every twisting move he tried to make. I wouldn't be able to hold on for long. *Come on, Garner.*

Sounds from the hallway, then a gunshot.

What the hell?

Another gunshot.

Nikki? I failed to anticipate another twist from Bennett, and he rolled to his back. Everything slowed. His gun moved toward me. I rolled away. A shot rang out, deafening in the small space.

"We need her!" Nikki screamed.

My ears rang from the shot, from her words. Bennett sat up, and in his eyes was something inhuman, desperate, unhinged. He swung the gun toward me. I had nowhere to go. I was going to die. *Aunt Irm. Christian.* Another shot, and his eyes were no longer frenzied. His eyes were no longer there.

Nikki leaned on the half-wall, a gun in her hand, her expression impossible to read and terrifying at the same time. Her mouth twisted in a sort of monstrous smile.

I lay back under the cabinet, out of view, and hopefully out of the line of fire. I scanned the area for another weapon. Nothing.

"Come on, Kate. Let's get out of here," Nikki said.

She'd had the gun the whole time. I wondered where, then I knew. The baby. She knew I wouldn't unwrap the baby.

Bennett's gun was just out of reach, still in the hand that rested on his abdomen, everything covered with blood and bone and brain.

"You killed your baby," I said.

"I wasn't going to give Cantwell his goddamn legacy. That bastard paid my mom to abort. He wanted to kill me before I was even born. Then he marries some barren hag and comes back wanting to play daddy? He tried to bribe his way into my life, just like he bribed his way out." In spite of myself, I found her view of the events fascinating, completely twisted, but fascinating. "I showed him. I took everything away. His beloved Kadence, his reputation, his grandchild. The look on his face when he saw her."

"Your daughter, Nikki. She was your baby girl." I reached my hand toward the gun.

"And when that grandchild hid a gun." Her laugh was nothing short of grotesque. The baby was merely a pawn in a horrific game of revenge.

"You killed him, too, didn't you? Your baby, your father, your husband."

"And now the father of my baby." Said without an ounce of remorse. Maybe even with pride.

I leaned out just far enough to catch a glimpse. Her face was pale, her lips barely pink. She was bleeding again.

"Come on, Kate. The car's waiting. Everything's planned."

"Where are we going?" I stretched further.

She leaned against the wall, her lids drooping. I grabbed the gun from Bennett's inert hand. Another shot rang out and searing heat crossed my arm. I jerked back, dropping Bennett's gun, and it clattered to the floor. A streak of blood crossed my forearm, only a graze.

"Ian loved you."

"Ian didn't love me. He loved sweet, weak Nikki Yarborough, not strong, determined Nikki Simmons. Cantwell destroyed my mother. She was going to be a brilliant doctor, and he took that away from her. All he cared about was his career, and all I cared about was ruining him. That's why I went to medical school and became a cardiologist and married a desperately boring man who worked in his lab."

Poor Ian was a means to an end.

"Our plan was perfect, you know, mine and Dale's. Ian was the fall guy. He would die, of course, but Dale set him up to take the blame. Except Ian couldn't handle it. Once you showed up at the cabin and told us about the crash . . . It's not like I didn't warn Dale that Ian was a coward." The sound of her voice changed.

I dared a peek. She was leaning heavily on the half-wall.

"It still might have worked if you hadn't . . . your aunt was a mistake. Made it too personal."

"She knew, by the way. She didn't trust you."

"But you did."

"I couldn't believe you would hurt your own patients."

"That was Dale. He went off-script. I chose them carefully so they could be resuscitated." She *chose* them. *She chose Aunt Irm.*

"I took care of one of the crash victims," I said. "A pregnant woman just your age. Her husband was killed and she required an emergency Cesarean and hysterectomy. The baby suffered neurological damage." I prepared to leave my hiding spot. "That child is your legacy—fatherless, with a widowed mother, and facing life challenges beyond anything you can imagine. All because you needed revenge." I moved to a squat. "You better pray that little boy sees past his traumatic beginnings, because you are the Victor Cantwell in his world."

"Cut the holier-than-thou crap. We're not so different, you and I—widows who lost a baby. I may have wanted Ian dead, but I didn't pull the plug. And you made me bleed . . ." Her voice trailed off.

I looked again. No Nikki. Staying low, I stepped over Bennett's body, grabbed his gun from the floor, and paused by the opening. I peeked around the corner. She sat on the floor in a pool of blood, her gun pointed directly at me, as mine was at her. "Put the gun down and I'll stop the bleeding," I said.

Her face screwed up in confusion. "You killed me? I told you we're not so different." She fell to the side.

"Nikki?"

No answer. I moved cautiously to her side. She lay motionless. I took the gun from her and tossed both of them aside. The door opened slowly, pushing Cantwell's body toward me. I saw first a rifle, then a face under a helmet. It was Garner. He stepped over the corpse and came to my side. "Leave her. Let's get you out of here."

A team of paramedics appeared. I told them about the makeshift balloon and how to inflate it. My gaze caught on the small bundle, Nikki's baby. I couldn't leave her on the floor. When I reached for her, Garner stopped me. "Part of the crime scene."

"It's a baby." For the first time, tears threatened.

Garner spoke to the paramedic examining Cantwell. Her eyes went to the baby and she nodded.

"She'll take care of it. Let's go."

As Garner led me to the door, I heard someone say, "No pulse. Begin chest compressions."

I tried to turn back. He stopped me. "They have it."

As he led me out, I noticed two bullet holes in the door. "I should have known she had a gun."

"The officer was wearing a vest. He'll be fine."

I glanced back again. "I only meant to incapacitate her."

"We'll talk about it later." Light spilled through the open door-way and broken windows. It wasn't until we reached the threshold that I realized it was night. The blinding light came from enormous panels erected around the front. Raised voices from the left drew my attention. "Let him through," Garner said.

Christian ran to me, his beautiful face still bruised, but his body strong and warm.

"Aunt Irm?" I asked.

"Safe. Everyone is safe."

Not everyone.

Garner ordered me to an ambulance where I sat on the back bumper, facing the building. *We're not so different, you and I.* It wasn't true, but I'd crossed a line tonight and my head needed time to be okay with it. I doubted my heart ever would be.

A paramedic helped me change out of my blood-soaked clothes and into a disposable jumper that ballooned around me. My clothes went into an evidence bag. She examined my face, performed a quick neuro exam, and washed and dressed my arm wound. "Do you want something for the pain?"

"No. No pain."

"You'll need to use antibiotic ointment."

I wasn't listening. I stared at the door, waiting for Nikki. Garner came out first. One look at his face and I knew. "This was self-defense, Kate. You saved my officers by ending things on your own."

"I could have overpowered her without . . ."

"She had a gun."

Christian's grip around my shoulders tightened. "Can I take her home?"

Garner nodded. Christian helped me from the ambulance and into his passenger seat. Without a word, we held hands all the way to his house. I knew I should ask what happened, how they saved Aunt Irm and the other patients, what was going on during the whole ugly scene. Instead, I turned off. Aunt Irm was safe. Christian was safe, and I was safe. That was all that mattered for now.

CHAPTER FORTY-NINE

WE ARRIVED AT Christian's house to find it fully lit and every adult awake, including Nathan and a very excited Shadow. Aunt Irm cried and we hugged for a long time. With coaxing from Christian, everyone agreed to wait for the story until morning.

"It is morning," Christian's brother Luke said, pointing at the clock.

"Four a.m. is not morning," said Mrs. O'Donnell. "We're glad you're safe, dear." And she headed to her room. Everyone else drifted away, except Aunt Irm and Christian.

"I need a shower," I said. "Let's go home."

"Stay, please," Christian said. "You can have my room."

Though the thought of staying safely under Christian's roof was almost unbearably tempting, I couldn't do it. They had just lost a family member, and I needed space for my own mourning. "I need clean clothes and my own bed." We headed toward the front door, Shadow glued to my side. "Besides, Aunt Irm snores," I said quietly.

"I do not snore."

"Guess my ears are still ringing, I meant to whisper."

"Oh, you did, kindchen, but I have excellent hearing."

Only when we stepped outside did I remember my car was still at the hospital. Christian came out behind us. "I'll drive you."

I didn't argue, and sat in the back seat with Shadow. "You were right, Aunt Irm. Nikki was part of it the whole time, maybe even in the lead. How did you know?"

"That night she did not enjoy my sacher-torte."

In spite of everything, I grinned. It would be an interesting fix for the legal system.

"I mean, that night, she did not behave like the other doctors. She did not appreciate anything. She was engaged in only herself. That is not a good person, and she was not your friend."

But I'd thought she was. Between work and Aunt Irm, I took little time for friends, and Nikki was one of the few. I had not chosen wisely. "I need you to teach me."

"For now, trust me, kindchen."

I rubbed Shadow's soft ears as he rested his head on my thigh. "She took a drug to abort her own baby."

Aunt Irm suffered numerous miscarriages early in her marriage and a sob escaped. "She is an evil woman."

"Yes, she was."

"She is dead?" She turned to look at me.

I nodded.

She grunted.

It wasn't actually her death I mourned. I didn't know the woman who died. How do you grieve for a friend who never existed?

At home, I thanked Christian for the ride and went straight to my room, turned the shower as hot as I could stand, and let water run over my hair, my body, washing away Nikki's blood and Dale Bennett's . . . everything. If only memories could be washed away as easily. She'd been responsible for so many deaths in the name of revenge. So many ruined and grieving families.

Try as I might to clear my mind, questions tormented me. I might never know the answers. One thing I knew, though, my blind faith in Nikki Yarborough was ill-conceived and, in the end, dangerous. Which made me wonder whether there were others in my life whose motives I should question. Fortunately, the water began to cool.

I toweled off and heard the murmur of voices. Part of me hoped it was the television. Another part didn't. The second part won when I opened the door to find Christian trying to convince Aunt Irm to let him make up the couch. Both stilled when I approached. Aunt Irm came to me, kissed me on both cheeks, and disappeared into her room.

"I'm sorry, Kate, after everything that happened tonight, I need to . . ." We were both moving and came together in a tight embrace.

"Me, too." I pulled his face to mine and we kissed long and hard, with the desperation of the night and the need to feel alive and whole.

I led him to the couch where we sat together, his arm around me, the unbruised side of my head on his shoulder. We didn't talk, just sat. I concentrated on the rhythm of his breathing, slow and steady and constant.

I woke to the sound of running water, my head in Christian's lap. We were still on the couch. He smiled down at me. I sat up. "I'm sorry. You should have told me to go to bed."

"I slept just fine here." He rubbed a hand gently through my tangled hair and gave me the most knee-weakening smile. Good thing I was sitting.

Delicious smells wafted from the kitchen—pancakes, bacon, eggs. We joined Aunt Irm at the table and ate heartily. The conversation ranged from travel to books to movies and completely ignored the only topic on any of our minds. Christian received a text. "Garner would like to come by." He looked at me for an answer.

I nodded.

Aunt Irm stood. "I will make more pancakes, and I will invite Nathan. He has been texting all morning." It was barely eight.

Christian offered to take Shadow out while I dressed and brushed my teeth.

When Garner and Nathan arrived, Aunt Irm brought an over-loaded plate of pancakes and placed it before them. They might have already eaten a full breakfast, but both dug in.

With my permission, Garner switched on a recorder and asked me to start with the events at the hospital with Cantwell. I related them mostly in order, occasionally having to go back and add in a detail. In deference to the meal, I left out most of the medical details about Nikki. "She asked me to leave her alone with her dad, so I made an excuse to go down the hall. That's when Cantwell was killed. She said it was suicide. It didn't feel right, but I didn't press it."

Garner shook his head. "You were correct. She told him she was behind it all."

"You could hear," I said.

"As you suspected, we had a listening device in the duffel. Nikki told him she joined his department intent on destroying him and everything he'd built. She convinced faculty to quit and others to decline job offers."

"And then complained about the hard work she brought on herself." Aunt Irm shook her head, mumbling unintelligible words that might have been German.

I'd commiserated with Nikki, encouraged her to stand up to him. She must have loved that. "In her mind, damaging her father was more important than any pain she might suffer."

"She told him it was her idea to hack the Kadence and destroy MDI before the sale," Garner said.

"If she'd let the sale go through and killed him after, she would have inherited a crap-ton of money," Nathan said.

"Not her goal," I said. "She used Dale Bennett, too."

"I can believe that. Doesn't make him innocent though." Nathan put half a pancake in his mouth.

"Agreed," Garner said. "At that point, she apparently handed Cantwell the baby and told him she aborted on purpose to prevent his legacy."

Aunt Irm stared, her eyes shining. "That poor child."

"The gunshot came soon after," Garner said.

"Did you know it was her?" I asked.

"Not then." Garner added more syrup to his pancakes. "What happened when you got back in the room?"

"I took care of Nikki, and Bennett went back into the control room. I looked for the gun and assumed he'd retrieved it, but I guess Nikki kept it. I searched for anything I could use to stop him. That's when I found the packet of pills and started to wonder if she'd aborted. After that, things sort of fell into place—the strange way Bennett looked at Nikki and the baby, plus the fact he wouldn't leave her, made sense when I realized he was the father. I also wondered why Cantwell would shoot himself rather than Bennett. I should have put it together then."

"There was much going on, kindchen. You figured it out in time."

"We told Bennett the car was available," Garner said. "Then the generator started, and we heard nothing else for a while."

"A really long while." It was the first words Christian had spoken. He sat beside me with his arm on the back of my chair, his hand on my shoulder.

"We had to restrain Rambo here from storming the building." Nathan gestured to Christian.

I smiled.

"You think he's kidding," Garner said.

Christian made no apologies but blushed a little.

Garner looked at me expectantly.

"She told me she was sorry but had the oddest look on her face. I can't explain it, but that was the last straw. I unclamped the intrauterine balloon knowing the bleeding would resume. I hoped it would incapacitate her so I could end it. The plan was to reinflate it in time." Tears threatened. I held them at bay.

"It was a brilliant move," Garner said. "I know it went against everything you believe in, but it was your only play at the time."

I wanted to believe him. "What happened next?"

"With the generator noise, we sent in two officers to try to get eyes on the scene."

"And Nikki shot them through the door."

"That's why they wear vests."

"Thank you for that. What happened with the radio signal?"

"Nothing," Nathan said with pride. "Once Garner mentioned the radio tower, I knew exactly what you meant. Christian and I figured there was no way to get all the Kadence patients to safety, so we decided to go after the tower itself."

"They made me sit in a windowless room," Aunt Irm said. "Luke tuned a radio and we heard only static. For hours, we sat there."

"Remind me to thank him. I'm betting you weren't great company."

"Oh, posh."

"Christian rejected my idea." Nathan's grin was mischievous.

"You wanted to blow up the tower," Christian said.

"It would have been awesome. Instead, we severed the connections from the building to the tower. Amazing what you can find on Google. It wasn't nearly as cool as explosives but probably safer for you inside the building."

"You think?" Christian said.

"How'd you disable Bennett?" Nathan asked.

"I tackled him."

"Katherine Rose." Aunt Irm's exclamation reminded me of adolescence when she would catch me playing sports with the guys.

I smiled at her. "All that roughhousing came in handy."

"Hmph. You still do not know proper limits."

"Thank God for that," Garner said.

Christian squeezed my shoulder.

"I couldn't hold him for long. He pulled away and . . ." How to describe the wild look in his eyes?

"And he shot you, kindchen."

I lifted my bandaged arm. "Actually, that was Nikki. Bennett missed, and then Nikki killed him." It hadn't occurred to me she saved my life while I was slowly killing her. "I hid out of range until she fainted."

"We heard the conversation," Garner said. "You did a great job keeping her engaged."

I kept her engaged for too long. I could have overpowered her earlier, before she bled out.

Aunt Irm read my expression. "She was killed by her own choices. That a choice you made contributed is not relevant." She emphasized the last two words. "Her survival would have risked more lives."

"She's right, Kate," Garner said. "We would have had to follow and anything can happen in a chase. You did the right thing."

I nodded, sort of. Choices are a funny thing. In my job, we are often forced to make them with incomplete data. Does this patient with low blood pressure need fluids or blood, or drugs to strengthen the heart, or pressors to tighten the blood vessels? We make an educated choice, watch what happens, and adjust as necessary.

It is not so different in life. We make choices based on our perception of events and situations, and adjust as necessary. My perception of recent events would be revised with time and distance, and hopefully my choices would feel justified. But today was not that day.

CHAPTER FIFTY

MICHAEL O'DONNELL'S FUNERAL was on Saturday. Aunt Irm and I sat with the family. Christian held my hand firmly throughout. Jackie, the eldest sister, gave the eulogy. She'd been closest to Michael growing up and told childhood stories that earned chuckles and a few tears. The stories ended when Michael distanced himself from the family in high school. Jackie said they all regretted losing touch, not knowing Michael better in adulthood. She blamed it on busy lives and distance. She said the siblings would ensure some good came from this tragedy, bringing the family closer. I thought it a beautiful send-off, a three-tissue send-off for me, more for Aunt Irm.

The internment would be up north, in a family plot with his father and other relatives. While the O'Donnells thanked the attendees, Aunt Irm and I left to set out food for the reception. We had cooked all morning, as had the O'Donnells. Even if every funeral attendee brought friends and family, we'd still have food left over.

With a week's grieving under their belts, the O'Donnells conversed and laughed and reminisced with distant family, making the day more a celebration than a wake.

In the late afternoon, I excused myself to attend a much smaller service for Dr. Cantwell. He had no family there and few friends. Mr. Samuels, his partner at MDI, was notably absent. Some hospital and College of Medicine dignitaries made an appearance, including Dr. Cantwell's secretary and Annabelle Kessler, the fellow, but there were no tears. A generic eulogy was offered by the officiant, more a reading of selections from Dr. Cantwell's resume than a heartfelt commentary on his accomplishments. When he invited words from others, no one volunteered.

Something in me couldn't let that be the sum of his life. I stood. "I only recently had the opportunity to get to know Dr. Cantwell. My first impressions were . . . less than warm." A few chuckles. "But I came to learn he valued family and regretted the single-minded focus that enabled his academic success but deprived him of so much else that matters. Though I didn't know him well, I think he might be gratified if his death caused others to consider their own choices, as the consequences echo unpredictably over time."

As I sat, my own words rang in my head. Nikki made choices throughout her life that led to a miserable adulthood, the ruining of others, and her own premature demise. That I played a role in her death was unfortunate, but I, too, was responsible for my life choices. I could choose to feel guilt over her death, or accept the events as inevitable—horrible but necessary, and influenced by her choices rather than my intent.

The same analysis could be applied in other areas of my life. I could choose to continue fighting with Greg's brother or accept that Adam no longer deserved my attention. I could choose to continue my self-imposed mourning over Greg or accept my loss and move on to embrace life. Most importantly, choosing not to choose is in itself a choice.

I left the chapel, nodding only to Annabelle as I hurried to my car and back to the O'Donnells. Besides the family, only Aunt Irm, Garner, and Nathan remained. The children played with the dogs in the yard while the adults sat around folding tables across the back porch. Shadow acknowledged my return with a quick bump into my legs for a pet, then returned to the unending game of fetch.

Christian offered his seat next to Aunt Irm, then pulled over another for himself.

"Finally," Luke said. "We've been pretending to be interested in Garner's stories while waiting for you."

Garner tossed a wadded-up napkin at him. It landed in his beer.

"He is going to tell us the news about our case." Aunt Irm nodded to him to begin, which made me grin. Though I wasn't eager to rehash the events, it was time to get it over with so we could move on.

"After reviewing communications between all parties, the picture has cleared considerably," Garner said. "In 1987, Dr. Cantwell was engaged to an up-and-coming medical researcher when he had an affair with Nikki's mother, a medical student at Emory University in Atlanta. She became pregnant and they agreed to keep his paternity a secret. She never returned to school. Dr. Cantwell set up a fund for her through an attorney, but none of the money was used until recently."

"Nikki claimed he paid her mother to abort," I said.

"The first installment may have been, but he continued to add funds over the years. After Nikki's mother died, he had his attorney invite Nikki to make contact. She refused, and his identity was not disclosed."

"That is good of Dr. Cantwell to keep his promise," Aunt Irm said. "The mother's pride was unfortunate and needless. A father should support his child."

I saw both sides and didn't want to think how I would react in the same situation.

"We found a photo of her parents in Nikki's apartment with other mementos of her mother," Garner said. It had to be the photo I'd seen in the flap of the baby album.

"Her mom died after Nikki graduated med school," I said. "I'm guessing she found the photo soon after and planned her career and even her marriage around getting close to him." She spent her childhood despising an anonymous father figure. Once he had a name, she focused on his ruin. Everything she did was designed for revenge. The similarity to her father's focus on the Kadence was not lost on me.

"Her Ian is not without blame here," Aunt Irm said. "But this was certainly her idea."

"A year ago, Nikki and Bennett worked together on a research paper and started an affair," Garner said. "When the FDA wanted bigger studies to allow use of his technology in the Kadence, he sent some angry emails to the examiners."

"Always a good idea with federal agencies when you don't get your way," Luke said.

"He shared them with us in the lab," Nathan said. "Believe it or not, the ones he sent were way nicer than the earlier versions."

Garner continued, "He was offered a job at MDI, which was rescinded soon after. He considered going overseas and starting a competing company away from the FDA. He even invited Nikki to join him. Then he found an investor and decided to start a company in Georgia."

"Who would invest in tech the FDA had just rejected?" Luke asked.

"Nikki Yarborough," Garner said.

Nikki complained about student loans. Except he'd just mentioned funds set aside by her father. "You're kidding. She took money from her father to invest in a company to compete with his?"

Garner nodded. "Under an alias, of course. Even Bennett didn't know it was her."

"Wow, devious," Nathan said with something akin to respect.

"It was Nikki's idea to keep the two-way communication in the software. She said it would help her with research to convince the FDA. To get the code installed, Bennett gave Ian the final version late, which made it easy to convince him to rush the testing."

"He was preparing the back door in case things didn't go his way," I said.

Garner nodded. "After the university and MDI refused his demand for control of his patent, he and Nikki came up with the misfire scheme. We can't be sure whose idea it was, but Bennett is the coder so he created the app."

"Probably to Nikki's specifications," I said. "All they needed was a fall guy, so they convinced Ian that MDI could have kept him on, but chose not to."

"So revenge as a motive for him, too," Nathan said. "It's theme night."

"He never knew of Nikki's involvement. Or her affair as far as we know," Garner said. "Then the misfires and blackmail began."

It occurred to me Nikki timed all this to deliver a pre-viable baby to hurt her father. Truly sick.

"Nikki chose the victims," Garner said.

"That woman did not deserve to be called 'doctor' or 'wife,'" Aunt Irm said. Mrs. O'Donnell agreed.

"Ian turned out to be a bad choice for a fall guy," Garner said. "After triggering you, Aunt Irm, he wanted out. He sent Bennett a text saying he knew the victim and might have been recognized."

So it was him outside the clinic. I despised him in that moment.

"Bennett reassured him. Soon after, though, Bennett and Nikki had an argument by text about Ian."

A week ago, I would have assumed Nikki defended her husband. A week ago, I was blind.

"She wanted Ian eliminated. Bennett refused, then she sent the threats to Cantwell and Samuels about their families."

"Ha, she threatened herself," Nathan said. "You have to admit that's kinda funny, considering how it ended."

"She wished to worry her father." Aunt Irm shook her head in mock disappointment. She was well beyond disappointment. So was I.

"She used their disappearance to manipulate Bennett," Garner said. "She didn't tell him about the threats or her plan. He sent numerous texts that went unanswered. Finally, he sent an ultimatum that she answer or he would proceed with the next patient on the list."

Christian's family, rapt since the beginning, looked on.

"That patient was Mr. McCann, the one who caused the accident," I said. "He was on her list for the next day when he had a clinic appointment."

"He was the very first patient to receive a Kadence," Garner said.

"She would attack her father's pride and joy," Aunt Irm said.

"She might have planned to do it right in front of him. Since there's no cell signal or Wi-Fi at the cabin in Georgia, she probably didn't know Bennett planned to trigger him early."

"Her texts back to him the next day went from angry to apologetic," Garner said. "They were quite a pair. She finally convinced him that Ian had become a liability."

"He had to be eliminated," Aunt Irm said matter-of-factly. I felt a little sorry for him, the way he'd been handled by both Nikki and

Bennett. I wondered how much he knew of her betrayal, whether she pulled the trigger, or if he died protecting her and the child he thought was his.

Garner summarized the rest of the story, which ended with the final two deaths. Only later did I realize the twinge of guilt never came.

"The autopsy revealed—" Garner paused and looked at his notes—"placenta accreta?"

I explained that one. "It's when the placenta grows into the uterine muscle. It can happen when a patient has had prior surgery on her uterus, which she'd had. She wouldn't have stopped bleeding without an operation and maybe a hysterectomy."

There were several more questions and clarifications, and then it was over. I hoped forever.

"Thanks for putting up with us through all of this," I said to Garner.

"Nonsense," Aunt Irm said. "Lieutenant Garner is grateful for our contributions."

I laughed.

"She's right," Mrs. O'Donnell said. "He told us himself."

"I also told you not to share that with Kate," Garner said.

* * *

At long last, Christian and I sat alone on the end of the dock, our bare feet dangling in the cool water.

"How do you feel?" he asked.

I thought about my answer. *How did I feel?* "I'm okay. I've decided not to blame myself for the consequences of others' choices."

"Wow, that's big."

"Yeah, it's a work in progress. Speaking of which, can you help me with another legal matter?"

"What's that?"

"I want to be done with Adam. Remove myself as executor of his mother's estate and give him everything."

He raised an eyebrow.

"His apron strings are strangling me. Aunt Irm is right—Greg wouldn't expect me to continue to look out for him after all he's done."

"If you're sure, of course, I'll help, but can I make a suggestion?"

I waited.

"In her estate, I noticed Greg took out a five-hundred-thousand-dollar life insurance policy on himself that paid her upon his death."

"Really?"

"He did it when he was commissioned, right after college."

It shouldn't surprise me he would make arrangements for his mom in case something happened.

"If you like, we can hold that money back for his charity. It comes out to far less than half of the estate's value."

"Wow. Yes. Thank you." I felt lighter than I had in months. Adam would be out of my life, and I had ample seed money for the charity. I was choosing to close the door on my life as a member of the Downey family but open a window that honored Greg's memory.

"Tell me about your promotion." I tried to sound upbeat, but Christian's home was in south Florida, not here.

"I turned in my notice."

"You . . ."

"Over the last couple of weeks, I realized I don't want to help corporations grow at the expense of employees. I'm ashamed to say that, until now, I didn't think much about the lives affected, the collateral damage. It's not who I want to be."

I trusted myself only to nod.

"I've decided to start a legal consulting company, working for myself so I can choose my own clients." He turned more fully to face me. "If you haven't hired anyone and would trust a rookie, I'd like Greg's foundation to be my first project."

I stared in his gorgeous eyes, warm and genuine. "That would be amazing." It was a lot to take in. "That's huge news. Quitting your job, starting your own company."

His eyes remained on mine. "I have a lot to learn. Staying put would be easier, but the wrong choice. I want something different. And I want to be here, with you."

The lump in my throat grew as warmth settled in my middle. With effort, I choked out, "I'd like that." We sat like that for several moments. Christian wasn't leaving. My world was shifting once again, this time in a good way, into alignment.

He wrapped his arm around me. "We make a good team, and I think, when you're ready, we can be a great team."

Lost in his eyes, bright in the moonlight, I said, "How about we make a great team now, minus the whole hunting murderers thing."

"Garner will like that last part."

"Aunt Irm won't."

AUTHOR'S NOTE

Misfire is a work of fiction, of course, but AICDs are real, and in fact, can be hacked. In 2019, the FDA issued an alert that several models made by Medtronic Inc. were vulnerable. While he was Vice President, the wireless function of Dick Cheney's AICD was disabled "to prevent would-be assassins from interfering with it and causing a fatal heart attack." Any such attack, however, would require close proximity to the victim and there is no evidence any device has ever been hacked. Meanwhile, AICDs save lives every day. Don't turn yours off.

The process of medical device development, clearance by the FDA, and the acquisition of small-tech companies by larger ones all advance the medical care of patients. I was privileged to experience firsthand all the critical stages leading to the introduction of a maternal-fetal monitoring device developed with my husband's company. Of course, I sped the process up quite a bit in *Misfire*—and added a few felonies along the way.

BOOK CLUB
DISCUSSION QUESTIONS

1. Kate seems to believe we are lucky to find one truly compatible life partner. How do you think she handles the balance of holding on to the memory of Greg, her first husband, and moving on?

2. What do you think about Kate's great-aunt Irm's sixth sense and her contribution—other than her "misfire"—to this medically focused plot? What does this say about multigenerational relationships?

3. Do you agree with Kate's disposition of her mother-in-law's estate? What would you have done differently? Separately, were you surprised by Christian's decision to help Kate with her former husband's charity?

4. Were you surprised by the facts presented regarding FDA approval of medical devices—for example, that they only know what is reported by the manufacturer?

5. At what point in the novel did you suspect the eventual ringleader? After the revelation—were there signs that were missed?

6. In the end, Kate makes a difficult choice, the consequences of which she must live with. Was it the right choice?

7. Unrequited love—did this plot motivation come as a surprise? Do you think this happens relatively commonly or quite rarely within families?

8. Thinking back to Kate and Nikki—does friendship interfere with our ability to recognize pathology in those we care about?

9. What do you think the future holds for Kate and Christian?

PUBLISHER'S NOTE

We hope that you enjoyed *MISFIRE*, the second book in the Kate Downey Mystery Series.

The first in the series is *FATAL INTENT*. The two novels stand on their own and can be read in any order. Here's a brief summary of *FATAL INTENT*:

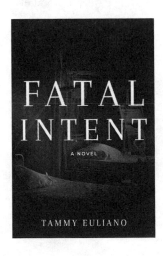

Elderly patients are dying at home days after minor surgery. Natural causes? Malpractice? Or a serial killer? And why doesn't anyone care? Anesthesiologist Dr. Kate Downey wants to know why, but her unorthodox investigation threatens her job, her family, and her very life. The stakes escalate to the breaking point when Kate, under violent duress, is forced to choose which of her loved ones to save—and which must be sacrificed. The ultimate ultimatum!

"*Fatal Intent* rings with thrilling authenticity. Tammy Euliano writes with convincing authority, immersing us in a world only a doctor truly knows."

—Tess Gerritsen,
New York Times best-selling author

We hope that you will enjoy reading *FATAL INTENT*, Tammy Euliano's first novel, and that you will look forward to more to come.

If you liked *MISFIRE,* we would be very appreciative if you would consider leaving a review. As you probably already know, book reviews are important to authors and they are very grateful when a reader makes the special effort to write a review, however brief.

For more information about Tammy Euliano, please go to her website at www.teuliano.com.

Happy Reading,
Oceanview Publishing
The Best in Mystery, Thriller, and Suspense